The Voynich Deception

Michael Lancashire

First of all I'd like to thank my parents…No, wait.
That's the Oscar acceptance speech. Wrong file.

To the vanishingly small but colossally important
group of people who matter. You know who you are.
I enjoyed this. Thankyou.

All my love,

Michael.

"Men are so simple and yield so
readily to the wants of the
moment that he who will trick
will always find another who will
suffer himself to be tricked."
Nicolo Machiavelli: *The Prince*

Anteprologue

Day -7034
18:33

Gezim Petrela was buzzing and not from a high. According to the rules he and Valon Bogdani had come up with for these little expeditions he wasn't allowed to be high for it to count. He was buzzing 'cause he enjoyed this.

He was standing in the porch gripping the bolted on handles of an improvised battering ram made from scaffolding filled with sand. Valon stood behind him.

He made everyone in the gang do this occasionally and he was a great believer in leading by example. Anyway, he enjoyed it. He didn't want to turn into some desk jockey. He wanted to keep his hand in. He wanted everyone to know he could still do the jobs himself.

The rules of the game were simple:

> 1. It had to be a random innocent. No settling scores. No getting paid for it.
> 2. It didn't count if you did it on your own. Someone had to vouch for you.
> 3. You had to be stone cold sober.

Insisting they all did it kept the gang tight and sharp, they all knew they were in this together and no one lost their edge. If they were going to survive amongst the more established London families he couldn't have anybody going soft.

No one was going soft yet though, in fact they'd probably have to calm it down a bit soon. A few of the lads were getting a bit carried away. At the moment the police saw them all as separate incidents and he really didn't want them stringing it all together, that'd cause him no end of bother.

"*Gatshëm?*" He asked Valon, checking he was ready to go in.

"*Gatshëm.*" His friend replied.

Their plan of attack was simple and direct.

He would open the door and steam in. Valon's job today was to sort the doors and the battering ram while Petrela stormed through the place and dealt with the people inside.

The idea was to smash their way in and seize control as quickly as possible. Shock and awe. Once they'd got control of the place they'd slow down and draw it out a bit to savour the moment.

Petrela levelled the battering ram at the lock on the door. It was funny really how much attention people paid to alarm systems when they ignored physical security like doors.

*

"Dad! You said you'd play Super Mario Kart with me." The boy stood in the doorway to the garden, evidently bored.

"And I will do. Go and set it up ready. I'll be there in a minute. Just let me finish this before Mom gets home." The man standing at the sink put another plate on the draining board.

"But she'll be home soon and then we won't be able to do it anyway."

The man rolled his eyes, the washing up would have to wait. Lorraine would understand. He lowered the glass he'd started cleaning back into the bowl and began to take off the washing up gloves.

Before his son had even begun to move a huge noise exploded from the hall and he spun his head left, horrified, in time to see the front door crash against the wall, raining shattered glass down on the floor.

*

Petrela dropped the battering ram and stepped over it into the house.

Standing directly ahead of him in the kitchen was the man they'd chosen earlier in the day. He was staring open mouthed at Petrela wearing, for some inexplicable reason, a single pink rubber glove.

Petrela rushed at him with his gun raised and whipped him across the face with it. Completely unprepared for a physical attack the man fell instantly to the floor.

"You! In there now!" Petrela shouted at him and pointed towards a room he'd sprinted past on his way in.

The man on the floor looked towards the back door and it was only then that Petrela became aware of a child standing there watching him.

He lunged at the boy and grabbed him by the hair with his left hand.

"I said get in there!" Dragging the boy with him he half kicked and half pushed the prostrate man with his foot towards what was obviously their lounge.

The man clambered to his feet and stumbled into the room.

Petrela shoved the boy towards a settee in the corner and pointed the gun briefly at him. The boy backed off until his legs hit against the settee but he remained standing.

"Stay!" Petrela commanded and swung back to the father.

Valon joined them a second later having shut out some of the noise behind the porch door and propped the front door shut with a chair so nothing was immediately obvious from outside. In one hand he held the battering ram upright like a staff, in the other there was a revolver.

Now they were out of sight Petrela could enjoy himself, let the situation evolve as it would. This was why it was still fun. It was the people. The things that happened were basically the same every time but the people and the way they reacted were different. Some would fight back, some despair, some started begging instantly. Eventually they all did that, begged.

He'd made up his mind as soon as he saw the boy that this was what would be different about today. This is what he'd enjoy. He wouldn't kill the child that was repugnant even to him. Unless, of course, he did something stupid to bring it on himself but looking at him, small and weedy, there was no way that was going to happen.

No, he'd come for the man so it'd be the man he'd do. But the boy would be his route to making this one unique.

"You! On knees." Petrela screamed at his victim.

The man sank to his knees and, doing his best to arrange his bloody face into a smile, looked across at his son.

"Just do as they say." He said. "It'll be alright."

The boy stood frozen with his fists clenched beside him and nodded once at his father.

"Ha! 'Do as they say'. This is bad advice from Daddy. Do as you feel not what other men tell you, yes? What do *you* feel like doing?"

"I feel like killing you." The boy said, the softly spoken words sounding oddly earnest in his childlike voice.

Petrela laughed aloud and clapped his hands together in delight.

"Good, good." He crossed the room in two steps, stood in front of the boy and glared at him. There was no response. He had expected the boy to quail but he met his eyes and held them.

Cocky little... He thought, and how old? Maybe 10, maybe a little younger?

No, he definitely wouldn't kill him unless he had to but he'd quite happily knock the privileged little snot down a peg or two.

He grinned maliciously and held out his hand.

The boy looked down.

In the hand was another gun Petrela had produced from somewhere. Held butt first towards the child, although he was careful enough not to point the barrel at himself. The boy took it and looked at Petrela coldly.

"*Gezim, çfarë jeni duke bërë?*" Valon asked from the doorway, his own gun still trained on the man on his knees.

"*Ai nuk do të bëjë asgjë. Dhe nëse ju jeni të shqetësuar, të shikojnë atë.*" Petrela reassured his friend without turning from the boy. Valon raised his gun ever so slightly to take in both the father and son.

"You can't stop Daddy dying now." Petrela continued to the boy. "See my friend here? He is going to kill Daddy. But he is work for me. I am bad man. But you can make me pay can't you?" He indicated the gun. "All you have to do is point at me and pull trigger. But that will make you a killer yes? Your choice. Life all about choices. What would Daddy think of you then before he died? What do you think he should do *Baba*?"

The kneeling father ignored the question but since he had the chance to speak he fixed his son's eyes firmly.

"I love you." He said, loudly and clearly.

"I love you too Dad." The boy's voice wavered and he showed the first sign of emotion.

"Look after your mom."

For half a second the boy's eyes made a series of rapid fire saccades between the gun in his hand and his kneeling father's eyes.

"I will." He replied eventually.

"Enough. Bye bye Daddy." Petrela said and, still without looking away from the boy, he gestured at Valon.

The shot rang out from Valon's unsilenced revolver.

*

The single shot entered the top of the man's head from the left.

The bullet was not particularly high powered but once it had punctured the skull it didn't need to be.

It tore downwards at an angle through the man's left parietal lobe and burnt and ripped a path through his jelly-like brain.

Slowed by the corpus callosum it finally came to a halt midway through his right temporal lobe.

By the time the bullet stopped 'he' was no longer a 'he'. It was dead.

The corpse was thrown forward and to the right by the momentum of the bullet and collapsed on the floor, exposing the open wound at the top left of its head.

Most of the blood pooled inside the skull but enough leaked out to destroy the carpet.

*

Petrela never took his eyes off the boy but he was disappointed by the reaction. Or rather, lack of.

What the hell is wrong with this kid?! He still hadn't moved but at no point did he seem scared or even upset. If he was angry then it was a white cold type of anger Petrela had no experience of.

This wasn't turning out to be anywhere near as much fun as he'd hoped. He tried to stir the boy up a bit.

"Now you want make me pay, yes?"

The boy didn't speak but he looked away from his father's corpse and remade eye contact with Petrela. If Petrela had been forced to describe his expression he would have said that it looked like he was concentrating. Concentrating?! As though he were doing a particularly difficult calculation in his head.

Petrela tried again. "You're thinking you could have saved him. That you could have shot me and my friend before we killed him. Maybe you could. But you chose not to try."

Still nothing.

Petrela didn't like the kid. There was something weird and unsettling about him. Who the *qij* didn't cry when they watched their dad get shot?

He'd had enough.

"*Nisemi!*" He shouted at Valon. He grabbed the gun from the boy, resisting the urge to hit him in the face as he had his father.

Valon, obeying instantly, headed for the front door. Petrela followed but when he reached the door to the lounge he turned back to face the boy who was still stationary.

"Remember you chose not to save your *Baba*. Life is all about choices kiddo."

Prologue

Day 0
17:37

Seth Mortimer, genius, criminal mastermind, planner of 34% of the unsolved significant crimes in London and (hopefully soon to be ex-) insurance clerk, hopped off the bus. He swung his satchel over his shoulder, took a deep, welcome breath of cool air and began the walk to his apartment.

He couldn't stand public transport.

In fact to be fair, it wasn't public transport he had a problem with. There was nothing wrong with the bus per se, the double decker was even a fairly neat solution to the question: "How can you carry lots of people at the same time?" No, it wasn't public transport. It was the public. People. Like the ones at work. *Oh God, the ones at work.*

He knew intellectually that they couldn't be the worst. On the assumption that irritating little people were normally distributed they must surely represent a fair cross section of irritants. Usually he was able to rub along without any problem, they didn't matter enough to annoy him. People not involved in his plans occupied essentially the same mental slot as furniture. They were obviously there, you had to remain distantly aware of them as you moved through life because otherwise you'd keep bumping into them but they weren't particularly interesting. But God it didn't feel that way at the end of a whole day spent insuring customers with them. It was like he'd stumbled across some weird sort of halfwit cluster.

He almost smiled at the thought that his new idea would mean he'd have to give notice. No more wearing the mask, no more pretending to care about their inane prattle and minor dramas.

He stopped the premature smile before it reached his face. He hadn't checked the idea yet, hadn't worked it all through so couldn't be sure it was actually viable.

Still, just for a moment he imagined leaving. Imagine the questions from co-workers about what job he was going to. *Because you'd have to be going to another job if you were leaving this one.* That was the way the world they lived in worked.

So few of them thought for themselves.

He'd always believed there were two types of people in the world: people who made paths and people who followed paths. Little people all followed paths laid out for them by others. Even when they thought they were rebelling they did so in neat little patterns, following somebody else's carefully positioned "Rebel Here" signs.

The job had been a necessity, still was in fact, but it'd be nice to stop squeezing himself into such a tiny role for a while. Even doing it part time he'd felt his brain beginning to atrophy.

Enough of this. He made a conscious decision to suppress this line of thought. What if the idea didn't pan out? The current plan was still perfectly good, he'd get what he was after but he wouldn't get to leave the insurance company.

And that will be OK, I can cope with it. I. Can. Cope.

*

To keep his mind occupied with something else he decided to review last night's game of Go.

Although it was less popular outside of China and Japan, Seth much preferred Go to chess. At least a thousand years older and with a vastly larger number of legal moves he felt it was a more strategic game. He also enjoyed the fact that while chess computers could now routinely beat even grand masters there were no artificial intelligence programs that could play Go at a professional level.

Last night's game had lasted an hour and twenty minutes or 211 moves. The first half was clear and he was happy enough with his performance. In the second half though something about the game had triggered this idea for a rewrite of the plan. While he'd normally be able to box off any ideas that occurred and concentrate on what he was doing this one had distracted him and he'd lost *sente* for a good portion of the game, ceding control to his opponent. Although he'd still won it had been a lot closer than it should have been.

That last night's lack of focus was not a one off was confirmed when his thoughts were derailed again by the new sign outside the church at the corner. It now read:

PREPARE TO MEET YOUR GOD.
IT'S HARD TO FALL WHEN YOU'RE ON YOUR
KNEES.

Instantly his mind dumped the game and started critiquing the sign.

First: the particularly poor choice of light blue writing on a neon orange background that would cause a significant fraction of the people who saw it to see the colours vibrate.

Second: the fact that the sign was written in Calibri, which, since all of their previous signs had been in Times

New Roman, meant that the church had just updated their software package to at least Office 2007.

And finally: most important of all the words. 'It's hard to fall when you're on your knees'. *If you're on your knees you've already fallen,* he thought in an associative flashback to heated debates with his grandfather. The old man within fought back vigorously.

He was still arguing with the mental model of Grandad when he reached Taunton House and let himself in. As he did so he stood aside and held the door for Mrs Pauli from number 204, smiling and nodding hello, earning a reprieve from Grandad.

He was going to have to avoid churches from now on, the inner debates with a man who could never genuinely win because he existed only in the head of his opponent, occupied valuable mental real estate and despite his best efforts to recondition himself he was still unable to stop it.

He pressed the call button for the lift.

*

Taunton House was an eight storey apartment building in a fairly cheap part of town. Four apartments to a floor, a mixture of studios and one and two bedroom flats. Seth rented a studio flat on the seventh floor which allowed him to come and go openly and have use of the communal spaces just like the rest of the residents.

Unlike the rest of the residents though he also owned the building (or rather, under a series of aliases he was the sole shareholder of a management company whose only asset was Taunton House, which amounted to the same thing).

The building had gone through a perfectly normal build process until it had been signed off by building regulations. Then before any marketing took place he had made a couple of key modifications:

1. Substantial upgrades to the sound proofing between the seventh and eighth floors prevented any noise from above being heard on the lower floor.

2. Installation of a heavy fire door, kept locked and alarmed at all times, at the beginning of the staircase from the seventh to the eighth floor. The addition of a nice big sign, clearly marked "Roof. Authorised Access Only. No access to residents / guests." provided an answer as to what was behind it should anyone ever notice it and wonder. (He had considered removing the stairs altogether but decided it would be the height of irritation to die in a fire and have his last thought be, "Why didn't I leave in the staircase?")

3. Replacement of the eight button lift control panel with a seven button one. Access to the eighth floor was switched via a scanner embedded behind the wall above the panel. You needed both the key card and the knowledge that the scanner was there to persuade the lift to finish its journey.

And with those three changes the eighth floor had disappeared, not so much from view but from notice. All of the subsequent marketing literature (none sent to the regs people of course) had referred to it as a seven storey building, seventh floor flats were described as top floor and priced accordingly.

The only person who knew of the changes was Jacob, his... what? Apprentice? Assistant? Field ops manager? Well, whatever. Jacob was the only person who'd seen the eighth floor and when Seth had first shown it to him he hadn't understood how no one had spotted it. He'd pointed out a couple of times that the whole thing would fall apart if someone just stood outside and counted the windows.

"Did you notice?" Seth had asked him, referring to the two times previously he'd been to the studio flat.

He had to admit he hadn't.

"No, I didn't think so. If you're ever forced to choose something about humans to rely on choose indifference and a lack of observation."

"Someone will notice eventually." Jacob had insisted.

"It's certainly possible. I've made a contingency plan just in case. But I bet I won't have to use it before I move on."

For a laugh Jacob had taken the bet. Seth hadn't lost yet and he didn't expect he would. People seldom really looked at anything.

*

When the lift arrived he stepped inside and, as there was no one else in there, pressed his wallet to the wall just above the control panel and waited while the lift took him straight to the eighth floor.

The doors opened at the eighth floor onto what looked like the inside of the lift shaft, dark except for the light spilling from the lift itself. Two feet in front of the lift was a brick wall covered in exposed metal surfaces with wires running along them. Between the lift doors and the wall was a thick steel cable plummeting down to disappear in the pitch black beneath the lift. Seth ignored all of it, pushed the taut looking cable aside casually, stepped over the gaping chasm (which in reality stopped three feet below the lift floor) and pushed the back open to reveal the "shaft" was a fake built around the lift exit as a final distraction to anyone accidentally carried here. As he left he sent the lift back to the ground floor.

He was now standing in the lobby of what had been envisaged as four, eighth floor flats and was now his 2000 square foot apartment. Given the location it would be ridiculous to call it a penthouse but in terms of both size and quality of décor it was the envy of many penthouses. He slung his bag and jacket over a 1930's hat stand in the lobby, kicked his shoes towards the shoe rack beneath it and headed straight to the bathroom, stripping his clothes off as he went.

He turned the shower up to full power and stood there letting the water pound the traces of the outside world from him. This was a part of the day he loved. His own personal equivalent of a decontamination unit from some post-apocalyptic sci-fi world. He'd been sorely tempted to have a shower installed as a kind of airlock in the lobby. No getting into his sanctuary with any trace of the unpleasantness outside.

Mind might well be its own place but when the particular variety of hell you were in was diminishing your mind each day then making of it a heav'n became a bit of a tall order. He was quite sure even Lucifer would have struggled.

Finished with his shower he pulled on a robe, nuked a supermarket own brand patatas bravas in the microwave, threw himself into the overstuffed settee in the lounge and began a race to see if he could eat his micromeal before the settee ate him. He just won. Having conquered both his dinner and the settee he flicked on an old episode of Frasier. Nothing like a bit of mindless American comedy to complete the wind down process.

Above him a projector sprang into life. Despite loving films he'd long since decided he didn't need a television, they just occupied space and he could stream anything he wanted from the internet. If he wanted a bigger screen he just dialled up the projector. He still bought a TV licence though, no sense attracting unwanted attention.

Kelsey Grammar appeared and did his thing for 22 minutes, sandwiched between framed copies of the Tiananmen Square tank man, Dali's Christ of St. John of the Cross and cross sections of Seth's own brain (from an fMRI scan courtesy of the NHS, nothing wrong with him the doctors confirmed, he could have told them that, the main reason for seeing them was to get these prints, thankyou data protection act).

While Frasier berated Seattle for not fully appreciating him Seth thought about his apartment and how there was more of himself in it than anything else in the world and yet it struck him now for the first time that there wasn't really a single identifying factor here. Unless of course someone was somehow able to pattern match the brain scans but he didn't believe that was possible yet. And he was pretty sure that he'd know about it if it was. Interesting then, why had he left so little a mark? Was there not enough of him somehow to leave?

Now, he thought in a mid-Atlantic drawl as he looked carefully around, *who would live in a flat like this?*

The drones at work put up photos and things on their desk, always desperate to personalise any little space they had, the oh, so polite human equivalent of scent marking trees...Very modern office, we hot desk here, we can work from anywhere, get the hell away from my desk, didn't you see my stuff?... He'd always thought it was pathetic but at the same time he'd assumed it was natural, that on some level he did it too. Evidently not. Fine, just another way he was different. And who would want to be normal?

Making it. The building. That was what he'd left of himself here, that was what had engaged him. He hadn't seen himself because he'd been looking too closely. To see the impact people like him made you had to stand back. There didn't need to be some photo of him gurning in front of the Taj Mahal or the local ice rink to stamp his personality on the place. Anyone who knew him, really knew him, would see him in the ingenuity of the solution. The whole place reeked of him. Of course no one did really know him... Anyway screw it, he had work to do.

He dragged himself out of the carnivorous furniture and hurried into the library. He could just as easily have worked in the lounge but he found the library more conducive to planning and right now a change of scenery seemed a good way to knock his thoughts into something more useful.

In the middle of the library was a floor goban which he walked over to and began absentmindedly arranging the stones into their positions at the crucial point of last night's game. That he could remember the precise positions of 247 stones did not strike him as as unusual as it would an outside observer, his eidetic memory had long been a key part of his identity. He picked the stones from the rosewood bowls and felt their smooth regularity between his fingers. Unlike chess where the pieces themselves could be as ornate or beautiful as the imagination of the craftsman allowed, there wasn't a lot of room for decoration in either the goban or the stones used in Go. Instead he'd satisfied his craving for something befitting the status of the game by scouring antique shops until he had found a genuine kaya goban. It was the single most expensive item he owned. It had an exquisite tenmasa grain and the kaya used to create it was from the Miyazaki prefecture. And, most beautiful of all, the sukiya-daiku who made it had taken account of the perspective of the players and made it slightly longer than it was wide, so that as you sat to play the board formed a perfect square. The stones were polished jade and were attractive enough in themselves but lacked the intellectual dimension that the foreshortening of the board gave.

As he set up the board, punctuating his thoughts by placing stones, he thought about the choices he'd made that had brought him here.

Click. His career, not the one at the insurance company obviously, that was the very definition of a job not a career, began by stealing cars. He had stolen four of them (well, if stealing is getting to keep the thing you've taken, then really just three, if it's just taking it off the owner then four, call it three and a half) before he realised that the bit he was good at (notwithstanding the half, obviously) was coming up with ways to steal them and that he could make more money and stay safer if he just developed the plans and sold them to others.

Click. Pretty soon he had saturated the market in normal car theft, learning a valuable lesson in economics (steal a man a car and he'll drive for a day, teach him how to steal and he'll steal forever… and not need you again) and the inapplicability of the royalty model to low end car thieves ("Why the hell would we keep giving you a cut? You've not done anything.").

Click. Step one was to make himself useful longer term, so, sell plans for specific thefts of individual high end cars rather than general approaches. Much better. Yes the thieves still learnt stuff but they were dependent upon you for longer. And since he fed data on the weaknesses to the car companies as well after a decent interval, the dependency was pretty much evergreen.

Click. Step two was to move out from cars altogether, first a similar approach with luxury boats (niche market, never really became a big earner) and then plans for different crimes entirely but still within a traditional model, product thefts, cash thefts, kidnapping, extortion, a couple of single sales of smuggling devices, murder.

(He'd only ever killed one man directly himself, and then only as a proof of concept, but he had no illusions regarding his responsibility for dozens of deaths, most never considered homicide by the police.)

Click. Step three was information based crimes, middle man for computer viruses, tactical and strategic plans for wars between rival gangs, money laundering approaches (that last one had blurred the line in his usual client base, two of his clients in the last four months had been fronts for governments, though he wasn't supposed to know that).

Click. Finally, he had started to offer a kind of corporate restructuring for organisations, introducing layers of automation and encryption as cut-outs to ensure that orders couldn't be traced to the individuals at the top.

Click. Along the way he had disappeared from view almost entirely. His clients knew him only as 'the Architect', the police didn't know him at all (though from his monitoring he knew that they were beginning to suspect the presence of a single mind behind a number of recent jobs).

Click. These days, as the Architect, he effectively ran a one stop shop, management consultancy for criminal enterprises. He had brought both the scientific method and the knowledge based economy to the world of crime. He was good at it and he enjoyed it, it was varied and interesting work, as far as he knew he had invented the field and he was the only service provider within it. And it had served him quite well financially.

Click. He was fully aware that being comfortable with this line of work was further evidence of his unique nature and indeed that by the definition of the DSM-IV he was a psychopath (though of course it didn't call it that, antisocial personality disorder being the preferred term) meeting four out of the seven factors it measures against.

Three was the cut off point for a diagnosis of psychopathy.

However, he disagreed with the assessment criteria and had written an article (under a pseudonym of course) which was awaiting publication in the British Journal of Mathematical and Statistical Psychology demonstrating that the scale was inherently subjective and therefore invalid and in any case applicable to most great leaders through history. Real men invariably made their own rules.

A much better scale, though it was still imperfect in his view, was Hare's PCL-R (on which he rated a score of 24 which was only borderline psychopathy in the UK). The different results between the two tests served only to validate his point.

He looked down at the goban board as though noticing it for the time, saw that he'd finished setting it up and concentrated briefly on the game. In a moment he saw where he'd gone wrong and what he should have done. Satisfied he left the goban and walked over to a large partners' desk in the corner, running his hand along the bookcases that lined the walls as he went.

Once installed at the desk he called up another projector and displayed the current version of the plan. It was interesting that it had changed once he'd developed and started executing it. Changing plans in flight was extremely rare and betrayed the fact that this one was emotionally driven. He would have to watch that. Carefully.

Most of the plans he sold were three or five day plans. Plans he had developed for himself had gone as high as eighty nine days (that one being Taunton House) but were usually less than that. This was different. In its original form it would have taken 183 days to execute, of which 34 had already elapsed, easily his most involved to date.

Last night's changes blew that out of the water. He'd work it out properly this evening but he could see the broad shape of it in his head already and by dead reckoning it would take closer to a year assuming no contingencies had to be invoked. A realistic contingency budget would bring it in under 15 months or round about 450 days. Much of that was risk avoidance obviously, it could be done faster by doing less preparation and building in higher levels of risk. But this had one real shot, failure would mean starting again with a whole new identity somewhere else. Not impossible but bloody irritating.

He went to work.

*

Day 1
03:08

He had it.

The most optimistic, contingency free view would be done in 411 days, worst case complete or exit was 484 days. Despite the irritation he'd felt at his inability to focus over the last 24 hours… he checked his watch, no, 29 hours… he was glad of the revision, the plan was much better this way. It was beautiful really, no other word for it. More importantly it was more personal and, after all, if he couldn't make this one personal why bother doing it?

Jacob would have to be based out of here for the duration. There were a couple of parts of the plan that would need him anyway but most importantly he'd coordinate the team in the event of any of the contingencies being triggered.

There were a couple of loose ends but he'd work them through with Jacob tomorrow. Oh and he'd have to work out a way to amend his eating and exercise regime to fit in, he added that as an action before he shut down the machine.

Shame I didn't do this a fortnight ago. He thought. Sixteen days earlier and his new plan could have been heralded by a modern day Star of the East as Jupiter, Venus and Mercury had all lined up in a rare conjunction. *That would have been one in the eye for God and Grandad. One more planet than he'd needed for his Bethlehem job. Never mind.*

The only real irritation was that the revised plan would mean Seth would need to put his helicopter lessons on hold. That was really annoying. Maybe he'd go this weekend and get in a last one. On the plus side, he'd definitely have to leave the insurance company.

When the thought of giving notice tomorrow came back to mind the smile he'd denied himself earlier in the evening crept to his lips. He was doing it for the plan of course but it was good news anyway.

Jesus, he thought, *this is how most people live their whole lives, trapped inside small jobs. No wonder the world moves so slowly.*

Another thought occurred, maybe when it was done he wouldn't even replace the day job. He needed to give that a bit more thought, find a suitable cover. Perhaps he should arrange a lottery win? Big enough to be seen as able to retire if anybody probed but small enough to join the ranks of the inconsequential rich.

Hmm. How to do that? Faking it wouldn't stand up to scrutiny. Rigging it was just too hard and the risk of getting caught had to be considerable. It'd need to be a legitimate win then. Find a winning ticket and get it off the owner before they claimed it, that should be simple enough. A small hack into the Camelot system to see where winning tickets had been sold, track down several winners, find the most appropriate one (that is, the one most easily taken before the owner spotted it) and the job'd be done. Definitely something to work up in parallel to this one.

Life posed relatively few insurmountable obstacles if you were prepared to think a bit. And then make your own path.

1

Day 311
13:57

Oliver Delaney, rare book dealer and amateur expert on the Hanseatic League, sat nervously outside the office waiting to be called in. While he waited he went over again the lines he'd rehearsed repeatedly already and ran through all of the things he'd need to know to get through this. Most of what he needed to say had been scripted in advance, and he reckoned he'd worked out most of what he'd be asked as well. He knew he'd have to think on his feet a bit, there were bound to be questions he hadn't prepared for but he was sure he could handle it. If he wanted the money at the end of this he'd just have to.

He caught sight of himself in the mirrored surface of the wall opposite, sitting with his hands in his lap and nearly laughed aloud.

Just like being sent to the headmaster's office, he thought.

Except as far as he was aware, his headmaster had never been suspected of drug running. Or armed robbery. Or killing people.

Of course, in reality the man he was here to see had never been accused of those things either, he wouldn't dirty his hands himself, but nonetheless it was a poor comparison for old Mr. Daniels!

How on earth did I get here? He knew the answer, though. He was here because after years of slogging away he finally had a shot at something big and he recognised good luck when it bit him on the ankle. However difficult today was he was determined to make it work. But he'd only get one shot at it so he went over his material again from the beginning.

Oliver Delaney wasn't a crook, had never done anything illegal in his life to speak of, and when the idea of getting the money from these people first struck him he'd rejected it out of hand, why would he involve himself in their world, for that matter how would he even get in touch with them? But then, the opportunity was too good to miss, how could he pass it up? He had tried a couple of other avenues to get the money but as he'd suspected none of them had panned out. In the end, when he decided that this was the only option left, finding them had been remarkably easy, in fact it made you wonder why the police struggled! Still, now he was here, it really didn't seem like such a good idea.

The door opened making Oliver snap his head up in time to see what looked like some sort of troll but was presumably a ridiculously oversized man, bend his head under the lintel and come to loom over him.

"You can go in now." Troll-Man said, in a flat monotone before turning and walking back to the door, apparently unconcerned about Oliver.

Oliver stood, pulled the sleeves of his jacket down to cover his cuffs and followed him into the office to meet Gezim Petrela, head of the crime family that bore his name, known to all simply as The Albanian (in Oliver's head you could hear the capitals when it was pronounced).

The office was empty.

"Sit here." Troll-Man said pointing at a chair beside a desk covered in paper. Oliver took the seat that was offered to him.

"I thought I'd be meeting Mr Petrela?" He said, confused.

"You will. In a minute." And with that the giant left the room.

Oliver looked around the room, whatever he'd been expecting this wasn't it. But then, what had he been expecting? A 3D map embedded in the table with enemy territory marked out? A swivel chair containing an evil, cat stroking Mr Big? That would all probably have been a bit clichéd. One thing he definitely had been expecting though was the man himself. This whole thing was pointless without him. There'd be no hope of getting the money if he didn't show.

After a couple of minutes Troll-Man came back in with a mug of tea for himself, none for Oliver.

"Boss'll see you now." He grunted.

"Right." Oliver said, still confused, were they going somewhere else? But Troll-Man answered the question before he had time to ask by picking up a remote from a shelf and aiming it at the television in the corner. The screen sprang to life and showed the outline of a man that Oliver imagined must be The Albanian. Troll-Man took up a station in the corner of the room next to the door, effectively blocking anyone else from getting in or, for that matter, Oliver getting out.

Oliver half rose from his chair in greeting. "Sit down," The Albanian said from the television's speakers, his silhouette gesturing expansively and his voice digitally disguised. "Sit down." He had picked up something odd about the voice the first time but when Petrela repeated the instruction he realised what it was, the television was distorting the voice. Presumably it wasn't an accident.

He waited for the image to clear so that he could see Petrela but it didn't happen. Obviously the point of the video link was to let Petrela see him not the other way around. Presumably having an image on this side at all was just to make sure he looked in the right direction during the conversation. Oliver shifted in his chair uncomfortably "Sorry, uh, nobody mentioned that we'd do this by video conference, I wasn't expecting it."

Petrela chuckled, "I hope it doesn't cause you any problems Mr Delaney. A man in my position, you must understand, it doesn't do to be in one place too often, nor to be openly associated with certain conversations. This," another wave of the hands in the air to indicate the video screen he was sitting within, "was a bright idea from one of my assistants. Should the need to explain our whereabouts ever become known, we can both easily demonstrate that we were a long way from each other. We have in fact never met." Oliver nodded, it was a clever solution for a gangster to have come up with. It also meant of course that Petrela could have this conversation, without having any impact on the rest of his life. "We are not like our American cousins here. I do not wish to be a household name."

A pause stretched on long enough for Oliver to feel he should speak, "Erm, no." He half agreed, half questioned.

"Quite so. This means that I expect you to respect my confidence in this matter Mr Delaney."

"Oh," Oliver suddenly understood what Petrela was driving at, he wouldn't want anyone knowing this, it would ruin the point. "Of course. You'll have my complete discretion sir."

"Good. It is natural. I expected as much but it is better to be clear, no?"

"Absolutely." Oliver agreed completely this time.

Petrela nodded. "So, my colleague here says you have a business proposal for me."

Oliver plunged in, there was no point in being shy now, his whole future depended on the performance he could put in now. "I do," he said. "I do. I think it's very interesting. That is, I think you'll be very interested in it."

"So tell me about it."

Oliver launched into the spiel he'd prepared, "I'm a book seller," he said. "Rare books, old books." Petrela nodded. "Have you ever heard of something called the Voynich manuscript?" Petrela shook his head. "No, not very many people have really." Oliver said, warming up slightly to his subject. "The, erm, do you mind if I give you a bit of history?"

"It's your half hour," said Petrela with a shrug.

"Right. So, you need to know all of this to understand what I'll tell you at the end, to understand the opportunity."

"Okay. Go ahead." Said Petrela.

"Yes, right. Go ahead. So, in 1912 a man called Wilfrid Voynich, a Pole who ran a book shop in London, announced to the world that he'd found a medieval manuscript like nothing anyone had ever seen before. It was written in a language no one could understand and covered in weird drawings. Since then lots of people have been trying to decode it, hundreds have tried and failed. In 1914 Voynich set sail for America, tried to sell this manuscript but couldn't find a buyer. It ended up being donated to a library at Yale University." Petrela looked bored.

"Hm. So why are you telling me this?"

"Because of what is in the manuscript."

"How do you know what's in it, I thought you said nobody had decoded it?"

"Well, I don't think that's totally true. Nobody has officially decoded it but I have found something... I said I was an antiquarian bookseller."

"Like your Mr Voynich?"

"Yes, like Voynich. Well in a house sale I went to I uncovered a letter from Voynich to his wife."

"Yes?"

"Describing what he'd found."

"So what had he found?" The Albanian said, his accent, previously undetectable, was starting to show through now that he was becoming irritated. Oliver wasn't concerned though, this was what he'd been leading to, the hope of hooking Petrela.

"Gold, sir. He'd found gold."

*

Oliver had paused dramatically following his dramatic denouement but it didn't have the effect he had anticipated.

The screen was silent for a moment as Petrela looked blankly from the other side before erupting in laughter, "You want me to finance some wild goose chase, some treasure hunt?!" When he saw it was safe to do so Troll-Man joined in from the corner with a laugh that sounded like gravel being spun in a cement mixer. "This isn't *i përgjakshëm* Dragon's Den!"

"It's not a wild goose chase. I know the gold is there." Oliver said calmly.

"Where?" The accent had completely taken hold now.

"Well, I don't know exactly."

"You don't know 'exactly'?"

"No."

"Just how 'inexactly' do you know?"

"Well, I know it's in London. Well, England. Probably London."

"England. Probably London." Petrela mimicked slowly. Oliver nodded, missing the rising tension in the room. "But you don't know where?"

"No," admitted Oliver. "But it's out there somewhere."

"Well England is a small place, yes? No problem to find gold." Even silhouetted the effort Petrela made to stop speaking was visible. Finally Oliver caught the undercurrent of menace. But just as he began to think he'd blown it and the whole thing would come to a crashing end, the silhouette relaxed. Petrela had obviously come to the conclusion that it was worth hearing him out a little longer. He supposed Troll-Man could always throw him out afterwards. "Okay Mr Delaney, let's pretend this *is* Dragon's Den. I'm interested for now but you must answer my questions." Oliver nodded eagerly. "How do you know Voynich wasn't making it all up? And even if he wasn't, how do you know someone else hasn't found it since? It has been hundred years, yes?"

"I know he wasn't making it up because he went overnight from plain broke to owning three shops in London. And I know no one else has found it because like I said no one has ever been able to decipher the manuscript."

The silhouette leant forward to the camera and pounded the table. "Wait! You say no one has deciphered. Then you said Voynich decoded then no one again. Which is it?"

Oliver felt his face flush, he was getting tangled up in the story and was tempted to ask if he could start again but that would have been unprofessional. Petrela's display was clearly meant to cement his role as unstable, big time gangster. Asking to start over would not have gone down well. He just had to recover it from here.

"I'm sorry sir, I'm not explaining myself very well. Voynich decoded something, that much is clear from his letter and his letter speaks of a proof that he found. I think that proof was a smaller deposit of gold because he was able to open those shops I spoke of but I don't think he was able to decipher all of it and I don't think he found most of the gold. And I know nobody else has deciphered it because it'd be all over the news. Besides everyone looking at it thinks it's written by aliens or some secret religious sect or something, they're looking at the wrong things in the wrong way."

Petrela sat back, "So what makes you think you'll be able to do it?"

"I wouldn't." He'd anticipated exactly that question and prepared what he thought was a clever answer but it clearly misfired so before Petrela could explode again Oliver hurried on, "I mean, I don't think *I'll* be able to. That's why I need you sir. I'm going to recruit a team of specialists to do it."

"What sort of specialists?"

"I have some CVs I could send you. They are basically a language expert and a code expert." At the mention of CVs Troll-Man snorted, reviewing CVs obviously not being in the character of a mob boss as far as he was concerned. Petrela though continued as if he reviewed CVs all the time, which of course he might well do for all Oliver knew.

"A cryptographer." Petrela said.

"Exactly." Oliver nodded. "And the cryptographer is also a computer expert. Between them they bring the skills needed to decipher it and find the rest of the gold."

"So what do you need? What is your 'business proposition'?"

"The proposition is simple. Decode the manuscript. Find the gold. Split it 50:50. We will be able to decode it because we will pay professionals to work on it as their day job."

"So. Let's say this is good idea. Why do I need you?"

Another question that had been anticipated, "I'll manage the team, you don't want to be doing that every day. Also you don't want to be openly involved until it succeeds."

"And maybe not then."

"Maybe not, that would be up to you."

"Hm. So how much do you need?"

"I need five hundred thousand to get the team on board and pay their salaries so they work on this full time."

"Five *hundred* thousand!" Petrela shouted but Oliver remained calm again. With the exception of the hysterical initial response this was going pretty much according to his script, he was starting to settle in to the situation and felt about as in control as could be expected.

"Yes, five hundred. It's a lot of money to me but to a man like you it would be achievable, I think."

Petrela paused, pleased despite himself by the obvious flattery. "And how much gold is there? What is the…upside? If this works how much are we going to get?"

Oliver hesitated. The truth was he didn't know. "I… er… I don't know exactly."

Petrela banged the desk again. "Again with the 'exactly'! You don't know?! You walk in here and ask me for half a million pounds to pay a bunch of *ndyrë shkencëtar* to look at some old book and you don't know how much I'm going to get at the end of it?"

"No."

"This is not business plan. This is stupid suicide mission. Get out. Valon, get him out." Troll-Man, whose name it turned out was Valon, instantly lunged from the corner and had hold of Oliver's shoulders none too softly.

"No, no, wait. Millions. It'd be millions." Oliver called out.

"What?" Petrela spat, his accent now evident even in the single word. Troll-Man / Valon stood with his huge hands still resting on Oliver, waiting for his boss to give him the nod again.

"Well, I don't know exactly how much it is but it must be millions." He cringed as he heard himself use the word 'exactly' again but Petrela ignored it this time.

"Go on." Petrela said roughly.

"It must be millions. Each one of those shops Voynich bought would be worth between £2 and £2.5 million today. And he bought them with just a tiny fraction of the gold. The whole lot must be worth several millions. At the very least you will more than quadruple your money."

That seemed to do it. After a minute's thought Petrela grunted at Valon, "Let him go." And Valon retreated back to the door. "Right. Okay Mr Delaney let's say I'm interested. Though not at 50:50. Pah! 50:50. So if we do this what do you get out of it?"

"What do I get out of it? Apart from untold wealth you mean? Fame. I crack the puzzle. People have tried this for a hundred years and not succeeded." He hesitated, unsure of how to address the percentages, "Not 50:50 then?"

"*Jo*. Not 50:50. 70:30"

Oliver didn't know whether to argue for the sake of it, 70:30 was completely acceptable but what was the right etiquette when negotiating with gangsters? How was he expected to behave? He settled on grudging acceptance. "70:30 then. Okay."

"Ha! You should have pressed harder Mr Delaney but too late now. So, half a million pounds... And this will work?"

"It'll work. These people are the best."

"Okay, right. Five hundred thousand pounds then. But you've got six months. No longer and I want results. At end of six months you find the gold or I get my money back. One way or another."

"Six months. Yes, okay."

"And I want to be in regular contact. Send updates every week letting us know the progress. Valon will give you email details. Do not refer to names in it."

"Of course, no names, weekly emails. Absolutely. No problem." Oliver said, in a hurry now to leave in case it somehow went wrong from here. "I'll send you the business case I prepared before for the banks and the CVs of the team as well." He was babbling now as he stood and headed for the door.

"That's great yes, attach them to the first report. So we have an agreement then. Do not let me down Mr Delaney. You can go now. Valon see Mr Delaney out, on the way get his bank details and give him an email address to reach us on." He cut the connection and the screen went blank.

*

Day 311
14:06

Once Valon had got rid of Oliver he went back into the office and called his boss from the desk phone.

"*Po.*" Petrela said curtly.

"It's me."

"Valon. So, old friend, what do you think?"

"Of Delaney or the idea?"

"The idea. Delaney is just a worm."

"I don't know Gezim. I know you like all this history stuff but it doesn't seem like your kinda thing."

"This *is* my kinda thing. You don't read enough Valon. You need to get smarter. Read more, watch some documentaries or something."

"Yeah. Okay it's your thing but maybe it doesn't seem like *our* thing, the family's thing."

"Maybe our thing is getting old. The Architect is always saying we should have some wholly clean, legitimate interests."

"Buried treasure? Someone else's gold. Is that legitimate?"

"If you find it you get to keep half and the robbing *shtet* has the other half, nice and legal. I know these things Valon. And maybe some of it goes missing before we halve it, eh?"

They both chuckled before Valon spoke up again, "Do you believe him?"

"What you think he's scamming us? That guy?"

"No, not really. He wouldn't dare. Look, you know me *krye* I'll do whatever you say but I just don't like it. He thinks he's cleverer than us."

"People always think they're cleverer than us Valon. And they're always wrong no? You and me we've been together for a long time, don't we always make it work eh? Don't we always come out on top?"

"Yeah Gezim, we do."

"Yes. Trust me Valon. We can handle this guy and if he steps out of line you'll squash him. In the meantime we get to be heroes, we get to solve the mystery, make lots of money and be famous."

2

Oliver left the station and crossed the road to the park opposite feeling quite good about himself. The other day had gone really well and it was definitely the start of a new chapter in his life. He intended to take this opportunity and capitalise on it as best he could. Obviously now he was thinking about it again there were a couple of things he'd have delivered differently given another run at it but then there always were. In a strange way he'd even quite enjoyed the challenge, having to improvise a bit. It was good.

About twenty yards inside the park he almost bumped into a man walking the other way. Oliver stopped and sidestepped right but the man moved the same way. He assumed it was a mistake until he moved left and the man did the same again. Oliver raised his head and looked at the man properly. Jesus he looked awful. He was obviously homeless and was going to hit him up for some change or something to eat. Oliver's fingers closed around his wallet in his pocket intending to give the guy some change.

"Where's the stuff?" The man growled.

"Pardon?" Oliver said, surprised.

"The rocks, man. The crack. Where's the goddam crack?" The man said, getting more agitated.

"I don't have any crack. I think you've got me mistaken for someone else." Oliver said abruptly and went to move past him quickly but the man grabbed him by both arms.

"Give it me now." He hissed, pulling at Oliver's sleeves.

"Get off me!" Oliver shouted and tried to pull away but the man just held on tight and pulled even harder.

As they struggled they stumbled and fell backwards onto the path. Somehow Oliver's arm ended up beneath him in the fall and smashed into the concrete, taking the full weight of both men. He cried out in pain.

"Hey! What's going on over there?" A jogger in the distance shouted and began running over.

"Give it me now!" The man growled again.

"Help!" Oliver screamed desperately to the jogger. "Get him off me!"

The addict, because that was obviously what he was, stayed on top of Oliver keeping him pinned to the floor but wriggled around to free his own right arm and bring his hand up to Oliver's face holding a knife.

"Where is it?!"

Oliver turned his head towards the approaching figure and started to shout again, "He's got a…" but didn't finish as the knife slid under his chin and cut off the words in a gurgled yell.

The druggy pulled himself up off Oliver and scrambled away seconds before the jogger reached them.

3

Day 433
18:30

When the intercom buzzer went Sarah was glad of the distraction, she pulled her head out of the textbook on Cauchy-Riemann equations that she'd been reading more from obligation than interest and glanced at the clock. It was later than she'd realised. *This'll be Ben*, she thought and her eyes crinkled as she smiled involuntarily. She jumped up from the reclining chair she'd been reading in and ran to the hall to answer. Ben had a key of course and would have taken it with him to fencing but he always buzzed with some stupid message and she wanted to beat him to it this time.

She stood to the side of the intercom so the camera couldn't see her and punched the speak button, "Good evening. Madame Laplace's brothel. What service will you be needing?"

"Erm. Hello?" Said a man's voice she didn't recognise.

Damn. Already going red she spun round in front of the intercom to see the display and show herself to the camera, "Sorry about that." She said and looked at the two men standing downstairs, neither of whom had the decency to be Ben. "Who is this?"

"Hello. Is a Mr Ben Jarvis there? Please?" The first man asked hesitantly.

"Oh. No, he's not at the moment but he should be back in a couple of minutes. Five at most."

"Oh okay. Thankyou. Perhaps you could help us until he gets back?"

"What is it?"

"We are looking for a missing person and think Professor Jarvis might be able to help."

"A missing person? From the university?"

"No, not from the university."

Sarah realised that he was obviously reluctant to talk outside and that the only reason they were still having this conversation through the intercom was because of how awkward she felt.

"Do you want to come up and wait inside?" She asked.

"If it'd be no bother."

"Of course not. I'll buzz you in. Just push the door and come on up."

A moment later she opened the door to the flat, "Hello again!" She said, brightly. "Sorry again about earlier, I was trying to play a trick on Ben."

"No problem Miss. Do you want us to take our shoes off?" the first one said, the other still not having spoken though this suggestion prompted a faintly horrified look from him. Sarah was tempted to say yes just to see what it was that could cause such fear at the idea of removing your shoes. She could only assume that his socks were in a fairly dreadful state, his mother would no doubt be ashamed. She decided against testing her hypothesis.

"No, no need." She said, "Can I get you a drink? Tea? Coffee? Orange juice?"

"Thankyou, that'd be very nice. Orange juice?" He phrased it as a question directed at his taciturn friend who simply nodded. "Two orange juices then thanks."

"Coming right up. Help yourselves to a seat." She waved to the settee and disappeared into the kitchen.

The two of them moved from the little hall into the slightly bigger room that served as the lounge of the single bedroom flat she shared with Ben.

"Sorry," she called through, "I didn't catch your names."

"Nigel Johnson, Miss and this is my partner Paul Davies."

"Hi." The other man finally spoke through a fairly heavy accent.

She joined them in the room holding out two glasses.

"Hello." She said, passing him a glass.

"Thanks." The irritatingly loquacious Davies replied.

Johnson was in the corner examining a complicated metal device which stood on the circular dining table. Four columns of what looked like brass gears were held together by a frame with a handle on the far right. Underneath the handle was a further set of gears that transferred the motion through to the columns.

Johnson's hand was poised as though he was desperate to turn the handle but knew he shouldn't.

"What's this?" He asked.

"It's a mechanical computer. Have you ever heard of Charles Babbage?" Johnson shook his head. "Neither had I, doesn't matter, he was just a Victorian who did something similar. Anyway this isn't exactly the same as his, Ben designed and made it."

"Looks good. Why did he make it?"

Sarah hesitated, nobody had asked that before. "He likes clockwork. He said it was hard to work out the maths and mechanics so it kept his mind occupied."

"Does he need things to keep his mind occupied, Professor Jarvis?"

Sarah didn't know what to make of that. "Anyway, you said something about a missing person."

"Yes. Oliver Delaney. Do you know him? He's been working with Professor Jarvis."

"Oliver Delaney? I don't think I've ever heard Ben mention anybody called Oliver."

"And you don't know him?"
"No, I don't know him."

*

Downstairs Ben brought his bike to a halt at the door to the building and pressed the intercom button. "Hi honey. I'm home." He sang into the microphone, opened the door and dragged his bike inside without waiting for an answer.

*

"Oh, here he comes. You can ask him yourself." Sarah said. *Thank god you're back*, she thought and walked quickly to the intercom to let him know they had company. By the time she reached it he'd already let himself in so she opened the door to the flat, stuck her head out and waited for the lift to arrive.

A minute later the lift doors opened and Ben's bike lead him out, still wearing his fencing mask.

He caught sight of Sarah standing outside the flat and grinned at her invisibly through the mask, "Panic not love, Dogtanian still lives!"

Sarah walked towards him and spoke quietly, "Ben, there are a couple of men in the flat who want to talk to you."

Ben lifted the mask to the top of his head and dropped the grin. "Talk to me about what?" He asked.

"Somebody called Oliver Something you've been working with. He's gone missing."

"Oliver... Oliver... Not Oliver Masters?"

"I don't think so, no. Who's Oliver Masters?"

"Lecturer in Microbiology. Doesn't matter. I don't know any other Olivers."

"That's what I told them. They're a bit… odd."

"Odd in what way?" Ben bristled.

"Nothing bad, just something a bit off about them. I'm sure it's nothing. I was half asleep reading when they buzzed. Oh! And then I said something stupid on the intercom." She said making him raise his eyebrows at her questioningly. "I'll tell you about it later. Forget what I said just now, they're fine I'm probably just thrown. Let's go see if you can help them."

They both went back in to the flat, Sarah calling out, "Here he is gentlemen."

Ben leant his bike up against the wall in the hall and walked into the lounge. Davies was still sitting on the settee but Johnson had gone back to looking at the clockwork computer. Ben placed his mask on top of a phrenological bust on the side table and dropped his bag at his feet.

"Hello, I'm Ben Jarvis." He said. "I understand you wanted to talk to me about somebody going missing?"

"Yes. Hello Professor Jarvis. I'm Nigel Johnson, this is Paul Davies. We were just discussing it with Miss Thorpe here." Johnson walked over with his hand extended and they shook.

Ben perched on the arm of the settee with his hand resting on Sarah's shoulder. He pointed at the chair opposite for Johnson to take. Johnson hesitated as it was covered in Sarah's textbooks, notepad and mobile phone.

"Just move my things, it's okay." Said Sarah.

He smiled at her, made a neat pile of the things, placed them at the foot of the chair and sat down. "Very impressive erm… computer." He said to Ben.

"Thankyou. So about this Oliver person?" Ben asked.

"Ah, so you know him then?" He said with a note of triumph, looking over at Davies as though he'd caught them out.

Ben looked perplexed and shook his head, "No. Well, at least I don't think so. Sarah told me his first name but couldn't remember his surname. Look do you mind starting at the beginning, I feel like I've missed half a conversation here."

"We're looking for Oliver Delaney."

"Delaney? I don't know anybody called Oliver Delaney."

"You've been working with him."

"Is he a student? I'm pretty sure if he is he's not in the linguistics department."

"That's where you're a professor?"

"I'm not a professor I'm a sessional lecturer. It's a hell of a way off being a professor. But yes, that's where I teach."

Johnson looked at his partner who just shrugged.

"Teach? You decode stuff."

"Not really. I teach linguistics. What is this about?"

"Oliver Delaney. We need to know where he is."

"Well, I can't help you. I've never even heard of him."

"Professor Jarvis you must understand we already know that you've been working with him. Working to decode some manuscript. The Voynich manuscript."

"The Voynich manuscript." Ben tilted his head slightly as the name sparked a faint recollection, "Oh right yes, I remember now, I did get an email about that. It could have come from someone called Delaney now you mention it. I can check but it was months ago and I ignored it. I certainly haven't been working with him."

Davies shifted on the settee.

"Listen Professor Jarvis… Ben… this will go much easier on you if you help us. Where is Delaney?"

"Did you say you were policemen? Could I see some ID?"

Johnson paused before eventually answering, "No. We didn't say we were policemen."

Ben stood, his lips pinched shut and he took a deep breath through his nose, "I think it's time for you to leave." He said slowly.

"I don't." Johnson pulled himself from the chair and stood up.

"If you don't go now I'm calling the police." Sarah said and picked up the phone from the table next to Ben's mask. Davies and Johnson exchanged a look but neither of them moved to stop her, instead Davies flicked his eyes to Sarah's mobile lying beside the pile of books on the floor by the chair Johnson had just left. Johnson nodded.

"Why don't we just do this the easy way?" Johnson said to Ben, ignoring Sarah. "We know you work together. You're working for him. You must know where he is. Just tell us."

"I've told you I don't know who the hell he is." Ben shouted.

"Ben!" Sarah interrupted. "The phone isn't working!" Her voice rose with panic. The corners of Johnson's mouth lifted slightly and any possibility of it being a coincidence disappeared. Her eyes darted to her mobile and Johnson shook his head slowly and stepped purposefully to one side to stand in front of it.

Ben slowed down, so far he had just been acting out his annoyance but these guys, whoever they were, were obviously dangerous. He'd have to start being a lot more careful now to make sure this didn't go wrong.

"Please leave." He said calmly. "I can't help you and I don't want anything to happen to...us." He glanced across nervously at Sarah as he spoke and Johnson picked up on it.

"Ben!" Sarah sobbed.

"Don't worry love," he said in as soothing a voice as he could call up. "They're not going to do anything to you here. Everything will be alright." He wanted to move to her, to comfort her but was rooted to the spot.

"We're not leaving until you tell us where Delaney is."

"I can't tell you where he is." Ben said shooting another look towards Sarah.

"But you wouldn't want anything to happen to that lovely wife of yours would you?" Johnson asked quietly.

"She's not my wife yet." Ben said, incongruously. "And is that meant to be a threat?"

"We're used to getting what we want Ben." Johnson said and came over to stand face to face with Ben. He turned and nodded at his partner.

Davies's hand shot out and he grabbed Sarah's arm in an iron grip. Sarah screamed more from shock than pain. Only once he had her tightly did he stand up slowly, almost causally, from the settee he'd sat on throughout. He positioned himself behind her and bared his teeth in a jackal-like grin at Ben.

Ben made to leap towards him but Johnson pushed him back onto the settee.

"Stay there!" He said firmly, pointing at Ben and then, when he had Ben's eyes, moving his finger to point at Davies who was now holding a knife against Sarah's throat. Sarah whimpered. "Now. You are going to tell us, right now, where he is or she's going to tell you to in a minute."

"Sarah, it's going to be okay. Everything is going to be okay." He turned back to Johnson. "Please don't take her."

"Then tell me what I want to know."

"I can't!"

Ben jumped towards Sarah. It didn't work. Johnson was much bigger than Ben and knew what he was doing. Besides which Ben had clearly telegraphed the move even as he decided to do it and the single punch that landed on Ben's solar plexus caught him exactly right. Ben went down, bouncing off the settee and hitting the floor. He pushed himself up onto all fours and tried to stand. "Sarah!" He gasped. "No! Don't take her! Don't take her!"

Johnson pulled back his leg and gave him a mighty kick in the stomach.

Ben felt all of the air rush from his lungs and lay on the floor fighting for breath. Johnson spun and pointed at Sarah who had started screaming as soon as Ben was hit and hadn't stopped, "You. Shut up or I'll finish him." She managed to stop herself screaming but the sobbing wouldn't stop.

"Now, perhaps you'll rethink. She's coming with us to help focus your mind. Don't move from here, we'll be in touch shortly for an answer. Oh and if you speak to the police it won't go well for her." Johnson turned his back on Ben, picked up his glass and downed the remaining orange juice.

"I think Professor Jarvis needs a little sleep to get over his trauma, can you help him?" He said to Davies. He stooped and pocketed Sarah's phone before taking hold of Sarah and heading out of the room.

Davies bent over Ben and Ben saw the excitement in his eyes. "Bye bye." Davies said and elbowed Ben hard on the side of the head. Ben instantly felt his world close down, the last thing he was aware of was the door to the flat slamming shut.

4

Day 434
19:10

Sarah sat on the wheel arch in the back of the van, holding on as it crashed over speed bumps and turned corners too fast. She had stopped banging on the walls when it became obvious that no one could hear her above the roar of the diesel engine. Or at the very least no one was going to do anything about it if they could.

She'd been sitting like that for about twenty minutes when she was thrown from her perch by a particularly vicious sharp turn and the van crunched down onto what sounded like loose stones.

*

In the front seat beyond a metal panel Ardian Bogdani and Zef Kadare (the thugs formerly known as 'Johnson' and 'Davies') were arguing. Zef drove the van through the front of a scrapyard weaving between stacks of cubed cars the tallest of which were 11 high.

"Don't talk crap. Pascal would never go to Arsenal."

"'s'not what it said on the website."

Strewn apparently randomly across the front of the yard the car cube towers were in fact carefully placed *Drachenzähne*, they allowed cars through to the offices and lock ups at the back but no faster than about 10 mph. A ram raid or drive by was rendered completely impossible and the slow approach channelled vehicles through a turkey shoot.

"You believe everything you hear?"

"I do if you aren't saying it."

Zef manoeuvred the van between the last couple of towers and pulled it into a large open fronted garage. Ardian kicked open the door of the van and dropped himself down to the floor.

"You're an arse." He said and slammed the van door closed making it rock slightly. "Hey! Where's Valon?" He shouted over to a guy standing over a microwave in the little kitchen area at the back.

The man jerked his head backwards, "Office." He shouted back.

Ardian turned and walked back out the way they'd come without acknowledging the man any further. Zef fell in behind.

"What about her?" Zef asked, catching up with Ardian.

"Ah, leave her there. She can't get out and she's out of the way."

They left the lockup and walked across the yard, heading for a set of four portacabins stacked two by two.

This place remained the hub of Petrela's operations even though he himself hardly ever came here anymore.

The top two cabins were knocked through and used as a sort of clubhouse or hangout by the Petrela family. On the ground floor one of the cabins was a sort of reception with a front desk on the off chance that they'd get customers turn up who didn't know any better. A doorway had been blowtorched from this reception into the second of the ground floor portacabins which now served as an office.

Ardian heaved open the door to the reception and stood aside to wave Zef in. Zef raised his eyebrows in surprise at this courtesy but his world made more sense again when Ardian then shoved him into the doorframe as he went to walk past. They both fell through the door laughing.

At the moment the reception was being manned by a young girl just over from Albania. She reluctantly raised her head from compulsively Facebooking just long enough to confirm Ardian and Zef weren't actual customers, seemed distantly amused by their entry and then the elastic connecting her face to her phone snapped her back.

Valon was nowhere to be seen but Ardian assumed he was in the back.

"*Hej bukur, është Valon Xhaxhai im në atje?*"

"Yeah." She replied without interrupting her relationship with her phone.

Ardian walked past the desk, pushed the door open and waved Zef ahead again. He didn't fall for it. After a second Ardian smirked at him and walked in.

"Uncle." He said in English throwing his arms wide.

"Ardian." Valon nodded a greeting but certainly didn't get out from behind the desk he was at to embrace his nephew. "How did it go?" He asked switching to Albanian for the rest of the conversation.

"Well, we did as you said. We went to the professor's place and asked him about Delaney." Ardian pulled out the desk chair opposite his uncle and dropped down into it. Zef nodded across the room at Valon and took a chair along the wall.

"And what happened?"

"He held out on us."

"What do you mean he held out on you? You were just supposed to be asking him where Delaney is."

"Yeah, well. He made like he'd never heard of him. And then he was like, 'oh yeah I think I might have heard of him but I don't know him.'

"You're not making any sense Ardian. Slow it down a bit and tell me what happened from the beginning."

"Okay so when we met him we let him think we were detectives or something."

"Didn't he want to see ID?"

"Not then he didn't, no, we were convincing. Later he did."

Valon was about to press this then decided to leave it for now, if he didn't step Ardian through it point by point he'd jump about all over the place. "Okay, never mind. Carry on with what you were saying. He thought you were detectives."

"That's right. I did the talking, Zef just sat there ready to help in case we needed it."

"So you said to him…"

"I told him we were looking for Delaney and needed his help. But he said he didn't know him. So I told him we didn't believe him. That we knew he'd been working for Delaney and should tell us where he is. I told him we could take him down to the station and make him talk to us there. That made him more talkative." Ardian said getting into his stride with the story. Valon knew his nephew though and the sight of Zef studiously examining the floor was enough to tell him that there was, as always, some embellishment going on here. Still it'd be accurate enough in most of the important elements and the rest he'd just let wash over him. Though if this weren't his little sister's son he'd have been long gone by now. "He admitted he knew him then you can bet but he still said he didn't know where he was. And he said he hadn't been working with him."

"Hadn't been working with him?"

"That's what he said."

Valon glanced across at Zef to confirm this, when he saw Zef nod his head he returned his attention to Ardian. "Why would he say that?"

"Dunno. Anyway it's obviously crap so I turned the screws a bit. He didn't like that. Typical geek type, loads of books all over the place but can't look after himself. Came in with these swords as well, thinking he's all that. Muppet."

"He attacked you with a sword?!"

"Well. No. Not attacked me with." Ardian resisted the urge to spin a tale involving a swordfight. "But when he came in he had them with him. He'd just been you know, like when people sword fight for fun?"

"Fencing." Valon said flatly.

"Yeah. So after I'd…"

"Wait. What do you mean 'when he came in'? How come you were already there?"

"His girlfriend let us in. Anyway, he said he hadn't been working with him and I told him we knew he had. Then it got a bit ugly. He wouldn't admit he knew where he was so I got us an incentive. In a bit I'm gonna go back and then he'll tell us what we want."

"What do you mean Ardian? What do you mean you got an incentive?"

"The girl."

"His girlfriend?"

"Yeah. I took her and told him if he doesn't give us what we want I'll carve up her pretty face."

"You idiots! You kidnapped his girlfriend?" Valon shot out of the chair, knocking it back against the wall behind him. "Where is she now?"

"In the van. Look don't worry Uncle. I've got it under control. I'm going to leave her here and go over to him again and finish this."

Valon looked at Zef, briefly surprised he'd allowed it to happen, then caught himself. Kadare was just as bad as his nephew that's why they hung out together.

"Ardian, you drove the van here with her in the back. Here." Ardian nodded. "After you'd thrown her in there in full sight of how many people?"

"I'm not stupid." Ardian said, causing his uncle to raise his eyebrows. "She walked out herself and got in the back. I told her Zef would kill her fella if she did anything." Ardian looked pleased for himself and Valon had to acknowledge that was better than he'd expected.

"Okay, that's not too bad. Right give me a minute to think, I need to work out what we're going to do now. How we're going to use this."

"If you're bothered we could just put her back."

"Put her back?! God, just shut up for a minute..." Valon paced around the office thinking. "Right, look perhaps this isn't so bad after all. If Delaney's made off with the money then this guy must know where he is, yeah?" Neither of the others responded, unsure if he was really asking them their opinion or just thinking aloud. "I said, yes?!" He shouted, removing their doubt.

"Yeah. Definitely." Ardian said.

"Guess so." Zef mumbled at the same time.

"Right. Well let's go with your idea. Turn the screws up, get him to cough up Delaney. How did you leave it with him?"

"I gave him a good kicking and then took the girl. Zef stopped to make sure the girl behaved."

"I knocked him out." Zef said.

"I meant, what did you say to him would happen next?" Valon asked slowly as though dealing with imbeciles.

"I told him not to call the police and that we'd be in touch. It's a good plan Uncle, he really didn't want the girl involved. He'll do anything to get her back."

"Right, I'm going to speak to the boss. You two get out. Go and put the van in the lock up out of sight."

"Already done that. That's where it is."

"Well then go and make sure nobody else is in there then!" He shouted. "I don't want her overhearing anything that might let her know where she's been. This is still a cock up Ardian don't think it isn't. Never do anything like this again without checking with me first. Understood?"

"Yes."

"And you? Understood?" Valon said, pointing at Zef.

"Yes *krye*, I understand."

"Good , now get out the pair of you. But don't leave the yard until I say. I'll call you when I need you."

The two of them left the office taking care to close the inner door gently and let the outer one slam. The receptionist looked up, amused. She'd heard the shouting even above the siren call of her social networking. Everyone knew what a cocky git that Ardian was. He could do with knocking down a bit. She knew what all the other girls said about him as well, but maybe she'd let him take her out. And then, well who knew?

Back in his office Valon picked up the phone, irritation still coursing through him. That bloody weasel Delaney, he knew this'd be trouble, now how the hell was he going to tell Gezim?

*

Day 434
19:30

Petrela answered on the third ring. His voice echoed through the speakerphone in his gym. He was working out.

"*Krye*, it's me."

"Huh." Petrela grunted as he lifted another set. "What is it?"

"Can you talk?"

"Yeah. What's up?"

"It's this Delaney thing. I sent Bogdani and Zef Kadare to go see this professor."

"Yeah."

"The idea was that they could sound him out and get some info on where Delaney is."

"Yeah. I re...member. So... what... happened?" Petrela's speech was broken by the repetitions he was doing.

"Nothing useful. They ran into a spot of bother and Jarvis wouldn't give them anything."

"Jarvis?"

"Ben Jarvis. The professor."

"Right." Petrela dropped the weights and grabbed a towel to mop up the sweat. He needed to focus. "Go on. I'm with you." He said, picking up his mobile from the bench it had been lying on and switching the call to it.

"He wouldn't crack. Told them he didn't know anything about it. But his story didn't stack up so they grabbed his girlfriend and brought her back here to persuade him to open up a bit."

"Jesus Valon, this was supposed to be legit."

"I know but I think that Delaney is trying to screw us."

"You reckon this professor is in on it?"

"He must be. Delaney said he couldn't do it himself didn't he?"

"And they've cracked it and don't want to share nicely."

"That's what I reckon. Why else would Jarvis be protecting Delaney?"

"Hmm. Yeah. But then if he'd decoded it and got a load of gold why is he still living in some dumpy flat?"

"Cause they're going to meet up later."

"So why has Delaney disappeared now?"

"Alright, maybe Delaney's ripped him off as well. Took it all for himself?"

"But then he'd tell us that wouldn't he? Why say he didn't know him? None of this makes any sense."

"I just don't know boss. This is way too complicated for me. We've got the girl I can just go and squeeze her until Jarvis talks."

"Sounds like your boys already tried that. And he's a professor for God's sake, he's not going to hold out on them is he?"

Valon paused, confused. "Gezim, I have the girl. I can try it my way but you're right, I think if he knew anything he'd have already said. I don't get it. You've always been the brains of the outfit. I just do as I'm told."

"I am not losing half a million pounds to some little *budalla*."

There was a moment while each man tried to think of a solution.

"What about the Architect? This feels up his street." Valon proposed.

"Yeah. That's a good idea Valon."

*

Day 434
19:40

Seth was sitting alone when his mobile phone buzzed to inform him that he had a message streaming. He entered today's password to the phone and was pleased to see the request for a live session was from the Albanian. He acknowledged receipt and began the log in process to the website he had created some years ago.

The idea was to provide a way for his clients to contact him in case they had a need for immediate advice. It hadn't been used very often, his clients tended to use him for plans, in the world they frequented there were very few emergencies that required the sort of cerebral services he offered. However, it had come in useful during a couple of territory disputes last year and in any case from his perspective its main aim was to enable him to charge a small retainer.

Once suitable authorisation checks had been carried out the website opened and completed a dedicated connection with the requesting machine. The screen presented him with two single lines. The top line displayed what had just been typed by the person at the other end, the bottom line was effectively a command line interface that allowed him to type a response.

Nothing very clever or difficult so far. The more interesting part was what it did in the background.

The website's first action on being opened was to shut down the pagefile and prevent any access to the hard drive or any other storage mediums on the system. The whole session was mediated through RAM alone meaning that no record was kept of anything once the machine was turned off. Next it generated a one-time pad for encryption which it based on live internet traffic statistics, established a dedicated connection between two machines and exchanged the pad with the target system. If the target accepted then you were good to start exchanging messages (which you'd better do quickly because failure to send a message in less than fifty seconds terminated the session, and you'd better be able to type as well because there was no ability to copy or paste in the command line) and it entered an encrypt, transmit, erase work cycle. It also had a fairly neat hash function he'd developed himself to detect errors in transmission but that really was geeky since he'd only done it to be sure he could.

Once the session had been completed or terminated the application forced a system reboot to clear the RAM.

The end result was something designed purely for live communication of fairly short messages that both ends knew could not be recorded. (It would obviously be possible to take a photograph of the screen but that would count for nothing in a court).

It was massively over-engineered but he'd been bored when he built it and clung to the hope that it might come in useful one day. In the meantime it meant there was no possibility of him being tied to any of his clients through electronic means.

The login finished and the screen showed him the Albanian's message.

ALBN: Need assistance.

This promises to be interesting, he thought as he typed out his response.

*

Petrela saw the Architect's response appear on his laptop beneath his request for help.

ARCH: What is the nature of the problem?
ALBN: Need to discuss on the phone.

ARCH: Can you summarise?

ALBN: Struck a deal with man to manage a team to do a job. Significant ££ given for it. He is out of contact. Team claim not to know him. Time is critical.

ARCH: Why time critical?

How should he word this? Petrela understood that the technology was supposed to be untraceable but there was no point exposing yourself unnecessarily.

ALBN: My team have brought me a guest to incentivise another team member.

There was a pause while the Architect digested that and then,

ARCH: Where is team member now?

ALBN: His flat.

ARCH: Being monitored?

ALBN: Not yet.

ARCH: What was the job?

ALBN: That is the long bit. I will explain on phone.

ARCH: Understood but what category does it fall into?

Seth had established categories of business opportunities for his conversations with clients, each referred to by a code word. It meant that requests for his services could be handled more efficiently and, strictly speaking, had the benefit over straight encryption that code words are unbreakable without inside knowledge. None of the categories fit this though.

ALBN: No category.
ARCH: How long have we got?

Petrela thought about that, the real ticking clock was how long Jarvis would stay in his flat waiting to be contacted without calling the police. But how to know how long that would take? Everyone was different.

ALBN: Prob 1 or 2 hours before team member takes regrettable action.
ARCH: 1 - Get someone watching him now. You need to be sure he isn't speaking to anyone else. 2 - I need information to formulate response. How do I get up to speed on the job before our discussion?
ALBN: I have reports on it.
ARCH: Reports?
ALBN: So I could see progress. No category.
ARCH: Understood. Send them to this email address: x1hg00fy01c00gte11str10@gmail.com I'll go somewhere private and log on. Fee will be usual consultation rate.
ALBN: Agreed.
ARCH: I will call you 45 minutes after receiving the reports.
-CONNECTION TERMINATED-

Petrela disconnected as well. He waited for his system to reboot and typed up a quick summary of what Valon had told him about the professor's interrogation. He attached everything he'd received from Oliver Delaney, the initial business case, the CVs for the team and the reports he'd sent before he disappeared and sent the lot to the email address the Architect had provided.

Then he called Valon and got him to send over somebody he could trust to keep an eye on Jarvis' place.

Finally he grabbed his things and called his driver to take him to the scrapyard and Valon.

*

Day 434
20:35

Forty five minutes later Petrela and Valon were together in the office, Petrela now behind the desk, Valon in the seat opposite. Everybody but the two of them and Ardian and Zef had been sent home. The two younger men were kicking their heels in the second lock up a safe distance away from the van that had become Sarah's prison cell.

Precisely on time Petrela's phone rang. The number was blocked. He answered it anyway.

"Yes." He said.

"The reports are made up." The electronically disguised voice of the Architect said flatly.

"Why do you say that?" Petrela snapped angrily.

"You can tell from the language he uses. When people are lying they don't use personal pronouns as much, stay as vague as possible most of the time and claim to be able to remember little details we'd admit to forgetting when telling the truth. It's obvious. Well, strictly speaking it gets more obvious as the reports progress, the early ones might be true, I can't be sure. The last few definitely aren't."

Petrela was livid. "Fascinating but I do not want lesson on deception. Tell me what is going on, that's why I'm paying you. Where is Delaney? Is Professor Jarvis in on it as well? If not why is he protecting Delaney?"

"That's the thing isn't it? That's the bit that doesn't make sense and it doesn't make sense because we haven't got all the information. But I think the men you sent to Jarvis' house know everything we need to. Though they don't realise it. Can you get hold of them and ask them a question while I listen?"

"Will this get me that little *mut* Delaney?"

"I don't know that but it'll get you answers."

"Argh! I am tired of this." Petrela roared, slamming his left hand down on the table. "That man has my money and I want it back. Get me my money back."

There was no emotion at the other end when the Architect said, "I have an idea which might explain what has happened but I need to test it with your men. We do not have to do that, as you know this is not a service I usually offer. I am happy to end this call now if you wish."

Petrela made a huge effort and calmed himself. "There is no need for that, I apologise." On the other side of the desk Valon struggled to contain his surprise at this. "I want to know what has happened to my money, I want to know where Delaney is and then I want to have parts cut off him and listen to him screaming. Anything that gets me closer to that I will try." He pulled the phone away from his head and spoke to Valon, "Get those two in here."

"When they're in with you then I want you to put me on speaker so I can hear them. I'll go on mute so they don't know I'm here, this is just you and them as normal but I need you to ask them to tell you precisely what Jarvis said when they asked him about Delaney. I'll play a beep through your phone when I've got what I need and they can go."

"Right." Petrela was subservient now following the Architect's threat to walk.

A couple of minutes later Valon came back into the office leading Ardian and Zef, both of whom now looked considerably chastened. A visit from the overboss as a result of their afternoon's fun was not what they had in mind. When everybody else was sent away they had seriously discussed the possibility that they might be disposed of, although they thought it was unlikely they were still scared, not that either of them would admit it to the other.

"You two." Petrela placed his phone on the desk and pushed it close to the furthest edge.

"*Krye*." Zef nodded so deeply it was almost a bow.

"*Krye*. It's good to see you again." Ardian said trying to ingratiate himself.

"The same cannot be said the other way around Bogdani. If your uncle was not my closest friend you would be dead now." He waited to let that sink in. "As it is you can try to redeem yourself. You can *both* try to redeem yourselves."

They fell over themselves to agree.

"Yes *krye*. Whatever we can do."

"Anything, yeah."

"I need you to tell me exactly what was said between you and Professor Jarvis when you mentioned Delaney to him."

"It's like I told Uncle Valon." Valon cringed, not the right time for the boy to trade off his relations, when this was done he was going to have a bloody good talk with him. "He said he didn't know him and then he changed his mind and said he had heard of him but didn't know where he was."

"What made him change his mind?" Petrela asked.

"I don't know."

"It was when you mentioned the manuscript." Zef said.

"Go on." Petrela prompted.

"Yeah, he's right I..." Ardian began to say.

"Not you. Him." Petrela barked without even looking at Ardian.

Zef looked nervously at his friend but then continued, "He said he'd never heard of him and then when Ardian said we knew he was working on the manuscript he said that somebody had sent him an email about it but he'd ignored it. He said it could have been Delaney."

"'Could have been' that's all he said?" Petrela asked. His mobile emitted a quiet beep from its position on the desk.

"I think so. Yes."

"Did he say anything else about knowing him?"

"Not that I can remember."

"And you? Can you remember anything else?" Petrela asked Ardian.

"No. That was about it."

"Is what Zef said right?"

"I guess so. I don't really remember, I was quite keyed up."

"Hm. Well that's all I needed from you. You can go."

"Al...alright. Thanks." Ardian headed for the door but Zef beat him to it and held it open for him, Ardian just scowled at him and walked through. Zef looked back once at Valon and Petrela and followed.

Valon began to speak but Petrela raised a finger and they sat in silence until they'd heard the outer door slam shut.

Then Petrela spoke to his phone. "They've gone. It's just us and my associate." Valon was surprised, he hadn't realised the phone was still connected.

"Thankyou." The Architect said. "So that cleared it up. Oliver tried to set up the decoding exactly as he'd told you he would. He got no buy in from Jarvis and couldn't find anyone else to do it either so after a number of months he gave up and ran with the remainder of your money."

"What makes you think that little *kopuk* didn't just plan the whole thing? He could have just taken the money and run." Valon asked.

"I considered that but why bother trying to recruit a team in the first place? If that was his plan he would have left you and gone straight to an airport. No, something changed after he'd secured the money from you. In the initial business case he gave you there's a section that talks about the team being in place. They weren't. And they turned him down when he tried to get them on board. Or at least this Ben did. Sometime between then and now Delaney panicked and scarpered. We could probably work out when with a more careful analysis of the text in the reports but it doesn't really matter. He's gone. I know you don't want to hear it but it's true."

"And Professor Jarvis?"

"Was telling the truth. And he isn't a professor by the way. I looked him up. He's a graduate student who teaches, a lecturer of sorts."

"I don't care if he's the bloody Pope. What do I do now? How do I get my money back."

"It's not just about your money now."

"Oh no? What else is it about then?" Petrela snapped barely containing his temper again but Valon shook his head, he had figured it out.

"The girl. Since those idiots thought with their adrenal gland not their brain you now have that problem to solve as well."

"I can deal with her, don't worry." Valon said, eager to avoid Petrela focussing on Ardian as the cause of his problems.

"Then you'll have to deal with Jarvis as well." The voice from the phone said. "I think I've got a better option."

"I'm listening." Petrela said.

"There are two possible plans that present themselves. First, cut your losses, accept you've lost the money. Now that Jarvis and the girl are involved you'd need to kill them both. There's no way you can keep them quiet. If you want we can then develop a separate plan to try to locate Delaney, £500k won't have got him very far though so your chances of recovering your money are remote."

"I can still make him hurt."

"You can, it's a viable option. But there is another. You keep the girl where she is and use her as leverage to make Jarvis do what Delaney tried to get him to do. Get him to find your gold."

Petrela hesitated, he didn't know what to make of it. "Can he do it?" He said, finally.

"I've read the business case and initial reports. There's nothing wrong with the idea. I don't know if he can do it, in truth nobody knows but his CV is credible. Delaney reckoned he could do it and he'd spent a long time looking for the right team. I'm convinced he was not trying to con you then. Perhaps with the right incentive to concentrate his mind Jarvis will lead you to your gold. Then Delaney doesn't matter."

"What if he can't decode it?"

"Then when he fails you follow the first plan anyway and you're no worse off. Get rid of him and the girl and move on. You're not going to get to cut bits off Delaney, at least not any time soon, and you won't get your money back but you have the same chance of making more of it that you did when you chose to pursue this manuscript thing originally. If it was right for you then it's right now. That's what I recommend but it's your choice."

"You're right." Petrela said, looking across at Valon, who shrugged in a what's-to-lose fashion. "We'll do that. Thankyou for your assistance today. Will you be able to remain on call if we need your services again?"

"I always am. I will send an email address to your mobile phone as an SMS shortly. If you send information there regularly I will ensure that I keep up to date and give the subject some thought amongst my other projects. Obviously payment will only be for the time you call on but it is an interesting situation and that way if you need me you will not need to bring me up to speed again."

"That would be most appreciated."

"I would also suggest if you are going to pursue this option then you provide Jarvis with a number he can contact you directly on. I am sure you trust your men but why put temptation of this scale in their way?"

"Right. Yes. I suppose I will."

5

Day 434
18:50

Ben slowly became aware that he was lying on the floor.

Why am I on the floor? Then the last hour gradually broke through the surface of his mind and he groaned.

Sarah! What had they done with her?! He braced his arms against the settee and the coffee table and pulled himself up. He took a step towards the window, his head swam, he stumbled and saw the carpet approaching again. Fast.

"Sarah." He half mumbled and half sobbed, and the world disappeared again.

*

Day 434
19:20

When he came around for the second time he more or less instantly he knew where he was. Evidently at some point he had stopped being truly unconscious and drifted into something approaching a normal sleep. This time when he stood he was completely steady. He ran to the window and looked out. There was no sign of Sarah or the men who'd taken her but then he had no idea how long it had been since they'd left. He turned and looked at the clock, 19:20. That didn't help though, he didn't know what time it had been when they'd taken her. He shook his head to clear it. He still felt rubbish, his head hurt where he'd been hit and it felt like he was thinking through porridge. Wait, they'd been here when he got back from fencing which would have been roughly half past 6, say they'd spoken for about 15 minutes, so he must have been out for about 35 minutes. They'd be long gone by now. With Sarah.

He dropped to the floor again, though this time through choice, and sat there forcing tears to come. Crying was not his natural response to anything but it felt like the right thing to do under the circumstances.

Before long though he'd had enough of that, it was slightly cathartic but otherwise unhelpful, so he decided to do something. They'd said they'd be in touch. He went to his kit bag and fished out his mobile to check he hadn't got a missed call. He hadn't. Holding his phone he seriously considered ringing the police, surely he should do? How could they know if he did? Wouldn't it be strange if he didn't? But then if he did he would lose control. And if they did find out and did anything to Sarah he'd never forgive himself. Again he reminded himself, they'd said they'd be in touch. To get what they wanted they'd have to get back to him. So he just had to wait.

He pulled a chair from the dining table over to the window, placed both the landline and his mobile on the window sill and sat there staring out. Waiting.

About half an hour later he saw a pimped up Vauxhall Astra reverse into one of the parking bays in front of the flat. The two men inside made no move to get out of the car, they simply settled down looking up at the flat. Obviously they were here to watch him, presumably to be sure he didn't try to run or contact the police. They were welcome to watch as he had no intention of doing either.

*

Day 434
21:15

Since the van was being used as a holding cell for Sarah, Ardian had borrowed a beat up old Peugeot 106 for the evening from the scrapyard. He wasn't amused, he wanted his BMW but he couldn't let it be seen here in case it was traced. The van had been a risk earlier, he was pretty sure they'd got away without being seen but there was no point pushing your luck. He pulled the 106 up next to Pjeter's Astra and he and Zef got out and spoke to the lads who had arrived earlier.

"Anything doing?"

"He's been sitting there staring out of the window at us the whole time. Sometimes he talks to himself the nutjob!" The driver, Pjeter, said and laughed. "Anyway why are we watching him?"

"Never you mind." Ardian said, "If you needed to know we'd have told you. If you don't get told don't ask."

"Right. Thanks for the advice." Pjeter sneered at Ardian and gunned his engine. "Catch you later." He shouted above the noise and drove off.

Ardian and Kadare got themselves comfortable where they could watch the window. They could see Jarvis sitting up there looking down at them. Kadare waved up at him.

"What are you doing?" Ardian asked incredulously.

"Messing with his head. Doesn't matter if he knows we're here."

"Good point." Ardian stuck his tongue out and made a slow licking motion at the head in the window.

Kadare laughed, "There's something really wrong with you." He said.

Bogdani's phone rang. It was Valon.

"Uncle."

"Ardian. Listen to me. I'm sending Pjeter back to you with an iPad. When you've got it you're going to go into Jarvis' flat and set it up so we can have a video call right? Call me when you're ready."

"No problem. Do you need us to soften him up a bit?"

"No." Valon said firmly. "We're going to use him so we need him healthy. The boss is going to talk to him. You're just going to set up the stuff, call me and then wait in there with him until we tell you what to do next."

"Okay Uncle. Do I need to take Zef in with me or should he stay in the car?"

"Well, since you don't seem to be able to take a leak without him you should probably take him in huh?" Ardian reddened and stole a sideways look at Kadare to check he couldn't hear what Valon was saying. He was staring out of the window, oblivious. Ardian lowered the speaker volume anyway to be sure while his uncle continued. "Just try not to cock it up this time right? I'm already covering for you with Petrela."

"Yes Uncle."

"Pjeter'll be there in a minute. Call me as soon as you're done." He said and ended the call. Ardian looked again at Kadare, he was still looking the other way so couldn't know the call was finished.

"Yes Uncle." He said, louder to be sure his friend was listening to his end of the call. "What do I think we should do? I'll send Pjeter away. I don't trust him. This needs someone close. Someone inside the family. I'll sort it." He paused. "Yeah, thanks. I know."

He turned to Zef, hit him on the arm and when he'd got his attention made a show of turning off the phone. "Pjeter's dropping off some stuff and we're going in there." He flicked his head towards the flat. "They want someone they trust to lead this. That's me. Oh and Valon said that Petrela thinks we did the right thing snatching the girl."

"Nice one." Zef said. "What's the stuff Pjeter's bringing? We going to mash up the geek?"

"Not that sort of stuff. An iPad so the boss can talk to him."

"What about?"

"This old manuscript thing. I don't get it but who cares, it's getting Petrela's rocks off so we get work to do."

Ten minutes later Pjeter roared back into the road (having forgotten to lower his music this time) and pulled up next to them. He opened his window and passed a folder full of paper, an iPad, a charger and a stand through the window to Zef.

"Cheers." Zef said.

"Now you can get the hell out of here." Ardian said leaning across to call through the passenger window.

"Whatever." Pjeter sneered back. He started reversing and said something that made the lad next to him burst out laughing.

"What did he say? What did he say?" Ardian growled at Zef. "He's going to get his, I'm telling you."

"Come on Ardian, let's just get this done, yeah?" Zef said getting out of the car.

"*Pidhi!*" Ardian called at the retreating car as he opened his door.

*

Ben buzzed in the men he knew as Johnson and Davies. They breezed past him into the flat as if they were old friends. He was desperate to ask them about Sarah but didn't want to give them the satisfaction. He reckoned he'd find out soon enough in some way connected to the iPad they were busy fighting to stand up on the table with a cheap easel.

Eventually they managed to arrange the bendable legs so that they'd hold the tablet and stand up. 'Johnson' pulled out his mobile and made a call.

"It's ready…Yeah, will do." He pocketed the mobile and rounded on Ben. "Sit there." He said, pointing to the chair they'd pulled in front of the iPad. "You're gonna get a call." Then he went and threw himself down on the settee and started leafing through the folder of papers they had brought for the professor to read. He wanted to know what the hell this was all about.

Ben sat in the chair and waited. On the iPad's first chirp 'Davies' bent forward, pressed the answer button and knocked the iPad over again. "*Mut!*" He exclaimed and then picked up the iPad and said into it, "Sorry, give me a minute." There was no response from the iPad.

Three awkward seconds later the iPad was upright again displaying a silhouetted figure in the main panel and Ben's own haggard looking face top right. Having sorted the damn tablet Zef went and sat with Ardian, reading the pages as he discarded them.

"Good evening Professor Jarvis." Petrela said.

Ben refused to behave as though he were scared of these people. They must need something from him to do with this Delaney or else why would they have kidnapped Sarah and come back? And if they needed something there was no need for him to act scared or even polite. "It's Mr. Where is Sarah?"

"I understand this but is honorary title, yes?" As always when dealing with outsiders Petrela laid the accent on thick.

"I don't care. Where is Sarah?"

"Ah yes, she is here. She is unhappy but perfectly comfortable and in no immediate danger I assure you. In fact let me apologise for the overzealous nature of my employees. They sometimes get a little… carried away."

Ben caught the threat and was inclined to react but what could he do? He was who knew how many miles away from this man and he was trapped in a room with two heavies who would presumably do anything their boss (because this must be their boss) told them to. He settled for the curt, "What is it you want from me?" Said with as much dignity as he could muster.

"So, what do I want from you? I like that Professor, a man who gets to the point. Well, the first thing I want is for you to understand the relative positions we are in and then I want you to read some material that my colleagues have brought you. Then we will speak again."

"I think I already understand our positions."

"Still, permit me to make sure that we are completely clear. You are a man whose girlfriend is being held… prisoner? Captive? Well, you are no doubt more articulate than me, I'm sure you can select the most appropriate word. Suffice it to say that she is currently indisposed. Of course, I would like to be able to release her this evening but unfortunately this isn't possible. Clearly to a man in my line of work, which we will save time by assuming you have worked out, reputation is incredibly important. As a result I am afraid that I cannot simply release her to you without being seen to secure something in exchange." Petrela's silhouette spread its hands and shook its head to indicate how truly unfortunate the man behind the outline found this state of affairs. "Which means she needs to remain with us until I can demonstrate that you have helped me. Now, I am a man of some influence, I can ensure your Sarah's safety for a period of time Professor. But, as you have seen, the type of men in my employ are, shall we say, impetuous. They have poor impulse control. At some point my influence will run out. At that point…"

He raised his hand, "But I am also a man with a problem in an area for which you have a certain expertise. So it appears to me that we can help one another. You can solve my problem for me and I, in return, will protect Sarah until I can release her to you."

"But I told your…employees earlier, I don't know the man you're looking for. I can't help you."

"Ah yes, I believe you. Again, an unfortunate misunderstanding. Still men of action deal with the situation they find themselves in yes? No whining about what is unlucky? You will know why there was such a misunderstanding when you have read the papers my men have got to give you. But it has recently been pointed out to me that this misunderstanding does not matter. You can still in fact help me. You can solve my problem for me."

"Something to do with this manuscript I guess?"

"No need to guess Professor, you can read and know. When you have read the material return this call from the iPad. I will be waiting for you."

Ben got up and collected the papers from the settee where Ardian and Zef had thrown them as they'd finished skimming and tore through them as fast as possible.

*

Day 434
22:05

There was only one number shown in the call log so he assumed it was the number he was supposed to use and Facetimed it. The silhouette answered.

"How do I know that Sarah is okay? Let me speak to her."

"No Ben. This is not the movies, eh? You only know that she is okay because I give you my word on it. And she is. Physically okay that is. She is a little distressed as you might expect. Still she will be comforted to know that you are out here and will be working to bring her home safely, no?"

"What if your word isn't enough? I need to speak to her."

"Help me fast then and you can speak all you like."

"But not before?"

"Not before. I am a simple man Professor. Simple but uncompromising, it is how people have learnt to rely on my word. I have said you will not speak to her so you will not speak to her."

Ben hesitated and then surrendered, "I've read your stuff." He said.

"So now you understand?"

"I understand the pitch this Delaney bloke made to you and I understand why you thought I knew him. Oh, I've also gone back and checked my emails while your guys here watched and it was him who wrote to me. I never even bothered replying, I thought he was a crank. What I don't understand is how you think I can help. What makes you think I can decode it when nobody has before?"

"Because you have an incentive like nobody has had before. And Delaney said you could do it."

"Delaney's ripped you off. And he didn't know me. What difference does it make what he thinks?"

"Perhaps you are right. What Delaney thinks doesn't matter. But what you think does, and you think you can do it. I see it in your eyes." Ben reflexively looked away from the iPad. "More importantly we both lose nothing by trying Ben. If you try I stand a chance of getting my money back or even making more and you stand a chance of getting Sarah back. If you do not try I lose my money and you lose… well, you just lose, eh?... Anyway, let us not beat the bush Ben. You have already decided to do it, this is just your pride making you argue. I like your pride Ben. I think in another life we could have been friends. But we men do not pine after might-have-beens. Better to just get started now. You are running out of time."

"Wait." Ben interrupted, "what do you mean I'm running out of time?"

"You have read the material. There was always a cut off point in the agreement. Recent events mean that it must be finished faster."

"Faster?" Ben echoed, numbly.

"I explained to you that my ability to keep Sarah safe has certain natural constraints related to the appetites of men and their limited capacity to resist those appetites." Petrela's tone sounded as though he were the voice of reason itself.

"How long?" Ben asked flatly.

"If you have not solved my problem in a week then I am afraid I will not be able to guarantee her safety any longer. Who knows what will happen then?"

"If you harm her…"

"Ben, come now. No empty threats, eh? In any case a deadline… my apologies, an unfortunate word… still, a deadline focuses the mind does it not? A man of your abilities should be able to accomplish this feat if you bring the full powers of your intellect to bear on it."

Ben was silent for a moment. The other man was completely correct that he had made his decision a long time before. But if this was going to work like he planned then they needed to agree some ground rules.

"I will try. But there are some things I'm going to need if I'm going to do it."

"And what might they be?" Petrela asked.

"I'm not going to be able to do this on my own. Delaney was going to get this Siobhan Leyton," he waved some of the paper at the iPad, "the GCHQ girl, to work with me. I will need her to help me."

"That was not the deal."

"You've said it yourself it's not in either of our interests for me to fail. Without help I will fail." Petrela said nothing and for a minute Ben thought he was going to refuse and it would be over before it began. There was no way he could make this work without Siobhan. "It doesn't have to be her." He said into the silence. "Do you know of somebody else who can do what she can?"

"No."

"Me neither. Look, I thought this through as I read." Behind the silhouette Petrela smiled to himself. He knew Jarvis had decided to help before he'd got back in touch. He prided himself on being able to read people. "You can send somebody to her place in Oxford. The profile says she hasn't left it since her accident. She's perfect for you to be able to control. But I need to be able to have freedom to speak to her."

Petrela made his decision. "Yes, I can send somebody to her house. Once they are there you can speak to her."

"They may need to stay there for a while. I don't know how long this will take."

"It will take no more than a week Ben, otherwise we will not be so friendly, yes?"

Ben glared at the onscreen version of Petrela and took a deep intake of breath, "Look, you need to stop threatening me. You have Sarah, I'm going to do what you want. But I don't respond well to threats." No answer at all from the iPad. So he continued with his list, "I need access to the internet and my phone. I assume these goons are going to be following me around, they can check I'm not doing anything I shouldn't. In any case, I have no intention of calling the police while you have Sarah."

"All conversation must be on speakerphone. But agreed." Petrela knew that Ardian would keep an eye on Jarvis, there was no way he was going to step out of line. "Anything else you were going to ask for?" He said patronisingly.

"I've already asked you for the most important thing. And you said no."

"You cannot speak to her but I tell you what Professor, as a show of good faith, I will send you picture every day so you know no harm has come to her. What they call proof of life. How is that?" Petrela was surprisingly impressed with Jarvis, he was not the weak academic he had assumed.

"That would be good."

"So. What I need from you you already know. Solve this code quickly. Get me the gold that Delaney promised me and I will reunite you with your Sarah. Ardian will stay with you throughout. We will speak again soon Professor. Bogdani, Kadare, come here!" He shouted the final words and both Ardian and Zef sprang to their feet and hurried over to the iPad. Ben moved back so they could get in front of the display.

"Valon has sent somebody over to you. I would rather they knew as little as possible about this job but they are there to help you if you need numbers. Kadare I need you to take one of them and go to the code breaker's house, the address is in the papers there. She will not pose any major problem to you, she is in a wheelchair and stuck in her house. When you arrive call Ardian and let him know. Ardian you and the other *ushtar* are going to stay with Professor Jarvis. Make sure he behaves himself. When Kadare rings you then the professor can speak to this code woman. I want you both to keep in contact with

Valon, he is to know everything that is going on at all times. Do you both understand?"

"Yes *krye*." They chorused.

"Good. Go then. Professor?" He called.

"Yes?" Ben said.

"No threats, yes, but a reminder. I am sure it doesn't need to be said but if you are tempted to outwit young Bogdani there it will not end well."

"You're right. It didn't need to be said." He was damned if he was going to be polite to this jumped up thug. Then something occurred to him, "I don't know your name."

Habit made Petrela hesitate but he knew very well that it would make little difference in the end so there was no harm in telling him, "My name is Petrela. Gezim Petrela."

"Thankyou."

"Good luck Professor. Do not let me down." Ben didn't respond so Petrela cut the connection.

6

Ardian snatched the papers off the table as he headed for the door.

"Give me your keys." He barked at Ben. Ben handed them over without speaking. "Don't go anywhere." He said and walked out with Zef.

As soon as they were in the lift Ardian waved the papers at Zef and asked, "What do you make of this then?"

"I don't know. I reckon Petrela's losing it." Zef replied testily.

"Watch it."

"Well, he is. Ancient codes, hidden gold, he's watched too many movies." Zef said, irritated at having to drive all the way to Oxford to look after the woman. Today was turning out to be really crap.

"Yeah. I know what you mean." The lift came to rest on the ground floor and they walked outside. "Could be real though, I've seen a load of documentaries where they found like, really valuable old stuff under carparks and things. And there was that guy found all that Viking gold in the news last year, or was it the year before?"

"It was Anglo-Saxon."

"What?"

"The gold was Anglo-Saxon not Viking. Anyway look, if it's real we aren't going to find it are we?"

"Why not?"

"That guy in there? I just don't buy it, he doesn't look all that bright to me. Where the hell in London is there buried treasure that people haven't already found and dug up?"

"Petrela thinks he can do it."

"Petrela's just pissed 'cause someone fleeced him. He isn't thinking straight."

"Yeah, that's what I think." Ardian said, unconvincingly. "Be cool if we did find it though, wouldn't it?"

"Well, we'll see. I'm going to be babysitting some cripple anyway so I'm not going to see it whatever happens."

"I'll save some for you." Ardian said.

"Yeah? You're all heart."

Just then the roar of an engine told them that their help had arrived. It was Pjeter again.

"That little *mut*. Not him."

"I'll take him with me." Zef said, wearily. He really didn't need the scene that Ardian was about to kick off. "You have the other one. We need to get this done Ardian. We don't need Petrela on our case 'cause you can't play nice. Get this done and then you and me'll finish the jumped up *pidhi*. We'll burn his pretty car with him in it." Ardian's face lit up. "But not before this is done."

"Yeah. You're right, good call. What's the other one's name?"

"Don't know."

While they spoke the car pulled up next to them, Pjeter opened his window and grinned at them both.

"Looks like we're going to have some fun tonight." He said.

"You and me are going to Oxford." Zef said to Pjeter before Ardian could respond. "You," he said, pointing at the passenger. "Get out. You're staying with Bogdani."

He used Ardian's last name to help reinforce who would be calling the shots.

Zef got into the car and Ardian banged on the roof to end the conversation. "Go babysit then. *Shihemi neser.*"

"Guess that depends on how quick your man gets this over with." Zef called back.

As Pjeter drove off Ardian turned and looked up at the flat window. Finding the gold would be like nothing before. He'd always liked adventure movies, they got his blood up for a good night in afterwards. Shit. Teuta. He was supposed to be taking her out tonight. He looked at his watch. She'd be mad. He'd have to ring her. Zef was right, the sooner this bloody thing was over the better.

"What are we doing then *krye*?" Asked the young man subserviently. He knew Ardian's reputation and without Pjeter around his earlier laughter began to seem like a really bad idea.

"What's your name?" Ardian snarled.

"Burim."

"Well, Burim. You're standing there while I make a phone call." Ardian said. "Watch that door. Be sure nobody comes out of it."

He kept his eye on the door to the flat and hit his girlfriend's name in his recently dialled list.

*

Day 434
22:22

As soon as he could see Bogdani and Kadare outside Ben grabbed his phone and dialled the number he had seen on Siobhan Leyton's profile and had committed to memory.

It rang out.

Damn. She couldn't be out, she must be asleep. He thought computer geeks were supposed to be up all night. He tried again. This time she answered.

"Hello?" Said an irritated voice at the other end.

"Hello. I'm very sorry it's so late. Is this Siobhan Leyton?"

"Who's asking?" He took that to mean yes.

"My name is Ben Jarvis. This is all going to sound very strange. It's not a wind up. Please listen to me."

The urgency in the caller's voice stopped Siobhan hanging up. "I'm listening." She said.

"In about half an hour a man is going to call at your house."

"I don't know who you are but this isn't funny."

"I know. It isn't a trick I swear. You can help me. They've got my girlfriend. I've only got about a minute before I have to go. I'll call you back when they're with me but I wanted to talk to you on my own first."

"Why don't you go to the police?"

"Because they'll kill her if I do."

"Why are you calling me?"

"Do you know somebody called Oliver Delaney?"

"Yes. Is he alright? I haven't heard from him in weeks."

"I don't know. These men are looking for him. I think they're gangsters or something."

"And they're coming to my house?!" She shouted in shock. "I'm going to call the police."

"No, no! Please. They will kill her. I can't let that happen." She didn't speak, but she didn't hang up either so he carried on more calmly. "The man who is coming to your house isn't going to hurt you. They just want you to help me."

"Help you do what?"

"Translate some document."

"The Voynich?"

"Yes. Did Oliver tell you about it?"

"Of course. I've been working on it with him."

"Have you solved it?" Ben asked with a glimmer of hope in his voice.

"No. I'm getting nowhere really."

"Okay. Most of this we can talk about in front of them." Outside Zef drove off leaving Ardian and a new man on the pavement. Almost immediately Ardian started to walk back to the house. "I don't have long. But I wanted to warn you."

"You said they've got your girlfriend?"

"Yes and if I don't solve this manuscript for them they're going to kill her but I can't do it on my own." He watched as Ardian stopped and pulled out his mobile.

Siobhan was scared. "I'm really sorry about this but what has it got to do with me? Why me?"

"Because Oliver got his money from them and he's disappeared. He said you and me could translate it so they think we can."

"And if we don't?"

"They'll kill Sarah."

"That's your girlfriend?" She knew it was a stupid question as soon as she'd said it but the fear made it difficult to concentrate.

"Yes."

"So what do we do?"

"I don't know. For now I want to go along with it."

"See if we can decode the manuscript?"

"Yes."

"We're not going to be able to do it. I've run all sorts of analyses and attacks and I think…"

"Siobhan," he cut her off, "I'm sorry but I don't have a better idea. If I don't give them what they want we're all dead."

"All?"

"Sarah, you, me. All of us."

"Why me? I don't want to be involved."

"Because you're already involved. You know too much."

"I can pretend I don't."

"If you're no use to them they'll probably just kill you anyway."

Siobhan's brain turned over, quickly evaluating any possible options but came up with nothing. "I don't know what to do." She said, quietly.

Ben's voice softened, "Neither do I. But I do know the only advantage we have right now is that we're cleverer than them. I've seen a profile Oliver wrote on you. You're a smart cookie. I know you don't know me but I'm no slouch either. As long as we stay alive I've got a chance of getting Sarah out. And you and I have a chance of coming up with a plan. But to do that we have to stay alive and to stay alive we have to stay useful to them."

She hesitated. "I understand."

"The only other thing I want us to do right now is come up with a way of talking to each other that they can't hear. I've convinced them that to get them what they want I need to be able to talk to you whenever. They've agreed but once that guy turns up at your place then we have to assume they're monitoring everything we say and do. Physically and virtually. And we might need to find a way around it."

"The computer isn't a problem, I can come up with a way of blocking any surveillance they put on there."

"Okay but remember they'll be watching you in the real world as well. We need to think of a way around it. Can you do that?"

"I can try."

"Okay we'll talk again when they tell me I can call you. I'm so sorry you've been dragged into this."

"Me too. So the plan is to just play along and stay alive long enough to… come up with a plan."

"Basically yes." Down below Ardian started walking again. "I've got to go. Be careful. And remember next time I call you we've never spoken before and you'll be learning all this for the first time." He hung up.

*

Day 434
23:06

Ardian and Ben were in the lounge when Ardian's phone rang. Ardian had sent Burim off to the bedroom to catch some sleep as soon as he'd arrived. The plan was that Ardian would stay up with Jarvis until they knew what was going on, then he and Burim would swap.

He looked at the screen on the bleating mobile and saw Zef's name.

"You arrived?" He said by way of answer.

Zef wasn't fazed by his friend's abrupt greeting. "I think so. It's the address I wrote down but it's a bungalow, like where old people would live. You sure this is right?"

Ardian looked across at Ben questioningly.

"Yeah, she's in a wheelchair, stairs are a problem." Ben answered for him.

"It's the right one. Kick the door down, we need to get the bitch on side fast."

"No!" Ben said. Ardian looked at him like a cat might look at a mouse that had suddenly turned and bitten it on the nose. "Sorry. I mean hold on. If he scares her she'll be no use to me for ages. Petrela wants this solved as fast as possible doesn't he?" Ardian nodded. "Let me call her now he's there and tell her what's going on. When we've done that he can go in and make sure she doesn't do anything she shouldn't."

Ardian had to admit that Jarvis was right. "Okay Prof. Fair point. Zef hold back. Watch the place. She can't leave anyway can she?"

"She can, she just doesn't." Ben answered, though the question wasn't directed at him.

"Whatever. Just watch the place for now. We need her to be able to do geek stuff. I'll tell you when to go in."

"Ask him if she can see him where he is now?"

Ardian repeated the question and Zef replied, "No. I'm not an idiot."

"He needs to be somewhere she could see him. I'm going to let her know he's there and I want her to be able to see him then she'll let him in." Ardian looked at him like he was mad again. Ben raised his hand, "Look if this doesn't work do it your way but let me try this first."

"Did you catch what Jarvis said?" He asked. Zef had so he moved out of the cover he had automatically found for himself when he'd arrived and went and sat down on the front wall of the bungalow opposite in full view of Siobhan's front window.

"Done." He said.

Ardian left the connection to Zef open while Ben made a show of reading Siobhan's number out from the paperwork and dialling with one finger.

"Put it on speaker." Ardian said. Ben did as he was asked and they both listened to the sound of ringing for too long. Ben panicked, what if his earlier call had freaked her out? It had been designed to prevent that but it might have done just the opposite.

"Hello." Siobhan answered eventually.

"Hello. Is this Siobhan Leyton?"

"It is." Ben's winced inwardly. To his ears she sounded very stilted, like she was reading from a cue card, and surely someone at this time of night would ask why you were calling. But Ardian didn't seem to notice.

"Hello. My name is Ben Jarvis. I believe you may know Oliver Delaney?"

"I do." Came the robotic response. *Oh God, loosen up a bit Siobhan.* He thought.

"You do." He hammed it up a bit and looked over at Ardian giving him a thumbs up. "Do you know where he is?"

"No, I don't. I was about to ask you the same question."

"Oh right." More hamming of disappointed faces at Ardian. "Well, anyway, there are a number of things I need to talk to you about Siobhan, can I call you Siobhan?"

"Yes."

"Thanks. Okay, well, like I said, there are a number of things we need to talk about. The first is that we need your help decoding the Voynich Manuscript."

"I'm working on it with Oliver." This time Ardian looked across at Ben with a pleased expression. "Why would I help you?"

"That's the second thing I wanted to talk to you about. Now, I don't want you to panic here, can you move about the house with your phone? Is it cordless?"

"Why do you care?" That's better Siobhan, more realistic answers to a man you've never spoken to before.

"Because I want to show you something outside your front window. Please trust me."

"I'm going there now. What am I supposed to be looking at? There's nothing there. Just two men sitting on my neighbour's wall. Are they what I'm supposed to looking at?"

"Yes. Like I said, there's no need to panic but those men work for the people that were paying Oliver."

" 'Were' paying him?" Much better, keep it up Siobhan.

"Yeah, there's been some issue, I don't know what, don't ask, and Oliver isn't around at the moment. But they still want to get the manuscript decoded."

"Okay. I'm not getting very far but if they want me to work for them direct this is the weirdest interview I've ever had."

Hurry up. Ardian mouthed, while making a wrap it up gesture with his hand.

"It's not an interview Siobhan. They do want you to work for them. In fact you are going to work for them but it isn't like an ordinary job. Those men outside need to come in to your house now."

"I beg your pardon? They most certainly will not!" Her acting was making it more realistic but unfortunately it was also making it much harder for Ben to keep her to the script he'd worked out in his head. He wasn't a gangster. What did you say in situations like this? The ludicrous idea that he should refer to an offer she couldn't refuse popped inappropriately into his head. He resisted the urge.

"Siobhan. The people who gave Oliver all that money. They are…" he looked across at Ardian, he didn't even know what should he call them. Was gangsters offensive? Was it flattering? Ardian just gave a disinterested shrug. *Oh well,* Ben thought, *a rose by any other name and all that. Besides, whatever I call him now someone else will have called him worse.* "They are gangsters. Oliver got the money from gangsters and they want us, you and me, to finish decoding the manuscript for them."

"Oh my god!" She said, in horror, though thankfully she didn't fake a scream. Ben wasn't sure he could have taken it. "I'm not letting them into my house."

"Siobhan you have to. If you don't let them in then they'll break in anyway and then they'll be angry. I said I'd talk to you, I said this was the better way of doing it. That you'd listen and do as I said." He emphasised the last part hoping she'd drop her fake outrage. Mind you for all he knew it was genuine outrage, he couldn't remember if he'd told her earlier that someone would be with her the whole time? Too late now. Lay it on thick for Ardian. "Siobhan, they've got my girlfriend. If I don't help them they're going to kill her. I don't want the same thing to happen to you. Please let them in, the man in charge's name is…" Again he shot a look at Ardian for a prompt.

"Zef Kadare."

"His name is Zef Kadare. He won't do anything to you if you don't give him a reason to." He nodded at Ardian who looked less than convinced. "They need us."

Siobhan paused. "Alright, if you think it's best."

"I do. I definitely do."

"I'm unlocking the door. They can come in." She triggered the door lock from the console mounted to her wheelchair.

Ben muted the phone and said to Ardian, "You heard her. Tell Kadare he can go in but be gentle with her. I need her to be useful."

"I can but there'd better not be anything waiting for them inside."

"She's in a wheelchair for God's sake."

But he unmuted the phone and said to Siobhan, "Siobhan one of them is here with me now on speakerphone. He's just going to tell his mates there to come in but don't try anything heroic will you? I did that earlier and got knocked about for my trouble. We just need to do what they say." Ardian nodded approvingly.

"I'm not planning anything, there's only one of me here. Tell them to come in." Ardian heard her and spoke to Zef in Albanian.

"He is doing now. He should be there in a minute." Ben said.

"I can see him, he's getting up and coming this way. I'm going to my desktop. If this is about the manuscript I'll need my data."

"Okay, tell me when you're there." He muted the phone and spoke to Ardian. "This is going to take a while. I need to understand what she's done so far." Unmute. "Can you give me a précis of what you've done so far?"

"Do you have access to the internet where you are now? I'm going to give you access to everything. Do you use Google Drive? Dropbox? Any sort of document sharing site?" She asked.

"Yes, I'm in my flat. I can access the internet. And I have an old Google Docs account I used on an old project at the university. I haven't used it in a while though."

"That's fine, they moved Docs to Drive. Do you remember your username?"

"bnjrvslngst@gmail.com" He spelled it out.

"No vowels."

"That's right, the project was about establishing the minimal sign sets for information transmission. I'm a linguist." He was surprised at how quickly she'd spotted it.

"Yeah I get it, consonants are the information carriers." She spoke as she booted her machine and connected to her Google Drive account.

"I didn't realise you knew anything about linguistics?"

"I don't particularly but crypto is all about information."

"Well, the belief that consonants are information carriers is a good example of linguists' bias towards recorded rather than spoken language. There was a study done in 2007 that showed that in speech vowels actually carry more information than consonants. In writing we've known for thousands of years that it was the other way around."

"Hebrew doesn't have vowels." She said distractedly.

"Written Hebrew, yeah, amongst others."

"There, I'm done," she said. "You have access. Log in and you should see a shared folder called MS408. It's all in there."

He logged in. Sure enough the folder was there. He glanced inside it and saw the long list of titles.

"Okay, where should I start?"

"I think you should read it all but Ben, listen to me, you're not going to like this but we need to sleep. We aren't going to solve this in a single night's work. If we're going to help your girlfriend we need to be fit to carry on for at least a week don't we? And that means sleep."

Ben hesitated, "I suppose you're right. He said. "But I'm going to read this through and then in the morning I'll be ready to keep up with you."

"Okay."

Ben looked up from the screen at Ardian. "She's right we need to sleep. What happens now?"

"We're going to stay with you." Ardian said. "We don't leave your sides until this is sorted." There was little point in arguing so Ben simply nodded.

"Siobhan, did you hear that? Zef and the other guy..." He looked across at Ardian questioningly.

"Pjeter." Ardian said.

"Pjeter," Ben repeated to Siobhan. "Are going to stay with you this evening. Are you alright with that? Do you have somewhere they can sleep?"

"I don't really have a choice do I? They can use the guest room."

"Thanks." Zef said in the background.

"We'll call you at 8am tomorrow."

"Right, speak to you then."

"And Siobhan?

"Yes?"

"Thankyou."

*

Ben scanned through the contents of Siobhan's shared folder trying to find somewhere sensible to start. There were lots of articles on the manuscript and a set of what looked like work notes on the various approaches she had tried so far.

She appeared to have grouped them in chronological order according to the technique they used.

Whilst it might be incomprehensible to the lay person, judging by some of the material in Delaney's reports this was at least the sensible end of Voynich analysis and speculation. Siobhan had concentrated on the cryptanalytic work and avoided the hare-brained ideas that others believed according to Delaney.

Scattered throughout the denser stuff there were occasional non-technical summaries which Siobhan had written for Delaney to incorporate into his reports. Ben focussed on those first in the hope that they would give him launching off points into the other work. He read bits of it out loud and supplied a running commentary on what he was doing. Partly to keep Ardian informed, partly because saying it aloud would help him remember it but mostly because it helped keep him awake.

"She's reviewed all of the existing attacks against the manuscript. There was a significant effort by serious cryptologists from the Government Code and Cipher School in the UK, that was like the forerunner of GCHQ, and the NSA in the States from the 40's to the 70's which she describes here but it came to nothing."

"The NSA looked at this thing? What the hell is it?" Ardian had never heard of the British organisations but he was familiar with the NSA from a number of action films over the years. As far as his understanding went they were a shadowy US government body responsible for breaking into other governments' (and their own citizens' depending on the film) secrets.

"The NSA themselves never officially looked at it but all of their top people did in their spare time, apparently for fun, and they used it to train up new recruits."

"And they didn't crack the code?"

"No. She reviews all of their work and then she starts applying crypto techniques developed since most of the serious people stopped working on it."

Having devoured all the non-technical stuff he went back to the articles and Siobhan's notes. Where to begin?

D'Imperio, Mary. 1979. *An Application of PTAH to the Voynich Manuscript.* Don't know what PTAH is, that won't help.

D'Imperio, Mary. 1978. *An Application of Cluster Analysis and Multidimensional Scaling to the Question of "Hands" and "Languages" in the Voynich Manuscript.* Multidimensional scaling? Next.

There's no point looking at the earlier stuff, he thought. It had been around for a long time and he gathered from the summaries that the NSA's crypto super geeks (not just the crackpots) believed there was something in the manuscript but all of the analyses they'd done didn't back up their intuition. So jump to the more recent stuff.

Jaskiewicz, Grzegorz. 2011. *Analysis of Letter Frequency Distribution in the Voynich Manuscript*. Okay, he understood what frequency distribution was but it felt a bit basic. If he was going to get anything from this surely someone would have sorted it by now? Put that one down as a maybe.

SL - Linear cryptanalysis. Presumably her notes on a technique. He opened it and fairly quickly dismissed it. For it to work you needed to know lots of plaintext-ciphertext pairs.

SL - Differential cryptanalysis. No use, apparently this was what they called a chosen plaintext attack. It meant you had to be able to generate more cipher texts. How the hell could he do that?

SL - Brute Force. He understood this one and her idea was intriguing, carving up the task and using Amazon's Mechanical Turk to distribute work parcels to people who'd do bits of it but she hadn't pursued it. Why had she dropped it? One to discuss tomorrow.

SL - Integral cryptanalysis. No good, another chosen plaintext attack.

Finally giving up on the idea of finding the right place to start Ben just jumped in to reading one at random and fired up Google on his machine ready to query anything he didn't understand. He'd do this the slow, thorough way.

The slow, thorough way turned out to be very slow, he discovered.

Following the demoralising line, "Exposition is sparing since the methods employed in this article use only elementary cryptanalytic techniques assumed to be familiar to all readers." He got as far as the second paragraph before finding something he neither knew nor understood. He reached for his keyboard and typed in the first of what he suspected would be many queries. It had been a long time since he had faced something he just didn't understand. Particularly something that was apparently "elementary". It was not a feeling he enjoyed.

After reading for a little while though he began to understand why she had taken the chronological approach both in her filing system and in her attacks on the manuscript.

He had assumed that the newer, more powerful, computer based techniques would easily crack whatever code was in the manuscript but that obviously wasn't true. Not so much like using a hammer to crack a walnut, it was more like using a hammer instead of a screwdriver. It's possible to put a screw in with a hammer if you bash hard enough but try using a hammer to undo a screw. It's just the wrong tool.

These techniques were phenomenally powerful, beyond the imaginings of the fifteenth century author of the manuscript but they were for the most part inappropriate. Siobhan obviously knew that and had been picking amongst them and applying a mix of her own ideas as well.

He ploughed on. A couple of sentences further on he got to the equations, or at least the maths, he suspected they weren't technically equations but something else. Google failed him altogether and he started to skim read. Further skimming (or perhaps by this point it would be better considered flying since his skips didn't touch down very often or for very long) brought him to the conclusion of the article. It wasn't a conclusion he felt justified in sharing but it was at least written in English.

New plan.

He began reading simply the abstract and conclusion of the articles. Both of these could be trusted to employ mostly words he understood, which is to say, words as opposed to maths. When he didn't understand he could consult the internet with more hope of success.

He could have sworn this approach was working until he was shaken awake, with his face resting on his shoulder in a patch of drool, by the man Ardian had brought in with him.

The man, whose name Ben couldn't remember now, said, "Bed's free if you want it, Professor."

Ben looked around groggily, saw Ardian asleep on the settee, considered for a minute trying again with Siobhan's stuff and took himself off to bed in disgust.

7

Ben had set the alarm on his phone for 06:30 but was awake twenty minutes before, instantly alert. He lay still for a moment mulling things over.

How was he going to help Sarah? He thought back on last night's reading and shook his head. How could he possibly get up to speed with 50 years of serious cryptography and hundreds of years of history in one evening? Or even a week? And then, even assuming he somehow got up to speed with the techniques, if the best people at GCHQ and in the NSA had failed to decipher this thing what made him think he could do it? He'd need to invent something completely new. Not very likely really in a week.

But Petrela had nailed it when he'd said that he might as well try. If he didn't then this would only end one way and he didn't like that one little bit. But how?

I need a shower, he thought. That would help him clear his head.

He could think of a way around this. After all he didn't need to have a detailed understanding of cryptography. He had Siobhan. He just needed to be able to effectively communicate with her and act as a sounding board. And sound convincing enough to Petrela so he didn't just go straight to Siobhan. Regardless of how realistic it was Petrela had to keep believing that he was going to be able to decipher it or his plan wouldn't work and Petrela would kill Sarah. But keeping one step ahead of Petrela didn't strike him as too difficult.

He got out of the shower feeling committed if not exactly confident, got dressed and went to make himself some breakfast. He found Ardian and the other guy in the kitchen.

"Morning professor." The other guy said. Ardian gave him a withering look. Ben joined in. They were hardly going to be good friends.

"I didn't catch your name yesterday." He said.

"Burim." The lad replied a little too eagerly.

"Well, Burim, I'm Ben." He smiled benevolently, then dropped it as soon as the lad naively responded in kind. "Now get out of the way." Ben walked past to the kettle and filled it with water. "I need a coffee."

Burim looked hurt and huffed off in the direction of the bathroom. Ben found this a curious emotion for a gangster who was involved in the kidnapping of his girlfriend and was now occupying his house.

Ardian laughed at Burim's reaction. It was always good to understand the people you were with Ben thought, and Ardian was not a complicated read. Like bullies everywhere he enjoyed other people being made to feel uncomfortable. Without a lot of effort Ben could win him round and poor old Burim would be one of the ways he'd do it.

Ben filled the cafetiere and let it brew while he put a couple of slices of bread in the toaster and poured some beans into a bowl to microwave. He didn't know when he'd get a chance to eat today so he'd decided in the shower to have a decent meal before calling Siobhan. There was no way he was cooking for those two though so when he came into the kitchen and saw them the cooked breakfast he had intended had become beans on toast. A better than average breakfast for him but someway short of the cooked breakfast he'd intended.

When it was done he ignored Ardian who was playing with his phone, took his mug and food into the lounge and sat at the table idly turning the handle on his mechanical computer with one hand and eating with the other while he watched the gears mesh and turn together.

"Does it work?" Ardian asked, walking in from the kitchen.

"Well you can't connect it to a television and play Xbox games on it but it can do some calculations and keep a couple of numbers in a sort of memory."

"I meant what I said yesterday, professor. That thing is cool."

Ben resisted both the urge to be rude and the urge to ask *Yesterday when you took my girlfriend hostage and knocked me out you mean?* He intended to try to get Ardian as much on side as possible. "Yeah, thanks. I made it. Wheels within wheels. You into computers?"

"Not really. I was when I was a kid." It obviously didn't sit well with his self-image as dangerous gangster Ben thought.

"Me too." Ben replied and continued to eat in silence. As he ate he decided to try a bit more general background reading, emphasis on the general, before he spoke to Siobhan at 8 o'clock.

*

Day 435
08:00

Siobhan picked up on the first ring which lead to a moment's confusion as Ben's phone hadn't had time to simulate the ringing and so he didn't realise she'd picked up.

"Hello." She said.

"Oh hello, sorry, who's that?" He said, assuming someone else had rung him as he'd picked up the phone to dial.

"Siobhan." She said, confused.

"Oh. Oh right. Good." *Good start*, he thought.

"Are you okay Ben?" She asked. "Oh sorry, stupid question."

"No, no I'm fine. You know apart from the obvious." He said. "So let's get on with this, hey?"

"Yeah. Before we do, Ben, I've been thinking. What if it's just gibberish? What if we're trying to do something that just can't be done?" Ben recognised that attitude from his pre-shower self. Siobhan had obviously been tormenting herself with doubt as well. He couldn't let it come to a halt now just because she was scared of failure.

"But we know it can't be gibberish because of Voynich's letter."

"The letter neither of us have seen."

"Are you saying you think the letter doesn't exist?"

"I just don't know."

"Siobhan, I need you to keep on with me here. I know it's frightening but think how frightened Sarah must be. I need to solve this and I need your help to do it."

"I know, I know. But so many people have already tried, what if we're all just imagining the patterns?"

Ben lowered his voice, he had to steer her away from this line of thought pretty quickly, if any of Petrela's lot overheard her and told him they didn't believe it was possible the whole thing could fall apart.

"I read your notes last night. Well, not all of them but enough to know that you think you're on to something. You wouldn't have carried on otherwise. You believe there's order in it don't you? It isn't gibberish." The last part said nice and loud to reiterate.

She hesitated, "I do think there's something there yes. But I've been trained to be methodical, to look at what's in front of me, not to indulge in flights of fancy. I need evidence, a gut feeling just isn't enough. Even if it is my own."

"It wouldn't be enough to commit men to war, no." Ben knew her concerns sprang from the training she'd received in her former life at GCHQ. "And if your gut feeling in this was that little green men wrote it, I'd be sceptical then too. But you are an expert Siobhan. The gut feeling of an expert is enough reason to carry on investigating. Isn't it?" She didn't answer, was obviously still thinking, so he prodded her a bit more. "Tell me the reasons our expert thinks it's real Siobhan. Tell me why until last night when it got scary *you* thought it was real. Convince me."

She drew in a breath. She knew what he was doing but she appreciated the effort so she played along. "Okay. Apart from the sheer effort involved in faking something that big, a number of statistical characteristics indicate that it has an underlying structure like language. The index of coincidence is too high to be random text, the entropy level is similar if a little higher than human language, and the text adheres to Zipf's law."

"Mhmm." He said with no idea of what the words meant.

She carried on anyway, having got into her stride. "The distribution of the words seems to indicate some of them have the sort of thematic links you'd expect with real language conveying information and you shouldn't find in a hoax. Added to which the only method described for faking something like that uses a method which hadn't been invented when the manuscript was written." He was right, she did believe it was a code and she believed she could crack it. She just didn't know if she could do it in time. "Of course by some measures it doesn't look real…"

He jumped in and cut her off. "Okay, that'll do. Add to all that the letter we have from Voynich, the sudden influx of money he had and we can forget the "it's a fake" hypothesis. Yes?"

"Absolutely."

"Good, we need to carry on."

"Ben?"

"Yeah?"

"Do you believe it's real?"

"Yes. I'm sure everything you said is right but you missed out the best reason for me. If it's real I stand a chance of getting Sarah out of this. So I have to believe it's real. Now, ready to get started?"

"Right. Yes, of course." All of a sudden she felt awful, if she felt bad how must this be for him? His girlfriend was trapped by a murdering madman and the only way he could get her out was to decrypt some six hundred year old manuscript he obviously didn't really believe in. She had to help. "So where do you want to begin? Did you read the files I sent you yesterday like you said?"

"I tried. To be honest I didn't get a lot of it, I just had more questions."

"Well, maybe your questions will help us work out what to do next."

"Yeah, okay. I guess I need to know what you've tried so far so we don't go over old ground. When I read your files I concentrated on the newer stuff because I reckoned the older stuff hadn't worked before so probably won't work now. What do you think?"

"Yeah, that's probably true. I read up on all of it as you'll have seen from the files so I've got a grip on anything we need to know. If it's relevant I'll bring it up."

"Alright then. Give me the run down on what you've done."

"From the first time Oliver contacted me?"

"Yeah. Everything I'm going to need to know to stop me reinventing the wheel."

"I began with the standard attacks to get a feel for the manuscript. I did some of the analyses I've just mentioned, coincidence indexing, frequency counts, that kind of thing. I also did some analyses just to confirm to myself that it wasn't completely random, I did a Discrete Fourier Transform and a couple of compression tests, a Lempel-Ziv and the Maurer universal statistical."

"Why compression tests?"

"Because if something can be compressed it means it contains order and isn't random. Truly random collections can't be compressed, because compression relies on patterns. Anyway, so I convinced myself that it isn't random."

"But it led you nowhere?"

"Not really but it meant I was working with the material, becoming familiar with it and I've always found that valuable. I think you get a sort of empathy for it that helps that expert intuition you were talking about."

"Okay, so what did you do next?"

"First I attempted to remove duplication, lengthening or padding. Easy enough in itself but difficult to know when to stop. English has plenty of words with duplicated consonants, should you remove them from the words? Would you recognise it if you did? On the basis that even if I went too far it would probably still leave me with something recognisable I went ahead and pruned. I'm sharing some of my assumptions with you as I go along here, shout if you disagree."

"Will do. I'm listening, keep going."

"Then, having got myself a cipher text to work on I moved on to the first wave of attacks. They'd all been tried before but you can learn stuff from the feel of a cipher by playing with it. Obviously the code must be symmetric because of how old it is but I also assumed it was a product cipher. That would be unusual for that age of encryption but I reckoned that a straight substitution or transposition alone would have been cracked ages ago. But if it is a symmetric encryption, even a product cipher, however many rounds it had been put through to reach its current state then you just look for trace elements of the plaintext left in the ciphertext. It should have been simple." She paused. "But nothing worked. It's strange though 'cause it behaves like it is a natural language hidden by a symmetric cipher but then you get nothing with proven attacks."

"Okay I think I'm keeping up. Then where to?"

"Modern day techniques."

"Right. This is the bit I struggled on last night."

"Yeah, they involve fairly advanced maths."

"I noticed but that isn't what I struggled with. I can't understand why they all seem to assume you know the plaintext. If you know the plaintext you don't need to decrypt it do you?"

"Ah, no. They don't assume you know *the* plaintext you are looking for. They assume you know *a* plaintext."

"I don't see how that helps. If I wanted to know this plaintext why do I care what that one over there says?"

"That's because you think of all encryption as being like the letter swapping you did at school. Everybody thinks that. And those codes worked because you didn't tell anyone except your mate the secret way you were working it out. Modern encryption isn't like that. Basically all cryptographic systems used today stick to a rule known as Shannon's Maxim which says that you have to assume that 'the enemy knows the system'. That means the method should be able to be public and as long as the key is secret you still can't decrypt any specific message."

"I see, which means you could have plenty of examples of plaintext-ciphertext pairs is that right?"

"That's right. The type of decryption you're thinking of, and what we need to do on the manuscript, is called a ciphertext only attack. The problem is that all modern day ciphers are supposed to be secure against ciphertext only attacks so all recent cryptanalytic work focusses on knowing plaintexts or at the very least being able to choose a ciphertext."

"Hang on, I'm lost again, 'choose a ciphertext'?"

"Well, you don't so much choose it as force it on the enemy. In World War II the British attacked German subs and ships specifically so they'd report back in code including their location which of course the British knew. Then you can make a chosen-ciphertext attack."

"I get it. That makes sense. This isn't good news."

"Not really, no. And I happen to think it doesn't make much sense either, as a profession we're spending too long gazing at our navels working on theoretic attacks with no real world application. Most real world applications are much more like this. Ciphertext only."

"So is there nothing useful from the computer age?"

"It remains to be seen. I'm working my way through the options."

He hesitated. "Don't take this personally Siobhan but it's too slow."

"I know. If it can be cracked then I can do it but in the time…?"

"So, what are our other options?"

"What do you mean?"

"Well, we both agree it can be done but that the existing tools aren't up to the job."

"Yeah."

"So what can we do instead? I'm thinking of the copy you've used. Where did you get that and how are you looking at patterns in it without being able to read it?"

"I'm using a transliteration into the Latin alphabet."

"That's what I assumed. So did you make that transliteration or get it from somewhere?"

"I got it from the web."

"Okay maybe we should do our own transliteration. Make sure it's right. None of these earlier efforts has ever worked out, maybe it's just because the stuff they were all working from is wrong. In linguistics we call it a concordance of signs and it's the first step in translating an unknown script. I think we need the same thing here."

"It'd be a huge job to come up with a new transliteration."

"Not if we used something I read in your files last night. Mechanical Turk."

"I didn't say to use it for this."

"No, I know but it would work wouldn't it?"

"I suppose it might."

"And we could get it done in parallel with anything else we were trying out?"

"It doesn't matter if it doesn't work."

"Don't think about that now. We need to come up with more ideas. What about the idea you did have about Mechanical Turk? Brute force searching for key words. I thought that idea was good. There's only about 500,000 head words in the OED."

"Unless it's not in English."

"Hmm. Bad idea then."

There was a pause while they both tried to come up with ideas.

"Before all this happened I was about to finish setting up a programme to search for bigram and trigram frequencies. I'll continue with that." Siobhan said, uncertainly.

"What will that tell us?"

"It'll help identify the language it's in."

"But not what it says."

"No. I'm trying."

"I know, I'm sorry it wasn't a criticism."

"You've been looking at the sensible end of the spectrum. What about some of the other more way-out authors, have they ever had any good ideas that might help us?"

"Are you thinking of the 'it was written by Da Vinci before he was born' theory or the 'it was written by the reptile overlords / Illuminati' theory?"

Despite the situation he laughed. "I'd have thought the Illuminati would have arranged for those web pages to be 'lost'!" He said, the heavy air quotes around lost audible at Siobhan's end.

"Yeah, well, they haven't. They're all there if you go looking."

"Funny I always assumed if they didn't want you to see something it got taken out. So that's a no on the crazies then?"

"I'm being a bit unfair, it's not all as bad as that. They're not all crazies. It's just that I'm not sure we'd be able to spot the good idea if there was one. There are online groups that look at the manuscript and some of the people on them are fairly serious individuals. I'm kind of using them as my filter to be honest. The crackpot ideas get as far as the forums and then the better amateurs pull them apart, good ideas kind of rise to the surface in a Darwinian struggle to avoid ridicule. Then I only have to look at them. I don't think we'll gain anything from trawling any deeper. But you're welcome to give it a go."

"Fair enough. If we have nothing else send me the links to the forums anyway and I'll trawl, as you put it."

"I'm saving them in a document on the shared drive now. It's titled, 'links'."

"Thanks Siobhan. I need to take 5 minutes. Does that work for you now?"

"No problem, suits me too."

"I'll call you back in 5 then." He hung up, stood and stretched.

Ardian looked up from where he had been lounging on the settee with Burim watching television. Burim remained steadfastly staring at the TV screen. "Are you getting there prof?" Ardian asked.

Ben didn't quite know how to answer, the fact that he'd asked the question was good because it showed he hadn't been listening particularly carefully but what to say in response? Something honest because Kadare was at the other end and if they compared notes it wouldn't go down well. "It's going alright, we're working out the best approach to take."

"Well, don't take too long. Tick, tock, tick, tock." He said cruelly. Burim had obviously stopped giving him any amusement for long enough that he was looking for somebody else to torture. Ben didn't have the energy to fight. He turned and went to the bathroom.

*

Day 435
09:25

When he got back his first question was, "Right, what have we got then?"

"I'm going to work out a way to get a new transliteration by Mechanical Turk workers to establish a concordance and then while they're doing that I'm going to complete the search for *n*-gram cycles. You're going to search through the online forums for ideas that are worth pursuing."

"Hm." He paused, none of it would work in time.

"It's not enough is it?" Siobhan asked.

"It's all fine but I don't get the feeling we're onto something that'll solve it fast. Do you?" He didn't give her time to answer, he didn't need another spiral into the slough of despond. "It all feels incremental doesn't it? We need something that shifts us onto a new trajectory altogether. Something dramatic and completely new."

"Completely new but not completely stupid, you mean."

"Yes. Are we missing anything? Is there anything else?"

"I can't think of any other avenue of attack. Decryption is just slow work Ben, it's methodical. It feels incremental because it *is* incremental."

There was a pause while they both tried to think of something new. "Okay, let's go back to the beginning," he said. "What about the document itself? What do we know about it? Or Voynich the man?"

"Well, we know a fair bit of the outline of Voynich's life. You can get an overview on any one of a hundred websites. But it doesn't flesh him out much. We could try to find out more."

"Good. And the document? What do we know about that?"

"What do you mean 'what do we know about it'?" She was confused and a bit offended. "We know more about it than all but a handful of people on the planet, or rather I do. We have to know it minutely to decipher it. What do you think we've been talking about?!"

He didn't rise to the slight edge in her voice. "But that's just it Siobhan. That's my point, we're studying it minutely. I just wonder if we're too close. Describe it to me. Help me think."

She tried to calm herself down, there was no sense getting annoyed, he just wanted to find the fastest way to solve it and she couldn't blame him. If it had been someone important to her being held hostage she'd have probably been a blubbering wreck, at least he was still functioning, so she should cut him some slack. "Okay. It is a handwritten text, in an unknown language, as we both know."

"Script." He interrupted.

"Sorry?"

"It's in an unknown script, it could be in any language including, but not necessarily, one we don't know."

"True enough. Shall I carry on?"

"Yeah."

"Unknown script, and contains a number of diagrams apparently arranged into six themes. There is an astrological section, a botanical section... these are all just guesses though right?" She interrupted herself. "Based on the pictures. No one knows for sure if the text relates to the pictures. The botanical section has big pictures of plants but no one knows what the plants are. There's a weird section referred to as biological because there are lots of little naked women in it. I'm not convinced it's biological though because they're all in tubes or rivers or pipes or something and there's only so many biological processes you can describe with reference to little women in pipes. There's a section with lots of mandala type circles or wheels in it, a section people call pharmaceutical which has little plants and containers and finally a section that is just lots of text. That's referred to as the recipe section by some writers."

"Recipes?"

"The arrangement looks a bit like some known recipe sections in other books of the period."

"Right." He said.

She waited for him to say more, when he didn't she struggled to think of what else to add, "Erm… the vellum it's made of has been dated to the early 1400's and analysis of the ink indicates it was written on when it was pretty new."

"What's it like physically? How big is it? Have you been to see it?"

"No, the Beinecke Library restricts access to it. It's 225mm x 160mm, about the size of a hardback book."

"Are you remembering that?!"

"No, I've jumped to my notes. There are 240 pages, not counting the ones that have been lost. The pages are made of vellum like I said…" She hesitated. "Wait! What about the lost sections?"

"What about them?"

"I'm sure I read somewhere that they might have been removed."

"Who by?"

"That's precisely my point. I'd need to check but I think no one knows. They were already missing when the modern decipherment attempts began in the 40's. Although thinking about it there was some confusion over an early numbering system Newbold did in the 20's. Maybe they were there then. I have to check this."

"What are you saying Siobhan? How would it help us?"

"I'm saying that the reason they went missing is that Voynich removed them himself because they hold the answer."

"God! You could be right. How do we get hold of those pages?"

"I'm not sure. Nobody has ever seen them."

"Hang on though, if Voynich took them out himself to stop it being deciphered why was he trying so hard to get it deciphered? That doesn't make any sense."

"The whole thing could have been just a cover. Misinformation. If he knew that it couldn't be deciphered without the pages he'd removed then it would have made the perfect cover wouldn't it? Then again, remember he was trying to sell the remainder of the manuscript for a lot of money. Maybe he did hope to get a partial translation. It would have raised the value of what he was selling and at the same time he could have used the translation method on the pages he'd kept to find out where the rest of the gold was. Two for one."

"Siobhan, you're brilliant. I think this is it. It feels like a missing piece falling into place. If this is right we can fast track through this and get Sarah out."

"We still need to find them Ben. We haven't got a clue where to start yet." She said, trying to keep him grounded.

"I know what you're saying but at least we've got an avenue to try."

"What about the other attacks? Should we give up on them?"

Ben thought for a moment, "No. No use having all our eggs in one basket. I'll do some digging about the missing pages, see if I can find out where they are, and you kick off the other bits. They're the solid stuff, this might not work out."

Siobhan was disappointed but he was right, they had to divide up their efforts in the way most likely to get success.

"Okay, let's dial off now but keep in touch. Let's catch up in an hour or so if we don't need each other before, yeah? Say… quarter to eleven?" Ben suggested, looking at his watch.

"Okay. Good luck."

"You too."

8

"Thank God for that!" Ben said as he hung up on Siobhan. "Now we're getting somewhere."

"That sounds positive, Prof." Ardian got up and stretched as he walked over to the table.

"It could be. I think we've found a way in."

"Yeah? What's that then?" Daytime television had clearly failed to grip him. Ben reminded himself it was good to have him on side and explained what they were doing.

"We're looking at pages that are missing from all the copies of the manuscript that have been analysed since Voynich released it. We think that maybe Voynich took them out himself before showing anyone the manuscript."

"Sneaky git!" Ardian said with obvious appreciation. "So where are they then?"

"Well that's just it, we don't know."

Ardian shook his head. This guy was a complete muppet. "So how does that help you?"

"Because nobody else knows either. The problem with this whole thing is that there's so much that has been done by someone already and none of it has worked. If Petrela's going to get what he wants then I have to come up with something that nobody else has thought of."

Ardian shrugged, "He could have thrown them away for all you know."

"I don't think he'd have done that, he wanted to finish deciphering it himself didn't he? He'd have wanted to keep it somewhere safe."

"He might have made a copy for himself."

"Well, if he did we can just find the copy. If it would have worked for him it'll work for us." He refused to let Ardian get to him. Keeping him involved seemed like a good idea but it was tough going. Almost every interaction the man had seemed designed to wind up anyone he was with. Of course knowing that should make his baits easy to ignore. It didn't though. "And even if he made a copy I don't think he'd have thrown the originals away. He might not have wanted anybody else to decipher it but he was a book collector, an antiquarian. This thing's six hundred years old and his most prized possession. Even when the most sensible thing to do was to keep his mouth shut, he carried on publicising it. He was proud of it. He wouldn't have destroyed parts of it even if he didn't want anyone to see it."

"Makes sense, I suppose. You just have to find them then."

"First I have to be sure what I'm looking for and that it's going to lead somewhere useful. We need to find out what, if anything, is known about these pages. Everything I know about the manuscript so far is based on the pages that people have seen obviously."

"So what are you going to do now?"

"Research it on the internet to start with. See what we can find out, they must have caught someone's attention before now."

*

Day 435
10:06

Some work on the internet and he'd got a good idea of where the missing pages fitted in, both in the physical manuscript and its story.

The numbering confusion that Siobhan had half remembered was connected to an early attempt at deciphering the document by a professor in the States with the magnificent name of William Romaine Newbold.

Based on a table of page numbers Newbold had produced as part of his decipherment there was a theory that he might have seen some of the pages that were now missing.

Newbold had been obsessed with the manuscript from the moment Voynich had introduced him to it and had developed more and more fanciful, and less and less plausible, decipherment techniques to extract meaning from it.

The field of encryption is one where Occam's razor is not easily applied, the decipherer is, after all, dealing with an adversary who is intending to deceive him. Fanciful encryption schemes are therefore quite likely. Devious anagrams abound and devotees of decryption (particularly amateur, historical decryption on which men's lives do not depend) are quite happy to imagine an encipherer committing significant amounts of time and effort to the attempt to occlude a message. Credulity was stretched, however, when Newbold developed a new theory which suggested that each letter had been constructed of microscopic shorthand characters visible only through a magnifying glass. Intriguing though the idea might be for those in the present age to imagine the ancient code maker presaging microdots it becomes difficult to follow the august professor when the maths is carried out and it becomes apparent that using this method it takes approximately 10 minutes to produce each character.

Patience with the idea (and in some quarters the professor) finally evaporates entirely when it is realised that the manuscript contains around 250,000 such characters.

Today Newbold's attempts at decipherment were used as examples of 'how not to do it' in cipher classes.

Checking the photostats he produced along with his table of numbers also showed quite clearly that the missing pages were already missing when he saw the manuscript. He had simply miscounted in the table. So much for that approach.

Newbold aside, however, there were definitely pages missing from the manuscript.

The numbering on the pages themselves (or more properly folios) clearly had gaps in. Since the recent ink analysis had confirmed the numbering had been done after the manuscript was bound in its current form but long before Voynich introduced it to the modern world this must mean that at some point between those two dates the pages with those numbers on had disappeared.

By this, presumably accurate, method there were fourteen pages missing from the manuscript. A bit more work though convinced Ben that those fourteen pages were not created equal.

After a short detour into the way medieval manuscripts were constructed it was obvious that most of the missing pages had come out in sections. Two *quires*, or whole sections, were missing (containing two pages each). Then a further four *bifolium*, that is sheets of parchment folded to make two pages, were missing from the middle of their quires (making a further eight missing pages).

It occurred to Ben that if a book made like this of a number of quires, each in turn made of a series of these bifolium sheets, were to fall apart this pattern of missing pages is exactly what you would expect to see. In each case the missing pages had been in the middle of a section. So far, so nothing sinister.

The last two missing pages however were different. The last two, folios 12 and 74 were only half a bifolium each. Their opposite pages, folios 13 and 73 were still there in the manuscript. This made no sense at all to him until he looked at the images. On the images of the neighbouring folios he could clearly see the remains of pages 12 and 74. Unlike all of the other missing pages, these two hadn't fallen out.

They'd been cut out.

*

Day 435
10:30

Although the manuscript itself didn't give any clues as to who had removed the pages Ben was pretty sure he could mount a convincing argument that it was Voynich. The cuts in the document when taken together with the letter made a good, if circumstantial, case against him. If anything the care with which the pages had been removed made it more likely it was him. A thief would have taken the whole thing, a vandal done more damage. It was hard to imagine it being anybody else.

So where did that leave them? As he'd told Ardian he couldn't see Voynich destroying any part of the book. So what would he have done instead?

He imagined that the natural conclusion to draw was that he had taken them with him to the States. Of course if Petrela or even Siobhan believed they were in the States then this was over. And he couldn't allow that.

He was aware that as far as arguments against an idea went, 'because I want it to be wrong' wasn't very persuasive. Nonetheless he continued to operate on the assumption that whatever he needed for the manuscript could be reached within the week. Was there any reason to believe that though?

Well, oddly there were a couple of reasons. Again, it was all circumstantial but it must have seemed to Voynich that having pages he had taken from the manuscript in the same place that he was trying to sell it would be riskier than leaving them here in the UK.

And then he may well have been worried that it would not be possible to smuggle it into the US. He may not have known what sort of procedure he would have to go through as part of immigration and the manuscript was distinctive enough that even if they didn't recognise it, which wouldn't have been likely since it wasn't famous at this point, any border guard would still want to know it was. Records would be kept. Records which could later be examined when he was selling the remainder of the manuscript.

No, there were enough good reasons for the pages not to be taken to the States that Ben figured you'd need to come up with a reason to take them there in the first place, and he couldn't. That was good enough for him, he would assume they were still in the UK.

Before he knew it it was time to make the call to Siobhan.

*

Day 435
10:45

"Hey Ben." Siobhan said in answer to the phone and was then relieved when she was right and it was him.

"Hey yourself." He replied. "How is it going? Do you want to tell me how far you've got?"

"Yeah, I've kicked off the Turkers on the transliteration. Well, more accurately I've designed a process for them to follow and submitted it to Amazon along with parcelled up copies of pages of the manuscript and the funds. It should be kicked off shortly."

"Funds?"

"Yeah, you have to pay these people Ben. You have to preload the account with funds so I've used my credit card."

"Oh, I'm sorry Siobhan. I wasn't thinking. I'll pay you back obviously."

"Well, let's just see where we get to, shall we? Don't worry about it for now. I have a feeling that one way or another it isn't going to matter very much."

"Okay, thanks. We'll sort it later. And the trigram bit? I know it's only been an hour so don't worry but have you got anywhere with that?"

"Not really. I finished with the Mechanical Turk stuff about twenty minutes ago and started on the trigram but I haven't really got very far. I thought it was more important to get the Amazon bit going, I can then develop the n-gram program while they're working on the transliteration."

"That's great Siobhan, it really is."

"So how's it going on the missing pages?"

"Really well. I'm dead certain it was Voynich who did it now." He outlined what he'd found to her.

"Cut out?" She said. "That's better than I'd hoped. So we know which pages to focus on then."

"Yeah, and even better, because they were cut out of sections that are still there we know what the missing pages probably had on them. Page 12 is most likely a botanical page and page 74 is probably an astrological chart representing Capricorn and Aquarius."

"Why would Capricorn and Aquarius be taken but the others left?"

"I don't know, I read something that said perhaps it was one of the previous owner's horoscopes but we know that's not true. It was Voynich and it was related in some way to the code."

She paused, unsure of how to keep him from getting carried away. "Look Ben, I don't want you get too excited about this. I agree it seems like he did it but we don't know for sure. And even if he did, maybe he removed them to sell them one page at a time? Perhaps they aren't the key at all."

"I don't believe that and I don't think you do. They'd be worth more if they were part of the original manuscript, anyway he never did try to sell them singly from anything I can find. I mean, it makes sense to want to sell individual pages and I see how that means he might have cut it up but then why hide them? It's not a very good sales technique is it?"

"I agree. But I want you to keep it in perspective."

"I just think it's the right lead. Siobhan, it was a fantastic idea. But I am keeping it in perspective. As Ardian pointed out…"

"Sorry, who's Ardian?"

"One of my babysitters. I have them too. Anyway as he pointed out I still have no idea where the pages are. That's what I'm looking at now."

"Want some help?" She asked hopefully.

"No you keep on with the text analysis." He could sense her disappointment over the phone. "Hey listen, I know you can do this but I can't do what you do. We need to cover as much ground as we can and splitting it this way we can do more. I may need to call you to bounce some ideas off later though if that's okay?"

"Sure, yeah, whenever. I'm going to have my head stuck deep in code for a bit so I'll welcome the distraction."

"Okay. I'll call as soon as I've got something. I reckon I've ruled out the US already."

"How come?"

"Lots of reasons. The biggest one is the same as earlier. If the pages are there then I can't succeed and I need to believe I can succeed."

She heard the desperation in his voice. "We'll do it Ben, try not to worry."

"Yeah, thanks. Shall we check in again in an hour or leave it a bit longer?"

"Make it about an hour and a half unless you have anything earlier. It'll give me time to get a fair chunk of this done." She said.

"Okay, speak at 12:30."

*

So, he thought, *if he hadn't taken it to the States with him where could it be?*

Ben flicked through internet pages with half an eye on them while he mulled it over.

Here was something. Voynich had made a donation of books and manuscripts to the British Library. Significant enough that they referenced him by name on the shelves which wasn't something they did very often. No, it wasn't any use, the donation was made in 1906 before he'd even found the manuscript. Presumably it was just stuff he couldn't shift. But when he entered the name Voynich into the Library catalogue the search brought back a reference to a MS facsimile 439: "*Rotographs of fourteen pages of MS. 8 in the possession of Wilfred M. Voynich, alleged to contain the cypher of Roger Bacon (ff. 1-56 of the MS. are reproduced in MS. Facs. 461)..."* Presumably a rotograph was an early form of photocopy and MS. 8 must have been what we now called the Voynich manuscript but the next bit caught his attention, *"...together with related correspondence, notes and articles."*

What were these related correspondence and notes? Was this what he was looking for?

He hurriedly linked through to the manuscript's online community web pages. Following Siobhan's advice he wanted to see whether they were already aware of this British Library reference and if so what they made of it. He was disappointed but not surprised to see that a number of them had already comprehensively researched it and thrashed what little value it had to begin with out of it by means of turgid debate on a number of discussion threads.

Drawn too far into the thread until he found himself reading completely unrelated Voynichiana he concluded Siobhan was right, if there was anything to a topic this group would sniff it out. They certainly weren't likely to ignore a lead until it was clear it couldn't take them any further. False positives, now that could be a problem, but ignored leads, no.

He took a deep breath. This could turn out to be really slow.

"What about this Kraus fella who had it after Voynich carked it?" Ardian asked, betraying the fact that he had been (a) reading up on the subject while apparently watching the television; and (b) listening to Ben's conversation with Siobhan. "What if he's got the missing pages?"

"No, firstly he's dead. Died in 1988. Secondly, if he had had them he'd have made them public, he was trying to sell the manuscript. It has to be someone who doesn't know what they've got or who has no interest in it being deciphered."

"Or an interest in it not being deciphered." Ardian said, conspiratorially.

Oh God, Ben thought, *he's one of those*. Reading paranoid rants online and being in the same room with them was going to prove too much.

"Who wouldn't want to decipher it? It leads to gold. This isn't a game. There isn't some secret group trying to hide knowledge away from the world. And there's no albino monk after us either." Ardian looked annoyed but the offhand way that Ben had said it convinced him he wasn't having a go, he was just preoccupied.

Had he kept the pages with another book? He remembered reading something about there being two books that were Voynich's prized possessions, the manuscript and another book called Valutius or something?

A quick search confirmed it was called the Valturius after its author, that Voynich had actually had two copies of it and that they were both now in the Library of Congress. After Voynich died they had passed through the hands of two other collectors, Kraus (who had owned the Voynich manuscript as well) and then a man named Rosenwald before he in turn gave them to the Library of Congress. That couldn't be it then. Both of the other men were experienced book collectors, familiar with the mystery of the manuscript and would no doubt have spotted and published any papers they could see were connected to it. Kraus in particular was trying to sell the manuscript throughout the whole period he owned the Valturius.

In any case Ben could see from the images he called up that the manuscripts looked completely different. Nobody, least of all experts like these two, would mistake pages from the Voynich manuscript for parts of the Valturius.

Both Kraus and Rosenwald donated large parts of their collections through life and most of the rest when they died. What had happened to Voynich's papers after his death? He thought.

"What do people do with their stuff when they die?" Ben asked aloud.

"What?" Said Ardian. Burim was now trying to ignore Ben altogether. Ben couldn't blame him and didn't need him anyway, if he sat there quietly it was perfectly alright with Ben.

"What do people do with their stuff when they die?" He repeated.

"They leave it to their kids."

"What if they don't have kids?"

"Then they leave it to their nieces or nephews. Or maybe their brothers and sisters."

"Voynich didn't have any of them either."

"I don't know. Then he'd leave it to someone else. Why you asking?"

"Why do you think he left it to anyone? Maybe he just locked it away somewhere and it just stayed there when he died, no one knowing about it."

"No, you said it yourself earlier, it was way too important to him." He'd been listening for longer than Ben realised. That was something to watch more carefully.

"I think you're right. So who could he have left it to?"

"His wife?"

"No, she was in the States. If we're right about it not going over there then she can't have it. What about Anne Nill?" Ben suggested.

"No, she was in the States too, she was looking after his missus." Ardian said.

Had he learnt all this stuff today? Ben wondered. It was certainly possible to pick up quite a lot in the couple of hours he could have been surfing. There was an intriguing possibility, though, that he was in fact cleverer than he looked and knew a lot more about this than Ben had thought.

"Who else do we know he was connected to in England? What connections did he have back here?" Ben said pensively.

Ardian pulled out his phone and started openly looking for answers. Ben carried on typing away at the keyboard while keeping one eye on Ardian.

After about 10 minutes Ardian said excitedly, "Hey, I've got it! What about his bookshop? Some guy called Henry Wreath was the manager of his London shop. Look," he said, standing up and practically running the twelve feet to Ben, reading aloud from a website as he did so. "It says here, 'Wreath and Nill remained firm friends until his death, exchanging letters on matters both business and friendly.' It's got to be him, there's no one else."

"It could be. Does it say anything else about this Wreath?"

"Apparently he left his papers on his death to UCL's Special Collection."

"What's that?"

"I'm just looking." They waited a moment while Ardian typed it into Google. "It's the university's collection of rare books and manuscripts and stuff. Things like personal papers. Medieval crap. If Voynich hadn't gone to America the manuscript might have ended up there."

"But it says Wreath's stuff did?"

"Yeah, it's listed here in the directory, Wreath Papers – MS ADD632. That's where we need to go then."

Ardian took over the keyboard from Ben and called up the website on the bigger screen of the laptop so they weren't both hunched over his mobile phone.

"Hang on." Ben said, "First we need to be sure that what we need is in there. Does it have any sort of description?"

"Yeah. You click on where it says AIM25 and that gives you a… there, the description of the contents."

Ben ran his finger down the list on the screen until he saw something that jumped out at him. *Assorted medieval texts in unknown, possibly Hebraic, shorthand.* He slowed his finger.

"That's it!" Ardian shouted. "That has to be it. A medieval manuscript in shorthand. Shorthand's like a code right? So they can't read it. That's got to be it."

"I reckon you're right. What are the odds of Henry Wreath genuinely having a set of medieval Hebrew shorthand notes? It must have been mislabelled by whoever catalogued it. We've found it."

"So where is it?" Ardian thought aloud.

"Look there, at the top of the page." Ben pointed to the top of the page where the Archive kept an Identity Statement, a standard set of information for all of the documents they had a record of. In that statement was a field labelled *Held At – click here to see details of the physical location of collection.*

They clicked there.

The Reading Room is temporarily located at The National Archives in Kew. Appointments to view material need to be made two weeks in advance through UCL Special Collections.

"Two weeks?!" Ben said, "That isn't going to work. I'll ring them, maybe it's just a standard statement. They might let us in today if we ask." He picked up the phone and began navigating his way around the UCL menu system with the phone's keypad and the flat with his feet.

*

Day 435
11:31

Six minutes later he got off the phone with an appointment to see the Wreath Papers in a fortnight and the promise of several application forms winging their way to him in an email. The woman had explained kindly that there was just no way he'd be able to see them today. Just giving him the appointment before he'd completed the forms was a sign of how helpful they were being. Maybe if the collection had still been at Gower Street they could have done something. He had to understand that places for readers were very short. He didn't bother asking her how this would have been alleviated by those same spaces being in a different building. He just politely thanked her and hung up.

Then he screamed.

Not the scream of a frightened girl but the scream of a man in pain. Half scream, half roar. At first it was definitely strangely pleasant, an animal release that his reasoning mind rarely had access to. Midway through though he lost the emotional connection, and that same reasoning mind began to reassert itself by trying out a couple of different graphs. On the x-axis was catharsis and on the y-axis, futility. They were pretty nearly inversely proportional.

His graph was clearly missing a dimension for attraction though as his outburst had brought Ardian back over to him and even made Burim run into them. He briefly tried to add a third axis but gave up. The relationship between the elements seemed unlikely to be linear.

"Ardian?" Burim shouted as he ran in. Ben looked at him and saw that he had produced a gun from somewhere.

"What's that?!" Ben demanded.

They both ignored him while Ardian spoke to Burim in a surprisingly calming manner. "Everything's alright. I'm guessing the professor's just been given an appointment that clashes with his diary commitments." Burim stomped off again muttering and Ardian turned to Ben. "What did they say then?"

"Why has that man got a gun in my house?" Ben asked loudly causing a final little spike on the x-axis before the graph folded in on itself and disappeared.

"Because we're the bad guys Ben. I thought you'd worked that out. Now what did they say?"

"They said we have to wait two weeks."

"That doesn't work for you, does it?"

Ben glared at him. "No. Can you call Petrela? I need to speak to him. I can make this work but he needs to wait and Sarah can't stay there for two weeks."

"I'm not telling him that Jarvis. And neither should you if you want to see your girlfriend again."

"Then what the hell do I do? We can't do anything without seeing those papers and we can't get them for a fortnight."

A minute went by and then Ardian said, "We may be able to get them if we try a different approach."

"What do you mean?"

"I'll make a couple of phone calls, we'll see what we can do. It's a library not Fort Knox."

"I'm not robbing historical documents." Ben said when he realised what Ardian was suggesting.

"Well, your choice, I'm quite happy sitting here for a week, but then…" He shrugged.

"Don't you think I know that?! We need it as soon as possible." More hesitation. "Alright. Make your phone call. But no guns."

"I don't think you're in a position to make the rules Prof, do you?"

"I'm going to the bathroom. Tell me when you're done and I'll speak to Siobhan and let her know what's going on."

*

Day 435
11:41

Ardian opened Ben's bedroom door without knocking.

"Valon's speaking to Petrela. I told him we'll make our way over there now. Then we're on site and can move fast if we need to. He's going to give us a call back when we've got the okay to go in."

"Okay, I'll call Siobhan." Ben said from the bed where he had been lying looking at a photo of him and Sarah in ski gear.

Ardian leant on the doorframe and slung the phone underarm towards Ben before turning and heading back out to the lounge and crashing down onto the settee next to Burim.

Ben picked the phone up from where it had landed next to him and dialed. It rang once before Siobhan picked up.

"We know where they are. The National Archives in Kew." He jumped straight into it as soon as she answered.

"Wow! How did you find them?"

"Lots of donkey work and a bit of luck. Ardian found some guy who used to run Voynich's shop and worked out where his things ended up after he died."

Siobhan lowered her voice. "Do you trust him?"

"Who, Ardian?" Ben asked quietly with an eye on the door.

"Yes. Don't you think he knows a bit too much?"

Ben paused. He did think it odd how much Ardian knew or how quickly he was learning but he hadn't really dwelt on it.

"I don't know Siobhan. I suppose I don't really trust him obviously but I don't have a lot of choice do I? If he knows more about this than he's letting on so be it. It's still a good idea, isn't it?"

For the time being she dropped it. "I guess," she answered. "But are the pages definitely there? What if it's just this guy's old stuff?"

"They're there. There's something listed as Hebrew shorthand, what else could that be? We're on our way over there in a minute to pick them up."

"What do you mean pick them up?" She asked, instantly suspicious. Her suspicion increased when he didn't reply. "Ben? Do they let you take stuff out? They're not running a lending library."

"They won't let me even see them Siobhan unless I wait two weeks. Two weeks! I don't have two weeks. In two weeks they'll have killed her. So I'm going to use a different plan. We're going to get them. It's not like it's the Magna Carta or something. No one but us even knows they're there. I'll send them back when I'm done, you know, anonymously."

"What if you're caught? What happens to Sarah then?"

"Well then she's no worse off than if I didn't try, is she? Look, I know this isn't good but I don't see what else I can do."

"Maybe they've got it scanned in. Loads of old stuff is online." She said.

"No, they haven't scanned them yet. I checked, it says they're working their way through their collection and we should be patient. I don't have the chance to be patient Siobhan. And it isn't like they're going to scan them tomorrow, is it? Some obscure London bookseller's private papers will be bottom of the list."

She didn't know what else to say. "I don't like it. I don't like it one little bit. But I understand. I'd do it too if it were me. When's it going to happen?"

"I'm not sure yet. Our babysitters are coming up with a plan for us. I'll know more then. For now we're just going to head over there so we're ready to go when the plan lands. Now, where are you with the n-gram search procedure?"

Siobhan gave him an update on her progress.

"Great, keep at it. We might need it if this doesn't work out."

"Okay. Good luck. Keep me updated won't you?"

"Of course. I'll let you know before anything happens. Speak soon."

He got up from the bed and walked into the doorway.

"I'm done." He called out.

Ardian hit Burim on the knee.

"Right. Go fill the car up, we're going to Kew. I'm going to call my girl and then we'll make a move."

*

Day 435
12:04

Ben and Ardian both arrived at the buzzing intercom at the same time, Ben from his bedroom and Ardian from making his call in private in the lounge.

"I'm back." Burim said.

Ardian pressed the button, "We'll be down in a minute." He said. "Come on Prof, we're going."

*

When Burim saw them come out of the lift and head for the door he turned and started walking back to the car. He was about twenty feet ahead of them when the old Nissan drove into sight.

By the time it drew level with the back of the 106 Burim's hand was nearly on the passenger door. And then everything happened at once.

*

The man in the back leant halfway out of his window and waved what looked like a stick at them.

*

"Gun!" Ben yelled and pointed.

*

Hundreds of small explosions went off all around them as the man opened fire with a Skorpion submachine gun.

*

Ardian slammed into Ben pushing him over and landing on top of him. He pulled his own gun and started firing at the disappearing car, the noise of each shot exploding in Ben's ears.

*

Burim ripped open the passenger side door and dived inside, cramming himself across the gear stick into the footwells.

*

Four seconds later it was over.

*

Ardian looked around and shouted, "Inside, now!" He dragged Ben up and pushed him back towards the door, Ben fumbling for his keys the whole way. Burim slid out of the car and ran as fast as he could to the building, as he reached the doorway Ben finally got it open and they all fell inside.

9

Petrela put the phone down from Valon. There was no way he was giving Jarvis another week. They needed those pages today. If necessary he'd give Ardian free rein and the young thug could just steam in in a smash-and-grab. The boy would enjoy that, putting the frighteners on a bunch of librarians was right up his street. Give him his due though, he'd actually thought a bit today. But it was bloody rare and probably stopped again by now.

He fired up the website to talk to the Architect again.

ALBN: Plan required today. 058.

He typed, using the code for a theft from a building.

That was the whole bloody problem with his outfit, it attracted the wrong kind of person, people who were too desperate to be seen to be the big man. Waving guns around and pretending they were gangstas. And putting it on bloody YouTube!

That wasn't the way you got respect in Petrela's world. He had no problem with violence, he'd done his fair share of the dirty work coming up but that had been necessary, he'd been building something, fighting every step of the way against a system that didn't want him or his kind to have anything. But that didn't mean he got off on the violence… well, no more than he needed to. This was a choice for him, a way to make a living, he didn't want violence. He wanted security and you got security by having power. And it had worked. He was a respected man now. He had made it. Clawed his way from nothing to a force to be reckoned with. Him and Valon.

These punks were different. They had everything handed to them on a plate. How many of them could have built all this? He needed better people.

When he'd sorted this he was going to have a sit down with Valon, maybe get some of the Architect's time and rethink the way they ran things. Like this cut-out stuff he'd come up with. That was clever. That was the sort of stuff they needed. Maybe he'd be prepared to come on board with Petrela full time. He could use a man like that. If only he was Albanian. Ha! That was the other problem, of course, his whole organization came from a network of families from around his home village. Nobody was allowed in unless you knew who his grandparents were. That was his fault. He'd unthinkingly followed the old ways. Well, it was time for a change. They needed some fresh blood. The world was moving on and they'd have to move with it or die.

He remembered the old men in his village, the ones who had worked in the textile mill. When the mill had been closed down not long after they returned from the war a part of them had died with it. Over specialized, dependent on just one thing, like modern day sabre tooth tigers. They just sat there for the rest of their lives bellyaching. And the rest of their lives had been short. Pointless and short. He had no desire to be a sabre tooth tiger. He would move with the world.

His screen flickered as a response appeared.

ARCH: What is the target?
ALBN: Government building. How quickly can you get a plan?

ARCH: Depends on the building and the item(s). Have plans for some on the shelf will just need tweaking, not for all. Which building?
ALBN: National Archive
ARCH: In Kew?
ALBN: Yes.
ARCH: I have that. And the item?
ALBN: An old document.
ARCH: Private collection or public display?
ALBN: I do not know.
ARCH: Do you have a reference number?
ALBN: Wreath Papers MS ADD632

Petrela entered the reference that Valon had given him from Ardian.

ARCH: Do you need the info in it or document itself?
ALBN: Need the document for the info in it.

Petrela obviously hadn't understood so Seth tried to clarify.

ARCH: Would a photo of document work or do you need original out of building?
ALBN: Need the original.

Petrela was guessing, as far as he knew nobody had asked Ben that question but what if there were hidden messages on the paper? He couldn't afford not to get this right first time.

ARCH: Discreet or open?
ALBN: 100% discreet if possible.

He didn't want attention drawn to the papers.

ARCH: I will investigate. I will let you know in 30 minutes if it is doable today.
-NO CONNECTION-

Petrela nodded to himself. He would have to make that man some sort of offer. He needed him on board.

*

Day 435
12:05

The driver of the Nissan rounded the corner and slowed back to a normal speed. With no one in sight he ripped off the distinctive wig he was wearing and threw it over his shoulder to the man in the back seat.

His accomplice grabbed it up and shoved it into the bag that had caught all of the spent shells.

Neither man said a word. There was no need, all had gone according to the plan.

10

Sarah wasn't given to melodramatics but she had spent quite a large part of last night in tears. This morning though she'd resolved to be more sensible. Crying was definitely Not Sensible and her mother wouldn't approve. She was a dust yourself off and carry on kind of girl. She'd been told so repeatedly. It wasn't that she was emotionless, just that there was a time and a place for emotion and being held hostage in the back of a transit van didn't seem to be either.

Having said that calling it 'the back of a transit van' didn't really do its current state justice.

*

Last night some time… (she wasn't sure exactly when because she didn't wear a watch. She'd always felt watches were vaguely anachronistic in an age with omnipresent digital devices blinking the time at her. She'd reached the age when she cared about the time at the same point as mobile phones had become completely ubiquitous, if she wanted to know the time and found herself in some peculiarly barren landscape devoid of other digital clocks, she looked at her phone. The thought that a watch would come in handy in case she was ever kidnapped and her phone confiscated was not something that had occurred to her.)…anyway, at some point after she'd arrived the back door had opened and a tall man stood there and told her not to move. Although he didn't have any obvious weapons and wasn't young, some preservation instinct told her to do as he said. A second, shorter, older man, clearly subservient to the first and who she thought of as Igor had thrown in some blankets, a bucket and a torch so that she could get through the night.

They left, the doors slammed shut again and the tears had come. Strangely she hadn't cried before that point but the shutting of the doors seemed to open an internal floodgate and she had cried until she had fallen asleep from exhaustion.

That was last night.

She had woken this morning huddled amongst a nest made of the blankets and strained to hear anything going on outside. There was nothing for a long time but eventually she heard somebody approaching. The van doors opened and she blinked in the light, through the glare she saw it was Igor. He was wielding a piece of pipe like a club in one hand and a pair of handcuffs in the other.

"Hands." He said.

Terrified of what he was going to do but convinced there was little point resisting, she extended her hands. He clambered into the van and clipped the handcuffs to her wrists. As he did so she saw that there was some sort of bike lock linked to the chain of the handcuffs, he attached this to the wall of the van and locked it.

She drew her legs up underneath her, scared. Igor looked at her a moment and then left the van leaving the doors open behind him.

Sarah was confused now as well as scared. She shuffled herself closer to the wall to put some slack in the chain, her heart pounding, and tried to take in as much as she could of the sight outside the van. There wasn't much to see, she was obviously in some sort of warehouse but then she'd already worked that out last night. Apart from that there wasn't much she could tell.

In less than a minute she heard Igor's feet returning and she tensed. He was carrying a drill.

Oh God, no! She thought, *Please, no!* But he didn't come anywhere near her. He stood with his back to her and drilled a hole through the bottom of the van door, inspected it, filed the edges peremptorily and stuck his finger in it to check the job. Once he was satisfied he left again. Sarah had no idea what was going on but she found herself relaxing slightly, whatever he was doing he didn't seem to intend to hurt her, not immediately at least.

Slightly longer went by this time, perhaps five minutes or so, before he reappeared, dragging a mattress behind him which he hefted into the back of the van. It was almost the same length as the van which led to a comic moment (if anything about this scene could be labelled as comic, perhaps by default it would have to be tragi-comic) in which she formed a bridge by standing, leaning over the mattress, balancing her hands on the side of the van and actually helped him by kicking it into position. How ludicrous it was that she was helping prepare her own cell struck her only later. In the moment it simply gave them the opportunity to exchange a first smile, him for her help, her for his efforts to make her comfortable.

It was a small and brief smile obviously, given the situation, but important nonetheless. It struck Sarah even while she stood there bridging the new bed in her prison that the wheels of society were greased with small tokens like this, fleeting microrelationships as you walk down a busy street, eyes meeting and agreeing without words on who will move where. This is how society worked.

With the mattress installed he left again. Another minute and he was back with an extension lead which he fed out through the hole he had made earlier before attaching a plug to the end of it. At Sarah's end of the lead he plugged in two desk lamps.

He bent down and scooped up the pipe he had been carrying earlier and gestured for her to back off into the corner.

She did so, panicking again briefly, before realising he had still left the doors open. Raising the pipe to make it clear that he could hit her with it, he leant over and unlocked her handcuffs, leaving them dangling from the side of the van on the bike lock. He backed away from her and hopped out of the van.

He flicked on the lamps and then looked up at her.

"When I bang," he banged the outside of the van to illustrate his point, "you put these on and hold hands up." He said pointing to the handcuffs.

She nodded and tried another little smile. This time his only response was a nod as he slammed the doors shut.

*

It had been some time before he had been back again and, strangely in the circumstances, she had fallen asleep on the mattress so that the bang on the side of the van woke her up.

She clambered up and fastened both hands to the handcuffs. It would obviously be easy to fake this and she filed away the thought for the future but there was no point in doing it now. She had no idea what was outside the van. What else was in the warehouse? Where was it? If she managed to get outside the warehouse what then? They obviously needed to keep her alive to persuade Ben to do whatever it was they wanted him to do but there was no sense in antagonising them.

Igor opened the door a little and peered in, she presented her chained hands to him. He nodded, threw the doors open wider and climbed in.

This time he had brought a newspaper and a camera. She'd seen enough films to realise that they must be intending to use it to prove to Ben that she was still alive.

He pressed the newspaper into her chained hands and mimed opening it out. She tried to open it but dropped it. It wasn't easy with her hands held together above her head.

He tried again and she managed to hold it but he can't have been impressed with the composition because when he stood back and looked through the camera he shook his head, took the paper back off her and propped it on her legs, the top half resting against her stomach. This time it must have worked for him as he took the picture.

When he'd finished he picked the paper up off her, seemingly taking considerable care not to touch her (a point that was interesting she thought, he hadn't touched her once) and took it and the camera out with him.

She thought that would be it but then she heard a scraping noise punctuated by his grunting and he reappeared once more half carrying and half dragging something obviously heavy that he struggled to lift into the van. He positioned it near the door next to the foot of the mattress and she saw that it was a chemical toilet.

One last return trip had him bring toilet roll, two bowls, a 2 litre bottle filled with what she assumed was water, a flannel, a towel and most importantly a plate loaded with toast and a mug of tea.

Once more he picked up his pipe from the doorway and advanced towards her holding up his wrist to indicate she should do likewise. She did so and he unlocked the cuffs. He backed away again and made a sweeping gesture with his hand to encompass the things he'd brought then left.

"Thankyou." She said quietly, as the door swung shut, it slowed slightly but then closed anyway and she heard him lock it outside.

When his footsteps had moved off she assessed the things he'd brought. She was forced to admit that it was quite impressive. As long as somebody provided food and drink for her and, she supposed reluctantly, emptied the toilet when necessary she had everything she needed to stay here for a long time. In fact she was quite sure she'd slept in some worse hotel rooms. If they got out of this she'd have to think about knocking one of these up for Ben and her, perhaps make the walls more attractive though she thought, oh, and lose the handcuffs and threat of death.

*

Day 435
??:?? Breakfast time

So now, having wolfed down the toast and drank the tea she sat there on her mattress reviewing things.

Firstly, her immediate situation. From all the work Igor had carried out she had concluded three things:

> 1. They wouldn't be going to this much trouble if they intended to kill her soon. This was a Good Thing.

> 2. They wouldn't be going to this much trouble if they intended to release her soon either. This was a Bad Thing.

> 3. Despite all of the work Igor had done he had made no effort to soundproof the van, which must

mean that they were somewhere that she couldn't be heard. This was also a Bad Thing.

Then, the general situation. What the hell was this all about? It must be connected to whoever Oliver was. She hoped they found him quickly and this could all be over. For a while she tried very hard to ignore the little voice in her head, strangely enough in her mother's voice, that reminded her she wasn't stupid. These people had made no effort to hide who they were from her or Ben. Which led to a further conclusion:

4. Whoever had taken her fully intended to kill them both once Ben had given them what they wanted. This was undoubtedly a Very Bad Thing.

And Ben hadn't seemed to know anything about it which, now she came to think of it, was quite unusual in and of itself. He always seemed to know everything that needed to be known. And when he didn't know he had no problem admitting he didn't because it gave him the chance to go and find out.

Thinking about him made here smile.

Different, that was Ben. She thought. Different in all sorts of ways. Mostly (but not exclusively, she smiled) good. But definitely different.

*

Day 112
10:27

The first time she had seen Ben had been for the grand total of 30 seconds on the first day of term. He'd managed to cram Different even into that.

When some idiot had bumped into her friend Emma and knocked the DNA model she was carrying to the floor Ben had been the only person to stop and help them pick the pieces up. She'd naturally assumed that it was the beginning of a come on until he'd finished, checked Emma was alright, smiled awkwardly at them both and carried on the way he was going, his head back in the book he was reading as he walked.

*

Day 147
19:30

He'd let her choose where to go on their first date. She'd chosen an authentic Japanese restaurant because neither one of them had ever had Japanese food before. And he'd been Different again.

"Can I get you some drinks while you look at the menu?" the waiter asked.

Ben had gestured towards her.

"Please." She'd said. "Can I get a dry, white wine?" She picked up the menu and seeing that it was printed completely in Japanese, looked across at Ben with a mock panicked expression. He smiled at her.

The waiter nodded, "And you Sir?" He asked Ben.

Ben spoke to him in a long string of what sounded to her like rapid fire Japanese, though she did catch the word "Coke" early on. She stared at him.

The waiter beamed at him and fired off his own rapid fire string in response then headed off to the kitchen.

"You speak Japanese?" She whispered.

"A bit. Not very well." He said without apparently picking up on the amazement in her voice.

"So what did you say?"

"I told him it was the first time we'd eaten Japanese and asked him to recommend some things for us to try. I hope you don't mind?"

"No, that's great. So you speak Japanese but you've never eaten Japanese food?"

"I don't go out much. And I really don't speak it very well, I imagine I sound like Tarzan to anyone who speaks it properly!"

She laughed, "So how many other languages do you speak 'not very well'?"

"A few I guess." Plenty of people would have said it to look good but there was something about him that stopped her getting that impression. The fact that she might find it impressive seemed not to have registered at all. When they'd known each other a lot longer she identified it as a sort of childlike enthusiasm. He enjoyed the challenge and impressing himself was obviously the main aim but impressing anyone else was just not relevant. When she, or anyone else for that matter, drew attention to it though he would get embarrassed and retreat into himself.

"Don't be embarrassed." She said. "I think it's interesting, tell me, what's a few?"

"Nine."

"Nine! How many of them fluently?"

"Fluently? Only the one, English. The rest I can make myself understood in and can understand enough to get by as long as people speak slowly for me."

"Can you read it?"

"Japanese?"

"Yes."

"Yes, I teach myself so reading is one of the first things I learn to do."

"I'd love to go to Japan. Would you?"

He gave it a moment's thought. "Yes, Japan would be interesting."

"Do you not like to travel then?" His delay was a giveaway. Her yes to almost anywhere would be instant. "I'd love to travel more. I want to see things."

"I like learning about places but to be honest travel kind of gets in the way of that."

"I'd have thought going places would give you more to learn?"

"I guess I'm a bit of a geek. The stuff I enjoy learning about tends to be in books. I went to Rome last year and saw the Sistine chapel."

"I'd love to do that."

"Yeah, only the thing is you know what? You can't see it as well as you can in books. The camera gets closer than your eye does. And you can't learn as much about the history of it standing there with the guards shouting *silenzio* every minute and a half!"

"But just being there, soaking up the atmosphere."

"Atmosphere's overrated. It's mostly just nitrogen and stuff people have breathed out."

They laughed.

"I'm being a bit unfair, being there is good for one thing. You know what Goethe said about it, 'until you've seen it you have no idea what man is capable of'? That's totally true. Books split up the pictures obviously so seeing it all as one unbroken mass is very impressive."

"I imagine it is."

Then, through their starter, he talked to her about Rome, a curious story that focussed on all the odd bits of the city. He began in the Sistine Chapel with how Michelangelo had painted most of the figures, including Christ, naked but that they'd had loincloths added after his death and then worked out from there across the city. She listened enthralled, although she wasn't sure whether she was enjoying hearing about Rome or just listening to him talk. He was right, he was undeniably a geek but somehow he was making it funny. And strangely attractive.

"And you learnt none of that from being there?" She asked when the waiter came to clear their plates.

"No, all from books I'm afraid." He grinned.

She flicked her eyes over at the waiter who was coming back to them, "How do I say thankyou?" She asked Ben quickly.

"*Arigatou gozaimasu.*"

"Okay."

When the waiter brought their main course she tried out her new found linguistic talents assuming she had mangled it but he turned one of those gigantic beams on her so he'd grasped her meaning. He replied with some Japanese she obviously couldn't understand and added, "You're welcome."

"Rome sounds wonderful." She said when the waiter had left again. "I should go."

"I'm not saying that, you still learn less than you would reading about it!"

"Philistine!" She said good naturedly, and he smiled. "I'd have thought you'd love travelling for the languages though."

"Yeah that's definitely worth it. You can't really beat trying them out on real people."

Later he'd walked her home and seen her into her building. He hadn't even tried to come in.

She rushed upstairs and hung out of her window, "You're weird!" She called out to him as he walked up the street, his head in a book he'd produced from somewhere.

He looked up and smiled naturally, "It's been said before." He called back. "Goodnight Sarah!" He waved and walked away.

Different.

*

Day 435
??:?? Lunch time

Igor interrupted her reveries by banging on her van. No, *the* van, not *her* van. She cuffed herself quickly and banged to let him know it was done. She guessed by how long had gone by that he must be bringing her more food.

He opened the door a crack and looked in.

She smiled at him and this time she was being at least partly disingenuous. She did genuinely appreciate the fact that he had gone to some effort to make her comfortable, in particular it spoke well of him that he seemed to be taking great pains to respect her physical space. But he was still responsible for holding her here. If he was really a decent person he'd just let her go wouldn't he? She had no intention of falling prey to Stockholm syndrome but she was not above seeing if it could work the other way around. So she would be nice to him and remind herself constantly that he was the bad guy.

"Thankyou." She said quietly as he placed a tray with a sandwich and a drink on the toilet.

"What's your name? Do you know why I'm here?" No response. "Are you allowed to talk to me?" She asked plaintively.

"Eat. You must eat." He said, picked up his pipe and holding it slightly less ready to strike now, unlocked her.

"I don't want to be alone." She didn't have to try too hard to put an edge of desperation into her voice.

He didn't reply, though again he hesitated as he left. But he still left.

*

Ben was one of the most capable men she knew, certainly the most intelligent, with an ability to grasp things faster than anyone she'd ever met. She had never known anything to faze him, so the best solution should have been to wait for him. But last night he hadn't had a clue what it was they were talking about so she had to work on the basis that he wasn't going to do what they needed. Besides, as well as being wonderful, he was cocky as hell and didn't do well with blind obedience. There was a better than average chance he was getting himself killed even as she sat here. For some reason that thought made her smile. Different. If you had to go down it was better to go down fighting. Her mom would have liked Ben.

Anyway, she was not some damsel in distress whose only hope of salvation was to wait for one of the 50% of humans who had a dick to ride in on a white horse and rescue her. (In fact she wasn't sure Ben could even ride a horse. *He probably can.* She thought with a mental roll of her eyes, still she was pretty sure he couldn't joust and storming what she assumed was a well defended compound didn't seem likely to be a talent he had hidden from her.) So then, all told it was not a good idea to wait for him.

And in any case there was still conclusion number 4, her mom's conclusion, certain death regardless. Which led her to her final conclusion:

5. She was going to work on getting herself out.

*

The bang on the van surprised her. It was too soon after lunch for him to be bringing her another meal. She didn't think the service would run to afternoon tea. She moved back into the corner and cuffed herself again.

Igor came in, put a small pile on top of her... no, *the*... mattress and came straight over to unlock her. The pipe was still at the back of the van. While he unlocked her cuffs she looked across at what he'd brought with him. There were a couple of magazines and a portable radio.

He climbed out, closed the door most of the way and then held it and stuck his head back in.

"I am Enver." He said without looking at her.

I am Sarah, she thought, *hear me roar*.

11

"What the hell was that?!" Ben panted, his heart pounding and adrenaline tearing a path around his body.

"Perhaps it was your albino monk!" Ardian laughed. He seemed to be on a high. Burim on the other hand didn't. He had gone a deathly pale colour and was shaking, Ben assumed it was fear until he spoke.

"Those *maskaras*. I am going to cut them up." His voice betraying the rage he felt.

"You said it boy!" Ardian said, laughing again. He turned back to Ben. "It was the Bridge Boys. You'll have to toughen up Prof, you'd never make it in my line of work. Occupational hazard. Good job spotting them though. Give me your phone." He said, gesturing. The screen of his own phone had been smashed. Ben handed it over.

"It's me." He said into the phone a moment later. "No, I'm not ringing about that. You said you'd tell me when we were good. We've just gone outside to head over to Kew ready for you and someone's taken a pop at us... Yeah... Yeah, I think it was. I reckon it was Martin driving. If it weren't for Jarvis spotting them we'd be dead... Probably followed Pjeter's pimp mobile over...Yeah, I know... No there's no need, we're leaving here now anyway, just wanted you to know...Yeah, alright, cheers. See ya." He hung up.

"Right." He said. "We're going to leg it back out to the car."

"You're joking? What if they're still out there?" Ben asked.

"They won't be, that's not how it works. We've got to get out of here before the police turn up. And I need to pick up a new phone on the way." He said throwing Ben's phone in the air. "Burim, d'you reckon the car'll work?"

"We'll have to check but I don't think anything hit it."

"Okay, we're all going to head straight for the car, walk quick but no running. Burim you're driving, everyone in and if it starts then drive, we'll work out where to when we're away from here. If it doesn't start then we all get out and walk to the left. When we're past that bend up there then we start running. Everyone get it?" Ben and Burim both nodded. "Okay, let's go."

At the car it turned out Burim was right, by some miracle nothing seemed to have hit it, it started without a problem and they drove off leaving Ben's neighbours to wonder what the hell was going on.

*

Day 435
12:10

Petrela's phone buzzed to tell him he'd got an SMS. Since he wasn't logged on the website automatically forwarded the message as a text to his mobile.

ARCH: Plan achievable today on basis described earlier. Details being worked up. Check email at liberatinglibraries@gmail.com at 12:45, password is your prof's name. If nec. return via this method. Email address will not work.

*

Day 435
12:11

Valon was about to give up as Petrela finally answered the phone.

"*Tungjatjeta* Gezim."

"Valon, great. I just received a text from the Architect, he can do it. He's going to…"

"Gezim, I didn't ring about that." Valon interrupted. "The Bridge Boys have just tried to take out Ardian and Burim and the professor. I'm getting together a couple of the boys to take it back at them, I was just calling to let you know."

"No Valon."

"Pardon?"

"I said no, we're not doing this now. We have to solve this manuscript thing first. When we've done that we can sort out the Bridge Boys, until then I don't want them touched."

"Oh. Right. Well, you're the *krye*. You're sure?" Valon couldn't hide his surprise. It wasn't the first time Petrela had played a deeper game than him but it felt wrong this time. Still, he supposed he would just have to trust his friend.

"Completely sure."

*

Day 435
12:37

Ben's phone rang breaking the silence in the car. Burim jerked the wheel as it snapped him out of his autopilot daydream state and they swerved while he steered it back away from the M4's crash barrier.

"It's Siobhan." Ben said and pressed the button to answer it. "Hello. Is everything okay?"

"Yeah. I want to help. I've had an idea." She launched at him.

"You are helping. What's the idea for, the n-gram work?"

"No. I'm doing that anyway. The archives."

"We're on our way there now. Siobhan someone shot at us."

"Shot at you?! Are you alright? Who shot at you? The babysitters?"

"Yeah, we're fine. And it wasn't them. I think it's somebody they're at war with." He looked at Ardian, who grinned at the use of the word 'war' and nodded his head.

"Is it connected to the pages? Or the manuscript?" She asked.

"I don't know. I hadn't thought about that. Hang on." He turned back to Ardian, "Siobhan says is the Bridge Boy attack connected to what we're doing?"

"I dunno. Wouldn't have thought so, it just kicks off every now and then. I told you, you need to relax." Ben ignored the last bit and went back to Siobhan.

"He doesn't think so. Anyway, you said you'd had an idea."

"Oh yeah. Well, I had an idea and I've done it. I've got you an appointment today."

"To see the papers?" He said excitedly.

"No, not them." She sounded deflated. "I couldn't do that because you asked about them this morning and they turned you down. They'd remember."

"So what have you done?"

"Well, according to their records a Mark Townshend has an appointment that was set up two weeks ago to look at collection number ADD631."

"The ones next to the Wreath papers."

"Exactly."

"Do you think they take you to them?"

"I've no idea, but I thought it'd be useful so you could get in and, you know, case the joint or whatever."

"Siobhan, that's great."

"You need the letter they're supposed to have sent you a couple of weeks ago, I've uploaded a copy to the shared drive. Can you access it and get it printed off?"

"I'll find a way, otherwise I'll just show them the email and hope they're okay with that."

"Okay. Speak soon then."

"Yeah, speak soon."

She hung up on him and he spoke to Ardian and Burim.

"She's got us an appointment to see the stuff in the collection next to it."

"How do you know what's next to it?" Burim asked.

"It's got the next number."

"That could be anywhere couldn't it?" He said sulkily.

Ben stopped. "I suppose it could actually, yeah. Anyway, she's got us this appointment so we can go in there and see what it's like before we use the plan you're getting." He said to Ardian. "Have they got back to you yet?"

"Not yet."

"Taking a look around first sounds good though. Get the lay of the land."

"Yeah. Siobhan said we should 'case the joint'!" They both laughed. Burim stared straight ahead without cracking his face.

"If your uncle doesn't come up with anything what do we do then?" Ben asked. "We need those pages if I'm going to decode the manuscript."

"We wait. I'm not doing a job that isn't approved. It could cause the family all sorts of trouble."

Ben sought for a change of subject.

"So who are the Bridge Boys then and why are they attacking you? I'm guessing you've got some sort of turf war going on is that right?" He managed to pronounce the quotes around 'turf war' even while fighting not to mime them.

"Yeah. They're a bunch of has-beens led by an old timer called Paul Bridge and his sons, Martin, Gary, Neil, Mark and Jack. They want what we've got."

"What they're gonna get is something else." Burim piped up.

Ardian looked at him amused. "They were bigshots before Petrela moved in. Now they're not. Simple as that."

"They don't seem happy about it." Ben pointed out.

"Hm. You think?"

And that was that, no more office talk.

*

Day 435
12:45

Petrela logged on to the email account the Architect had specified with his perverse sense of humour and discovered mail from another of the disposable addresses. He wondered whether the Architect set them all up in advance and simply remembered them or if he created them as necessary. There must be a way of finding out but of course none of his people would have a clue how to go about it.

*

From: hte1s10010sw0r0cdsf11@gmail.com
Sent: 12.16
To: liberatinglibraries@gmail.com
Cc:
Subject: Documents

Attached are two plans.

1. Discreet
2. Less so

The two requirements you specified, i.e. today and discreet, were to some degree in conflict. I have therefore provided two plans.

I recommend the first if you can wait as it is likely to remain undetected until the next time that the document is requested. For many archived materials this can be years. At that point it will be impossible to determine when the theft took place and therefore all the harder to associate with any individual.

The second can be put in place today and executed tonight but stands a much higher chance of being discovered. The theft that is, not the perpetrators, obviously.

On the assumption that you will wish to pursue the second option despite the risk I have taken the liberty of carrying out a preliminary intrusion of the security company's system and inserted a stub for us to use to this effect. I will need photographs of whoever is carrying out the job to complete the work. If you would rather wait and use the other plan the change can be backed out.

Also see attached architectural drawings for the building.

Return via usual process. Email address no longer in use.

Regards.

<Attachment_1>
<Attachment_2>
<Attachment_3>

*

Petrela quickly skimmed the first attachment, it was good and he was tempted to wait but it would have taken a week to set up properly and he wasn't going to wait that long.

So he'd go with the second plan but he'd have to make a change. It assumed only one person would be going in, there was no way he was relying on Jarvis to do it alone but it needed him because he couldn't be sure Ardian would be able to identify the papers.

He called Valon and told him to get hold of photos of Ardian and Ben and typed out a message to the Architect.

ALBN: Go with plan 2 but need 2 people inserted. Will email photos shortly. Please provide address.

12

Day 435
13:15

Paul Bridges opened his email, saw the weird email address at the top of his inbox and wondered why his spam filter hadn't picked it up. Then his eyes caught the title.

*

From: 11bd0zzzcv0vfd00bd0f1g1ek1w01z@gmail.com
Sent: 13.01
To: Paul.Bridges@hotmail.com
Cc:
Subject: Competitor info re: Petrela

Petrela is trying to make a deal with Turkish importers for a new product.

To ensure that he gets favourable terms he is likely to make a move against your business interests.

It would be in your interest to keep aware of developments and prepare yourself for an attempt at a hostile takeover.

Regards,

Your friend.

*

What the hell did that mean? Petrela wouldn't dare make any type of move against Paul. Not unless the old bastard had started smoking the crap instead of selling it.

And why hadn't he heard anything about Petrela setting up something new? Or anything about any new product? Just let him try. He'd have that wanker.

13

The sign above the garage read "Bridge Brother's Autos" with the irritatingly errant apostrophe. There was a single customer inside the office.

The four men in the stolen car down the road waited for her to leave, the man in the passenger seat taking the opportunity to practise his Albanian.

It was a shame about her car, she would probably look back on today as a really crappy day and tell all her friends in years to come how unlucky she was, completely oblivious to the lucky escape she'd had. If it hadn't been for the bloody traffic they'd have arrived slightly earlier and might not have seen her in the office. They'd have just gone in. The boss wouldn't have liked that, an innocent being killed would have got the wrong sort of attention altogether. And it would have been a much worse day for her than the damage that was no doubt about to happen to her car.

The men in the garage were little more than hangers on. Only one of them could be called connected and that was a stretch. Chris Bridge liked to talk of himself as Paul's nephew but in truth he was a first cousin once removed and he'd had nothing to do with him growing up. His parents had tried very hard to maintain an orbit that was precisely the right distance to count as neither dangerously impolite nor dangerously involved. It was not easy but they'd managed it. And then Chris had come of age, shown no interest in getting a job and proved, when forced to, that he couldn't hold one down anyway.

So he'd taken himself off to "uncle" Paul and asked for help.

His father, steeling himself, had gone and put his neck on the line for his son. He had spoken to his cousin and asked him not to help Chris. He understood that Paul was very successful, had always been proud to be part of the family, etc. but they didn't want Chris involved in whatever it was Paul did so successfully. Thankyou. Paul had looked his cousin in the eye and said he understood. And before he'd left the building had started making calls to set Chris up with this garage.

It was an arrangement that worked for both of them. Chris had to do nothing but got a decent living and, more important, respect from the sort of people he chose to hang out with and fear from the others. He converted both into the basic currency his brain worked in, booze and girls. Paul got another semi-legit cash based business through which he could channel money and the family name plastered over another piece of real estate. And one over on his toffee nosed cousin who'd always thought he was better than the rest of them.

The woman walked out, waved to Chris in the office, a courtesy wave, nothing more, got into a waiting car and her friend drove her away.

Over the road the man in the passenger seat reached into the glovebox and retrieved a mobile phone then nodded to the driver. The driver started the engine and reversed them up the road a little way to give the knackered old heap they were in enough space to get some speed up. All of the men buckled up.

The raid began as soon as the woman left the industrial estate and it ended not long after.

The driver swung the car into the open garage bay door and smashed straight into the back of a mechanic who was bent over inside an open bonnet. He let out a godawful scream as the car crushed his legs, threw him forward onto the exposed engine he'd been working on and ploughed both mechanic and car into the back wall of the garage.

The passenger looked at the crushed man clinically through the windscreen. Writhing in agony, pinned between the two cars, he was wailing piteously and would never walk again but he was alive.

"He'll do. He gets left." He said quietly to the others.

Then they were all out of the car. Fast.

Two of the targets were shot dead instantly by the men from the back seat even as they got out of the car.

The man from the passenger seat stood above the now crippled mechanic and shouted orders in Albanian.

The driver chased a man out of the swinging back door and caught him trying desperately to climb the back fence. It was chain link and for a fitter man would have posed no problem. Unfortunately for this chap he wasn't a fitter man, though he could have taken satisfaction from the fact that his doctor was wrong and fast food and beer didn't kill him. The bullets tore open his back and he fell backwards, dead before he hit the ground and his head burst like a giant bag of thick soup.

Chris and the man who really knew enough to run the garage were both in the office. The intruders found them hiding under the desk and put a bullet through the back of each man's neck while they cried and begged.

The whole thing was a massacre, not one of them put up a fight.

Slightly disgusted at how easy it had been, the four men calmly left the garage and crossed the road to a second stolen car, this one a medium term keeper with clean plates and an altered chassis number. The man from the first passenger seat, now in a second, checked his watch. Twelve minutes before Paul's collector would be round. Nicely done.

*

Day 435
13:55

The mug hit the wall and shattered, staining the paper with the remains of the coffee it held.

"That Albanian bastard! Scum sucking vermin! They are gonna fucking get theirs." Paul was red in the face from the shouting he'd been doing since he got the call.

"Dad, we need to find out what they're doing before we steam in." His eldest, Martin, said. "It's obviously something to do with this new product. We need to know what it is." He pointed at the computer.

"I don't care. Nobody hits my family and gets away with it."

"You'll care when business disappears. We all will." He said, looking around at his brothers for agreement and getting a majority of more or less reluctant nods in return. "We can kill them all anytime. I want to know what they're up to."

"Find out then!" His dad snapped. "But bring me that immigrant's head on a stick while you're at it!"

The boys, always called that but the youngest of whom was 31, filed out of the room leaving their old man still raging and throwing things.

14

In the end they had made three stops on the way to Kew. The first to pick up a new phone for Ardian, the second on the hard shoulder to take passport style photos of Ben and Ardian and email them to Valon and the third at a printing shop once they'd reached Kew to get Siobhan's letter printed out.

Check in time was at 14:00 so they were still early. The good people at the Premier Inn Kew let them in to their rooms anyway, managing to combine being helpful with letting them know the overwhelming scale of the favour they were getting by being allowed in 15 minutes early.

They had two rooms. One for Ben and his minder of the moment, the other for whichever of the lucky hoodlums was getting a break from Ben duty. Right now they were all in the one room to go over the plan and agree their next steps.

Ben booted up his laptop so they could all view the plan that Valon had emailed to his account. Thirty seconds into the launch process (it was a Windows laptop, the new and improved boot up procedure was still too long) the thought occurred to him that of all of the people involved in this Ben Jarvis's name was the only one that would have undeniably illegal activity associated to it. Great.

Valon had called Ardian not long after they had finished speaking with Siobhan. He'd informed his nephew that they had a plan for the National Archives and they'd be going in this evening. It did need photos of both Ardian and Ben though as they would both be involved.

The fact that the plan used Ben surprised Ardian, and irritated Burim, but the idea was to extract the necessary papers from the collection and Ben was obviously best placed to identify them. They certainly wouldn't get another shot at this so it made sense to put the best man on the job and that was Ben. The best man for their highly illegal theft from the headquarters of a government department was the mild mannered university professor. Ardian tried rolling that around in his mind a bit and wondered if he was losing his edge before deciding, with little attention paid to the tone of his recent conversations with his uncle or, more rarely, Petrela, that it was no reflection on him. Jarvis was necessary right now. He undoubtedly knew more about this stuff than Ardian did. But that was okay, he needed to keep his eye on the main prize, this job was just one step along the path, it wasn't the whole thing. As long as he kept Jarvis in check and made sure he delivered then when this was over Ardian would be in good standing with Petrela again. Maybe he'd take Valon's place, he was getting old. And if Petrela could hang on for a couple of years after that then he was a shoe in to succeed to the lot. Who else was there?

Since Ardian and Ben were both going to be going in this evening and the plan required them to be unknown to the Archives staff the only person who could use the opportunity Siobhan had given them was Burim. He was not amused by this. And he was even less amused by the success that Ben was having using him as a foil in his attempt to get Ardian emotionally invested.

"Does he need to go over there now? What time does it close?" Ardian asked Ben.

"Not until 1900 tonight."

"No rush then. Let's all run through the plan so we know what we're doing."

Since Burim had been driving and Ardian had been speaking to both Valon and Zef on the phone for much of the trip Ben was the only one who had had the chance to read the plan so far. So he took the lead and drove the laptop as he talked them through it.

First he showed them the blueprints of the various floors so they were familiar with the layout. Then he moved on to the plan.

"There are two main components to the plan. One, Ardian and I go in there as security guards and actually find and remove the pages. And the other is that on the outside one of your gang hacks into the fire alarm's computer system and triggers an alarm so that the place is evacuated."

"One of us? Who?" Burim asked. Ben shrugged and looked to Ardian.

"Never mind, it's under control." Ardian said. "And I'm guessing we don't evacuate?"

"That's right. For obvious reasons the Archives are not big fans of sprinklers."

"So what do they do when there's a fire?" Ardian asked.

"The storage areas with the records in are shut down with air tight seals and filled with Argon."

"What's Argon?"

"It's an inert gas. It starves the fire of Oxygen and kills it."

"So if you were in there you'd die?"

"You would if the gas was actually released. That's the point of the plan, we're going to fake the whole thing. The hack into their system will convince them there's a fire, sounding the internal alarms and sealing the storage area doors but it will also simultaneously disable the Argon dispensers. The guards then evacuate and Ardian and I walk into the records section and get the pages. There's a bit of camera work but that's about it. They investigate when it's safe to go back in and they'll find there was a computer glitch but the documents and collections and stuff are all fine so everybody is happy and we go home."

"Is that it?"

"Well, like I said the hacker does some stuff with the cameras so they don't have pictures of us. We have to make or get hold of some smoke bombs and it needs someone on standby to deflect the police and or fire brigade if they are called. But yeah, that's about it. I assume you're both going to read it?"

"What are the smoke bombs for if we're faking it?" Ardian asked.

"Verisimilitude." Ben said with a smile.

"What?"

"Realism. It's a case of no fire without smoke. If the alarm goes off but the security guards don't see any smoke they might get suspicious. With smoke visible they won't question it they'll just evacuate."

"That sounds sensible but unless you brought some from home I don't see any smoke bombs."

"There are instructions for how to build them in here if we need to but it also says that there's a paintball shop round the corner, if that's open we can just buy them there. That'd be quicker. It says to give them a bell though and check they're open. Apparently it's run by amateurs and they might not be there."

"Alright we'll do that while you're checking the place out Burim." Ardian said.

"So why am I going there?" Burim asked, his hand resting on the doorframe.

As the written plan clearly didn't need him to do it Ben had nothing to say, Ardian answered him. "I need you to check as much of what it says in here as possible. We've got the building plan but I need to know the things that don't get written down. The plan has lots of information about their security procedures and camera locations and things but is it up to date? You need to check."

Burim nodded sagely. He looked terrified to Ben. He was holding himself too stiffly, masking his emotions too completely to feel comfortable. He was like a woman covering up a spot by slathering on foundation. Sure you can't see the spot but you can see that you can't see it!

"How many of these sorts of things have you done before?" He nonchalantly asked Burim.

"None." The lad replied candidly.

Ben took his chance to turn the knife. "Jesus! None? What sort of a criminal are you?"

"The sort who kills people." Burim said with a glint in his eye causing Ardian to snort. "How many burglaries have you done, Professor?!"

"None. But then I'm not pretending to be something I'm not. Speaking of which, I'm a lecturer not a damn professor."

"Tell him to shut up or I'm not doing this." Burim said to Ardian.

"Yes, you bloody well are." Ardian replied, his voice like steel. "Now knock it off the pair of you, I don't want to be your goddamned dad. Christ, when did I get to be the bloody grown up? Burim you're going in as this Mark Townshend. Jarvis, give him the letter."

"How long have I got to stay there looking at this stuff?" Burim asked petulantly.

"At least an hour, you're supposed to be researching it." Ben took pleasure in seeing Burim's face drop.

"Why can't he do this bit?" He whined. Ardian just looked at him. "Yeah, alright. I'm going."

"Go and get yourself cleaned up and ready then we'll drop you there and go shopping."

Burim started to leave.

"Wait, I've had a thought." Ben said as Burim walked to the door. "If you can put some sort of tracker into the ADD631 box then we'll be able to find it quicker, hopefully 631 is next to 632 and we'll be sorted, otherwise we're going to have to work out the filing system when we get in there. The one thing this doesn't give us," he gestured to the plans on the screen, "is the layout of the stacks themselves. We don't know how they're organised."

"That's really good." Ardian said.

"Hey, what about if I put the smoke bombs in there?" Burim asked. "Then you haven't got to smuggle them in. And the smoke would really be in the right place."

"Yeah and we wouldn't be able to see a thing." Ardian said rolling his eyes.

"And the Argon might well really be released. And we'd be killed." Ben added in a kinder voice this time. Burim nodded an acknowledgment that it wasn't a good idea.

"But the tracker's a good idea. Where can we get one of them before you go in?" Ardian said.

"What about my phone?"

"Has it got a tracker on it?" Ben asked.

"I meant you could just ring it and follow the noise."

"Now, that's a good idea." Ben said and Burim beamed despite himself.

*

Day 435

17:30

Ardian and Ben spent the first hour and a half after Burim left running around Kew sourcing the things they'd need for the plan. Their shopping list, committed to memory rather than written down, made for an eclectic mix:

1. Smoke bombs and detonators – it turned out the paintball shop owner had opened up which saved a lot of home brewing in the hotel room but meant that they also had to buy sufficient paintballs to make it look like they might be going paintballing and endure a twenty minute conversation (read: monologue) about the best sites in the area.
2. Laminating machine – to laminate the ID badges they would be printing with the:
3. Desktop printer – to produce the badges they'd need and print logos on the:
4. Iron on fabric transfers – to transfer the logo onto the:
5. Uniforms – black suits, white shirts and shoes fit for a security guard. (Too many plans (all the way back to Richard III's) had failed because of inappropriate footwear.)
6. Black cocktail drinking straws, largest bore possible
7. Black children's plasticene
8. Sleeping tablets

Then they returned to the hotel room and within a short space of time it resembled nothing more than a factory.

Ben connected the printer to his laptop and produced the ID cards and a credit card sized map of the layout of the building for each of them in case of emergency. Then he ran through almost the whole pack of transfers trying to get the logo correctly on to the jackets and shirts. They had to leave the room twice, the first time to borrow an iron from reception, the second time to go and buy a replacement jacket for Ardian, cue curious looks from the shop assistant. In the end though he was finished and, while it should really have been embroidered to be correct, the uniforms would stand all but the closest scrutiny.

Ardian spent most of his afternoon (with the exception of the uniform manufacturing rescue trips out with Ben, both much needed breaks) on the floor transferring the contents of the smoke bombs to the drinking straws.

Each straw was packed full of powder from the smoke bomb and topped with the pleasingly small radio detonator, all of which he tuned to the same frequency, turning their tiny potentiometer with a cut up piece of plastic UHT milk carton (better than using it in the tea) in place of the jewellers screwdriver he didn't have. The last touch was to add a thin ring of plasticene to each one.

The idea was that the bombs themselves were far too obvious but the straws, dropped strategically, would be all but invisible in corners and at the edges of walls held in place by the plasticene.

Once Ben had finished he left Ardian hunched over his latest straw and rang Siobhan to tell her the plan.

"Who's going to be controlling the computers? That's a fairly sweet hack. Who've you got that can do it?"

"I don't know, the money man's covering that end of it."

"Does he need me to help with it?"

"I don't think that'd be a good idea. He's got the experts, let's leave it to him."

"Perhaps I can monitor the police. Give you early warning if they suspect anything."

"And the fire brigade?" He asked.

"Yeah, both of them."

"That'd be good. Another pair of eyes can't hurt." He glanced at Ardian, who was engrossed in adjusting another frequency, and said quietly, "Petrela's guy is supposed to be watching but I'd like it if you did too. That way if anything is going on you can text me."

"Of course." She said.

"Thanks. Within 12 hours then we should have the pages and then we'll be able to get somewhere."

"Do you know how Sarah is?" She asked, unsure if she should bring it up or not.

"I know she's still alive, they sent me a picture of her with today's paper. And I know she's in some room with metal walls. That's all I know. And I know I'm, *we're*, going to get her back."

"We are. Keep believing it. Get me those pages and I'll do everything I can to crack them."

*

Day 435
18:21

"It's Burim." Ben said in answer to the bang at the door.

"Let him in then." Ardian said from where he was stretched out on the bed texting his girl.

Ben opened the door and Burim walked in.

"Well, that was a waste of bloody time." He said.

"Why?" Ardian asked.

"'Cause there was nothing to learn. It's all like it said in the plan. Got some photos though." He said brandishing his phone.

"You were supposed to leave that in the box!" Ardian said.

"Got a new cheapo one from the supermarket on the corner as I passed. I left that in there. The number's in here." He waved his own phone again.

"Oh, alright, then. Can you hook it up to that so we can have a look?" Ardian said pointing at Ben's laptop.

"Not without a cable. I'll email them, what's your address?" He asked Ben.

"Here I'll type it." Ben said and held out his hand for the phone. "So what happened when you got there?" He asked as he typed. "Did you get to go to the stacks?"

"Stacks?"

"The place where they keep the collection. Did you get to go to where the collection was or do they bring it out to you?"

"No, they brought it to me. They have this room called a reading room just for the UCL Special Collection. They're like really proud of it. Once you've told them where you're sitting they bring you the books and things you ask for. There was only me there, thank God because I looked like a total idiot."

"Just like their standard process then. I hoped that they might be running a different process for the UCL stuff, if so we might have been able to get it more easily."

"Just stick to the plan Prof." Ardian said.

"Yeah, okay you're right."

"Of course I'm right. Now let's take a look at these photos."

15

Day 435
20:30

Burim pulled into the carpark an hour after the reading rooms had closed to be sure that all of the visitors had left and Ben and Ardian got out. Behind them Burim drove away.

Ben looked at the building with a riot of emotions roiling around inside. Terrified, determined, excited. He could understand why this would give people a rush. What was happening to Sarah now? Was she ok? *Whoa!* He thought, *Where did that come from?* He needed to focus on the task at hand.

"Is this going to work?" He asked Ardian nervously as they walked purposefully across the carpark to the side door they'd been told to use.

Ardian shook his head slowly, almost despairingly. He didn't seem to be suffering from any mixed emotions. In fact he didn't appear to have any emotions at all at the moment. Ben was actually quite impressed. He strolled up to the heavy metal fire door and pressed the intercom on the wall beside it, hard.

A voice answered. "Yeah? Who is it?"

"Hello, we're with SeQRty. Sorry we're late."

"Alright, be there in a minute." The voice said.

After a moment the door opened and a little man, who looked old enough that he should have his own specially treated room here rather than be guarding it, slid himself through the small gap he'd left and let the door shut behind him.

"So you're the new guys. I got the call from the office. They said you'd be joining me this evening. I'm Alan." He said extending his wrinkled hand.

"Paul Hodges." Said Ardian, taking the outstretched hand and shaking it.

"John Gates." Ben said doing likewise and suppressed the rules about handling parchment that leapt unbidden into his head as he touched the man's skin.

Alan checked his clipboard.

"Yep. That's you." He said. "They printed your IDs yet?"

"Yeah." Ardian said and they both produced their freshly minted cards.

"Need to get you lanyards for those. Still, it's more than they managed for me. Took two weeks to get mine sorted. Let's go in to the office and get a brew on and then I'll give you the tour."

"We know the layout." Ardian said.

"They covered it in our induction." Ben added quickly.

"Induction?! Well, things have moved on haven't they? Better to see it in person though, eh? And we'll do our first round at the same time, check no one's stayed inside with intent to cause grievous bodily harm to old documents!" He guffawed and led them away down the corridor that lay behind the metal door.

*

Day 435
21:12

True to his word Alan showed them around. He wasn't used to having anybody else with him through the night as it was a one man job, a fact he kept reiterating as they walked, didn't really need more than that. Ardian did a very good impression of a bored employee just following orders.

As they walked they were able to drop the smoke bomb filled straws along the corridor leading to the UCL Special Collection. By the time they had walked slowly up the dead-end corridor bewailing SeQRty's resource strategy and walked back down it discussing the futility of a bonus driven culture in a job with no appreciable targets they had lined it with enough of their smoke bombs to make it look as though a long extinct volcano had sprung into life beneath Kew.

When they had covered what felt like the whole building twice he took them to the *piece de resistance*, a glass enclosure containing five large books bound in wood sitting on top of a heavy wooden chest.

"Gentlemen." He said, humming a fanfare and sweeping his arm grandly to the display. "William the Conqueror's tax register. Domesday."

"I thought it was a book. Why are there five of them?" Ben asked. His question had been directed at Alan but it was Ardian who spoke.

"There are actually two Domesday books. The Little Domesday and the Great Domesday. The five books are just the way they split them up to bind them so they'd last longer. That's right, isn't it?" He asked Alan. Again Ben found himself surprised by Ardian's knowledge.

"That's right lad." Alan seemed impressed. "Those three are the Little and the other two are the Great."

"I looked it up when I knew we'd got this job." Ardian shrugged and tried to make light of it.

But Ben couldn't help but probe a bit, see how much Ardian knew. "If that one's called Little why is it bigger than the Great one?"

Alan smirked but Ardian knew the answer to this one as well. "The Little Domesday covered less of the country but had more detail in it. Like who owned how many cows and pigs."

Ben looked at Ardian quizzically. He was surprised.

Not to be outdone on his home turf though, Alan took the floor again. "See the box they're resting on?" Both men nodded. It was a dark chest covered in nail heads that wouldn't have looked out of place on a pirate's man-of-war. "It was made in the 17th century to house the Domesday. See those three locks?" More nods. "A different person had each key so all three of them had to agree to open the box and get the books out."

"Cool. Like a nuclear key."

"Exactly."

*

Day 436
00:11

A final button press and the exploits embedded in the National Archives servers earlier in the day came alive.

First a copy of the fire monitoring system code was taken and checked against the original:

```
function UserInterfaceInstance (INT Test_Timer)
Begin function
  Copy FireControlAdmin -> New_FireControlAdmin
  Create New_FireControlAdmin
  Sync New_FireControlAdmin with FireControlAdmin
  Set Test_Timer = 0
  Wait While Test_Timer < 500
        Test_Timer ++
```

```
End While
Begin If
        New_FireControlAdmin State <> FireControlAdmin
State
        Goto ErrorTrap
End If
Call FireControlAdmin (Set UserInterface = FALSE, Set
Alarms = FALSE)
Call New_FireControlAdmin (Set Telecoms = FALSE)
Exit function if successful
    ErrorTrap: Present_Error
End function
```

Next a small subroutine moved throughout the system disabling each Argon dispenser in turn:

```
function ArgonDispenserDisable (INT CountDispensers,
BOOL DispenserEnabled)
    Begin function
        CountDispensers
    Begin Loop
        For Each Dispenser in CountDispensers
        Set DispenserEnabled=FALSE
    End Loop
End function
```

Once these two steps were executed the new instance of the system had control of all of the user interfaces and internal building physical control measures, leaving the original with all of its connections to the external world in place but no real knowledge of what was going on inside the Archives.

Finally control was taken of the cameras and a timer kicked off:

```
function CameraControl (BOOL Job_In_Progress)
Begin function
    Initialize Job_Timer
        Call Hard_Drive(Set Record = FALSE)
    If Job_In_Progress = FALSE Then
        Stop Job_Timer
        New_Video = Copy Current_Recording - Job_Timer
            Call Hard_Drive(Apend New_Video)
    End If
End function
```

The cameras continued to see what was happening and output it correctly but the hard drive was now failing to record their input. When the call was received to say that they were finished the timer would be read and a section of memory of the right size extracted from earlier in the evening, the time stamps altered and the data spliced into the file.

With all of this complete the building was successfully isolated and a text message was sent to Ardian. They were on.

*

Alan snapped his head back up from where it had dropped to his chest.

"I'm sorry lads." He slurred. "Don't seem able to keep my eyes open this evening. Not normally like this, you know."

"No problem." Said Ben.

"Maybe it's our company!" Ardian said and chuckled. Just then his mobile beeped inside his jacket, he looked at it discreetly and nodded at Ben. "Perhaps we're just boring?"

"No, no, that's not it. I must just need a bit more kip."

Ben stood up and headed for the door. "Right then!" He said, a little too loudly. "I'm just off to the gents."

Ardian nodded at him and reached inside his trouser pocket and clicked a button attached to his keyring.

"Less tea for him tomorrow ni..." Alan began. He stopped in mid flow when one of the dials on the virtual dashboard on his computer monitor shot up into the red. He pointlessly tapped the screen.

"What's that?" Ardian asked.

"It's a temperature sensor in the Special Collection."

"Shall I go and take a look at it?"

"No need son." Said Alan, "We'll have a check on the cameras. It's probably just on the fritz."

He punched some keys on the keyboard, the dashboard shrank to the top right quadrant and the rest of the screen showed the view from the camera in the special collection repository. And quite a lot of smoke.

"Oh my God!" Alan said just in time for the alarms to start sounding.

"What do we do?" Ardian asked.

"Evacuate."

"What about those people in the offices earlier? Are they still here?"

"Grab that printout there." He said pointing to the printer which the alarm system had caused to spring into life. "It gives us a list of all the people still in the building. We meet them out front and check them off." Alan was standing and putting on a hi-vis jacket. "There's more of these in that locker over there, put one on."

*

Ben had left the security office and quickly made his way to the room housing the UCL Special Collection.

As he walked he rang the number he'd been provided with. It was picked up but, as the plan told him to expect, nobody at the other end spoke.

"Now." He said into the silence and hung up, still walking.

*

Unlock door number 27:

```
function DoorControl (INT Door_Number, BOOL Door_Lock,
BOOL Door_Seal)
    Begin function
        For Door_Number[i]
          Set Door_Lock = FALSE
        End For
    End function
```

*

Ben pushed on the door to the collection and it swung open. He stepped inside and called the number again.
"Inside."

*

Relock the door to the repository and add the airtight seals to avoid an error message appearing on the user interface:

```
function DoorControl (INT Door_Number, BOOL Door_Lock,
BOOL Door_Seal)
    Begin function
        For Door_Number[i]
```

```
        Set Door_Lock = TRUE
        Set Door_Seal = TRUE
    End For
End function
```

*

Ben looked around. The room was filled with column upon column of mobile shelves all pushed together to fit in. To get to any one shelf in particular you had to move it, and sometimes its neighbours, along tracks in the floor to make a space to walk down.

He rang the number of the phone Burim had put in box 631, moved the phone from his ear and listened for the ringing. Nothing. He looked down at the phone in his hand and saw that it had answered, he rammed it to his ear in time to hear the end of the voicemail message.

"Damn it!" He said aloud.

He looked at the shelf nearest to him, it was labelled OGDEN1. That didn't seem very promising. He run-walked along two or three shelving units worth of OGDENs, ascending each time by two, that made sense, presumably the even numbers were on the other side or something.

But where the bloody hell is ADD632?

Then he ground to a halt. Between OGDEN7 and OGDEN9 was ANGL11. Then it jumped to OGDEN27 and the numbers began to descend. So did his hopes of finding the box he needed. He began to panic. This wasn't going to work. Back to the phone. He dialled again.

Nothing.

Again.

Nothing.

Once more. Ah! Ringing! He pulled the phone away and strained to hear where it was coming from. Once he'd identified it he spun around, because it was behind him, and tore through the stacks to get to it. An internal voice chastised him for running in a library but, as though it recognised the gravity of the situation, it seemed half hearted about it.

He skidded to a halt at the end of the shelf that seemed to be ringing. The label at the end read ADD601 – 751. He shoved the phone into his pocket, frightened to hang up in case he needed the ringing to find the right box and looked at the shelf.

He grabbed hold of the handle and heaved. It moved easily. The no-running-voice felt strangely cheated, there should definitely be creaking, missing indexes and much dust to be blown off things. Still, oiled tracks and clearly labelled boxes were better given the circumstances.

He squeezed himself down the too narrow gap he'd made. Here the boxes were labelled and in order. He ran along the shelf until he discovered a single box labelled ADD632. Yes! He checked his watch. It felt like an eternity since he'd left Ardian and Alan. It had been four minutes. Okay, slow down, there was time to do this part carefully.

He removed the box from the shelf and started taking things out of it and placing them carefully on the floor.

*

Ardian and Alan were about half way to the exit when Alan raised his hand to his mouth.

"What about your friend?"

"He'd gone to the toilet, hadn't he? He'll make his own way out. Come on we can't stay in here."

They reached the door and Ardian spoke again, putting a note of panic into his voice. "Alan, I don't know what I'm doing. I've never met any of these people. You're alright sorting all the registering and stuff aren't you?"

"Yes, yes. Come on now lad, hold it together and stick with me."

"Thanks." He said, meekly. As Alan turned away from him back to the door, Ardian yanked off his tie, shoved it into his pocket, pulled out a black marker and scribbled quickly over the yellow SeQRty logo on his jacket. With his jacket covering the logo on his shirt there was now nothing to distinguish him from any other suit wearing office worker.

*

Day 436
00:17

Ben reached the door and made another call.
"Got it."

*

Unlock the door again to let Ben out:

```
function DoorControl (INT Door_Number, BOOL Door_Lock,
BOOL Door_Seal)
    Begin function
        For Door_Number[i]
            Set Door_Lock = FALSE
            Set Door_Seal = FALSE
        End For
    End function
```

*

There was a small huddle of people outside. Ardian and Alan joined them. Ardian instantly put just the right amount of distance between him and Alan to make it look to Alan that he was trying to be involved but too scared while to anyone else he just appeared to be part of the crowd.

He saw Ben slip out of the door, and nod almost imperceptibly in his direction before taking up station near the back of the little crowd and apparently becoming absorbed in his mobile phone.

*

Day 436
01:10

Ardian made the final call as he and Ben walked to the car park of the retail park to meet Burim.

"We're out." He said into the void and hung up.

In the distance Burim spotted them, started the car and drove towards them. He pulled up next to them and they climbed in, Ardian in the front, Ben in the back.

"How did it go?" Burim asked when they were in the car.

"All done." Ardian replied.

"Got it." Ben said exultantly.

"Nice one." Burim said.

"Yeah, we're brilliant. Any chance we could get out of here?" Ardian asked. Burim nodded and pulled away as Ardian continued, "Get us to the hotel and then get to Pjeter and give him the stuff for the girl."

"I called him when I saw you walking over, he should be leaving now to meet me." Burim said as he drove.

"Right. When you've given it him get straight back to the hotel and use the other room, I'll keep an eye on Jarvis. He needs his beauty sleep if he's going to crack this thing. First thing in the morning we head back to the his place."

*

As they drove away from the nearby car park the final piece of code was triggered and began removing the evidence of the new control instance and any record of the two 'security guards'.

*

Days later, when management concluded their assessment of the incident, it was clear that there had been a glitch in the computer system. There never had been a fire, which explained why the system hadn't summoned either the fire brigade or the on-call manager.

The coroner found that the incident had almost certainly been what triggered the old security guard's fatal heart attack later that night but that the fire alarm system company were not to be held responsible. Though it wasn't the official position the underlying tone of the inquest was that he was an old man and if it weren't this it would have been something else shortly after. Even his family agreed.

On the positive side the evacuation had worked like a dream. Everyone had left their stations promptly and the building was empty in just over 3 minutes.

The only thing that wasn't fully explained by this version of events was the curious smell of smoke that a number of people reported they could smell during the night. Presumably this was simply an interesting psychological effect of being involved in an evacuation no doubt enhanced by its taking place during the night when, let's face it, people aren't at their best.

*

The world today is an amazing place.

Until very recently an operation like this would have required a number of different specialists, all on site and all timing things together to perfection.

Lots of room for error.

Lots of humans to break confidences or just make mistakes.

Today everything is digital. And to the digital cognoscenti that means everything is available. And the commute is a hell of a lot better.

16

Day 436
07:30

Siobhan sat at her desk with the material Pjeter had brought back last night in front of her. She intended to work through the contents, scan them into her machine and then send them across to Ben.

The National Archives folder, complete with tag stating "Do Not Remove", contained a single foolscap envelope with Wreath's name scribbled in a hurried handwriting. Inside it was a letter, well, more of a note, from Wilfrid Voynich to Wreath and, matryoshka-like, another envelope with an official tag stating it had remained sealed until the Archives folk opened it to catalogue its contents. These contents were: a letter from Voynich to his wife, Ethel and (fanfare please) the two pages of the manuscript which had been cut out.

She started with the note to Wreath, it was a simple, in-the-event-of-my-death request to pass the enclosed envelope to Ethel.

This gave Siobhan pause. Why hadn't Wreath done as he'd been asked? He'd had ample opportunity, Ethel outlived her husband by thirty years and Wreath had remained in fairly close contact with her for a large portion of that.

On closer examination the outer envelope appeared to have been opened in precisely the same neat manner as the inner and she formed a working hypothesis. For some reason (no point speculating as to what) Wreath had never in fact opened even the outer envelope. He had therefore had no idea of his former employer's wishes with regards to the inner one, nor even any clue of its existence. This was hardly very satisfying from the point of view of a person preparing for death but had the feel of something ludicrous enough to have happened.

Happy enough with her explanation she scanned it in for Ben. Probably pointless but better he had sight of everything just to be sure.

Done with the note she moved on to the missing pages. She carefully removed them from their envelope one at a time and laid them out.

They were beautiful, she could hardly believe she was holding something that was six hundred years old. And that hadn't been seen by anybody for a hundred years and by precious few before that. They were clearly the missing pages, without a shadow of a doubt. She had spent long enough staring at the manuscript over the past few months to recognise the script, the drawing style, even the parchment.

She gazed at them for a while, hoping something would jump out at her. The fact that they had been cut out was pretty damn significant. But significant in what way? What was it that it signified? She hadn't got a clue.

She lined them up one at a time on her flatbed scanner and recorded the images. This had to be it. The answer had to be in these pages. She'd work on the transliteration of them herself this morning, there was no way she was pushing these image files out over the net, Christ the forums would be on it in seconds and she'd probably be arrested. Then when she was done she could add them to the rest of the transliteration from the Mechanical Turk workers. By the end of today she'd have the most complete version of the manuscript anyone had had since 1912. And she had the benefit of modern technology to process it. All of a sudden she was confident that she could do this. She'd decode it and she would be the first person to read it in… well, probably since it was written down. My God. All those people trying for so long and she would do it in, what? Two days? Three?

Oh and they'd save Sarah as well, of course, that was the main reason they were doing this. She thought, guiltily.

She'd better email these over to Ben. She grabbed the final letter out of its envelope, the one Voynich had intended Ethel to get if he died, meaning to scan it in quickly so Ben had the complete package and she could get on with the transliteration.

The letter was only a third out of the envelope when she stopped.

What the hell was this?

She pulled it out completely, stared at it and mentally reordered her morning's work. She would not be transliterating the new pages. Not yet anyway.

*

Day 436
07:42

"Ben, have you seen my email?" She blurted out as soon as he answered.

"I'm just in the restaurant. I can't see my email unless I get off the phone." He said, the irritation plain in his voice.

Assuming the irritation was directed at her she was taken aback. "I thought you were going back to yours? What are you doing in a restaurant?"

Now, *he* took offense at *her* tone. "Waiting for these two to finish eating. *I* haven't eaten properly since Monday lunchtime. It's not exactly my priority is it? But they won't leave until they've eaten." In front of him Ardian made exaggerated chewing and lip-smacking motions. Ben tried to ignore him. "So what's on the email? Is it good? Are we getting somewhere?"

"I think so. It's astonishing. Inside that envelope to Wreath there's a letter from Voynich to Ethel, kind of an in-the-event-of-my-death type thing."

"Does it tell us where the gold is?"

"Well, no because he didn't know, remember? All he found was this thing he called a 'proof' which Oliver reckoned was a smaller amount of gold."

"So does it tell us where that is?"

"I think it probably does."

"What do you mean 'probably does'? Does it or doesn't it?" He snapped at her.

"Most of the letter is a code Ben."

"A code?"

"Yeah. Take a look at your email and ring me back." She rang off shirtily.

*

Angrily stabbing at the screen for the benefit of Ardian and Burim, Ben called up his email on his phone.

The email from Siobhan was at the top of his inbox. He opened it and tapped the attachment titled V2E.pdf, assuming that it stood for Voynich to Ethel.

The handwriting was difficult to read on the little screen but when he scrolled down he soon saw what had got Siobhan so excited.

*

3rd Oct. 1914, London

Dearest Ethel,

I depart tomorrow for Liverpool and from there to New York upon the RMS Lusitania.

It is not my intention that you should read this letter, however, I write it anyway as men are not always masters of their own destiny. Travel is treacherous [Of course, Ben thought, *this is only a year or so after the Titanic sank making the same journey.] and if the worst should happen then I would rather you were aware of its contents and had the opportunity to profit from them.*

Enclosed are the two folios of the Bacon manuscript [Voynich believed that Bacon wrote what was now referred to as the Voynich manuscript.] which I believe are of the utmost importance to the secret it holds.

[This it. He thought as his eyes scanned further down the little screen. *This is what got Siobhan so worked up. Seven paragraphs of complete gibberish. It must be some sort of code.]*

PF TG BM TE OW DC UA UT AF CS TI SC GZ UZ TE OB SA UT CT FI ID EL GN DC SP WO EP WE CS PF FA QP OI QB KC GN AU GS FD CT LQ KF TK OA PQ OM BL TE ML VB FB XS KP EK TC CH PE WA OB ST FC EP PF DI DC SP PF NG AS WE GN EP WE UT PF PN KF TX IT CF ZG MD QP AN HZ QP GN WI SE

CT FS GP QP OW QP QP TF MH SG RV TG WG
QU ET PO CT ND FA SG PF PE KE ET BW EV

IK BY AI QU PL UF MI WR MU DA TC FC
ST XT OP MT KE PG DI TW MH PV QM VA
GZ UC KE SG AW SD ID PA MB TP ET BY AM
YP CS UF GS TE QP EP

FO EP UO ZL RY PT TK UB DR ZH MW SK
MD NI MW PQ SG PF FA HY DI PE TF TI TU
UO CT YF WO QM SL SG PF PG MT SB AF GZ
GN MP BY AM YP CS LU PQ GK TZ NG ZG AS
GP QP OW QP LR QY MB SG AW TE AM LP PI
ON TF IM DI BT YE MA SE SG AW DA SL IO
MF PQ PU PT AW OB SA UT AS FR QL FP CF
ZG RV TW QB FB FD SG AW TU PF CS HL WT
SX PQ FO EP MP SA GZ DU QU PQ PT TK UB
DB MD NI MW PQ SG PF FA AS DI CR CD
AW SE GP QU KD CS CF BU PB PA PS TK PF
PF FA BU PB SA OW ZC FI BL IO KP UO ZX
QU BG IF TU PA KE PS OW UP WA DB EL PF
NK FB RI PQ AU SE KA SP FI RM CT SA PW
WO FQ DF FC QH PQ PF CT BD IW KE SX PQ
TP EK EZ

TM OM BL OW OP GP DA MP AO UF AM
PF PT NK UT LI UT AF CS TE GP WU MD KI
OW UB BT MB AU UP CT FI RM BO CM ID
FB XS TU PA KE PS KC GN AW PO CT ND
FA PE DB PI ON ID CL SK SA PM TG PQ YQ
SG AW WQ SE GP BY SX AM MN OW DC MA
FB XS QP OQ XS MD SA SO MN PF UF FS GP
DA TC FC ST XT QY

AS DI TU VO WR SB SC UT PF FA CK AU
CL QP FA SG PF PQ PT AW OA GP OI CZ NI
MB NE WE RF DM TQ CU WP GP TP AT RT
KF PT GP TF TI PV QM CE WT HO QO QM UO
CT ZB UT XS MP FA AM ST IO IT EP UQ DT
EP FK TU HQ BT RP

PF DI ZC KE NP AN SG FQ WQ FG QU NO
SP DK XS NM TE TW UQ ON PT AW BY MW
DM TG QU QM MP NG XS TE GP DA MP PO
SQ KA ST PF PT CF TQ OA GP QP OI CS GS UQ
OA GP OI CZ NI MB NE AS TP DG AS DI VE
SA GZ FC KP CO SA LO DF UA MO PS AF SL
PD QM DF GT NA FB FQ WQ HS MB KN AD
WR ZL CT TP LZ QP BT MU BL IT PQ OW MB
PW QM VA GZ HC TX NG ZG ZG QW QA SG FO
EP OP GP TP AU SL UQ ON PG UF MI PF PN
UQ VD TP WO SX PS HQ TK EP QY MB BL PT
DA SL TM QS AR HV YF UA CT PO CT ND
FA PE GP QP OI CS GS UQ OA GP FM LZ QS SE
CT FS GP TC EY NH VB EW AW PF NK BT
MB AU UP OW DC WF SL WR OZ CD ZG SP
XS OY CT AO QU CT WP DB EL KF KA PZ QM
FB XS WO EP TC EI SG QS FR XY XT XT QP KC
GN AW FO WG QU FM MU PD RT TS WT WR
QC TU XA TU TF DN MF TK QP TE WE FB SA
AW WQ AE GP IV CF ZG PT AF OQ ZC AO UQ
OS FB NA YP NE KP SP FA FB BU PB AF SL
XP SA PF IT VE AW WQ LM ID EL QW MF TE
TK GS XS MP CS KN IK BY AI QU TZ CD ZG
KP FQ WQ FS RW QM AD WR ZL CT CR NA

*UT SD CL PG DV AW PD WT WR RL DI TW
MH EV*

I have not shared with you the fact of this secret until now because I wanted to solve it to my satisfaction before doing so. If you are reading this it means that I failed to do so before my death. Forgive my vanity. A woman of your undoubted gifts will, I am sure, be able to shed light where I, and so many others through history, have failed to do so.

Любовь всегда,

Your Wilfrid.

*

"This is it." He said, waving his phone across the table at his gluttonous companions. "We've got it!"

Ardian looked around the dining room quickly. There were only two other tables occupied, one in the furthest corner by a couple with eyes and ears only for one another and the nearer one by a family with three kids whose parents were desperately trying to keep them under control. And failing. That suited him fine, the extra noise would help mask their conversation.

Ben was already calling Siobhan back. She answered immediately.

"Why did he write to her in code?" He asked.

"Presumably because he didn't want anyone else to know what was in it." She was still annoyed at him.

"But what about the letter Oliver found, if he could read it that can't have been in code can it?"

"No but none of us have seen that."

"We've been over this. We believe it exists."

"Yeah. I'm just saying we haven't seen it so we don't know if it's coded. But he never said it was so assume you're right and it isn't."

"Why would he write one in code and one not?"

"I don't know. Isn't it enough that we've found this one that is?"

"I'm just trying to understand why there'd be two letters saying the same thing, one with a code and one not." He said.

"Well, the Oliver letter didn't say *what* or *where* the proof is, just that there was some."

"That's right."

"So perhaps this one tells her what it is and where he found it."

"That makes sense." He said, thoughtfully. "So we need to crack this as well then. But before that, what about the pages that were cut out? How are they?"

"They're amazing Ben. They're here. Have you seen the scans I sent you?"

"Briefly. Can you read them?"

She finally lost it at him. "Ben, Pjeter got back with them at 2am. I fell asleep looking at them at about 3am. I've had about 4 hours sleep. When I woke up I found this and called you straight away. So, no. I haven't deciphered and read the six hundred year old code just yet."

He was quiet for about ten seconds. Ten seconds is a long time to be quiet on the phone.

"I'm sorry." He said eventually.

Exploding a bit had helped her cool down. "Don't be. I understand. You've just got to understand too. These things aren't quick. I'm doing all of it as quickly as possible. Today the Turkers will finish their transliterations and I will stitch it all back into one piece.

That and these new pages together give us a really good chance of getting something." He didn't reply. "I know you were holding out a lot of hope for these pages but unless a street address was written on them in plaintext they were never going to instantly give us the answer."

More silence and then, "I know that. I just thought… we're getting so much closer… I just thought…"

"I know what you thought and I told you yesterday, we'll get her back to you. But let me do this, it's what I'm good at, yeah?"

"Yeah. Thanks Siobhan."

"Right. Now this code from Voynich to Ethel, it's got to be important. If all he had that we didn't were these two pages then the answer has to be in them. Agreed?"

"Agreed."

"But at the moment they don't mean anything more to me than the other pages do. He must explain what he did in this code to Ethel. I'd like to start by trying to decipher that. Does that sound sensible?"

"Yeah it does. But how do we go about doing it?"

"I'm glad you asked." And for the first time that morning he could hear her smile. "Are you sitting comfortably? Then I'll begin!" He laughed despite himself and she carried on, glad that the earlier tension had dissipated. "The code is a Playfair cipher. You can tell by the fact that it's grouped into twos. We call them digraphs."

"I'm a linguist Siobhan."

"Sorry, I slipped into crypto 101. Have you heard of the Playfair cipher?"

"Well, no. But I know what a digraph is."

"Okay, back to 101 then but the version for language nerds." He laughed again. "The Playfair is symmetric, remember symmetric and asymmetric from the other day? And it's monoalphabetic but instead of substituting single letters it combines the plaintext into digraphs and substitutes those. It makes deciphering it much harder because you can't just use a standard letter frequency analysis."

"But there are still patterns in digraph frequencies." Ben pointed out.

"There are but it's just harder to map them. There are six hundred of them and you need a lot more ciphertext to start spotting the patterns. It's not a bad system at all, the government used it up until World War II."

"How did Voynich know about it if it was a government system?" Across the table Ardian, the conspiracy-theorist-gangster, pricked his ears up and Ben inwardly rolled his eyes.

"Oh most educated people knew about it around the turn of the century. People used to leave coded messages in newspaper personal columns, at least those of them with the time and money to read newspapers did. Anyway, Playfair follows that Shannon's maxim I mentioned the other day. It doesn't matter if you know that's what he used, you need to know the keyword to decrypt it."

"So how was he expecting Ethel to decipher it then?

"Ethel Voynich had been a spy when they met. And she was George Boole's daughter. George Boole as in famous mathematician, inventor of Boolean algebra. Maths was hardly an unknown land for her. We can probably assume that she was familiar with several of the encryption techniques used at the time. She probably understood the digraphs meant it was a Playfair as quickly as I did."

"But you said she'd need the key."

"Yes. The key would have to be something they'd both know, something they'd agreed on beforehand or that he could be sure she'd work out he'd use."

"So do we try to come up with those?"

"Not really. There are 2^{79} possible combinations. We can have a try at a few if you like, you could do it on the drive back to your place, I'll send you a link to a website that'll let you enter some of the text and try out different keywords. No, what we really need to do is set up an algorithm to solve it. It'll take a while to run." He groaned. "Not a long while. I'm talking two hours for me to write it and three, maybe four hours for it to run. We could get dead lucky and hit it straight away but assume it'll take four hours."

"What do you mean 'get lucky'? Don't algorithms just take a specific amount of time?"

"Some do but the type I'm planning to use for this don't have a fixed runtime unless we build one in and then it just might not work in time. It's an artificial limit."

"I don't understand."

"The best way to crack this is to set up a shotgun hill climbing algorithm. That basically means it makes a random table of letters and tries to decrypt the text with that, does a letter frequency analysis on the result to see if it matches the profile of the target language, changes the table slightly, decrypts again, does another frequency analysis and compares the results. It keeps any improvements and changes bit by bit until the frequency of the decrypt attempts matches the frequency of the target language perfectly."

"Like a genetic algorithm?" He asked.

"Yeah, that's basically it." She said surprised.

"Why the funny name then?"

"Shotgun refers to the random starting position. The hill climbing bit is a metaphor from maths. Imagine the problem as a three dimensional plane, any improvement in the solution is a climb up a hill off the plane."

"Okay. So if you tell it to finish in a specific amount of time it can but it will just be stopping, it won't necessarily have really finished?"

"Yeah."

"So you're going to write one of these algorithms for the text."

"I am."

"Can I do anything to help?"

"Not really, leave me to it. I'll call you when I'm done."

"Will it work Siobhan?"

"It'll work. There are only two complicating factors. The fact that we don't know what language it is in, they both spoke several so he might have used any one of them, or worse a combination. So I'll need to keep intervening in the algorithm to see if I recognise words that it might move away from because it can't assess a jumbled up bunch of languages. Hopefully he didn't do that though. And the other one is that this type of algorithm has a weakness in that if it randomly starts out at a bad place it finds better and better versions of something that is inherently wrong. That's why the shotgun bit is built in, to randomly restart in different places on the plane and compare them. Again it just means I should keep my eye on it. Both of those things just make it harder though, they don't make it impossible. It will work."

17

Day 436
08:03

Knowing that Siobhan was now on the case, Ben had allowed himself some toast for breakfast. Neither Ardian nor Burim seemed to mind the delay, it just gave them an opportunity to have more.

Once they'd finished they had headed back to the rooms and made sure they were clear of any evidence of their stay. The only small difficulty this presented was finding all of the pieces of smoke bomb casings that Ardian had thrown increasingly further from him as his patience wore out. The plan was to take it all with them and dump them in a number of different public bins as they drove.

Rooms cleared and checked out Ardian announced that they'd be 'swinging by my uncle's place on the way' to Ben's to give Valon an update in person.

More like to point out how under control he has everything and get his face seen, Ben thought.

Apparently being a gangster was depressingly similar to every other human collective he'd encountered. University lecturers, office workers, gun toting kidnappers and drug dealers. It was all politics. Don't just do a good job. Make sure you're seen to do a good job. And if you want to get ahead and are forced to pick between the two, pick the latter.

However, since (a) any objection he made would count for nothing anyway and (b) they could contribute very little while Siobhan worked on decoding the letter, he said nothing but climbed into the back seat and turned on his laptop to reread Siobhan's scans.

*

Day 436
09:29

Jack Bridges was waiting in his souped up, black Audi S4 drumming his fingers impatiently on the steering wheel in time to the radio station. He and his three mates were watching the Albanians' scrapyard. They were parked about two hundred yards up the road, facing away from the yard while the lads in the back used binoculars to keep an eye on any comings and goings on the site. Martin was insistent that they needed to understand what Petrela was getting into. He was worried about being left behind if the Albanian got a jump on them with something that took off on the street.

Martin was the family thinker, the strategist, and he wanted info. That was fine. But Jack was more a doing kind of guy, he wanted action, he wanted revenge. Chris was his cousin... Alright, second cousin... And the little twat had got on his nerves on the few occasions he'd had anything to do with him... But family was family... And anyway, truth be told he fancied a bit of a rumble. Martin was getting his way at the moment but sooner or later the old man would snap and want blood. And as soon as he gave the nod Jack was going to be in there.

"Jack." Said Dave, the guy in the passenger seat.

"Yeah?"

"Isn't that Ardian?"

"Where?"

"Traffic lights." Dave said and pointed.

Jack looked across the junction at the beat up old Peugeot and squinted. "Yeah. It is."

He wasn't waiting any longer. He started the engine at the same time as he shouted. "Tool up, we're having him."

His mates, knowing the old man had said to wait had just enough time to be gobsmacked before he'd got the car started and was heading straight across the junction at the side of the other car. They quickly dropped the binoculars and grabbed an assortment of guns out from under the seats as the car crashed over the pedestrian crossing in the middle of the road, glancing off the plastic bollard impotently flashing its keep left arrow at them and sending it careening across the road.

Only Dave, unencumbered by surveillance gear, managed to get his gun out of the window and get off a couple of shots before the cars met but he only had an old revolver and his wildly inaccurate shots did little but send out a warning.

*

Burim saw the black Audi heading for them and assumed it was out of control until he spotted the man in the passenger seat firing at them.

He threw the car forward, slamming it into the back of the car in front. His quick reaction didn't get them completely out of the way by the time Jack's car reached them but they had moved forward enough that he only hit the boot, pushing the rear around and freeing up the nose rather than smashing into the seat Burim was sitting in. Burim held his hand on the horn and drove across the lights as fast as he could. In the backseat Ben crouched down. Ardian was swearing.

Burim veered to the right and headed for the scrapyard but Ardian twigged where he was going.

"Not there!" He yelled, "It's too slow!"

Burim spun the wheel and did a U-turn, cars screeching to a halt all around them and aimed towards the main road.

During Burim's momentary drive the wrong way Jack had got his car reversed and turned and was powering after them. It was never going to be much of a contest, the 106 against Jack's enhanced Audi, and he caught them before they'd even reached the other side of the lights.

He rammed their car from behind and kept the accelerator down. The Audi ploughed the little Peugeot ahead of it like a mascot tied to the front of a juggernaut as Jack headed them towards the pavement and the building site beyond.

There was nothing Burim could do to stop it.

They smashed through the fence surrounding the site, the flimsy metal screaming against the car as workers in fluorescent jackets scattered like ants.

Burim saw the wall approaching dead ahead of them and yanked the wheel to the right. The little car tried desperately to respond but the combination of the sharp turn and the speed that the Audi was forcing it along meant it stood no chance of handling it.

It flipped.

Jack slammed his brakes on and the Audi screeched to a halt.

Tumbling side over side, the 106 finally crashed into the wall on its side with its roof pressing against the wall, undercarriage on display.

A horizontal hailstorm of bullets from the Audi peppered the underside. The steady rattling of the two automatics in the back disturbed by the last few pops from Dave's revolver. None of it accomplishing anything.

"Have that!" Jack bellowed.

"Jack, let's go!" One of the guys in the back said.

Taking the advice, Jack threw the car into reverse and tore out of the building site clanging over the remains of the fallen fence.

The 106 teetered on its side, moved by the weight of the men within and then crashed back down to its wheels. As it landed Ardian looked past Burim and saw the Audi tearing away.

As they left a final shot rang out, the crazy echoes and his disorientation making it sound as though it came from the other direction. Instantly his face was covered in blood.

"Out! Out!" He screamed at Ben who had been frozen in the back seat unable to do anything. They both scrambled from the car and Ardian grabbed hold of Ben's jacket. "Behind that!" He pointed at a bulldozer that had been abandoned by its driver.

When they reached it they fell behind it gasping.

"What... happened to... Burim?" Ben panted. "Shouldn't we wait for him?"

"I'm wearing him." Ardian replied coldly and gestured to the blood covering the right side of his face, and matted in his hair. "We need to get away from here. Get another car." He checked his gun as he spoke. "Come on. Over there."

They hauled themselves up and staggered to the other side of the building site where the workmen had left the site door open in their terrified exodus.

"Where are we going to get a car? Your uncle's place?" Ben asked as they ran in a crouch.

"No, we can't go there looking like this. Half the time it's under surveillance by the police." He stepped into the road and pointed his gun at the first car to approach.

"What are you doing?!" Ben yelled.

The driver, panicking and unable to think of simply driving around, stopped. Ardian made his way to the driver's side door and opened it.

"Get out!" He screamed.

The man practically fell out of the car holding his hands palm outwards and shouting "Okay, okay. Take it."

Ardian got in. "Get in the car!" He shouted at Ben.

"I'm sorry. Sorry." Ben stammered at the man and got into the passenger seat.

Ardian tore off up the road leaving the driver standing there. Ten seconds later he started sobbing to himself in the middle of road.

*

Day 436
09:34

The lone man on the roof opposite allowed himself a small moment of satisfaction. He'd taken advantage of an unplanned opportunity and it had been a decent shot to boot. Much more satisfying than simply watching the scrapyard.

Still he'd have to move on now.

He typed out a text on his phone and began to pack up his sniper rifle.

*

Day 436
09:46

Ardian turned off the North Circular and drove calmly into the carpark of the first pub they came across. As soon as they stopped Ben opened his door, lurched forward and vomited.

Ardian looked at him over the bonnet. Now that they were at a safe distance he appeared perfectly calm again.

"It's exciting round you Professor, isn't it?" He said. Ben didn't reply, he was still bent forward holding onto the wall to try to stop the peculiar shuddering the Earth had so recently started. "We need to get to your place." Ardian continued, a mixture of amusement and irritation in his voice.

Ben looked up at last. "They've already been there. They might expect us to go back."

"They don't know who you are and they can't wait outside every place I've ever been can they?"

"Come on we need to be walking." Ardian had his phone out and was fiddling with the map application. Once he'd got what he needed he strode off down the road with Ben in tow and rang Valon. "They've had another go. The Bridge Boys... Definitely. It was Jack this time. The mental... They got the boy. No not Jarvis, our boy, whatshisname."

"Burim," Ben said quietly in the background but Ardian wasn't paying any attention and in any case Ben suspected he knew perfectly well what Burim's name had been.

"Hollow tip. Ripped him apart but lucky for me 'cause I just ended up covered in bits of his head instead of getting hit as well. We were right by you but I had to get us away. Expect the police before long. Can you get someone to pick us up and get us to the professor's place? We're just leaving the car now... Alperton tube station is a 20 minute walk. There's a hotel opposite, we'll be in the lobby there... Thanks. Uncle Valon, we've got to do something about these scumbags. They're getting too cocky... Yeah, okay well when he gives the go ahead I want to be in on it. Somebody else can look after the professor can't they?... Alright, yeah he's the *krye*, but tell him I want in yeah?"

*

Day 436
09:49

Valon made a quick phone call to one of his *miqs* to dispatch someone to pick up Ardian and then rang Petrela.

"It's me."

"Valon."

"What the hell is this thing Gezim? We've just had another attack on Ardian."

"By Bridges?"

"Yeah."

"And you think it's about the manuscript?"

"I don't know, why else would they suddenly be so interested?"

"It's probably just a push. We've seen it before. Bridges is on the way out and he doesn't like it."

"Well, whatever it's about let me take it back at them. Ardian wants to have a pop at them and he's right to Gezim. This is twice now, they need putting back in their place." Petrela grunted at the other end of the line. "I think we should let Ardian lead it, this is the sort of thing he's good at. We can get anyone to look after Jarvis. What do you say?"

"No, not now. I need to sort this first."

"Gezim why is this so important?"

"I will not be made to look like an idiot."

"Reputation? If we don't sort the Bridge Boys we're not going to have anything to need a rep for."

"I've made my decision Bogdani. We'll deal with them when this is sorted."

Valon hesitated before agreeing. "Yes *krye*."

"Good. Now tell me how it is going."

"I don't know. They were on their way here to give me a report when they were attacked *krye*. Ardian'll no doubt call me when he's been picked up. I'll have to ring you then."

Petrela paused, trying to decide whether to make something of Valon's tone. But no, the man was annoyed but he was going to do as he'd been told, there was nothing to be gained by belittling him further. "Right. Call me then."

18

Day 436
09:?? Just after the 09:00 news

Sarah's roaring, whilst clearly being a much better mindset than passive victimhood, had not yet come to anything.

At first she'd left the radio on because it gave her an idea of the time. Eventually though it became monotonous. Quite quickly in fact. The songs began to repeat after a distressingly short amount of time and the voices sounded the same even though the topics and presenters were different.

It all began to grate so she'd turn it off for a while and then turn it back on to re-orient herself to the time. It was amazing how quickly her sense of the passage of time drifted. She'd have to talk to Ben about it when they were back together. He was bound to be intrigued and probably tell her of some experiment done on it in the sixties or something.

He was interested in everything. When he did it badly it could be insufferable. And sometimes he did do it badly. She remembered him being intrigued at her neighbour's funeral, that had been awkward. And yes, she had had to tell him it might be a perfectly valid question to ask the vicar but expressing any interest in the mechanics of cremation at that particular moment was insensitive at best.

But that was unusual, his delight in learning about just about everything was usually endearing. She found that just looking at the world through his eyes made it all a lot more interesting. It was actually on the evening of the funeral that she'd realised that in lots of ways he reminded her of a child. He could take a refreshingly simple delight in things but at the same time show this surprising naivety, occasionally tripping into rudeness.

She pulled herself back to the moment. She'd been drifting again. She imagined everybody who'd been held prisoner went through this. The overriding sensation was one of boredom. She'd been terrified plenty of times in the last few days but boredom was the thing that was really getting to her. The lack of anything to occupy her mind.

She thought of people like Nelson Mandela and Terry Waite but in truth like most people she knew very little about either of them save that they'd been held prisoner (or hostage in Waite's case) for a long time. She had no idea what either of them did to prevent themselves going mad with boredom.

Maybe if you knew how long you were going to be held for that would be better? Perhaps it was the uncertainty, the thought that you might get out at any moment that made it all the more torturous? If you knew you were going to be held alone for years perhaps you could start some adventurous mental project. That's probably what Ben would do. Stone walls do not a prison make and all that.

Who'd said that? Wasn't that Wilde? He'd been sent to prison unjustly as well. Well, justly given the laws of time she supposed but still unjustly in her view. In fact there were plenty of famous people throughout history who'd been imprisoned unjustly for one reason and another. She tried to recall a list but drew a bit of a blank after Wilde, Raleigh and the Burmese dissident Aung Sun Suu Kyi.

In any case none of it gave her any comfort, if she remembered right Raleigh was killed and jail had pretty much broken Wilde. And neither of them were being held captive by gangsters trying to force their boyfriend (or significant other) to work for them.

She put the radio back on and looked around her cell. Her eyes lit upon the bike lock holding her handcuffs to the wall.

She knew now what she could do to pass the time. Her brother Darren had taught her this when she was little. Not that he'd ever used it to steal a bike, at least not as far as she knew, it had just formed part of his Houdini routine. Well, not so much a 'part of' as it happened, more the 'whole of'. Still, parents, grandparents, uncles and aunts alike admitted it was a very impressive routine, if routine was the right word for an act in one part. Which it wasn't.

As his younger sister she had earned the position of glamorous assistant (without being very clear on the selection criteria, though she now suspected that being gullible and not wanted in the audience may have been factors). More importantly for today as his glamorous assistant she had earned the knowledge of how the budding escapologist carried out his trick.

The idea was simple. By putting the cable under tension it was possible for her to work out the combination. If she turned the wheel furthest from the "key" end slowly then when it landed on the right number she would feel the faintest of tugs in the chain as it loosened from the lock. Once she'd got the first, or rather last, one she would move along to the next.

It wasn't a fast process (which also gave Darren's 'routine' a bit of a knock in the suspense stakes!) but it worked.

She settled down on the mattress, pulled down on the cable and began to work it out. It was delicate work and required paying close attention to the feel of the combination lock as it turned. Unfortunately it didn't require a great deal of mental energy so she was soon drifting off in thought again.

*

Their friends thought it was funny how much in love they were, putting it down to a honeymoon period. It didn't fade though. She put it down to working at it and not getting complacent. Her friends didn't get it. Why work at it? You shouldn't have to work at it. They said. But perhaps work was the wrong word she thought, it isn't work if you enjoy it. It was just important to keep trying. And he always seemed to keep trying.

A couple of months after they'd met, just before they'd broken up for the Christmas holiday (they weren't living together by then but they might as well have been, they both had keys to one another's flats and spent very little time apart) she'd arrived home from classes and he had been in the kitchen sitting cross legged on the work surface reading a book.

*

Click. There! She felt it. Fantastic, she'd got the first one. She glimpsed up at the number. 6.

*

He was always reading a book. She had joked that she wouldn't recognise him without a book but there was some truth in it. She couldn't think of an occasion when he didn't have a book in his hand or at the very least within arm's reach. Well, alright one or two occasions.

She'd probably have found it annoying or even upsetting if it wasn't for the fact that she could interrupt him at any point and he would engage with her completely and then, when they had finished, pick up where he left off as though there had been no break. He never used a book mark either and even when he had a few books on the go at the same time, as he often did, he always seemed to remember where he was in each of them. Reading was just like breathing for him. He read watching television, he read making tea, he read eating, he read walking. She'd once pointed out what she referred to as this astonishing ability of his to multi-task and he had disagreed.

"I don't multi-task particularly well," he'd said. "I can't do the things you do. If I try cooking a meal you get the choice of half cold or half burnt. What I can do is process multiple sources of information quite well."

He was right about the cooking. She always cooked for them. If she didn't cook she wasn't convinced he'd eat at all. She wasn't really sure how it was he'd survived before her.

"Sandwiches." Had been the answer. Of course, food you can eat with one hand while holding your book with the other.

*

Click. 0.

*

So, there was nothing particularly unusual in coming home and finding him sitting in an unusual place reading.

What made this time memorable was that next to him was an old fashioned picnic basket full of her favourite foods, a list he hadn't explicitly asked for but which he had obviously mentally collected through their conversations over the course of months.

And that was what she meant by work. It was paying attention to the other person, so that you knew what they liked and disliked. Surprising them with unprompted effort, not gifts necessarily, though that was nice, but effort. Giving over what he called 'mental space' to them. Putting in effort, effortlessly.

Above all she knew without a doubt that she was the most important person to him, he proved it in lots of tiny ways every day. And he was to her.

The picnic had been great fun. And they'd learnt a lot, chiefly:

1. That he paid very little attention to the outside world, to the point of being surprised when she delicately pointed out that it was December.

2. That she didn't particularly like the cold and that picnics were designed for summer not December. The addition of a coat did not apparently turn it into a good idea.

*

Click. 0.

*

3. That they were food opposites. If she had a favourite food on her plate she would eat it straight away, presumably due to a combination of:
   a. millions of years of small mammalian ancestors burning pathways into her brain to

fill her with the overwhelming desire to hide away important foodstuffs; and

b. her own meta-desire to satisfy her desires as quickly as possible.

He, on the other hand, would always leave a favourite anything for last.

4. That the densely packed, needle like leaves of the Yew tree were particularly good at keeping the rain off when there was a wholly predictable rainy afternoon.

5. That picnics were designed for summer not December. Such a valuable lesson that she had decided they should learn it twice. He had obligingly agreed.

*

Click. The last one fell into place quickly. 1.

*

The lock came apart in her hands. Success. She looked at the combination, 1006, memorised it and relocked it immediately.

Then she had another thought, she listened out to be sure Enver wasn't approaching and then moved one of the digits back so it read 1005. Now she'd only need to slip that last dial one click and she'd be off the wall. Still handcuffed and trapped in the van but providing Enver unlocked the door she would have a way of getting out. And if she could take the keys from him she'd be out of the cuffs too, that couldn't be too hard, he hadn't even bothered with the pipe this morning and he was an old man. She was sure she could overpower him if necessary.

The question now was when should she do it? There was no point getting free only to roam around a slightly bigger cell outside. She'd need to have a chance of getting out altogether or there was no point. And once she was free she'd need to get hold of Ben and let him know. How to do that? She didn't even know his mobile phone number, it was on her phone so she'd never bothered. Did anybody know phone numbers anymore?

The university, they'd have it. As long as she escaped during opening hours her first call would be to them, get the number then tell Ben to make a break for it.

The unwelcome little voice in her head spoke again pointing out that it wasn't a great plan, really. She couldn't really disagree but it was what she had for now. Besides, she had time to tweak it while she waited for the right opportunity.

19

Day 436
07:50

Siobhan put the phone down to Ben excited and scared at the same time. Him saying he hadn't eaten had reminded her how hungry she was. She needed to eat and to get a cup of tea or she wouldn't be able to think properly. She never started the day without a cup of tea but this morning she'd leapt into action as soon as she'd got up.

She looked over at the settee where that Pjeter man was lying on it, still asleep though she'd made no effort to be quiet. And wasn't about to start making one now.

"I'm making tea, does anybody want any?" She shouted chirpily to be unkind and disturb them.

Zef lumbered out of the spare bedroom rubbing his eyes. In a different situation she'd have found this pair funny, they were really quite amateurish as far as guarding went. Pjeter had been supposed to be keeping an eye on her while Zef slept. When she'd come in to the lounge this morning she'd found him asleep on the settee. She didn't know what the ones with Ben were like but if these two were the future of criminals in this country then she felt quite safe. Zef was slightly more impressive than Pjeter but they were both basically boys play acting at being bad guys. Oh, she had no doubt that they could each be very unpleasant if the need arose, or even if they were just let off the lead and they'd almost certainly enjoy every minute of it, but neither one of them was going to be running the show and if you'd given them an easy path to a non-criminal lifestyle as they grew up they'd probably have taken that instead. This was just what they saw around them. It was the default, no thinking option.

"Please." Zef said as he walked into the lounge and kicked Pjeter. "Get up. You were supposed to be watching her."

"I was. I must have just shut my eyes for a minute or two."

"Yeah. A minute or two while she had a complete conversation with the professor. Well done. Lucky for you I was listening from the other room." Pjeter went to speak but Zef cut him off again. "If you need a kip go and get one in there properly. I'll wake you in a couple of hours. You need to be alert." Pjeter dragged himself off the settee.

"Look," Siobhan said to Zef as he seemed to be the closest there was to the brains of the outfit, "I'm focused on trying to decode this thing. I don't need watching the whole time. I'm not planning on trying to run away." She smiled and gestured to her chair.

"I didn't think you were. You know. Thinking of running away." He looked embarrassed and, like so many people, wouldn't look at her chair but didn't want to be seen looking away from her chair so compromised with himself by almost never looking in her direction at all.

Bloody hell, she thought, *real gangster material.*

The weird part though was that she had been telling the truth. She really hadn't been thinking about getting away. Why the hell not? She hadn't been outside in a long time, in fact she didn't want to think about how long it had been. It didn't matter. She had everything she needed in here. But surely they had to come up with a plan for getting away from these people? If they didn't then she had to assume that at some point they'd kill them all. Even these guys couldn't be that amateurish could they?

She wheeled her chair under the worksurface and filled the kettle. She had to admit though Ben's point was a good one, it was better to stay useful until they came up with a plan. But they should be working on that plan and she didn't know about Ben but she hadn't been.

For now though she needed to focus on writing the algorithm.

*

"So what you doing Siobhan?" He asked sipping his tea as he walked over to stand behind her. Since he had not been interested in anything other than watching porn since he arrived she assumed he was trying to be polite out of some deep seated instinct to repay her for making him a cup of tea. She didn't like rude people pretending to be polite all of a sudden and expecting everybody else to play along. So she told him exactly what she was doing. In detail.

"I'm afraid it's all a bit beyond me." He had the decency to admit when she'd finished her high speed and unnecessarily detailed explanation of local optimisation algorithms and the history of the mathematical plane as metaphor. The latter including a couple of diversions which were tenuous at best and she'd included only because they sounded complicated.

She tried to turn the knife again, she took his honesty and stood on it. "Oh? Ah, yes, I see. Well, never mind, it isn't important." She nodded allowing just enough condescension through in the desperate hope that it would remind him of the many other times he'd disappointed people in his life. *Ha! The wrath of the geek*, she thought. "Basically I'm trying to stop your boss killing Sarah."

Sadly Zef wasn't quite as stupid as she thought, he knew when he'd been insulted and certainly wasn't one to take a slap lying down.

"I'd have thought somebody in your line of work was used to killing people." He said. "Or don't you like to get your hands dirty? That is what you did isn't it? Cracked codes for the government? I don't imagine they were coded shopping lists do you? You can't be very good after all if nobody died because of your work. I'd have thought somebody as bright as you would know that."

She was begrudgingly impressed but wasn't about to get into a moral debate with this man who had invaded her home. "I need to get on with this if we're going to get it done. You do want it done don't you?"

"Sure." He smiled viciously, knowing he'd won. "Carry on." He waved to the computer.

She turned from him, picked up her tea and a pencil (she couldn't think without some sort of writing tool regardless of how much she ended up writing) and started to jot down pseudocode for the algorithm.

There were definitely some pluses to work with, she was completely sure it was a Playfair and Playfair wasn't very good at diffusion. That is, small changes in the matrix it was based on tended to make small changes in the ciphertext. That sounded obvious of course but modern day ciphers were designed to amplify any change in the key or the plaintext into a big change in the ciphertext. It was another of Claude Shannon's findings and it greatly increased security. Purely by chance the Playfair wasn't bad at it for a cipher developed before computer attacks, but in an age where desktop computers in every home could run through millions of calculations per second anything that hadn't been specifically designed to accomplish it was going to struggle. Which meant that it was ideal for the kind of attack she had in mind.

The biggest downside she had to contend with was the one she'd told Ben. If she was Voynich she would definitely have made it harder for people by spelling stuff wrong and using multiple languages. That would throw off any frequency based analysis but leave the message completely interpretable to Ethel. In fact it would still work today.

She couldn't do anything about incorrect spelling since she wouldn't have any idea beforehand if he'd done it at all and if so which words he'd misspelt and how. So ignore that for the purposes of the algorithm. On the language front there was more she could do and the real question was how far did she go?

She knew Voynich knew several languages but how many did Ethel know? Or rather how many could Voynich be sure they both knew well enough to communicate what was presumably an important message in? Russian certainly 'cause she was famous for it (and indeed in it, translations of her novel were a bestseller in Russia). English, obviously. She hadn't heard anything about it but she'd also assume French and Latin on the basis that most educated people knew them at the time. And she'd better add in Polish since it was his mother tongue and he might very well have taught it to his wife. That gave her five languages for which she had to include digraph frequency tables for the algorithm to assess against.

She mulled it over as she looked about on the net (no sense reinventing the wheel). There were plenty of general purpose hill climbing algorithms and even a few that focussed on Playfair decryption but, in the way of much of the internet, they all assumed a monoglot English population.

Abandoning the internet again she considered building all five languages into the same code set and including a weighting function that would learn which was the most likely as it went. After twenty minutes of scribbling she gave that up, it was intriguing but she could feel herself getting sucked into it and it would take too long balancing and optimising. In any case there was a simpler solution.

Inspired by the numerically small but politically powerful monolingual minority who had colonised cyberspace first, she would simply create five separate instances of a monolingual algorithm but give them each a different language to work on and she'd set them off at the same time. If four of them failed and one was a success so be it. Once she'd started them running she'd give some thought to cross pollination between them but at least things would be moving this way.

She finished the algorithm within the bounds of the prediction she'd made to Ben. The program finished compiling an hour and a half after she'd put the phone down to him.

To prevent them competing for CPU resources and give them the best chance of success she set all five going on separate machines. Luckily she had several. These were five of her best. She had others. She arranged them in alphabetical order of the language they were running in, set them off and sat back.

Great. More tea was called for. And no offer to Zef this time.

*

Day 436
10:06

The first alarm sounded from the second machine. The one running French. That was odd, she hadn't expected that. She wheeled over to it and looked at the output it had flagged. And then realised she didn't speak French. Or Russian. Or Polish. And her Latin, while better, was thirty years old.

She'd have to write a dictionary look up with a variable number of wildcards to allow for the inaccuracies in the key table as it evolved.

As it was she didn't need it this time. It was obvious that while this might meet the frequency analysis it was gibberish. She kicked the machine off again, effectively triggering a new start table or location in her plane and quickly knocked up a lookup program with a call to an online dictionary. The next time each of them stopped she'd patch it into them.

*

Day 436
11:24

It didn't take her long to complete the transliteration of the two new pages. She looked over at the machines whirring away as they tried out various permutations. There was nothing she could do there except continue checking. She needed something to occupy her mind. Picking up that debate with Zef would probably occupy her but she rejected that idea in the interests of retaining her sanity. Her eye fell on the missing pages. Perhaps she'd try out her new idea. The Capricorn / Aquarius astrological page had pushed something up in her head she hadn't thought of before, though she must have noticed it. The astrological charts were all labelled with western zodiacal symbols (that is, the pictures at their centre were each of a zodiac sign which anybody in the west would recognise today from a thousand cheap newspapers). But there were a couple of zodiac signs which had more than one representation. A couple where the same animal was drawn, one coloured and one left blank. And in every case both pictures were labelled with the same "word".

She would take the zodiacal titles and attempt to use them as a crib to force the rest of it. Start by cataloguing the words for the zodiac signs in western languages, follow it up with a syllable count on each. Perhaps she could match the lengths of the words to the syllables they encoded? Then when the transliteration was complete use the letters in the names as cribs against the wider text. See what it threw up.

There was little hope of it succeeding but she couldn't stand by and do nothing. She needed to feel as though she was doing something.

*

Day 436
14:56

She didn't hurry when another alarm sounded. This was something like the thirty first alarm. Who was she kidding? It wasn't something like the thirty first, it was exactly the thirty first and she'd begun to get a bit irritated. Human involvement had seemed like a good idea, and truth be told it probably was, but as the particular human concerned she'd got really fed up of it really quickly.

She finished the bit she was working on and made her way over to the machine.

She reached out, fingers poised over the command combination to trigger a restart and froze. That looked like English. She looked closer.

My God it is. She thought.

It wasn't complete, there were obviously still errors in the key table but you could start to see order and meaning rising out of the mess like watching somebody familiar walk out of a mist. Assuming the algorithm focussed in on this solution now (and didn't decide the moment had come for a random restart) it shouldn't take long. She responded to the code's request for input with a command to continue assessing the current effort.

This time she didn't leave it. She sat and watched as, each time it reran, a little more of the message emerged from the fog.

*

Day 436
15:01

"Ben I've got it."

"The letter?"

"Yes the letter. I've cracked it."

"Brilliant! She's done it!" He called to Ardian who was in the lounge on the phone. "What does it say?"

"I've emailed it to you. Can you see your emails? Are you at home?"

"I am. I'll log in now." He got up, went in to the lounge and plugged in his laptop. "Does it give us what we need? Please tell me it does."

"It does. Ben, it does." She couldn't keep the excitement from her voice. "I'll read it to you if you like but it's quite long, if you can log in it'd be better for you to see it."

"No, that's fine I'm just logging in now." He said, navigating to his email. "You wouldn't believe this morning." He said as it logged in.

"Why?"

"Because we were forced off the road by that rival gang and shot at all over again. And Burim's dead."

"My God Ben! You should have called me.

"It was more important that you did what you've done, anyway I'm alright."

"But this Burim? Who's he, one of the babysitters?"

"He was, yeah." He said, distractedly as he was now opening up her email. "I've got your email."

"Did he die when you were shot at? Did they kill him?"

"Yeah. Can you give me a minute to read this?"

"Do you want to ring me back?"

"No, no. Are you alright to hang on?"

"Yeah, no problem."

"Thanks."

He skimmed as quickly as he could through it. She had emailed only the decrypted text not the rest of the letter but it seemed to stand alone. It read:

The first folio contains an illustration and a single line of text in that remarkable coded language. After much study I have been able to translate this line. The little text on the page was all directly relevant and therefore rewarded my efforts. Translated the text says:

Capricorn holds your final answer. To see his words you will need to visit Briset's priory in Oldestrete.

After much research, my love, I discovered that Briset was a Norman who founded the Hospitallers' priory in Clerkenwell. I therefore hurried to St. John's but was disappointed to find a modern restoration. I thought all my work had led to nothing. However, after still more research I discovered that it is built on the original crypt. Beneath that crypt I found a chamber. My work had not been for nothing. The chamber contained a quantity of gold larger than I have ever seen.

So much for the first folio. The second contains the zodiac for Capricorn and Aquarius. I have not been able to translate this but since it is referred to on the previous folio I have removed it. It must hold the final answer.

It is now my opinion that Bacon created the rest of the manuscript to hide only these two pages. He was, as you know from our many conversations, a master of steganography.

This unexpected good fortune gives us two routes to provide for ourselves, the first remains the sale of the remainder of the manuscript itself. It is still a beautiful document and should fetch a good price. If you can secure a purchaser for it you will be well looked after. The second route holds the promise of even greater riches. Find somebody who can translate the remainder of the document and then apply it to the Capricorn folio and you will never want for anything again. You have often asked me how we were able to afford our shops. Now you know. Know also dearest that I took the smallest amount from that crypt beneath a crypt and yet it has stood us in good

stead ever since. Capricorn will be good to you if you can but convince him to show you his words!

"Siobhan, this is phenomenal. This is exactly what we needed."

"I know."

"Have you got any idea what the priory in Clerkenwell is?"

"I looked it up as I called you. Have you heard of St. John's Gate?"

"Yes, something to do with the Olympics?"

"I don't know about the Olympics but that's where it is anyway. There was an old priory there where the Knights of St. John used to have their headquarters before Henry VIII dissolved the monasteries."

"So the proof is buried under St. Johns Gate?"

"That's what the letter says."

"Siobhan, you're a genius."

"I know." She smiled. "What are you going to do? Are you going to go over there now?"

"Yeah. We've got to. This is it, isn't it? The beginning of the end."

*

Day 436
16:50

Having checked into yet another budget London hotel, Ben and Ardian walked around the outside of St. John's Gate.

It was an imposing building, a crenelated archway straddling the road separated from its large, vaulted, stained glass main window by a triplet of coats of arms. The whole thing was built from large blocks of stone and looked for all the world like part of a castle had been transported into the middle of a perfectly average London street. Which was about what had happened except that instead of the castle landing in the street, the street had grown up around the castle like some sort of masonry based enchanted forest.

They walked repeatedly through the archway but couldn't find a way in. After about five minutes of fruitless perambulation a door opened in one of the businesses at the side of the gate and a man stepped out blinking into the light.

He lurched backwards as Ardian shot towards him from the other side of the street and Ben did the same from under the archway. They reached him together and he tried to step back in through the door obviously thinking it was a robbery.

Ben broke into what he hoped was a smile and said quickly, "Hello! I wonder if you could help us? We're a bit lost."

"Oh! Yes, of course. What are you looking for?" The man answered, obviously relieved that they weren't attacking him.

"My friend here is researching the Hospitallers and was interested in seeing the crypt here." Ben said.

Ardian shot him a look but played along. "It's for a sort of family history project I'm working on."

The man frowned. "I'm afraid you've been given some duff information." The man said to Ardian. "There is no crypt here son."

Ardian looked at Ben again, bemused but Ben was none the wiser.

"No, someone's steered you wrong. The crypt is at the church." Now it was their turn to feel palpable relief.

"The church?" Ben asked.

"The Priory Church of St. John. Just up the road." He pointed.

"Do you happen to know if it's a modern restoration?" Ben asked remembering more of the letter.

"I do. I'm a St. John's Ambulanceman. I've been in a few times. The crypt is original. Twelfth century in fact. From what I remember the church has been rebuilt a number of times. I think the last time was after the blitz. I could be wrong though."

"That must be the place." Ardian said to Ben.

"Yes," the man continued. "It's a magnificent place. Beautiful church and the crypt has a couple of medieval effigies and things. That'll be what you're after if you want your genuine period stuff lad."

"Yeah that'll be it. Thanks." Ardian said. "It's definitely the genuine period stuff I'm after." He said with a fairly transparent sneer. Ben cringed but the man appeared not to notice.

"Which way did you say it was?" Ben asked.

"Just up there." He said, pointing to the right. "Cross the Clerkenwell Road and it's on your left. On, erm… Albemarle Street."

"Thanks, you've been a great help."

*

They reached the Priory Church at a run to find a red brick building which certainly didn't look any older than mid 20th century.

"They must have had a thing for grand entrances these Hospitallers." Ardian said, pointing to the massive iron gateway in the centre of the building. Flanking the gates were four Doric columns, supporting an ornate lintel topped by the eight pointed cross. Half hidden behind the gates was a beautiful looking garden.

"I don't think that's our entrance." Ben said and walked off to the left where a heavy front door, impressive in its own right but less so following the Gate and the gates, stood ajar.

They made to walk through the door but were stopped politely by a gentleman sitting behind a counter. He was wearing a uniform of sorts, dark trousers and a jumper with the St. John's insignia on the left breast and wielding a date stamper.

"Evening gents."

"Oh, hello." Ben said. "We were hoping to take a look around."

"I'm afraid that won't be possible, we're just shutting."

"Oh, that's disappointing." Ben said. What the hell were they going to do now? How could they get this far and then be stymied by the opening hours of a church? Weren't churches supposed to be open all the time anyway? He launched into his spiel regarding Ardian's passion for all things of antiquity again. "So, I don't suppose it'd be possible to arrange a private tour? You know for a history buff?" He gestured towards Ardian, conscious even while doing so that unless Ardian had even deeper unknown pools of knowledge than he thought, this whole thing would fall apart the first time the man asked a question. Then again Ardian had surprised him repeatedly with what he knew, perhaps he did know enough about the Hospitallers to bluff his way through if necessary. But it'd be better if they didn't have to find out.

The man hesitated, clearly wanting to help them but unsure of what to do. "Let me go and talk to Patrick." He disappeared, leaving Ben hopeful and Ardian irritated.

"What are you doing? I don't know anything about this. What if he asks for detail about what I'm doing?"

"I don't know, I'm ad-libbing. Just pretend you're enthusiastic but learning."

The Chap, because you'd have to call him a Chap, he exuded Chap-ness, from reception came back.

"It's a no go I'm afraid. We've got a wedding reception here this evening, one of the fellowship members. And we've got to get the place ready."

"Not even a quick look?"

"I'm afraid not."

"Okay." Ardian interrupted before Ben could carry on. "Tomorrow morning then. What time do you open?"

"10am."

"Thanks. That's great, we'll see you then." Ardian pulled Ben away.

"What are you doing?! We need to get in there!" Ben said when they were out of earshot.

"And we will but not by talking to Chumpy the Magnificent there."

"We can't break into a church!"

"We're not going to break into it. We're going to walk into it." Ben frowned, confused but Ardian just grinned and carried on. "We will probably need to break *out* when we're done though. Now come on, we've got to go and buy suits, we've got a wedding to go to."

20

Day 436
19:03

They'd been waiting in the café at the corner for about 10 minutes, nursing a cup of coffee and dressed in their newly acquired suits when the wedding party had started to arrive.

"Come on then." Ardian said, making to stand up.

"Hold on!" Ben said quickly, raising his hand. "How are we going to do this? We don't know anybody there, we don't even know the name of the couple."

"You never been to a wedding? No one knows everyone. Half the time even the bride and groom don't really know them. Either their parents insisted on inviting them or they haven't seen them for 20 years. Just throw yourself into the middle of it and look like you belong there."

"How do I do that?"

"God, I don't know. Look like you'd normally look at one of these things."

"I normally look out of place." He smiled.

"Yeah, I can believe it." Ardian said with disgust. "Just make sure you and me are talking then, talk to me about your work like we're catching up. If we're not talking just try to look bored rather than scared. If you catch anyone's eye smile at them and if anyone talks to you just say how beautiful 'she' looked as they made their vows or something. No one'll disagree with that to someone they've just met even if she looked like a pig squeezed into an inner tube two sizes too small."

"Got it. Phatic communication." Said Ben the linguist.

"If you like." Ardian replied, clueless as to what he was talking about and not interested as long as he stopped talking and started moving.

They stood, left the café and strode purposefully over to join the crowd that was starting to mill about, some with their face pressed up against the iron gates looking through into the garden where a photographer was taking pictures of the bride and groom, others outside the entrance Ardian and Ben had been at earlier, now resolutely shut against the jostling crowd of relatives, friends and passing acquaintances.

After what for Ben felt like an excruciating (appropriately enough outside a church, he thought) three minutes the doors were opened and the crowd shamble-shuffled forward.

Like all crowds it had subsumed the individual people in it and turned them into unitary-crowd-elements (or UCEs), reducing their freedom of movement. No doubt this model would be quite effective in a perfect world, each UCE would respond to the environment around it like an insect's legs, and the crowd would move in a coordinated fashion without the need for a central brain guiding it. Sadly human UCEs were buggy and tried to go their own way which slowed the whole process down. Eventually, however, Ben and Ardian reached the front.

Thankfully the man now standing beside the door was not the Chap from earlier. This one was more of a Gent. Dress uniform and everything.

Despite his best efforts to appear relaxed Ben held his breath as they passed him but the Gent simply nodded at them as he did at all but every eleventh person who passed. The eleventh received a "Good evening."

The Gent was a pro and evidently eleven-ish was a number that he had landed on as being some prime factor of crowds, enough to ensure everybody heard a greeting, not too much that everybody heard it repeatedly.

Ben became conscious he was rambling mentally and made a concerted effort to get a grip on himself as he was swept along through the round-fronted entrance hall and off to the right into the church itself.

The church was really quite beautiful. He was standing in the large doorway, flanked by pilasters to either side of him and facing up to the altar. Light filled the place, streaming through the hall behind him, the stained glass window to his left and the huge vaulted, leaded panes high up on the walls.

The floor was a highly polished black and white chessboard pattern interrupted in front of the altar by a gold encircled St. John's cross embedded perfectly flush in the floor. The gold arms of the cross were separated by lions and unicorns reflecting the light from the windows and the chandeliers above (which for some reason were lit despite the presence of enough natural light to give the women in the corner still wearing their expensive sunglasses enough of an excuse to get away with it).

He and Ardian made their way up towards the altar, attracted by the large double doors there. Presumably the stairs to the crypt were behind those doors.

Ardian reached them first and leant on them as though waiting for the bride and groom to make an entrance. When Ben got to him a moment later he tried them discreetly.

Nothing.

They were locked.

*

Day 436
19:24

After too long spent negotiating passage through groups of people engaged in small talk, and promising to catch up shortly with one man who seemed to be under the impression they were Colin's (the groom? they guessed) colleagues and would have good fodder for the speech he was going to make later, they found themselves in the courtyard where the photo shoot had taken place.

"Where the hell is it?" Ardian said.

Ben didn't reply, he had spotted a possible answer. Or at least a way to get one. There was a man in uniform lurking by the ornate gates having a crafty fag. Ben strolled towards him doing his best to appear nonchalant.

"You had enough too?" Ben said and blew out slowly, shaking his head. "Bit much these things aren't they?"

The man let out a snorting laugh. "You're telling me."

"Still, beautiful place you've got here."

"Oh yeah, it is beautiful."

"Do you know how to get back in?" Ben asked. "I came out for a quick one," pointing at the man's cigarette. "And now I can't find my way back in!"

"Yeah, it's just over there." He pointed to the fairly obvious door in the wall.

"Oh thanks. I was afraid I was going to end up in the crypt! There's one of them round here isn't there?"

"No, the crypt is back at the entrance hall you can't get to it from here."

"Oh I see, that's a relief. Didn't really want to call the whole thing to a halt while they searched for me! Cheers."

"No problem."

Ben walked quickly back to the door they'd come out of, flicking his head towards it at Ardian, who fell in behind.

*

On their way across the church, moving slowly enough to look like they were here for the party not to check out the building, Ron, he of the need for a speech, caught up with them. Ben panicked but Ardian spun him a tale generic enough to get away with but likely to cause a raised eyebrow on the part of poor Colin who had, as far as they knew, never thrown up on a cat.

In the entrance hall there was a perfectly obvious double width staircase leading down, presumably it had been invisible earlier because the crowd had blocked it causing them to lose twenty minutes and get a tour of the church and gardens.

A velvet rope, impassable guardian of all important historical sites, was stretched across the opening to the staircase. They ducked under the rope, outwitting the museum and heritage industry's greatest security minds and hurried down the staircase before the Gent, who was still standing in the doorway looking out, turned around and spotted them.

*

They had entered the crypt in the main chamber, a long low room formed of a series of bays with exposed ribs criss-crossing over the top of them. Half way through each bay there were electric lights on tall thin pedestals to brighten up the room when it was rented out. At the moment though it was not supposed to be occupied so the only light came from the elaborate stained glass window above the altar at the far end.

A combination of the narrowing perspective and gloom where they were standing conspired to make the altar seem radiant. Ben, who was not at all religious, was impressed. You could see how this whole set up would generate awe in the faithful.

"Right." He whispered, unnecessarily as no one above stood the least chance of hearing them through the centuries old, thick stone flooring. "We're looking for an entrance to another chamber. The letter said it was beneath this one so look on the ground."

They both pulled out the LED torches they'd brought and without speaking concentrated on one side each, scanning the crypt from side to side as they walked the length of it.

Ben reached the altar without finding anything. "I'm going to look in here." He called across to Ardian in a stage whisper.

"Okay." Ardian sounded distracted so Ben looked up to find him at the other side of the wall poring over the effigy of a bearded knight with a child lying at his feet.

"Have you found something?"

"Not yet, I just figured if I was going to hide a secret room under a crypt I'd put it under a fake tomb."

"Alright, keep looking. I'm going to check out the side chapel."

*

Fifteen minutes of minute scrutiny later, as Ben was exploring the chapel, he heard Ardian start moving and then, from the chapel on the other side of the altar came a loud, "Jesus!"

Ben ran over to him. "What is it? Have you found something?"

By the time he got there Ardian was laughing at himself. He pointed at a second effigy. For some reason the body had been carved to look like a corpse.

"I thought it was a mummy!" Ardian said shaking his head. Ben grinned at him and bent down to read the inscription on the monument and see if it gave them any clue. It didn't.

"It's their last prior." He said having read as much and began to straighten up but then stopped.

"This is getting us nowhere. How are we supposed to find it?" Ardian despaired. "We've been here a bloody hour, this is longer than I've spent in a church since I was 10. Doesn't that letter tell us anything else?" But Ben didn't reply, he was frozen in a half crouch. "Professor? Hello, Professor? Have you had a bloody breakdown?"

"What's that?" Ben asked, pointing past Ardian at a point on the wall.

"It's a wall Ben."

"On the wall. Here." He finished standing, pushed past Ardian and touched the wall at a point where two of the bays met.

As the great stone ribs on the ceilings approached the floors they came together at about waist height and the builders had added decorative pillars made to look as though they were supporting the ribs. Ben was tapping at a point on the pillar nearest to the 'mummy' effigy.

"It's their funny cross. It's everywhere." Ardian answered. It was indeed a Maltese cross, about six inches square, carved into the frontmost pillar and covered in dust.

"It's not quite everywhere. It isn't on any of the other pillars." Ardian looked around. He was right.

Ben blew into the depression to get rid of the dust and then looked closely at it. Beside him Ardian knelt down. "What do you think it is?"

"I don't know but if Voynich found this other room then there must have been something that drew his attention. I can't see anything else can you?" As they spoke Ben explored the cross, trying to turn it, tap it, pull it. Finally he pushed against it and there was a grating noise.

"No. I haven't seen anything. I…"

"Shut up!" Ben said without thinking. Ardian blinked in surprise and Ben caught himself. *Don't upset the gun wielding gangster.* "I mean, did you hear that?"

"I didn't hear anything."

"Listen." Ben pushed again and the stone seemed to give a bit more beneath him. More grinding.

"I heard that!" Ardian said excitedly. "Do it again."

Ben pushed again, harder this time and felt resistance from the cross. When he removed his hand they could both see that the cross had been pushed in and now the pressure was removed it was creeping forward again. It was the forward motion that made the noise. "This is it. This is definitely it." Ben said.

He pushed again and this time kept the cross pressed down until they heard a distinct click. Gently, he removed his hand.

As they watched the "pillars" slipped towards them as one piece, leaving a half inch wide gap between the right hand edge and the wall.

*

The two of them dragged the pillar door open to expose a hole behind it just big enough to crawl into. Ardian shone his torch into the opening and looked inside.

"It looks like a priest hole." He said thoughtfully. "But didn't you say that manuscript thing is from 1400 and something? I thought priest holes weren't invented until Elizabeth I? That's like, a hundred and fifty, two hundred years later."

Once again Ben was surprised at how much Ardian knew but now was hardly the time to let him start exploring anachronisms, they needed to get in there. "Well, I guess all secret chambers look alike." He replied, dismissively. "We should go in."

"What if it's booby trapped?" Ardian asked, as he pulled his head out and turned back to Ben, smiling cruelly. "After you."

It was Ben's turn to peer inside. This time more reluctantly. The light showed a tunnel deep with cobwebs. The air felt dry and he couldn't hear any scrabbling rodents. Both good signs. He crawled inside, the light from the torch in his mouth leading the way.

It turned out to be more of a thick doorway than a tunnel proper. After a meter and a half it opened out and he was able to stand up and see where he was.

"Oh my God!" He said loudly enough for Ardian to hear. "Come in, it's safe."

Ardian's head appeared seconds later. "What's in here then?"

"Have a look."

Ardian stood up and slowly moved his torch around the tiny room, no more than two meters square.

At first he thought the walls were made of wood but then he realised what he was seeing was a series of wooden chests similar to the one Alan had shown them yesterday evening (*God, was it really only yesterday?*) at the National Archive. None of these had triple locks like the Domesday chest but all had heavy metal hasps held shut by the biggest padlocks Ardian had ever seen. Three of the walls were lined almost to the ceiling with chests.

When the torch beam hit the only one that appeared to have been placed in the middle of the room, the one that had been opened, or perhaps never locked since he couldn't see a padlock anywhere, it reflected the gold and silver coins that filled it to the brim.

The second had obviously fallen, or been pulled, down from the top of the stack and smashed open. Its padlock still clung to the hasp of the metal band that surrounded it but the wood within it had splintered and the coins it had once contained had spilt all over the floor.

"*Ndyrë ferr!*"

"That's what I thought." Ben said.

Ardian flicked his torch at Ben's face in surprise. "You speak Albanian?"

"I'm a linguist. I can curse in all sorts of languages. Anyway, this is it. We've found it. Now Petrela can let Sarah go."

Ardian shook his head at Jarvis' naivety. "I doubt it Professor. He was after the big haul. This is just supposed to be the beginning, right?"

"But there must be millions here. Enough to do anything he wants to, he could…I don't know. Do whatever it is he wants to do. Buy an army and crush the Bridge Boys. Retire to a big hideout in the Italian mountains. Whatever." He paused for a beat. "Just your share is going to be colossal." Another beat. "He has to let Sarah go now." He finished weakly.

Ardian had crouched next to the open but intact chest and was running his hands through the coins thoughtfully. He picked one up and examined it. There was what looked like English letters in a circle around the outside though he couldn't read what it said, didn't even recognise the language, probably Latin. It was about the size of a £2 coin, had a full frontal head stamped on one side and two crossed lines on the back that split it up into quarters.

And it was made of gold.

And there were a lot of them.

Some of them were silver mind. But there were even *more* of them.

Ha! 'His share.' Yeah, right! Jarvis had no idea how Petrela operated. There was no way Ardian was seeing any of this.

"Just stay focussed." He said, not sounding very focussed himself. "He will want you to find the main thing. He doesn't go back on what he's said. Ever." He stopped speaking but carried on fiddling with the coins. Picking up handfuls of them and letting them fall from his clenched fist repeatedly. He appeared to be thinking. Ben didn't interrupt.

The silence continued for a long time.

After a couple of minutes Ardian suddenly placed his torch on the floor pointing upwards to illuminate the room and started taking photographs on his new phone.

Finally breaking the silence he said pensively, "I'm going to call Valon, let him know what we've found."

"You should get him to come and see it." Ben said casually, busy counting the chests bending over a pile of gold in the corner.

Ardian looked at Ben oddly and hesitated again before seeming to shake off whatever it was and crawling back out. "You stay here."

Ben couldn't help but notice that he had taken a handful of the coins with him.

*

Day 436
19:43

Valon saw that it was Ardian and picked up. "Ardian, how is it going? Has he found the proof yet?"

"What did Petrela say about me going after the Bridge Boys?" He asked instead of greeting his uncle or answering his question.

Valon was a little surprised but Ardian had always been like a bull in a china shop. It was hardly like it was out character. So he answered the question. "He wants to get this thing with the professor out of the way first."

"Why?"

Valon sighed. "That's his decision Ardian. He's the *krye*."

"For now."

"That's enough. Why did you ring?"

"I rang because we have found it actually." Valon expected Ardian to be sulky but there was something else underlying his tone that worried him.

"It was in the church?" It was only half a question, Ardian had been keeping Valon informed throughout, he knew full well they were in the church that evening.

"Yes." Ardian hesitated, unsure of how to say what was on his mind.

The hesitation bothered Valon more than the bullish way he'd opened the conversation. What was the boy thinking now if it made him pause before blurting it out? Perhaps he'd spent too much time with the geeky Jarvis. All that thinking was going to his head. Eventually Ardian spoke again. "There's millions of pounds worth of gold in here Uncle. Millions. Boxes and boxes of gold coins just sitting there for us." He turned one of the coins he'd pocketed over and over in his hand, staring at it as he spoke. In about forty five minutes the sun would set but for now there was enough sunlight left forcing its way through the stained glass to catch the coin and give it a lustrous glint.

"Great job. Petrela will be chuffed."

"Yeah…What's going on with him, Uncle? Why don't we move against the Bridge Boys now? They're making us look like a bunch of *budallas. He's* making us look like idiots. If he's not going to…"

"Ardian drop it."

"Uncle. We don't need him. He's lost it. He needs to retire, he's not even interested any more. You're running the whole thing, it's just a matter of time before he hands it to you anyway. And if he doesn't want it why is he stopping you from taking over?"

"Ardian, I want you to stop talking like this."

"You think we should be going after the Bridge Boys as well. Tell me you don't." He waited a second for his uncle to speak but Valon couldn't think of anything to say. "Yeah, that's what I thought. If he won't stand aside then *qij atë* there's enough here for us to start our own family."

"That's it. Shut up! No more." Valon snapped.

Ardian did as he said and was quiet but neither of them were fooled into thinking the damage was fixed. He'd said what he had and there was no going back. They might choose never to speak of it again but it couldn't be unsaid.

Valon continued, "Right. Now I'm going to call Petrela and let him know you've found the chamber. You got any pictures?"

"I'll send you some." Ardian's voice was flat, emotionless.

"Good. Wait there until I call you and tell you what to do next. Just stay there and make sure Jarvis doesn't go anywhere, alright?" Valon tried to calm his nephew.

He hung up and sat perfectly still, staring at the phone as if it were responsible for the mess he found himself in.

Today was Wednesday and Wednesday's were Petrela's card night. He hated to be interrupted during cards.

He sat and stared a while longer.

*

Day 436
19:47

Ardian crawled back into the chamber fuming. There was so much boiling around inside his head he felt like exploding. And normally when he felt like exploding he exploded, usually at the people around him though at a push he'd make do with inanimate objects. It took a huge effort not to just smash the place up, and *shkërdhat* Jarvis' face in, right then.

Jarvis was waiting for him to return, hopping from leg to leg looking like an excited puppy having fetched a favourite chew toy for the first time.

"I've found something. Over here." He said beckoning Ardian over.

"What?" Ardian snapped. Seeing the locked chests again, all that gold, was not helping his mood. He nearly roared at the futility of it all, what the *ferr* was Petrela going to do with all this? Nothing. *Shkërdhat* nothing, that was what.

Ben seemed not to pick up on the dangerous tone in his voice. "It's another passage, taller. I felt a draught, that's how I found it. It looks like some sort of escape route."

Ardian stepped forward, the small space robbing him of the satisfaction of stamping across, so that he could see what Ben was showing him. His step brought him next to the open box once more, he grabbed a fistful of coins reflexively and thumbed them one at a time back into the box.

Ben's find was in the corner opposite the entrance to the chamber. A break in the wall of chests showed a gap in the wall itself, no more than two and a half feet wide but five feet tall. A man could walk up it, as long as he was prepared to stoop and was neither fat nor claustrophobic. It wouldn't be exactly comfortable but it would be better than the entrance to the chamber.

"What do you think is down there?" Ben asked.

"Well we're not going to find out standing here are we?" He huffed. Angrily throwing down the coins and pulling his gun out he pushed past Ben into the tunnel entrance, finally getting the chance to stamp.

Three feet in he stopped and half turned, gun hand rising and his other hand spasmodically clenching and unclenching a fist. He opened his mouth to speak and Ben waited but whatever he was about to say he let go and stomped off down the tunnel.

*

After a minute Ben heard a guttural, primeval roar from the passageway.

*

Thirty seconds later Ardian reappeared, framed in the small opening, and gestured at Ben with his gun.

"End of the line Professor. We're not going any further."

The gunshot that followed dislodged plaster from the walls all around the tiny, old chamber.

*

Day 436
19:49

Petrela's phone vibrated. He didn't know why he brought it here. Once a *i përgjakshëm* week he came for a bit of space away from the family. Both families. No work, no wife looking after screaming grandkids. Didn't feel like a lot to ask. The phone buzzed angrily like a wasp trapped inside a glass, demanding his attention. He should ignore it. He did, for a whole minute, then he looked anyway.

The message was from Valon. Knowing Valon would not disturb him unless it was worthwhile, he opened the message.

Proof found. Can you speak?

The professor had found it! It must be eating Valon up to admit he was wrong but at least he knew to get in touch. Petrela smiled, he'd long since learnt to trust his instincts. Alone of the men playing at this table he had relied on his instincts, his *mendje*, to get him where he was. Not for him a handout from daddy.

He was feeling pleased with himself and typing a reply when his phone rang as he held it. A name appeared on the screen. A name that wasn't stored in his phone, so shouldn't have been able to. Seeing what it was, he wasn't surprised. He instantly stood up.

"Excuse me gentlemen. I need to take this." He said and stepped away from the table.

21

Day 436
19:52

"How did you get this number?" Petrela demanded. He didn't even bother to ask how the Architect's number had got into his phone. He was quite sure he wouldn't understand the answer.

"Information is my business, remember? Which is why I'm calling. I have some you should hear. Your man Bogdani and the not-professor have found the proof chamber."

"I know. Valon just told me."

"I'm sure he did. I also think you need to hear this. I'll be back when it finishes."

"What are you talking about?" Petrela said into nothing before there was a faint click and voices started up.

It took him a moment to tune in to what they were saying and to recognise Valon and his nephew. It was a recording of the conversation they had had earlier.

When it finished there was another faint click and, as promised, the Architect was back.

"I thought you should know." He said.

"How did you get hold of that?"

"Following our agreement that I would assist you in this matter I have been monitoring the young Bogdani's mobile."

"Learnt anything else I should know while you've been spying on my people?" Petrela was angry and came out fighting but the Architect remained composed.

"Not spying. Assisting. As per our agreement. And I've learnt that you should trust your pet 'professor'. He wants the girl back, he'll do as you say."

"Is that it?"

"That's everything that had happened until about 30 seconds before I called you."

"That jumped up little *pidhi*. I'm going to rip him a new *gomar!* Then we'll see who's lost it."

"If you nip it in the bud Bogdani is no threat. He is young and hotheaded. Were you any different?"

A pause but Petrela ignored the question.

"I never thought Valon would betray me."

"I don't think he is doing. Listen to what he says, he wanted none of it. But if you like I can put an ear on his phone."

"No, you are right. But lately…Yes, do. Oh, I don't know, do you think we need to?"

So Petrela and the Architect were a 'we' now? Seth noted.

"I don't think he means to go against you. It's not his style."

"Hmm… Maybe before but just recently he has been dis…Wait, I'm getting another call." His pocket was vibrating, it was his other phone. The one whose number he had given to Ben in case of emergencies. Jesus, what the hell was going on tonight?

"Shall I stay on?"

"Yes."

*

"Hello." He answered blandly in case it was a wrong number, or God forbid a telesales call!

"Is…is that Mr. Petrela?" Ben said, sounding terrified.

"Yes, Professor Jarvis." Petrela said with an effort to maintain a state of composure. If the little weasel was so scared why ring in the first place? "I understand congratulations are in order. I must remind you, however, that this phone was only for use in emergencies. Our normal channels would suffice for the good news of your success."

"Pardon?" Ben said, confused.

"You've solved the first part of the puzzle. That is presumably why you are ringing me."

"Oh… oh, yes. I have but I mean, no, it isn't why I'm ringing you. I have to… I'm afraid…"

"What is it man? For god's sake spit it out."

"Ardian tried to kill me and take the gold." He blurted.

"What?! Where are you now? Where is he?"

"He's dead. I killed him. But it was self-defence. I swear I'm not trying to get away. Don't hurt Sarah. I found the gold. The proof gold. I'll wait here until his uncle comes. He rang him earlier, he'll be on his way."

"Professor can you stay where you are or will the noise have attracted anybody?"

"We're in some sort of secret tunnel, I don't think anyone will be coming. I don't think they can have heard. I wanted you to know about it as soon as possible. I'm not trying to escape." The words tumbled out of him in a fluster.

"I know, I know. Your girlfriend is safe." Petrela took on the unusual role of comforter. He couldn't let Jarvis have a meltdown until he understood what was going on. "I need to have a conversation with someone to sort this Professor, can you hold the line open at your end? I will be back in one minute. Do not panic. I understand what has happened. I have people who help clean up these types of accidents. Do not panic." He repeated.

He put the phone on mute and changed hands to speak to the Architect on the other phone.

*

"Did you hear that?"

There was second's pause as the Architect unmuted his own phone. "I heard your end. Not his. What happened?"

"Ardian tried to take the gold and kill Jarvis."

"That was faster than I had expected."

"But Jarvis killed him somehow. I don't know the details. And Valon is on his way there."

If the Architect was surprised that Jarvis had killed Ardian the digitised voice filtered it out. "Are you sure?" He asked.

"Well, he said he killed him."

"No, I mean are you sure about Valon being on his way over there?"

"Jarvis said he was."

"Did Jarvis hear the call we did I wonder?"

"Why?"

"If he did and only heard what Bogdani said he could have misunderstood, it didn't sound to me like Valon was going to go."

"No, nor me. But I need somebody I can trust there. You could go. I'd pay you well."

"That isn't how this arrangement works. You know that. I think you're going to have to go yourself."

"What about the cut-out? I have spent a year following your advice distancing myself from any activity."

"It's your call but my recommendation would be that you get in there and take charge."

"What about Valon?"

"Well, I'd take him there too. Keep a bit of an eye on him for a while. I really don't think he's a problem but it's probably worth watching. Bogdani's ideas must have occurred to him as well."

Petrela was thoughtful. "I'm going back to Jarvis. Hold on."

*

"Jarvis?"

"I'm still here."

"I will come to you myself."

"You?! But what about Ardian's uncle?"

"We're both coming. Where are you?"

"I'm under the Church of St. John but you don't have to come in that way. We found an escape tunnel that leads to a cemetery."

"Which cemetery?"

"I don't know."

"Right, hold on again."

He switched lines again.

*

"Are you there?" He said to the Architect.

"I am."

"Jarvis and the Bogdani brat found a tunnel that leads from the church to a cemetery nearby. But he doesn't know which cemetery. Any way you can find out?"

"I've got the location of Bogdani's phone. Tell him to get it and take it to the cemetery. Let me know when he's done it and I'll tell you where he is."

*

"Jarvis?"

"Yes."

"Go and get Ardian's phone and bring it to the park. We'll trace you from that and be with you in half an hour."

"Okay. Good. Thankyou. What do I do until then?"

"Stay where you are."

"With the body?" Ben sounded like he might throw up.

"Yes. Now call me when you're at the park with that phone."

He hung up and went back into the games room to apologise to his friends. He would have to give this evening a miss.

*

Five minutes later the Architect called him back.

"He's at Bunhill Fields."

22

Day 436
20:18

Petrela stared silently out of the passenger window.

He had called Valon as soon as he knew where they needed to go, told him with no compassion (but no recrimination yet either) that Ardian had died trying to kill Jarvis and asked him to pick him up from his club. Valon, dependable as he had always seemed to be, had driven straight over and was now winding them through the streets of London towards Spa Fields Park.

Petrela was torn, he didn't know how to handle this. Outside of his wife and kids, who he never allowed anywhere near his business life, Valon had been the one constant part of the world he moved in. His mind refused to believe the idea that he might betray him. But, whatever the Architect said about it being unlikely, he also couldn't stop thinking about that phone call and how Valon had not disagreed with his nephew.

For his part Valon was mulling over the same conversation. How had it led to Ardian dying? Because it must have done. They were far too close together to be a coincidence. Did he feel sadness at Ardian's death? Yes, a little. If his sister had still been alive he'd have been more upset for her. Luckily little Donieta was long dead or this would have killed her. But it was hardly a surprise. The stupid, *kokëngjeshur* fool was going to make it happen sooner or later. But what the hell had gotten into him tonight? Why that phone call and then this? And how the hell had that geek managed to kill him?

"Were you going to tell me about the phone call?" Petrela interrupted his thoughts as though reading his mind.

"What phone call?" Valon said guiltily, instantly aware that somehow Petrela knew about it.

"What phone call?!" Petrela exploded. "The one where your nephew suggested I'd lost it and that you should finish me off."

Valon fought back. "He didn't say we should finish you off!" And then, "How do you know about that?"

"A concerned friend let me listen to a recording."

"The Architect." Valon practically spat the name out. "And how did he have a recording?"

"I asked him to help us with this didn't I? I need brains on this Valon. Where else am I going to get that? You?!" He waited but Valon didn't rise to it. "So tell me about the call."

"Ardian's just… Well, he *was* just… being stupid, letting off steam. Jesus Gezim don't you remember what we were like when we were that age? He wouldn't have done anything about it."

"Well, I guess it doesn't matter now does it because he can't anyway. I'm more worried about you."

"Me?! What the hell do you mean you're worried about me?"

"You haven't agreed with this since the beginning."

Valon hesitated before replying.

"I think this isn't our thing." He said after a moment. "You know that. We should leave the treasure hunting to other people. And I think there are more important things we need to be doing."

"Like taking on the Bridge Boys?"

"You know that's what I think Gezim. I've never pretended otherwise. But you also know I always do what you decide. You are the *krye*, you make the decisions, I follow your orders. I always have." He said.

Petrela looked at his old friend, eyes fixed tightly to the road. "You have." He nodded and fell into silence.

A minute later Valon spoke again. Quietly and calmly. "It bothers me how much we are relying on that man. I don't know why you trust him so much. You don't even know who he is. He could be police setting us up."

"The numbers speak for themselves Valon. Over the last year the jobs he has planned have brought in huge sums, the number of our men arrested has fallen. If he is the police he's not doing a very good job."

Valon had to agree but he didn't like it.

"He's still not part of the family." He sulked.

"That may be a good thing. Look where we've got with family."

The rest of the drive took place in silence, each man brooding over his own thoughts.

*

Day 436
20:51

Ben saw the two men cross the road. He was hopping up and down again, this time from fear.

"Professor Jarvis?" One of them said as they approached.

"That's me."

"Can you prove it?" The other demanded drawing a look from the first one.

"Prove it?" Ben said panicking. "I've... I must have my credit cards here." He started fumbling for his wallet.

"It's him." Said the first of them, shaking his head.

Ben recognised his voice, it was Petrela. Which meant that the man who wanted ID and already seemed pissed off must be Valon, Ardian's uncle.

"You said you'd be half an hour." Ben said to Petrela.

"So speak to my driver." Petrela said dismissively but got no reaction from Valon. "Now show me what I need to see."

"Follow me." Ben said and began to walk through the cemetery. None of them spoke. Eventually Ben came to a stop and pointed at a grave marker which appeared to be lying flat in the ground. "It's inside here." He said.

When you looked closer it was just possible in the fading light to see a small plank of wood stuck between the stone and the surrounding grass. Ben walked over to it and pushed the plank down, levering the gravestone up a little way. As soon as there was enough space he worked his fingers underneath the stone and heaved it aside revealing a rectangular hole underneath it only slightly smaller than the gravestone itself. He turned around and lowered himself down backwards.

Petrela shrugged at Valon and went to follow but Valon reached out and grabbed his bicep.

"Let me go first. I don't trust him." He said gruffly.

Petrela nodded his agreement and Valon knelt down on the edge of the grave and leant over it. He was surprised to see the top of Ben's head was only about two feet below ground level. Beneath him Ben switched on the torch he was holding at his side. He kept it pointed down to stop the light drawing attention and in its beam Valon could see that he was standing on a stone platform that took up about two thirds of the space of the grave. The other third, where the head would be, Valon thought, fell away in a set of stone steps.

"Are you coming?" Ben asked, looking up and moved down the first couple of steps to make space.

Valon did as Ben had done, turned and shuffled himself down to the platform. Now he was down there he could see there were two niches cut into the wall of the 'grave' making a sort of ladder you could use to climb up or down.

He went and stood at the head end near the top of the steps, placing himself between Ben and the back of the grave and called up to Petrela.

"Okay, it's safe." He guided his boss's feet to the holes in the wall and when he was safely down reached up and dragged the grave marker back towards the opening. "Should I leave this bit of wood there?" He asked Ben before pulling it all the way.

"No, that was just to stop it closing on me. We can easily push it up from underneath." He replied.

Once the stone was back in position he passed Valon the torch he had recovered from Ardian and led them down four steps and into the narrow tunnel that led back to the chamber.

"Why didn't you come in this way before? Ardian said you had to go to a church." Valon asked suspiciously.

"We didn't know it was here. The letter led us to the crypt in the church. I don't think Voynich knew about it either. Anyway it's blocked halfway down from the other side, until we'd opened that end you couldn't get in through here. Like a one way valve."

A minute passed with no one talking as they trudged single file along the passage. Then Valon broke the silence.

"You seem very calm for a man who's just been forced to kill someone." He said.

"I don't have a lot of choice do I? If I don't help you what happens to Sarah?"

Valon didn't answer that, there was no need.

"So what happened with Ardian?" He asked instead.

"He said he'd had enough of being a lackey." Ben answered loudly enough for Petrela to hear. "There was enough gold here and that trying to find more was a waste of time, he didn't believe it was real. He said if I was out of the way you could concentrate on the right things and then he came at me."

"He came at you? Then why aren't you dead?" Valon challenged.

"I don't know, there was a struggle, the gun went off. I'm here, he isn't."

They came to a stone wall and Ben turned to face them. Valon reacted immediately.

"It's a trap!" He shouted and started to move back towards Petrela, pulling his gun as he went.

"What is it?" Petrela asked unable to see anything past Valon.

"No, no, no!" Ben said quickly, raising his hands to show they were empty.

"What's going on?!" Petrela boomed.

"It's the door I told you about. Look." Ben bent down slowly to the floor as he spoke. Behind him Petrela pushed Valon down so he could see over him to understand what was happening.

Ben kept eye contact with Valon and groped around on the floor until he found a second plank of wood he'd take from the broken chest wedged in the bottom of what looked like a dead end. He slid both hands into the gap and pulled and the 'wall' swung aside with little resistance.

"I think it must be counterweighted. If you don't hold it open it swings shut so you can't open it from this side but there's no catch or anything, if you push from the other side it just opens. It looks like a dead end though."

Valon relaxed and helped pull the door open. The three of them passed through and let the door slam shut behind them.

"How far now?" Valon asked.

"About as far again." Ben replied.

*

Eventually they reached the entrance to the chamber. Ben stepped quickly through the gap in the chests and stood to one side to let the others see.

Valon looked around the room and said nothing. Petrela on the other hand was less discreet, even though he was out of sight Ben could tell the moment that he had seen the chests as the man's deep voice boomed, "*Jezu Krishti!* Good job Professor."

"Where is Ardian?" Valon finally spoke.

"I… I moved him over there." Ben said, pointing to the little tunnel that led to the crypt.

Valon shuffled past Ben, the small space making it difficult for the three men to manoeuver in. Petrela stepped forward out of the chest gap into the chamber proper, caught Ben's eye and flicked his head at Valon in a gesture that Ben interpreted to mean that they should give him a moment.

In the corner Valon bent his head to look up the tunnel. Sure enough Ardian's body was in the tunnel, doubled over as though it had been shoved there with some effort. He looked back at Ben. He still found it hard to believe that this man had beaten his nephew but with Ardian in a strop and with this tiny space making it near impossible for him to move about it was obviously possible. And he couldn't come up with an alternative. If Jarvis was trying to pull one over on them he'd have run wouldn't he? No, as much as he might like there to be someone to blame here, someone to take it out on, in truth it was just bloody Ardian being Ardian.

He shook his head angrily at the dead boy and stood upright.

"Right. What are we doing with all this?" He said, gesturing to the gold. "And what's next Professor?"

"We've got to get it all out of here as soon as possible." Petrela said.

"I don't know that we need to do that straight away." Ben said, pensively.

"Oh you don't think so do you?" Petrela said sarcastically. "So what do *you* think we should do *Professor* Jarvis?"

Ben caught his tone and immediately retreated. "I mean, you're right you should take this if it's what you really want… But I meant if you wanted to find the other place, you know the main stash. I thought that was what you wanted. If that's what you're after then we need to work out where it is and the letter said something here would help. This lot," he swung his arms to indicate the chests surrounding them, "has been here for hundreds of years and stayed safe."

Petrela looked around thoughtfully, calculating how many chests there were but didn't say anything.

Ben spoke again sounding nervous but committed to saying what was on his mind. "There are millions of pounds worth here. If you just have this then can we agree to let Sarah go now? I've done what you asked, I've found Voynich's gold."

"You haven't found it all though have you?" Petrela said. "I'm afraid you're right. I was, and in fact am, after the main stash as you put it. Thank you for reminding me."

"Isn't this enough?" Ben chanced his luck.

"This is magnificent. But if it is meant to be merely a proof, *o Zot!* What must the main hoard be like?"

Ben looked crushed and Valon, in spite of evidently trying to throw himself into this whole affair to (a) reaffirm his loyalty to Petrela and (b) distract himself from Ardian's death, didn't look much happier.

"Do not sulk, Professor. Keep up your end of the bargain and I will keep up mine. Your girlfriend will be free." Ben didn't believe him for a minute. "Now, where do we go next?"

Ben made a visible effort to get a grip of himself. "I don't know." He said. "The letter said to see Capricorn's words we'd have to come here. To see. What does that mean? There must be something here that will give us a clue."

"It's just a lot of gold." Petrela said.

"There must be something. We should start searching."

"What about inside the chests?" Valon said.

"I guess it must be. There's nothing else here." Ben replied. "You two start with those ones," he pointed at the two that were open. "I'll start moving the others and see if we can get into them."

"Don't smash them. We need to be able to get them out." Petrela said.

"I'm not going to. I'm going to see if I can see anything behind them and see if any others are open while I'm doing it."

They all moved to their assigned tasks. Ben struggled to move any of the boxes. Valon began sifting through the shattered box, now little more than a metal skeleton since Ben had cannibalised it for door wedges and props; Petrela started rummaging through the central box, lifting handfuls of coins and placing them in a pile next to the chest.

"What are we looking for?" He asked.

"I've no idea." Ben answered. "Anything that looks unusual or out of place."

"What if it doesn't look out of place?"

"I don't know!" Ben finally snapped. "Look, I don't know what I'm doing here, I'm making it up as I go along. You threw me into this and I'm blundering my way through it. I have no idea why but it's working so far so I suggest you just stop asking for a plan and start doing stuff."

Petrela raised his eyebrows at Valon who just shrugged. Nice to see the geek had a bit of spirit. Much good it'd do him in the end.

"What if Voynich took it, whatever it is, with him?" Valon asked, a minute into what felt like a fairly fruitless search.

"I don't think he can have done. He never cracked the code and anyway he didn't mention taking anything except gold from this chamber in his letter to Ethel." They both looked blankly at him. "His wife. His wife's name was Ethel."

More shrugging and they went back to it.

Twenty seconds later Petrela shouted incoherently and stood up, dragging something from the chest he'd been searching.

"I think I've got something!" He shouted.

Valon and Ben stopped what they were doing and looked over. When they saw what he was holding they joined him huddled around the central chest.

He was holding a metal disc, about 15 centimetres in diameter and 2mm thick. In the centre was a picture of a goat's head, front legs and body facing left, the rear of the goat was replaced by a fish's tail. Around the perimeter of the disc was a circle of writing in the familiarly unfamiliar script of the manuscript. Between the central goat-fish stamp and the outer ring of Voynichese were a series of apparently randomly placed holes. All but one of the holes were rectangles, curved so that if they were all extended they would form a circle (or in fact a number of circles since they weren't all in the same arc). The final hole was star shaped and positioned to the left of the goat's face.

The metal it was made of gleamed in the light, that and the fact that it took both hands to hold it comfortably were pretty good indicators that it was solid gold.

"The picture. Look." Petrela said. "*Bricjapi*. It's Capricorn."

"Not just Capricorn though." Ben fumbled in his pocket, got out his mobile and tapped away at the screen for a second or two. "That's what I thought. It's exactly the same." He showed them the screen with the scans of the pages from Wreath's papers that Siobhan had sent him. Sure enough the Capricorn pictures appeared to be identical. "This it. This is obviously it."

"But what do we do with it?" Valon asked.

"Siobhan has the original pages, we need to get this to her and see what she can do. It must be a clue."

"You're joking. I'm not letting anyone else have this." Petrela said turning and tilting the disc in his hands. "It's worth an absolute fortune."

"I didn't mean send the real thing, she doesn't need the gold, she needs whatever information is on it. It must be what we need to decode the manuscript somehow but I don't get it." He said leaning past Valon to try to get a good look. "Put it down somewhere I can take a picture of it and I'll send it to Siobhan. She can take a look at it."

Petrela looked uncertain but Valon gave him a brief nod, "Kadare is with her remember? It's safe."

Petrela put it down and Ben took three different pictures of each side, though the reverse appeared to be blank in this light, you couldn't be sure. "I'm going to send it to her then give her a call. Is that okay with you?" He asked Petrela.

"Of course. She is needed to help decipher it, you said so the other day."

"She is. We wouldn't have got this far without her."

"Go ahead then." He said.

*

Day 436
21:10

"Hi Siobhan. I'm sending you a picture I need you to have a look at."

"Where the hell are you Ben? The line's dreadful. Are you still in the church? Was it there?"

"It was there. Millions of pounds worth of coins, gold and silver all mixed together. Boxes and boxes of them. But Petrela isn't interested in it. He's hell bent on finding the main stash. But we found what I think is a key to the code. It's a gold disc, I'm sending you a picture of it now. It looks like you're meant to match it to the horoscope page, it's even got a picture of Capricorn on it."

But he'd been too eager, calling her as he sent the email.

"It hasn't landed yet." She said. "Tell me about the church then while we wait. How come no one's ever found it before if it's in a church?"

"It's hidden Siobhan. Behind a couple of pillars. You'd never see it if you didn't know to look for it. You have to go down a tunnel behind these pillars and the room was there, full of boxes. And then there's another tunnel that leads out."

"But surely somebody would ha… Okay, I've got it. Hold on." She said. "I'm just opening it now."

Ben waited. At the other end of the line he could hear the sounds of her working her machine.

The sharp click of a mouse button (he thought he could tell by the sound (though a smaller part of him acknowledged he was probably imagining it) that it was the right button, Siobhan was left handed).

The rapid but dull chunk-chunk-chunk of scrolling through an email with a roller wheel.

Finally the professional assassin's double-tap gunshot replaced with the professional hacker's double click on the offending file. Admittedly less dramatic than the gunshot but still that same satisfactorily terminal feeling.

And now the seemingly interminable wait that was the curse of modern life. Everything served up instantly and somehow instantly never quite instant enough.

A quiet chime indicated the machine had filled its end of the bargain and presented the image to her.

Now another pause while her brain processed it.

"Oh my God!" She said, an abominably long 12 seconds after she previously spoke. "It is steganographic after all. It's a Cardan grille. In the 1400s? That's phenomenal."

"And in English?" Petrela demanded impatiently.

"Who was that?" Siobhan asked.

"New babysitter." Ben didn't want to frighten her by telling her where Petrela fit in. He took a stab at translating. "You're saying that the holes in the disc show you what words are really the code?"

"Which words or letters, yes. Judging by the size of these it'd be words. The rest of the characters are just nulls. That's why no one's managed to decode it."

"Meaning that the rest of the book is just to hide these two pages? And most of the writing and pictures on this page is just to hide the bits that the holes show. So it couldn't be decoded without knowing which bits had real meaning and which were just nonsense?"

"That's it exactly."

"So how do we use it?"

"First we have to work out how to align the disc and the folio. Otherwise we'll be looking at gibberish. Problem is we have no way of knowing." She said quietly, talking to the others a little but mostly thinking aloud. She became aware of it and raised her voice. "Usually with a Cardan grille you'll see the answer leap out at you because it's written in plaintext. The message is hidden just by writing something else around it. That's how it works. The enemy isn't supposed to even know there's a secret message there. But this is a coded grille so even if we line it up right how are we going to know?"

"What about the star?" Ben said. "I think that must be meant to line up with one of the ones on the picture? What do you reckon?"

"Well let's try." Siobhan manipulated the images on her screen as she spoke, creating a transparency of the grille disc, resizing it to match the dimensions of her image of the page and rotating it around to try to find a star that lined up. All of them did. "Yeah, it'll work but which one?" She said. "Hold on... Oh my God! This is all I needed. Look at it." She was talking to herself again.

"What are you seeing Siobhan?"

"I've lined up the star hole with the star that's coloured in, there's only one on this page, and the rest of the holes frame a set of words perfectly."

"So what does it say?" Petrela asked.

"Well I can't read it. It's still in Voynichese." Siobhan sounded confused. As though it were perfectly obvious.

"So how does this help us?" He pushed.

"Because now I know which words were the real message I stand a chance of decrypting them."

"A chance?" Petrela said darkly, glaring at Ben.

"She'll do it." He said hurriedly. "Won't you Siobhan? Now you've got that you can do it?"

"Almost certainly." She said. "Still, assuming it's monoalphabetic we should have it quickly now. I'll start by running it through the hill climbing algorithm we used on the letter. We'll have it. The only question is what language to use on it. Start with the Europeans 'cause of the clothes. If that doesn't work we'll try further afield." Her voice had tailed off again as she began thinking.

"But this grille will not show you the right order for the words will it?" Valon pointed out, demonstrating he'd been keeping up.

"That's true but the order doesn't matter to the algorithm. It's doing frequency counts on letters, it's independent of the order, in fact it doesn't know the words are even there, it's theoretically possible that the right frequency count could be reached by complete gibberish, it's just unlikely by accident." Siobhan explained.

"So how will we know how to read it?" He asked.

"Well, it'll either be written in the right order which is great, and quite likely historically, or what I think is more likely, as like I said the idea here seems to be a bit different to the original Cardan grilles, they'll be the right words but we'll have to work out the order." Siobhan said.

"With some languages the order doesn't make a blind bit of difference to the meaning." Ben said.

"You're thinking it could be Latin?" Siobhan asked.

"It's always made the most sense given when it was written."

"Well, I've already got a Latin letter distribution and dictionary check loaded from earlier so if it is we should catch it quickly."

"Can you start with what you've got while you prepare the others?"

"Yeah, will do. This it Ben. We're going to do it." She said, excitedly.

"How long will this algorithm thing take to set up?" Petrela asked.

Before Siobhan could show the exasperation he expected her to, Ben jumped in. "I asked the same question earlier. Siobhan I'll explain, you get on with it. Call me as soon as you have something."

"Of course." She practically slammed the phone down in her rush to get started.

23

Day 436
19:39

"New plan boys." Paul Bridges said. "Martin's right, we need to know what's going on." Martin's face, visible to his brothers over his dad's shoulder, had the sombrely pleased look of a man who was right all along but is too magnanimous to crow over it.

"But we haven't learnt anything by watching them." His father continued.

Through some previously undiscovered facial sublimation process that avoided passing through any intermediate stages, Martin's expression had instantly become one of a man who knows he's just been insulted but can't quite work out how.

"What is this new drug? Who are they looking to hook up with? Are they importing it or are they going to cook it themselves? We don't know a bloody thing about it."

"So what's the new plan Dad?" Jack asked, desperately hoping it would involve a bit of a scrap. He'd listened to the news all morning until the fun at the building site had been reported but there was no mention of any bodies. It was reported as joyriders who'd run off, which either meant that they'd all survived and got away or Petrela had sent in cleaners in time to stop the police finding it. He'd have thought the workers would have mentioned the gunfire though. Anyway it had left him hungry for a bit more fun.

And it sounded like Paul was about to deliver.

"I want you to bring me Valon. He'll know what's going on and we'll make him tell us."

The room erupted as all of them spoke at once.

"Jesus Dad! It'll kick off!"

"Oh yes!"

"About time."

Paul held up his hands and his sons stopped. "What do you think Martin?" He asked.

"I think you're right." Martin had the good sense to say while wisely keeping his real opinions to himself.

"What do we do about the rest of them?" Gary asked.

"None of the rest of them know anything. Leave them, kill them, I don't care."

"What about Ardian? He might know something." Martin suggested.

"The poser? All mouth and no trousers. But yeah, if he's there bring him too. Valon's the most important one though, yeah?"

"So who's going?" Jack asked.

"You and Neil. And I want you to take a whole load of guys, I don't want any fuck ups."

"Nice one. When?"

"Tonight. When it's dark."

"Where we going to do the work on Valon?" Martin asked. Please God his father had at least thought through not getting them all arrested by torturing Valon on the kitchen table here!

"Chris' car place. They're going to learn."

They all liked that. Even Martin had to admit it was pleasingly ironic.

*

Day 436
22:29

Sarah was bored. Bored. BORED.

She'd been unable to get anything more than a glimpse of the warehouse or whatever where she was being held and no opportunity had presented itself to make a break for it since she'd worked out the combination to the bike lock. Even the small distraction of breaking the code had now faded.

She hadn't yet reached the decade long imprisonment stage where she'd be able to play a game of chess in her head and in any case she didn't have an opponent. And she didn't like chess. Instead she'd amused herself by making lists and prolonged the amusement by arranging the lists into a list of lists which ran:

> 1. A list of the things they needed to do around the flat (subdivided into a list of things he needed to do and a list of things she needed to do);
>
> 2. A list of things to do before she died (working assumption: she'd get out of here and have chance to do some of them);
>
> 3. A list of the places she'd like to visit (sublists: UK, Europe, rest-of-world);
>
> 4. A list, alphabetised, of the people she had been at school with (she didn't know any of the people he'd been at school with, he was admittedly poor at keeping friends);
>
> 5. This list of lists.

That had now been rung completely dry of fun. She'd only taken it this far because her obsession with making lists was a running gag between her and Ben and she wanted to be able to tell him about how she'd passed the time.

The final bit of entertainment to be gained from it would be to write them down and present him with them when they got out of this but she thought Enver would probably draw the line at bringing her pencil and paper. She had decided to ask him anyway next time he came back, good manners didn't really seem a useful survival tactic in a hostage situation. Well, at least not when you were the hostage.

The bang on the side of the van startled her and she realised she hadn't had the radio on for a while. She dutifully shackled herself up to the bike lock and banged back, the additional piece of communication they'd worked out without discussing it but that let him know she'd locked herself in.

He opened the door carelessly and climbed in carrying two mugs of tea. He placed one of the mugs within reach of her, worked his way back down the van and perched himself on the tailgate, legs dangling outside.

"I don't like football." He sulked.

"Me neither." She replied, surprised at the conversational gambit.

"They all watching it." Oh, he was bored too! Was she supposed to provide entertainment somehow? She briefly freaked out, flashing back to the panic she'd had when he'd first handcuffed her but she was convinced he was harmless. And even if he wasn't exactly harmless then he at least didn't intend to harm her. She couldn't imagine a rapist bringing her a mug of tea first. No, if she was expected to entertain him it would only be through conversation.

He sat in awkward silence for a bit and she watched him try to work out how to talk to her. 'How was your day?' was out obviously.

He looked almost relieved when a loud explosion sounded from some distance away. He jumped down from the tailgate and stood in the doorway listening. A second explosion followed and then a series of bangs that Sarah imagined must be what gunshots sounded like. He shot a look back at her cuffed to the wall and a peculiarly regretful look at his mug (as though the real irritation in any pitched gun battle was the wasted tea) and ran towards the sound of the noise, leaving his tea untouched.

And the door open.

This was it. Whatever was going on outside couldn't bode well for her and she wasn't going to sit around waiting to find out. Who knew when she'd get another opportunity.

She could hear Enver's feet hitting the warehouse floor and a door being thrown open as she scrambled to the back of the van, hands still handcuffed together in front of her. She got there just in time to see a door closing.

That must be it. The way out.

Having half rolled, half clambered inelegantly down from the van (the handcuffs making it (a) unwise to jump as she couldn't protect herself if she fell and (b) impossible to climb properly) she ran across the warehouse towards the door.

Twice on the short run she nearly stumbled, not appreciating how difficult it would be to run without the use of her arms for stability. Each time she regained her balance and after what felt like a lifetime her bid for freedom made it at as far as the door. She hesitated in front of it, unsure of whether she'd be spotted the instant she walked through. Steeling herself she opened the door a crack and peered through.

Into 1980's Beirut.

She slammed the door shut again and examined it more closely, looking for the clues she'd missed before that it was a Narnian portal. Unsurprisingly there weren't any and since she hadn't been unconscious when they'd brought her here she knew they must be within an hour or two of home. Which made it difficult to explain the men in ski masks brandishing automatic weapons.

She stood once more with her hand on the handle. No choice really, if she wanted to get out she couldn't stay here. Trusting to whatever was happening out there to keep them all distracted she opened the door and looked out properly.

Now she could see for slightly longer she was able to identify her surroundings as some sort of scrapyard, the jumbled piles of scrap, the towers of former cars and the still recognisable car shapes waiting to be crushed had all conspired in the dark to mimic a ruined cityscape in her first glimpse.

While what she'd thought were men with guns, turned out to be men with guns.

Most of them were focussing their attention on a blocky looking building some way away from her. There seemed to be two groups, one wearing ski masks who she'd spotted first that were obviously attacking the second group, maskless and, apart from a handful of isolated men in the yard, mostly holed up in that building. The ski-maskers had surrounded the building and were trying to get closer to it while the ones inside tried to hold them at bay by taking pot shots through the windows and doors. Even without any knowledge of tactics or military history or any frame of reference for this kind of thing she could tell it didn't look good for the maskless contingent. Unless help came from some of the stranded groups outside there was surely only so long they could hold out.

Having decided that in the melee she could probably run fairly openly without being seen she sidled out of the door and did exactly that.

Running as fast as her shackled hands would allow she headed away from the building that was the centre of attention.

*

Day 436
22:39

Once he'd agreed what Siobhan would do, Ben had managed, with a great deal of difficulty, to persuade Petrela and Valon to leave the chamber and return to the hotel room he and Ardian had checked into earlier.

Petrela had been reluctant to leave the chests, though he saw the wisdom of it (and in any case insisted on them taking as many coins as they could carry in their pockets without drawing too much suspicion). Valon had been reluctant to leave Ardian's body though he couldn't come up with any alternative that satisfied Petrela's demand that nobody else should find out about the chamber until they'd removed the gold.

Eventually they had made their gold laden way back through the tunnel and out into the cemetery, narrowly avoiding being spotted climbing out of the gravestone by a gang of lads drinking in the graveyard. They were now safely ensconced in the hotel in Shoreditch.

The mobile going off in Valon's jacket had rung for a minute before he reached it.

"It's all kicked off *krye*. They're after you." Enver said in Albanian, launching at Valon as soon as he got it.

"What do you mean 'after me'? Who's after me?"

"They've cornered a couple of the guys and I heard them asking where you are. But none of us know."

"Slow down. Who is after me and what do you mean cornered? What the hell is going on?"

"Punks in ski-masks are shooting the place up and want you."

"Who are they?"

"I dunno. It must the Bridge Boys."

"How many of them are there? Are they still there now? Where are you?"

"Yeah it's happening right now. I don't know how many there are, millions, they're all over the place."

"How many of our guys are there?"

"About sixteen of us. They were watching the match on the big screen in the cabin. They're trapped in there now."

"And how did you get away?"

He hesitated, reluctant to admit the truth that he'd run. "I was in the lock up when it started, I went over to the cabin and saw what was happening then I came back here to call you."

Valon turned to Petrela, "We're under attack. The yard."

Petrela held out his hand for the phone and Valon gave it him without a word.

"This is Petrela." He said. "Who's this?.. Right, Enver, tell me what is happening…yeah… mhmm… and what of the girl?" He glanced over at Ben and left the room. Ben watched him go, attentive for any sign of Sarah's state. The door shut behind him masking any words but a clue to the tone of the reply was given by the unintelligible roar that came from the corridor.

Ben stopped staring at the door and span round to Valon.

"What's going on?" He asked him nervously.

"Nothing for you to worry about Professor." Valon said. "You just concentrate on where we're going next. We'll handle this bit."

*

Day 436

22:41

The gunfire was limited now. The continuous scream of the automatics had stopped and been replaced by more sporadic shouts from what she guessed were handguns. Obviously one side had pretty mush finished and were mopping up what remained.

Sarah was crying. She was in pain, exhausted and bloody. She had cuts all over her legs, hands and arms where she had fallen repeatedly as she had tripped and various piles had given way beneath her. She'd lost count of the number of times she'd fallen over and each time she'd hit the ground it had been hard and sharp, cutting her again.

When she'd first run from the building she'd figured she'd be out in no time but she'd run straight to the back of this God forsaken place. She'd run along the high wall hoping to find a gap or way out, though knowing the kind of people she was dealing with she wasn't really surprised when she found nothing, she didn't expect they were very trusting. That was when she'd fallen the first time, she was pretty sure she'd twisted her ankle but she kept going, working her way from pile to pile trying to get to the front. If the masked men had got in she must be able to get out. But she'd fallen again and again and was beginning to think she'd been in the same place a couple of times. The dark and the weird silhouettes meant it was impossible to tell. And now it sounded like they'd finished with the building and were combing the place looking for survivors.

Through the half light she tried to pick a direction she hadn't already been in and stumbled on again.

*

Day 436
22:41

At the back of the scrapyard the four men on motorbikes sat and listened to the gunfight going on next door.

There were other ways to get intelligence of course but this was more visceral plus if there was a need for them to do anything they'd be on hand. A rapid response unit as planned.

The man in the middle put his hand to his jacket as his phone vibrated. Only one person had this number so he drew it from his pocket, typed in his passcode and checked the message.

THE GIRL IS MISSING. MAKE SURE SHE IS OK AND RETURN HER TO THEM. THEY MUST HAVE HER BACK. UNHARMED.

He flicked his intercom on. "Come on. We're going in." All four dismounted without a query and walked with him to the wall. One of them used a cordless grinder to open a hole just big enough for them to get through. Focusing on the mortar it took about a minute. As he cut the first man told them the objective.

*

Day 436
22:41

Petrela came back into the room trying to look composed. Ben wasn't fooled.

"So this Siobhan will ring you when her computer works out the message?" He asked Ben, ignoring Valon's apparent struggle not to spontaneously combust in the corner.

"That's right." Ben said distractedly. "The algorithm needs time to work its way through a load of possibilities, it could find the right one really quickly or take hours. The only sensible way to estimate is to halve the time it would take to work through all of the possible solutions." He said paraphrasing Siobhan's earlier explanation to him.

"Well, I suggest we all try to get some sleep." Petrela said. "You will need to be alert tomorrow."

Valon finally lost the battle with his tongue, though he kept it polite which he considered impressive given the circumstances.

"Can we have a minute?" He said and walked to the door. Petrela followed though there was a manner to his walk that said he'd have sooner not.

"The scrapyard then Gezim. Have you sent people round to help?"

"No. It's too late." Petrela said offhandedly leaving Valon bemused.

"But they're…" He began too loud, stopped and corrected himself. "But they're being slaughtered right now."

"They're expendable. We're both here. This is the only thing that matters right now, this is going to make us Valon." He spoke slowly as though explaining to a child. "Enver's going to tell me when the girl is safe. I should never have started that bloody proof of life business but as long as we can convince him tomorrow it doesn't even matter if she's dead. Easier if she isn't though. Do you reckon we can trust Enver to sort her?"

Valon ignored the question. He couldn't believe that Petrela was focussed on the girl when untold damage was being wreaked on the organisation they'd spent so long building.

"Then we're going to retaliate after." He said.

There was a pause while Valon's tone finally got through to Petrela. He turned his hard eyes at him. "Is that a question?" He asked.

"Of course it is." Valon replied, all too aware that this had somehow become a question of loyalty again. And that it was becoming a more valid question as the situation wore on.

"Then the answer is no. And anyway retaliate against who? We don't know who it is."

"But the Bridge Boys obviously." Valon's voice rose despite his best efforts.

Petrela kept a level tone. "So if it was them why did they want to get hold of you before shooting the place up?"

"Of course it was them. And I don't know why they'd want me."

"Perhaps they wanted to make you a job offer?" Petrela suggested.

Valon understood what Petrela thought was happening too late. "Gezim, I…" But Petrela cut him off.

"It doesn't matter if it was them or not, we are not getting into this until we've sorted the manuscript out. This business at the yard is just a distraction."

Valon almost spoke but managed to hold his tongue once more. Things weren't going to get any better until this whole bloody thing was out of the way and then he'd just have to see about how they could rebuild whatever state the organisation had fallen into.

"Yes *krye*." He said as enthusiastically as possible.

*

Day 436
22:49

Sarah was lying atop a pile of scrap metal, unable to drag herself up from where she'd fallen for the last time.

She couldn't, wouldn't, give up but she had no idea what to do. She didn't know where to run to, she couldn't shout for help because that would just draw the wrong sort of attention. She was out of ideas. So now she lay there hoping something would come to her or at the least that the pain would subside a bit and she could pick herself back up and move.

Perhaps if she could dig herself in and stay out of sight until they'd passed her she could make a break for it? Or she could stay here until the police came. The police must surely be coming?

"Hello! What's this?" A cockney accent said. She heard the sneering, lecherous quality of his voice through his mask and her pain.

*

Day 436
22:50

Once through the wall Jacob and his men split up and began working their way through the scrapyard, spaced out in a line to optimise their search for Sarah.

Black motorbike gear on and visors down they all but disappeared into the shadows. Whenever they came across another man, usually, though not always, masked, they skirted around him listening carefully to be sure he hadn't found the girl.

Jacob had told them if possible they were to avoid engagement. If possible. If not get it over quickly, they did not want to become the second front in an all-out battle here.

By the time they were midway across the yard they had only had to kill two of the other men, both of them masked. Jacob was satisfied enough with that, their prime directive style noninterventionist policy could bend as far as evening up the sides a little.

"Hello! What's this?" Jacob heard the cockney voice away to his right and moved as quickly and quietly as possible in that direction.

*

Sarah lay there looking up at the man in the ski mask waiting for him to kill her. Or worse. Her hand tightened around the piece of scrap it was resting on, it felt like a piece of pipe, if he came near her she'd make him hurt before he got what he wanted.

"You're a pretty little thing aren't you?" He sneered. A small part of her brain registered his words as nothing but an unpleasant threat, covered in blood and dirt she could hardly be described as pretty. The rest of her brain had shut down, retreating into an animal state to prepare her to fight.

He took a step forward and then abruptly halted, becoming aware at the same time as Sarah of the movement off to her left. They both turned to see a man in a black motorbike helmet rise up the mound.

Black-Helmet took in Sarah and the handcuffs she was wearing as he rose up the pile and in one fluid motion raised his head to meet the other man's eyes and his arm to point at him. For the briefest fraction of a second Sarah couldn't work out why he was pointing and then the oddly shaped gun in his hand spat. There was a noise like a can of pop opening and the cockney fell backwards.

"Thankyou." Sarah said from the ground, or the agonising mess of broken glass and jagged metal that passed for it here, as the man turned to her and reached down to her with his free hand. Assuming he was going to help her up she raised her shackled hands towards him but he dodged them with his and pressed a cloth to her face covering her mouth and nose.

She blacked out.

*

Day 437
00:18

When Sarah came to the only sensation she was conscious of was her pounding headache. Nothing else existed. On reflection she had probably not even opened her eyes.

Gradually her awareness expanded from her headache outwards. First to her mouth and throat, so dry, like she'd never known, it felt like she hadn't drunk for days. Presumably the biker had considered her saliva glands a threat and whatever he'd pushed into her face had been designed to shut them down. If so it had worked and they were no longer dangerous.

Next her groping awareness encompassed the pain in her right wrist. This brought her two pieces of information, firstly she was now handcuffed directly to something, no more bike locks, and secondly the something was the side of the van.

She was back in the van.

This realisation was the last jolt her brain needed to flick into fully conscious mode and she became aware of Enver sitting at the foot of the van. The back doors open, his legs swinging over the tailgate as though the last few hours simply hadn't happened.

She had no idea what had happened outside but within the lock up itself there was no evidence whatsoever of the attack. In fact, if it weren't for the absence of the bike lock and the cuts that covered every exposed piece of skin she had she might have suspected it was a dream. It wasn't.

She shuffled around to try to take some of the weight of her wrist and make herself a little less uncomfortable.

Enver spotted that she was awake and looked over at her. It was very brief but she was quite sure she spotted a half smile.

"You remind me of my girl." He said through his thick accent. "She too is one with spirit. This is good. But this not a safe place for spirit. Spirit will get you hurt. Stay in here and I will look after you while I can."

It was the most he'd ever said to her. She started sobbing even as the door closed behind him, by the time the lock slammed she was shaking uncontrollably.

24

Day 437
05:41

At first Ben incorporated the ringing of his mobile phone into the dream he was having. At some point later, presumably in reality mere microseconds but in his dream a long time, the illusion fell apart and he realised what it was, snapped awake and clawed at the phone.

Instantly his dream, ringtone and all, disappeared.

"Hello?" He said, hoping it was Siobhan but not having had the chance to check the number that was calling. It was her.

"Morning Ben." She practically sang down the phone. "I know it's early but I thought you'd want to know you were right. It was Latin. Or most of it was. There's one word that isn't but I'm working on that now."

He came fully awake at that.

"So what does it say?" He asked moving to the desk, grabbing the complementary pen and scribbling on the hotel's headed paper until the ink began to flow.

"It says, with apologies for the pronunciation:
Insula iaceo molaisi,
Sub pedibus Epidii,
Ubi lauat magna vertice experrectus Aurora,
A morsu Neptunus in tulit domus mea occulta."

He wrote as she spoke and Petrela and Valon, disturbed by the noise, leant over his shoulder trying to read it, both being of an age where learning Latin was normal. Unfortunately neither of them had ever been particularly good students so they quickly gave up and stood up straight again, now merely hovering nearby.

"I've emailed you a copy so you can have a go at translating it yourself." She continued. "Do you speak Latin? I assumed you did being a linguist and all, well if you don't I've also attached a machine translation. It obviously doesn't sound like poetry which I reckon the original was supposed to but with a bit of fiddling it makes sense, it says:

I lie on the molaisi island,
Beneath the feet of the Epidii,
Where waking Aurora washes the great summit,
My house hidden in a bite Neptune took."

Ben beckoned the Albanians back as he scribbled again, this time in English. They looked at one another in confusion when he put the pen down. Was that really it? "*Do* you know Latin?" She asked.

"Not really. Enough to get by."

"Do you know what *molaisi* means?"

"I'm afraid not. I don't know what any of it means. Well, I know who Aurora and Neptune were but I've never heard of the Epidii before. How does this help us Siobhan?" He sounded desperate but Siobhan tried to engage him anyway.

"Tell me about Aurora. What does it mean?"

He stared at the notepad. "Aurora was the Roman goddess of the dawn." He said thoughtfully. "So if she's washing something it won't be with water it'll be a metaphor, she'll be washing with the light of dawn. Oh! It must mean wherever this great summit is it's in the east. And the great summit itself is a clue. It must be on a mountain."

"I thought that but it can't be because of 'Neptune's bite'. Neptune's the god of the sea isn't he so he can't bite a mountain top."

"Lots of mountains are mostly underwater, it could be one of them?"

"I suppose it could but I think that's too complicated. It says something is hidden in this 'Neptune's bite'."

"Tell me then. You obviously think you've worked it out." He said getting a little annoyed.

"It's a cave."

"Oh God yes! A bite Neptune takes out of a mountain. A cave on the shoreline. Great! So what is the Epidii then?"

"Who."

"The Epidii."

"Yes, I heard you. I meant they're a 'who' not a 'what'. I'd never heard of the Epidii so I looked it up. They were a Celtic tribe. But they're only ever mentioned once that anyone knows about by a writer called Ptolemy in his *Geographia*. And the only thing he really said about them was where they lived. They lived on the Kintyre peninsula and the surrounding islands."

"So if the treasure is 'beneath the feet of the Epidii' it must be on the Kintyre peninsula?" Ben said. Over his shoulder Petrela's face lit up and even Valon looked more cheerful than the night before.

"Or more likely, by the sounds of it, one of the islands around it."

""Okay, so we've got it all apart from the *molaisi* bit. We need to find an island in southwest Scotland that has mountains with caves on the east side. Well, there can't be many of those, we can just check all the islands around the Kintyre peninsula and match them up to the description. Brilliant job Siobhan!"

"Hold on. I've tried that. It turns out there are quite a lot of islands around there. And most of them have mountains and caves. And no one's quite sure which ones the Epidii lived on apart from the peninsula itself."

He paused and then making a visible effort to keep the frustration from his voice said, "I'm sorry Siobhan, I'm sure I'm being thick but I'm not getting this. If we don't know which island it's on and there are lots of them, how is this helping us?"

Petrela deflated again and Valon shook his head and disappeared into the bathroom.

"Basically because we know it's in southwest Scotland. You're going to have to go there at some point so why not start driving now while I work on the *molaisi* problem."

"Oh, okay. That makes sense. We head for Kintyre and you try to narrow the target for us as we drive. Yeah. I get it. So tell me about this *molaisi* word. How is it spelt?"

Siobhan spelt it out for him. "It isn't Latin, or at least it isn't in the dictionary I loaded. I'm going to do more digging, the rest of the message is in Latin so I don't see why this wouldn't be. I'm wondering if it is a Latin word it's just rare or something and not in my dictionary."

"Have you got a plan?"

"Not as such yet. I wanted to tell you this bit first so we could be using the time better. We've already lost at least an hour all because of this word. The algorithm was still chugging away when I stopped it, it just got all tied up in a knot, it kept making changes to the solution it had found to account for '*molaisi*' but it couldn't converge on any better solution because every change degraded the rest of the message slightly. So it would generate another set of changes which gradually moved it back to this one. You can't see it minute by minute but if you graph it over a longer time period it's obvious it's just bouncing around this one imperfect solution like some sort of fixed point attractor. In the end I realised the rest works and this one word just wasn't going to so I stopped it."

"Alright, suggestion, have you considered looking at them as syllables rather than letters? If we assume those are the right letters…"

"They are." She interrupted.

"Okay, so we assume that. Can we extract the sounds from the letters based on the Latin and see if you can match them to any other language? Don't worry about the letters they're encoded with."

"Yeah, I see. So if whoever wrote it had heard a word but didn't know how it was spelt."

"Exactly. Can you use dictionaries with phonetic renderings in your word check stage?"

"I don't know Ben, it's a good idea but it could take ages to sort. I'll look at it."

"That's all I ask. I'll look at it as we go as well. I'll call you when we're on the road."

"Cheers." She paused. "Take care of yourself."

"You too." He nearly hung up. "Oh, one other idea. What if it *is* a Latin word but it's an anagram? That might be worth checking."

"Oh yeah, I like that. I can knock something up really quickly that generates all the possible anagrams and does a dictionary check for valid words. I'll do that first and see if we get anywhere."

He hung up and looked at Petrela and Valon, who was now back from the bathroom. "So did you hear that? She's cracked most of it. We need to head to Scotland. The southwest in particular."

"But she doesn't know where?" Petrela asked.

"No. See the word I went back and rewrote when I checked the spelling? You can see for yourself that it's key to the exact location but we don't know what it means."

"So where do we drive to? Scotland's a big *shkërdhat* place." Valon said, frustrated.

"The point is it doesn't really matter yet. There's a lot of 'head north' to cover first. These Epidii it talks about," Ben waved the paper with the riddle on. "Lived in the area around the Kintyre peninsula so if we get up as far as Glasgow and haven't worked it out then we'll have to decide whether to wait there or take a punt on somewhere else. But until we get that far it's the same route anyway."

"But if we know it was on the Kintyre peninsula shouldn't we just go there?"

"Well we can do but it says it's on an island and we don't know which one. A bunch of the islands aren't accessible from the peninsula itself. And it's a two hour drive down it. If we do that and then find we needed to be somewhere near the top we're going to waste four hours. Anyway like I said, the point is if we head to Glasgow now it'll be hours before it's an issue. Hours we can use to try to work out the rest."

Valon didn't look convinced but Petrela stepped in.

"Right then. It's agreed. Let's get going." He said. "Before we do though, send me that email, there's somebody else who might be able to help." He added to Ben.

"Does this place have toothbrushes? And can we get something to eat before we leave?" Asked Valon, the man who'd be doing the driving.

*

Day 437
05:50

Martin Bridges' phone rang waking him.

Who the bloody hell could this be? "Yes?!" He answered with what he hoped was more anger than sleepiness in his voice. Whoever it was obviously thought better of it because they hung up immediately.

Martin groaned and took his phone from his ear to put it down but as he did so a text message arrived from a number he didn't recognise, in fact a number he didn't think could be real.

+01111101110 - Petrela + Valon going north today for a meet re: subject of my previous email. M1 to Rugby. M6 to Gretna. Leaving about 0630.

He jumped up, pulled on the trousers he'd dropped beside the bed last night, grabbed his phone back up and started to make a call to his father. Paul had become an early riser as he got older, there was a good chance he was already up and about and if not he needed to know about this anyway.

*

"A text? And the email I got the other day. Someone's playing us." His old man said.

"I don't think whoever it is is playing us. They seem to be playing them. If anything they're helping us."

"I don't like not knowing who it is."

"Me neither Dad but I think I should go anyway and see what he's up to."

"Take Jack in case you need some support."

Martin rolled his eyes. "Is that really necessary?"

"Yes. You need to be able to work together, you're good at different things Marty."

"He never thinks. He just always jumps in."

"He'd say you don't jump in enough."

"Is that what you think?"

"No. You know that. I need you to help me look ahead. So does Jack but he doesn't know it. You need him to act for you. You do know it, that's the difference between you two. When I'm gone you'll need an enforcer. Men aren't scared of you son. They respect you but they aren't scared of you. The Albanians, now, people're scared of them. And Jack. You need that."

"They're scared because he's mental."

Paul sighed. "I can tell you to take him anyway Marty but that's not how you and me behave is it? I'm trying to help you. I want you to understand why I want you to do it."

"I understand Dad, I just don't like it. No, stop." He cut his father off before he could complete the interruption he'd been trying to make. "I'm agreeing with you. You're right, I'm just telling you I don't like it. But I'll pick him up on the way."

*

Day 437
11:13

Martin and Jack were waiting on a bridge that carried the A684 over the M6. Martin was resting his elbows on the waist high metal railings at the edge of the bridge and aiming a pair of binoculars southwards along the M6 trying to spot Valon's car. Jack was sat in the car grousing.

They'd been here since twenty past ten and, despite his protestations to the contrary to Jack, Martin was beginning to wonder if they'd missed them.

"They're not coming. Someone's having us on." Jack called from the car.

"Maybe." Martin acknowledged. "But I don't think so. Someone wants us to know what's going on here."

"Then it's probably the seller. They want a bit of competition in the price."

That's not a bad idea actually, thought Martin. *He could be right.* "Then we're not being had are we?" *But we might be too late.*

He was close to giving up when he thought he saw Valon's car in the distance. "Jack!" He shouted.

Jack hurtled out of car and joined him at the rails. Martin was peering through the binoculars. Jack held his hand out. "Let me have a look."

Martin handed them over. "Dark blue S-Type."

Jack put the binoculars to his eyes. He'd never been able to use binoculars, always closed one eye and used them as a cumbersome telescope. Through the half redundant glasses he picked out the car Martin was referring to and tried to see the people in it.

"That's them!" He cried, thrusting the binoculars back at Martin and running to the open car door. "Come on, get in! You're driving." He said, pulling his gun from the glovebox and checking it.

The car passed underneath them as Martin ran around to the driver's side and they set off making an immediate left and screaming down the slip road to join the motorway.

*

Day 437
11:17

The three men had eventually got on the road at about 7am once Valon had had his breakfast. Since they still weren't clear on where they actually going, and none of them relished the idea of a day spent in the car with the others, nobody grumbled at the delay. Even Ben who wanted all of it over as soon as possible didn't think they were losing anything significant for the loss of an hour or so. Still, it struck him as he sat there watching Valon eat that two motel breakfasts in the company of gangsters in one week was more than anyone should have to endure.

At first Petrela and Valon had made several attempts to speak to one another but it soon became apparent that every conversation they had veered back to a subject that wound one or other of them up. Unfortunately Ben had picked up on this faster than either of them had (well, that or maybe they just didn't want to give up (on each other or an argument)) so they had they had spent an unpleasant first couple of hours driving in the kind of low level carping environment reminiscent of married couples who can't stand one another but haven't yet decided to split up. Eventually they'd cottoned on as well, saving Ben the uncomfortable task of mediating. An uneasy silence had fallen over the car broken only by Ben's occasional muttering as he scribbled a note about the Latin riddle and the *molaisi* word Siobhan couldn't identify.

Valon was cruising along in the middle lane when the other car shot up from behind them, pulled into the outside lane as though to overtake then slowed to match their speed. Valon cursed the other driver for the idiot he was and looked across to flick him a V sign. His hand dropped back when he saw the man grinning maniacally from the passenger seat was Jack Bridges. And he was lining up to take a shot at them.

*

Jack held his semi in both hands resting on the window frame. "Hold it steady!" He shouted to Martin above the noise of the wind rushing in through his window.

*

Valon slammed his foot on the accelerator and swung to the left. The car lurched forward in response.

Inside lane.

Ben's notepad went flying from his hands. Petrela sat bolt upright from where he'd been half dozing.

"What the hell are you doing?!" He shouted.

"Car next to us. Jack Bridges." Valon answered in a staccato, his attention consumed with avoiding the dual causes of imminent death that were the Bridges' gun and the other traffic on the road.

Petrela looked past Valon to the only car that he could mean. All but one of the cars around them were now trying to avoid the maniac they assumed Valon to be. One was speeding towards them clearly trying to catch them.

"Jesus." Petrela said. "Have you got a gun?"

"Arm rest. False bottom." Valon said, through gritted teeth.

Petrela opened the arm rest between the two front seats and looked inside. It appeared empty but there was a small piece of material sticking up from the front edge, he pulled on it and the bottom came up revealing a compartment with a revolver nestling inside, he took it out and held it ready.

*

Behind them Jack was half leaning out of the window and taking shots at them.

Most went hopelessly wide as the car swerved all over the road but one clipped the wing mirror, shattering it.

*

Second lane.

"Why don't you shoot them?" Ben shouted at Petrela.

"Not enough bullets, we can't afford to waste them. If they get close enough to take one of them out I will, otherwise we keep them in case they manage to stop us."

Valon pushed the car as fast as possible. Trying desperately to outrun them he weaved in and out of the traffic like so many slalom flags. Just as it was becoming obvious that he wouldn't be able to shake them off a sign flashed past advising them that they were a mile away from junction 38.

"Shall I come off here?" Valon asked Petrela urgently, swinging the car again.

Third lane.

"No." Ben piped up from the back seat before Petrela could answer. Petrela spun in surprise to see him bent over his phone, fingers tapping and swiping away on a mapping application as he spoke. "But can you trick them in to taking this junction? If they do then they'll have to do a massive loop to get back to us. We can come off at the next services, they're two minutes further up with a load of little roads leading away from them. If we can get to there we can lose ourselves amongst them and they won't be able to follow us."

Valon glanced quickly at the geek in the rear view mirror with a new admiration and looked ahead trying to judge the best way to do what Ben had suggested.

The back windscreen shattered as a bullet passed through it and buried itself in the dashboard inches above where Valon's arm was gripping the gear stick. The glass held together, just, but was now completely opaque veined with tens of thousands of cracks.

*

Jack watched his last bullet slam into the back of the Jag.

"Have that!" He shouted and clapped his brother on the shoulder. Martin was gripping the wheel so tightly his knuckles were white.

The Jag hadn't lost control though so he couldn't have got Valon. Jack scrabbled inside his pocket for another clip for the gun.

*

Valon floored the car and they shot across the River Lune as he to tried to put himself beside the lorry that was just ahead of them and over in the inside lane.

Second lane.

He brought them level with the front of the lorry, waited a beat to be sure Martin had a good sight of them, swerved right in front of the lorry and flicked on his indicator at exactly the same time.

*

The lorry driver leant on his horn and kept his hand there pulling off a passable impression of a flatlined patient.

*

Behind them Martin thought he knew what they were doing. Years of driving meant that without consciously taking in the indicator he somehow knew they were planning to come off at the next exit and were planning to use the lorry to hide it.

No you don't! He thought, swung across two lanes and pulled in right behind the lorry.

"Get ready." He said to Jack. "They're going to come off at the last minute." He hung the car off the back of the lorry and hugged the side of the road as far left as he could go.

"There they are!" Jack shouted, peering forward around the left hand side of the lorry. The wing of Valon's car was just visible edging over to the slip road. "You were right."

Gun reloaded he shuffled in his seat to get in the best position to make this count.

*

They were at the slip road.

Valon slammed on his brakes and released them instantly. Behind him the lorry and presumably the Bridges were forced to do the same in a high speed version of a Newton's cradle.

He accelerated and swung left sharply to show himself to Jack, now driving along the rumble strip separating the slip road from the motorway proper.

In the back seat Ben cried out as the window gave way and thousands of pieces of glass rained down on him.

*

Martin edged forward behind the truck.

*

The lorry driver, immensely frustrated that the single tone of his horn didn't have a more expressive range to demonstrate the depth of hatred he felt for this idiot, pushed his machine as fast as it could go until he was sitting about a foot from the rear bumper of the Jag.

He didn't really intend to go through with ramming it but he'd sure as hell scare the jumped up little prick.

*

The truck ahead accelerated and blocked Valon from Martin's view.

"Get out of the fucking way!" He shouted, slamming his hands on the steering wheel.

*

At the last possible moment Valon floored it and spun the wheel to the right, smashing over the grass verge and pulling back onto the motorway.

*

Martin sped along behind the truck until they were halfway up the slip road and then caught Valon's car in his peripheral vision down on the motorway.

"No!" He shouted, skidding to a halt and grabbing at Jack who was hanging out of the window again trying to see around the lorry.

Jack clambered back in and realised what Valon had done. He screamed with rage.

"Up there!" He said, pointing further up the slip road. "Fast. We'll be able to get back on the other side. Go!"

Martin got the car moving again and shot over the crest of the exit ramp expecting to find an island with a slip road beyond to re-join.

There was none. They roared around the road, circling a lake, separated from the other carriageway that was heading for the motorway by a crash barrier. Forty seconds later it became obvious they weren't going to catch them and Martin stopped the car again.

"We've lost them." He said.

"Bastards!"

*

Day 437
11:26

Valon kept the speed up until they reached the services where Ben had said they would be. He brought them off and they wound their way through the car park and out the back onto a warren of single track roads.

"Find somewhere to stop for a bit." Petrela said.

"We can't stop!" Ben said. "We need to get away from them."

"We've got away from them Professor. If we get back on the motorway now there's a good chance they'll catch up with us again. We'll wait here for a bit until they've got bored and moved on."

There was little point in arguing so, with Ben directing in the rear from the satellite map on his phone they buried themselves in the Lake District looking for somewhere they could stop.

*

Day 437
11:23

The brothers stood outside the car, an open map on the bonnet. Jack had demanded one and they'd pored over it for about a minute before agreeing that trying to find them now was completely futile. If either of them had believed there was any chance the Albanians would stick to the motorway it'd be worth a shot but there was no way they'd be that stupid.

"You want to call the old man while I drive?" Martin asked.

"More a you thing really, don't you think?" Jack said cravenly.

Oh yeah, he could learn a lot from his brother, Martin thought. "Yeah, no bother."

His dad answered on the first ring.

"Martin. What's going on Son? They turned up yet?"

"They did but we lost them Dad." No point in going into detail with him, he wouldn't care.

"Where the hell are they going?"

"They're heading north."

"What the hell is there in the north?"

"I don't know but Jack and me reckon they must be planning to make this new stuff. Jack recognised the bloke he saw with Ardian at the building site. And he doesn't look Turkish, he looks like a right pencil neck. He must be the chemist."

"Alright so maybe our email friend was wrong about the Turks but those bastards are up to something. Get your asses back here and we'll work out what we're going to do next."

25

Day 437
11:43

Eventually Valon pulled them across a field and into an outbuilding that looked like it might have deserved being called a barn in more glorious days but had fallen on hard times. It was perfect for what they wanted, out of the way, invisible from the road and had enough space for them to move around and stretch their legs in.

"How did they know where we were?" Valon said, as much to himself as either of the other two.

"Yeah? I wonder." Petrela said sarcastically, shooting him an accusing look.

Valon, reserves drained from the chase, snapped. "What the hell does that mean?!"

"Well, they were looking for you last night and now they seem to know exactly where we are and you're the one driving."

Valon looked incredulous. He pointed at Ben. "He's the one who said we should go to Scotland and you're the one who agreed. Unless you want to spend a week touring bloody England there's only one way. Isn't there? Where else do you want me to drive Gezim?" He turned and stomped off to the other side of the not-quite-barn.

There was another awkward silence. After about thirty seconds Ben couldn't stand it any longer.

"If it's alright with you I thought I'd take another look at the disc." He said to Petrela. "I'm not getting this *molaisi* thing and I wondered if we've missed something on the disc itself that'll give us an idea."

Petrela looked irritated at the interruption to his fuming but controlled himself. "Yeah, whatever. It's in my bag." He said gesturing to the car.

Ben wandered over and bent over the passenger seat for a minute before sticking his head back above the car and calling over.

"This bag?" He held Petrela's bag aloft and waved it surprisingly easily for a bag with a one and a half pound lump of precious metal in it.

"Yeah."

"It's not in here." Ben said.

Petrela jumped up. "What do you mean it's not in there?" He said as he walked to Ben's side, took the bag from him and started rummaging through it. It didn't take long, it wasn't that big a bag. After about three seconds a panicked look came across his face. "Where is it?" He scrabbled frantically, and pointlessly, once more through the bag.

"Maybe you put it in the wrong bag by mistake?" Ben suggested, opening the back door and looking carefully through his laptop bag. He held it open to show Petrela. "No, nothing."

Then his eyes fell on the driver's side compartment. He looked away quickly but Petrela had seen where he'd been looking. He stormed around the side of the car, threw open the driver's door and pulled the disc triumphantly out of the pocket where it was nestled behind a window shammy.

"*Çfarë dreqin është e ndyrë kjo*?!" He yelled, spinning around and brandishing the disc at Valon.

Valon looked up lazily and, a champion sulker, refused to be drawn into an argument that quickly. "Looks like your disc." He said with perfect nonchalance.

"Then what the hell is it doing here?!" Petrela threw the disc angrily onto the driver's seat and stamped towards the corner.

"I'm not getting you." Valon said

"Why is it not in my bag where I put it? Why is it down the side of your door?" Petrela raged, face red and spit flying from his mouth with every hurled word.

"I don't know. Perhaps he put it there."

"What, Jarvis?!" He spun wildly and gestured contemptuously at Ben who was standing on the far side of the car, cringing and trying his damnedest to become invisible or at the very least look innocent. "It was you. You wanted it for yourself and you were going to take it with you to the Bridge Boys or whoever it is you're working with."

"You're losing it. In the *shkërdhat* head!" Valon tapped his head for emphasis and strode across to stand face to face with Petrela in the centre of the not-quite-barn. "If you want to talk about someone working with the Bridge Boys why don't we talk about you? You're the one who won't let me take the fight to them. We're sitting around like *pidhis* waiting for them to come and cut us down."

"I'll crush the Bridge Boys! They're nothing! But they just don't matter now. Why can't you see that? This is going to make us!"

"Make us what Gezim? Honest men? Forget it. You are what you are. *I përzënë*. And you were good at it. Those men you play cards with are nothing compared to you. You and me." He punched first himself and then Petrela in the chest. "*I përzënë* , together."

"We can be more Valon. Our children could be proud of their fathers. Those men I play cards with can put their children through school. They can give them jobs. Men respect them."

"Your children are long grown, Gezim."

"Grandchildren then." He said petulantly.

"Everybody respects you, respects us. All those men you let die last night. They respected us. And the ones who were lucky enough not to be there last night, will you let them die tonight or tomorrow or whenever while you play at being a treasure hunter? Who will 'crush the Bridge Boys' then? Not you, not without anyone to do it for you."

"I will do it myself. I don't need them. I'll start it all again."

Valon shook his head despairingly. "Ever since this cut-out thing started you've been losing touch. The men don't even know who you are anymore."

"But they know who you are, don't they?"

"Yeah 'cause I'm there with them. They can see me."

Petrela suddenly thought he'd seen the answer. "So that's what it is. You're not going to work for Paul Bridges. You want the *organizatë*. My *organizatë*. You think you could do a better job than me?" Petrela thumped his own chest. No communal chest bashing for him.

Valon hesitated, genuinely searching his feelings. "I never did before. I do now." He said coldly. "What's happened to you? The Petrela I grew up with would have dropped this madness at the first sign of the Bridge Boys acting up and ground them under his heel. You? You do nothing while they attack our people." By now Valon was red in the face as well, waving his arms and shouting in Petrela's face. Petrela took a step back, spluttering and dropped his arms to his sides in what Ben assumed was resignation but some dam inside Valon had burst and there was no stopping it. "You even did nothing while they attacked us in the car. Us! You and me. They attacked you and me and you sat there with a gun in your lap doing nothing. Nothing! Even Jarvis was more use than you. Ardian was right you've gone soft. He was wrong about one thing though, you're not losing it. You've lost it. You're…"

And then lots of things happen at the same time (though whenever Ben replays the scene in his mind later he will remember seeing the images first and not hearing the sound until afterwards, like seeing lightning before hearing the thunder).

    1. Petrela raised his right arm;
    2. Valon clutched his stomach, began to double over and stumbled backwards;
    3. A loud bang echoed off the hole-filled walls of the not-quite-barn;
    4. The fallen man made a curious noise, a sort of mix between the pained exhalation of a man who's been winded and the wet, gurgling, bubbling sound of a child blowing once, very hard, into a drinking straw.

Petrela turned from his friend before he had even hit the floor, took a step away as though having lost interest completely and then caught himself. He turned on his heel and walked back to stand above the prostrated Valon, looked down at him for ten long seconds, spat on him and hissed, "Traitor."

This time he walked away without a backwards glance. Halfway back to the car he cast aside the gun he had borrowed from, and then used to kill, his friend.

Ben rushed to the dying man and knelt beside him, shaking his head in apparent disbelief and muttering under his breath.

Valon's eyes widened as he stared up at the geek above him whose fault all this was and, to his credit, asked for no help.

He died without another word.

26

Day 437
11:54

Petrela called Ben while he was still kneeling beside Valon.

"Come on then Professor! No time to lose. Let's take a look at the disc and see if we can see anything." He sounded upbeat but, hardly surprisingly, there was a manic quality to his voice Ben didn't like. He got up and leant over Petrela who was now sitting in the driver's seat holding the gold disc in his lap, rotating it this way and that.

Ben crouched down so he was on a level with the disc and reached out for it. Petrela let him take it.

It was the first time he'd had a really good look at it in natural light since they'd taken it out of the crypt and he pored over it hoping to find a clue they'd missed. But there was nothing. With the exception of the circle of Voynichese and the stamp of Capricorn it was completely blank. Ben even tilted it to see if there was anything on its edge or inside any of the holes. Nothing.

He turned it over. The back was completely blank.

"I'd have thought they'd decorate it." Petrela said.

"I guess you need to know which way up to use it." Ben said. "It's a circle isn't it? So if you put it with the wrong side facing up the holes would reveal the wrong words even if you lined up the star."

"Oh yeah, of course. See anything useful?"

"No. Nothing." Ben replied and returned the disc to Petrela.

They both stared at the disc for a minute longer as though simply wishing would make something appear.

"Do you think there could be a hidden message on it like invisible writing?" Petrela asked.

"Hm, I don't know. All of the secret inks I know about that existed when it was made would just run off metal. They'd have to be done on parchment or paper." Petrela looked crestfallen. "We could ask Siobhan though, she might know of something that would work." He paused. "I should ring her anyway and see if she's found anything."

Petrela nodded so Ben dialled the number and put his phone on the top of the steering column with its speakerphone activated. Siobhan answered straight away again. Every time he rang her he was surprised how quickly she got to the phone and then had to remind himself that she could answer it from her chair so never needed to get to it at all.

"It's me." He said. "Just ringing to see if you've got anywhere with the riddle."

"Are you alright Ben? You sound terrible."

He hesitated but there was little point in describing the morning's events to her. "I'm alright. I'm tired. I just… I just want to get Sarah out and go back to a normal life." He looked significantly at Petrela who stared back blankly at him.

"I know." Siobhan said. "We're getting there."

"So, have you got anything on *molaisi* then?"

"Lots of dead ends I'm afraid. I got nothing with the anagram approach. Well, I got lots of anagrams but none of them tell us anything. So while that was running I did a search for *molaisi* on the internet. You know, I wondered if it was a person's name. And it is but not someone we want. I spent about half an hour looking into a Saint Molaisi. He's an Irish saint and he's associated with two islands so I really thought I'd found what we needed but neither of them can be right, one's an island in Ireland and the other is Iona off the tip of Mull."

"I thought that was someone called Columba." Ben said distractedly.

"It was, Saint Molaisi was like his mentor or something and was the one who sent him to Iona apparently."

When Ben didn't reply Petrela looked up at him from where they had both been staring, in the unnecessary way people on teleconferences do, at the phone. He appeared completely lost in thought.

"What is it Professor?" Petrela asked him.

"Wait. I need a minute. Something you just said Siobhan. Something you said..." He began to get out of the car.

"What are you doing? Where do you think you're going?!" Petrela shouted at him.

"Nowhere, just shut up! I need to think!"

Petrela blinked, surprised at Ben's ferocity but let him go. Ben began to pace up and down outside the car.

"Ben? Are you okay?" Siobhan said from the phone balanced behind the steering wheel.

"He's left the car Miss..." Petrela said, unable to remember her name. "I think he's thinking... So that sounds like it could be it, yes, this Iona? Is that where we need to go?" He asked.

Siobhan had no idea who he was but recognised his voice from earlier as one of the gang that Ben had referred to as the babysitters. There was no point in antagonising him by refusing to talk to anyone but Ben so she ploughed on.

"I thought that too but then I discovered that the Epidii didn't live on Iona, it was a different tribe altogether called the Creones. Assuming that whoever wrote the riddle knew that, and they seem to have known their stuff, then it can't be Iona. Which pretty much rules out the *molaisi* as person idea. So then I tried Ben's phonetic dictionary idea. That's interesting and if we had longer it might well work but without knowing which language to try it's like looking for a needle in a haystack. It's also harder than it sounds to code. At the moment I've written a routine that does a fuzzy search for close phonetic matches but I'm then reviewing them myself for connections to Scottish islands. Writing something that would automate that last bit but give us a decent confidence level isn't the work of a couple of hours. I can keep trying but it hasn't found anything promising yet. And to be honest I'm not sure how I'd know it if it did."

She paused, she didn't want to say it but that was her done and she knew that if they didn't narrow this down then their trip to Scotland was pointless and just took Ben further away from Sarah.

Petrela looked out of the window at Ben but he was still stomping around, waving his arms in the air apparently still trying to figure out what it was that he'd just missed. "Professor Jarvis is still thinking Miss... We were wondering whether there could be a secret ink on the disc. Something written on it that we couldn't see."

Siobhan thought for a moment. It would be possible today of course, you could write on anything in ultraviolet ink and then only see it under an ultraviolet light, both of which were easily available. But they weren't available in the fifteenth century. "I don't think so... I mean, I suppose there could have been but I wouldn't expect it to last very long and I get the feeling whoever made this intended it to be readable for a long time. People make things out of gold because it endures."

"And because it's valuable, hm?"

"Well, yes. But if you're dealing with messages the fact that it's valuable just helps its longevity. Gold is a relatively inert material so it won't corrode but also its desirability means you could be quite confident that this thing would survive even if it changed hands a lot."

"So why does that mean there wouldn't be an invisible message?"

"Sorry, bottom line it'd rub off. The secret inks that were known back then are all organic and wouldn't adhere to metal. What we've got here is a device for transmitting a message which will endure for a long time. So it's just unlikely whoever made it would have gone to the trouble if anything important was going to rely on an ink that would likely only last being handled a couple of times before wearing out."

"So that's…" Petrela began but Ben threw open the door and cut him off.

"I think I've got it!" He shouted at the phone. "Siobhan, you said you looked up *molaisi* thinking it could have been a person?"

"Yeah. But like I said it didn't help."

"And I bet you were really careful with the spelling? *molaisi* with an 'i' at the end?"

"Yes. Exactly like it's spelt in the riddle, I was very careful."

"Are you connected to the internet now?"

"Always."

"Try the same searches but for *molais* without the 'i'. It's just the genitive."

"God, of course." Siobhan said and then fell silent except for the rattle of a keyboard.

"What does this mean?" Petrela asked.

"Remember your Latin lessons." Ben said. "In Latin, and a bunch of other languages too, you change the ending of words to show what they're doing in the sentence. The 'i' ending show's that something, in this case the island, belongs to whoever or whatever *molais* is."

"So this person's name isn't Molaisi it's Molais?"

"Well, if it is a person. And actually it could really end in any other letter as well, the 'i' will have replaced it. But searching for it with an 'i' will stop it finding the others."

"Oh my God!" Siobhan said. "This is it. Eilean-Molais is an old name for Holy Isle, a small island off the coast of Arran. Arran is another island which is tucked between the mainland and…" She paused for dramatic effect. "The Kintyre peninsula."

"The Epidii." Petrela said.

"That's right." She said, excitedly.

"Hold on, we need to be sure. Check for mountains Siobhan." Ben said.

A pause while she clicked around, muttering to herself. "Crap, wrong Holy Isle." She mumbled as she clicked on the wrong link. "Hold on. Sorry. Here." Then slightly louder, broken as she read. "There are two hills. Technically I don't think they're mountains 'cause they're not tall enough. The tallest one is called a Marilyn, whatever that is. But they do rise pretty quickly from the coast. Hang on, get this. The tallest one is called Mullach Mor which is Gaelic for great summit."

"Like in the riddle." Petrela said.

"Exactly."

"Come on. Let's go." Ben said to Petrela and then to Siobhan. "We're on our way up there now. How do we get to the island?"

"You get on the road and I'll look into it." Siobhan replied. "Get going."

"Thanks Siobhan." Ben said. She hung up.

He looked at Petrela. "This is it then?"

"So it would seem Professor. Your girlfriend will be pleased, no? Do you drive?" He asked.

"Yes." Ben answered.

"Then do so."

"What about him?" Ben asked, sweeping his arm towards Valon's body.

Petrela followed his arm with his eyes appearing to take in the body of his friend for the first time and froze for the briefest moment.

"Fuck him." He said. "But we will take this." And wondered over and picked up the gun that was next to the body.

27

Day 437
12:23

Ben's phone rang as they reached the M6 but he was concentrating on driving Valon's car.

"Can you get that? It's probably Siobhan." He asked Petrela. "Inside my jacket." He took his left hand from the steering wheel and turned slightly to expose the pocket.

Petrela reached across and fished out the other man's phone.

"Hello?" He said.

"Erm, hello. Is Ben there?" It was Siobhan.

"He's driving Miss Leyton. Do you know how we get to the island yet?"

"Yes. The only way to get to Holy Isle is from the Isle of Arran and to get to Arran you need to take a ferry. There are only two ferry routes, the closest one to you is from a place called Ardrossan."

"Do you know the postcode?" He asked, firing up the satnav.

She gave it to him. "There are two ferries you could get today. The first one is at quarter past three. I'm trying to book you tickets on it but I need your registration number."

"Registration number?"

"For the car. They need to know what car you'll be going on in. Unless you want to leave the car and be a foot passenger? But I figured you'd want the car on the other side."

"Oh, yes. We should take the car."

"Okay, so what's the number?"

"I don't know. Professor, do you know what the number plate of this car is?"

"No idea, why?" Ben answered.

"Miss Leyton needs it to book us tickets."

"Tell her to hold on and I'll pull over and find out."

A minute later they were mobile again having stopped on the hard shoulder and confirmed the number to Siobhan.

"Thanks." She said. "I'll sort the tickets and let you know when it's done but you have to get there by 1445 or they won't let you on and then the next boat isn't until 1800. Can you make it?"

Petrela checked the satnav's ETA. "We can."

*

Roadworks in Darvel meant that despite Petrela's confidence they'd scraped into the harbour at 1457. The officious, hi-vis jacketed man in the booth directed them to the lane on the far right, the ferry queue equivalent of being made to stand in the corner wearing a pointy hat. As he did so he made it abundantly clear that their failure to meet the clearly stated boarding times meant they had forfeited any right to board the ferry and that merely being in this rightmost lane guaranteed them nothing. If they were to make it on board at all it was due to the good graces and startling Scottish efficiency of the much-put-upon ferry company.

Ben thanked him effusively and steered the car rightwards with the distinct impression that even if this harbour master / receptionist had known of the breaking and entering, high speed car chase and pitched gun battles they'd been involved in in the last 24 hours, he would still

322

have ranked arriving twelve minutes after the published boarding time as the day's greatest transgression.

Twenty minutes later boarding started for every other line until, after a further nerve jangling ten minute process the naughty line was finally allowed to start boarding and they drove onto the ferry with a sigh of relief.

*

Day 437
17:12

Petrela wanted to be sure that they left no indication of where they were going just in case anybody followed them. There was no way he wanted anybody interrupting them or, even worse, becoming suspicious and finding the gold themselves. Ben rated all of this as incredibly unlikely but was overruled.

Unfortunately as soon as they had landed and made their way around the coast road to Lamlash, the village from which they would be able to get to the Holy Isle, they discovered how difficult it was going to be to get where they wanted to without anybody knowing.

After surveilling the village harbour and studying the ordnance survey map of the area they bought on the trip over from the mainland, Ben enumerated the following facts:

1. The Holy Isle was about as close to a rectangle as nature could achieve.
2. It lay in a natural bay with its west face directly opposite the village and both ends in view.

3. It was owned by a Buddhist community who placed an emphasis on peace and tranquillity for the island's residents, both human and animal.
4. There was therefore only one ferry that operated between Lamlash and the island.
5. That 'ferry' could hold about ten people.
6. There currently weren't even ten people looking to go across.
7. The last ferry returned at 18:45.
8. The east side of the island (where they wanted to be) was a nature reserve completely off limits to humans.

And from these facts drew the following conclusions:

1. There was no way they could use the ferry without everybody knowing where they'd been and furthermore expecting to pick them up in about an hour.
2. Renting a boat and heading to the west side of the island would have been visible to an observer either on the island or in the village.
3. Renting a boat and heading to the east side of the island would have been apparent, if not strictly speaking visible, to anyone in the village as they disappeared from one side and failed to appear on the other.

As a result they settled on renting a boat and telling the rental shop that they were staying up the coast in Sannox and would moor there for the evening before returning the boat tomorrow.

There was no way to avoid being remembered but at least this way no one would know where they'd gone.

As they'd agreed Petrela took the boat to the north towards Sannox. Their plan was to hug the coast of the bay until they rounded Clauchlands Point and disappeared out of sight of Lamlash. Fifteen minutes later, when the hypothetical, harbour based, treasure hunting, spy who was watching would have lost interest and stopped paying attention, they would turn and head southeast for a couple of miles to come up on the east side of Holy Isle.

*

Day 437
18:11

Petrela kept the little fishing boat on a bearing of 157 degrees, effectively running parallel with the edge of the island. His intention was to bring them up to a position level with the trig point of the highest mountain, or Marilyn apparently, where the cliffs moved back a little way from the shore and exposed an area which, though you couldn't call it a beach, they could at least walk on.

He glanced back at Jarvis in the back of the boat. The professor sat, knuckles white where he was gripping the edge of the boat, staring at the coastline of Holy Isle and scanning it for any obvious caves through a pair of pocket binoculars they had bought when they'd landed.

"You do not like boats Professor?"

I don't mind boats, it's the sea I don't like. Ben thought, but he had no intention of talking to Petrela any more than he had to so he remained silent.

Petrela snorted. It was obvious from the look of grim determination on Jarvis' face that he was thinking that very soon all this would be over. Hopefully he was right. Though that did prompt the question in Petrela's mind as to what he would do with him and the girl once they found the gold. Could he get shot of the girl but keep Jarvis busy for a while? Probably not. He would have to give it some thought.

Until they did find it though he was indisputably useful. And even after that he could save himself for a bit by providing labour until Petrela could get in touch with people from his *organizatë* and bring them out here. The right people. People he either trusted or were expendable. Valon had proved beyond a doubt that there weren't any of the former so for now he'd have to settle for expendable. Luckily Jarvis met that definition perfectly.

"Look at this!" Ben said suddenly and passed Petrela the binoculars.

Petrela grabbed at them. "Have you found it?" He asked as he raised them to his eyes.

"No, no the goat, look." He pointed.

Petrela looked in the direction Ben had been pointing and understood his excitement. Somehow finding purchase on the seemingly vertical cliff face was the biggest goat he had ever seen. The excitement though wasn't due to its size or even its evident acrobatic abilities.

"*Bricjapi!*" He said. "It's from the disc."

The white goat on the cliffside could have been the model for the picture of Capricorn on the code disc. He recognised the long, wide curling horns and huge beard flowing into a long coat that covered its body. The goat on the stamp wasn't just a generic goat. It was one of these goats.

"But how did a goat get here?" Petrela demanded as though Ben had put it on the island himself.

"Apparently the Vikings left them on lots of islands they passed as a sort of living fast food drive-through for when they came back."

"How do you know that?"

"I read it on the way over." He answered.

"Well, however it got here, this proves it, Professor, this is where we need to be. We are so close now!" He threw the binoculars back at Ben. "Keep looking for the cave."

Confident now that they were in the right place he turned back and gunned the throttle, feeling the wind run through his hair. Unlike the land loving professor, Petrela loved boats. Well, a boat like this anyway, beaten up and basic as it was, that put him in charge. Not the ferry they'd been on earlier, that was more akin to a floating car park than a proper boat.

*

Day 437
18:42

There was no mooring on this side of the island and they had no dinghy to reach shore but the little boat only had a two foot draft and the coastal charts indicated that the seabed was a mixture of mud, coarse sand and broken shells so Petrela risked beaching it.

"Brace yourself, Professor." He warned at the last minute.

The boat grounded and Jarvis lurched forward. Petrela smiled to himself.

"Come on." He said. "Over we go." And swung himself over the side, splashing into the shallow water and wading ashore. Behind him Jarvis followed somewhat more hesitantly.

Despite the fact that they were intending to go exploring the island's caves the only equipment they had brought were the binoculars and a couple of head mounted flashlights. If the cave they wanted was deep inside the mountain they'd obviously need potholing gear but they'd established on the ferry over to Arran that neither of them had ever been potholing so there seemed little point bringing anything.

The vaguely sketched out plan was that they'd spend this evening recceing the caves. With any luck they'd be able to access the gold, if not then they hoped to at least find where it was and then Petrela would have to engage someone with the necessary skills. He was quite sure that between his own contacts and those of the Architect he'd be able to find somebody if necessary. Hopefully it wouldn't be.

"Right. Which way now?" Petrela thought aloud.

"Well, I didn't see anything on the way down and getting back there on foot is going to be a nightmare so do we start by looking south?"

Petrela joined Jarvis looking northwards at the cliffs they had sailed past. Jarvis was right, they had to hope that the cave was to the south or it was going to be incredibly difficult to access. They both stood for a moment each thinking the same thing, there was no good reason to believe it was the easy way. Eventually Petrela found them one.

"I guess whoever put it here would have struggled up there as well though, yes?"

"Good point. South then." Ben turned and started picking his way along the rubble strewn shore edge.

There was very little space between the edge of the mountain (he couldn't help but think of it as a mountain, particularly staring up at it as it shot up practically vertically next to them) and the sea. And the rocks were wet and covered in seaweed so on several occasions each of them slipped and almost brained themselves or fell into the water. God only knew how the goats managed it and now to add insult to (almost) injury they were joined by a brown sheep that followed them along effortlessly about twenty feet up.

"Get lost!" Petrela shouted at it, throwing a stone at the unfortunate animal. The unfortunate animal refused to be unfortunate, it merely skittered aside and immediately sauntered back to the same spot again, staring at him unfazed throughout. "More Viking snacks?" He asked Ben.

"No, they're Soay sheep from St Kilda. They were only brought here in the 70s. They're descended from some Mediterranean sheep that were the first ever domesticated apparently. They're about as pure sheep as you can get. Soay even means sheep in Old Norse." He paused. "So it's a Sheep sheep. It's like sheep royalty."

"It seems to know." Petrela huffed and started walking again. Above him the sheep squared followed. He let it. "Are there any other royal animals here I should know about? Emperor dogs wearing collars made from my gold?"

"Only the ponies but I don't think they've found the gold."

"Ponies?" Petrela repeated, looking around as though expecting one to be sneaking up on them.

"A couple of herds, brought here at the same time as the sheep but I guess they stay further up the hills."

*

Fifteen minutes of hard scrambling later, having covered very little ground, Ben called out to Petrela who was about twelve feet behind him.

"What's this?"

Petrela lifted his head from scanning the floor to find less slippery footholds. Jarvis was addressing a rock about the size of a backpack.

"Have you found something?"

"Possibly. This rock shouldn't be here."

"Why not?" Petrela said, having clambered over to him.

"It's an erratic." Petrela looked blank. "They're odd rocks dropped in the wrong places by glaciers during an ice age."

Petrela looked at the rest of the rocks around, it was true all of the others in sight were a different colour to this one.

"So this is in the wrong place, no? So that is right."

"Well, yes but there shouldn't be an erratic here on the east side of this island."

"Oh, I see." Well he half saw, there was something odd about this rock, that'd do. He pushed past Ben, bent down and tried to lift it. It was too heavy to lift properly but he managed to get it to tumble forward. "Oh my God!" He said.

"What? What is it?" Ben asked from behind him.

"Underneath it. Look, the Voynich writing from the manuscript." He stood aside so that Ben could see. Sure enough on the bottom of the rock, partially obscured by algae and discoloured by seawater was a series of words in Voynichese.

"We must be here. It must be right around here. Let me just…" Ben began to get his mobile out to take a picture of the rock. "There!" He'd turned as he spoke and was pointing to the spot the rock had uncovered.

Petrela span around and looked at the hole in the ground the stone had opened. It was fist sized but it was a hole. And now he looked the rest of the rocks around it were obviously loose as well and bridging the edges of the same hole, covering it.

He grabbed hold of the nearest one as Ben leant forward and did the same and they both pushed, pulled and threw the rocks out of the way until they had cleared out a long narrow opening in the rock face. More like a letter box than the opening to what Petrela would think of as a cave but he could tell from the echoes made by the loose stones that fell inside that beyond the entrance it opened up considerably.

He looked at Ben excitedly.

"This is it Professor! We've found it!"

Ben was excited too. "We have. Can you imagine being the first person to see this treasure in six hundred years?"

Petrela got on his hands and knees to lower himself into the chamber but Ben put his arm on his shoulder and stopped him.

"Wait."

"What is it?"

"Sarah. I've done everything you asked. I've got you here. Do I have your word that you'll let her go now whatever is in here?"

"What do you mean 'whatever is in here'?" Petrela frowned.

"Well, what if somebody's beaten us to it? What if the gold isn't there anymore?"

Petrela shook Jarvis' hand free of his shoulder. "Yes, yes, of course." He said insincerely. "But it will be in there."

"I'm sure. But thankyou anyway." Ben said.

Petrela lowered himself onto his stomach and shone his torch inside.

"It looks very small." He said, before pulling the torch over his head and shuffling sideways through the opening.

Ben followed him.

*

The two men squatted uncomfortably close to each other, unable to stand up or move about much. The space was tiny and mostly taken up by another erratic.

"I've been in bigger cars." Petrela said.

"I've been in smaller hotel rooms." Ben shot back.

As he'd squeezed his way in Petrela had almost roared with rage when he'd realised this chamber wasn't full of gold. Then his head torch had illuminated the waist high erratic that was covered in Voynichese and was clearly covering another opening.

They squatted now examining it from all angles trying to work out what to do. They tried pushing it but it was far too heavy to shift and, like everything in here, slippery from where the last high tide had soaked it.

"There has to be some way of moving it." Jarvis said.

Petrela was running his hands over the surface of the boulder. "Got it!" He cried. He straightened up as much as he was able and found that if he leant forward over the erratic he could stand up completely. Directly above the erratic the roof of the cave swept upwards and left just enough space for him to squeeze his body into.

What he'd found on top was a series of projections on some sort of plate that felt distinctly different from the rock around it. He tried angling his head so that his head torch would light it up but he was too close.

"Can you shine your torch here?" He asked.

Ben shuffled over and did so. There wasn't room for both of them in the taller open space so Ben stayed stooped and simply lifted his torch above it for Petrela to see.

"Ah! It is the disc again." Petrela said.

"What do you mean?"

"There is another gold disc stuck into the top of this rock. But where mine has holes this one has little lumps.

Wait." He scrambled around in his bag for the gold disc. "Here." He lifted the disc from his bag and placed it on top of the erratic, turning it slightly to line up the holes with the projections on the plate. There was a metallic clunk as the two lined up and the disc from the crypt dropped onto its twin on the erratic.

From deep in the wall of the cave something made a grinding noise reminiscent of a great millstone grinding flour.

"Get back!" Jarvis shouted and Petrela felt hands shoving him backwards.

Petrela scraped his back on the ceiling of the cave and instantly dropped to his knees. The erratic inched its way upwards into the space that seconds before his upper body had been filling. If Jarvis hadn't pushed him he'd have had a lot more than a bad back to deal with. The force lifting that rock would not have stopped just because his chest was in the way. He'd be dead.

"Are you alright?" Jarvis asked when the noise had stopped and the erratic had come to a halt, its bottom now hanging in mid-air at roughly the level that the top had been previously. Both discs were trapped above it, closed off by the roof.

"I'm alright. Thanks for that." He grumbled.

Jarvis gestured towards the place where the erratic had been and where now there was an opening.

"Do you want me to go first?" He asked.

Petrela clambered up and shot him a look, not even bothering to reply. There was no *i përgjakshëm* way he was letting that little geek get the first look.

He crawled forward on his hands and knees, not so much from the pain, which wasn't really that bad, but because he had to anyway to fit through the hole in front of him. Once more he pulled his torch from his head and held it through the opening to see what was in there.

The little tunnel sloped upwards before opening out into a cave that, while still small, was much bigger than this one. Beyond the opening it would at least be possible to stand and walk around. In fact it was about the same size as the chamber under the crypt had been. And just like that chamber it was filled with chests.

He pulled his torch back on and crawled on all fours through into the room and his date with destiny.

28

Day 437
19:06

Petrela had got as far as the first chest when he heard the grinding noise start up again behind him. He span around just in time to see the erratic slam back down.

"Jarvis!" He shouted and ran back to the now closed entrance, slapping his hands on the face of the rock, panicked.

"Yes?" The voice outside called back, audible through a tiny gap where the erratic didn't quite cover the opening.

Petrela did a bit of a double take on hearing the voice, it was obviously Jarvis but, perhaps through some trick of the acoustics in the enclosed space, it was different, richer. Like seeing a news reader stand up from behind their desk. It was the same man but there was somehow *more* of him.

"What's happened? How did it fall back?!"

"I let it."

"What do you mean you let it?!" Petrela asked, confused and thrown.

"No, sorry, I'm not being clear. I didn't let it. I made it."

"Let me out of here Jarvis." Petrela put an edge in his voice which should have reduced the other man to jelly.

"That won't be happening. And my name isn't Jarvis. It's Seth Mortimer." The voice, Seth, said calmly.

But Petrela was barely listening. "What are you talking about?!" He roared. "If I don't get out of here your pretty little girlfriend is going to die."

"Oh, so we've stopped pretending to be civil now have we? I thought you were protecting her?" Seth's voice was mocking.

"I'll have them gut her like a pig." Petrela snarled.

Seth chuckled. "How are you going to do that then? Would you like me to pass the message on for you? Because I'm quite sure the signal in there isn't very good."

He glanced across at a rock in the corner of the outer chamber he was standing in. In the part of the spectrum visible to human eyes it was indistinguishable from all of the other rocks. He knew though that if he could see into the UHF band this rock would stand out. Unlike the others this one was broadcasting a constant stream of noise at 800 – 2000 MHz. Uncoincidentally this was a range that covered the bands used by UK mobile phone providers. He'd have liked to make it more precise but he'd installed it early enough that there was a risk Petrela would change phone provider before they got to the island so he'd had to cover all the bases.

Crude as it was, it had the desired effect of completely killing the weak phone signal that had been here before.

"Anyway," he continued, "when I leave here you're going to have them let her go."

"*Si qij* am I! How are you going to make me do that?"

Seth laughed again. "Oh I'm going to do it for you, that's the beauty of the cut-out system see? Total deniability for you, total accessibility for me!"

Petrela hesitated, for the first time getting an inkling that this wasn't a spur of the moment thing on Ben-or-Seth-or-whatever-his-name-was's part.

"How do you know about that?!"

"Jesus Petrela, you're not getting this are you? And to think I was worried you'd twig what was going on too early. I know about it because I designed it."

"You designed it?" He paused while his brain spun trying to process the new information. *"You're* the Architect?"

From the other side of the rock came a slow hand clapping. "Well done. I'd throw you a fish but it appears you're locked inside a cave with no access to the outside world."

"You *mascara*! You made me do all this."

"Actually I never made you do anything, you had a choice at every point. I just gave you the opportunity to do it to yourself."

"You did all of this just to get £500k? Or was it to get at the gold?"

"The gold is the £500k! And I couldn't give a damn about the money."

"All that gold was my money?"

"Yeah, you'd be surprised at how little gold you can buy with half a million pounds, that's why there's so much silver with it."

"So what then, to take over the *organizatë*?"

"No, no, that hadn't even occurred to me until this morning. I probably will now though." He said, thoughtfully.

"Then for God's sake why?!" Petrela shouted desperately.

"Benjamin and Lorraine Ferguson." Seth said with a quiet reverence.

"Who the hell are they?" Petrela snapped instantly without giving it any thought.

"Think harder. Benjamin Ferguson." He said and waited for a moment but Petrela was silent, the name meant nothing to him. "Benjamin Ferguson was the man you killed while his son held a gun trained on you. And didn't shoot."

Twenty odd years dissolved in Petrela's mind and he relived the moment and, despite the situation he was in, he smiled as he remembered it. Then he made the connection.

"You were the boy." He said pensively and then, as though it would make everything okay, an angry denial immediately came from his lips. "I never killed your mother."

"Yes, you did. Two weeks after you butchered my father in front of me I came downstairs in the morning to find my mum had killed herself in the night."

"So like I said I didn't kill her. She killed herself."

"You did kill her, you killed her that night, she just took a bit longer to die than my dad. But that wasn't even the worst of it. The worst of it was her face in the fortnight before she died. Every time she looked at me. She tried to hide it but we both knew she blamed me. So you did kill her. *We* killed her. You through what you did and me through what I chose not to do."

"So all this is because you blame me for your life? For who you are?"

"God no. I don't blame you, I credit me. I chose my life. Sure, what you did helped make me who I am, gave me a clarity I couldn't otherwise have got as quickly. But I'd have been who I am eventually anyway. And I like who I am. I just have to live with the fact that I'm glad I got that clarity as soon as I did and that means I wouldn't change what happened to them."

"So you're punishing me because you feel guilty?"

"No, you're not listening. I'm punishing you because I can and you deserve it. I don't feel guilty. I am who I am. And who I am is capable of punishing you when the rest of the world can't or won't. My parents were decent folk but they lived by other peoples' rules. They could never have made you pay for what you did, that's why my mum killed herself. Despair. I don't do despair. I make things happen. And today the thing I'm making happen is justice."

There was a long silence.

Eventually Petrela said, "So what are we doing here? Am I supposed to say sorry or did you bring me here just to kill me?"

"Yes, I brought you here to kill you so no, I wouldn't bother saying sorry if I were you."

"So get on and kill me then."

"I already have. To the rest of the world you're already dead, no one will ever see you again or know what has happened to you. But we both know you're going to suffer first. Those chests you thought were full of gold are full of military rations, MREs. They're horrid but if you're careful they'll keep you alive in there for about a year, give or take a few months. I've done my bit, I've removed you from the world. Finally squashing you will happen when Providence, or God, or the Parcae or whoever tire of you. You'll run out of MREs, or they'll go rancid, or there'll be a particularly high tide and you'll drown but however it happens Atropos will cut your thread and you'll die. Until then you'll sit here for months waiting, out of control, completely impotent." Petrela could hear the cruel smile through the rock. "They say that hell is being trapped with your friends for eternity. Yours is going to be being trapped with yourself. It could have been with your friend, of course, but you killed him remember?"

"Why did Valon help you? What was in it for him?" Petrela asked, still not understanding his friend's betrayal.

"Oh, Petrela are you really that slow?" Seth sounded genuinely disappointed. "Valon didn't help me. Why would I want help from a man like him? He was almost as big a scumbag as you are. He never betrayed you and had no intention of doing anything of the sort, I just made it look like he did. He was as much your lackey now as he was twenty years ago." He hesitated to let the full impact of his words sink in and then, just in case Petrela hadn't grasped it, he spelt it out. "You killed your friend for nothing and as he died I made sure he knew who did it and why."

"You *mascara*!" Petrela exploded again. "When I get out of here you're a dead man!"

"Was I not clear? You're not getting out of there."

"That rock isn't going to stop me. You shouldn't have left all this food in here. I'll stay alive and I'll get out. You're a dead man walking."

"We're all dead men walking. You taught me that. But I'll say it again for you, you're not getting out. When I leave here you'll stay where I put you."

"You're a coward, you're afraid to kill me like a man."

"I'm not afraid to, I just chose not to. You don't deserve to be killed like a man. You don't deserve even as little as a gunshot marking your exit from the world. You deserve to fade away like the pointless nothing you are."

"What makes you so high and mighty?! Eh? Eh? If you're the Architect your plans have killed hundreds. You're just the same as me." Suddenly another part of the last few days fell into place in Petrela's head. "In fact you killed Valon's nephew didn't you?"

"I certainly did." Seth said with the faintest trace of amusement. "A single gunshot to the head. You should have seen his face. He found the tunnel was blocked, came back to tell me and walked into a bullet. I made sure Valon knew that as well."

"So you're a killer just like me. How come you're any better than I am? You're no different at all."

"I'm not sure I've ever said I was better than you."

Petrela didn't know what to make of that so he ignored it. "So why not just grab me and bring me here then? Why this elaborate set up?"

"Honestly? Because I enjoyed it. I could have had you taken off the street and dumped here but it just wouldn't have been as satisfying. This way you'll know you chose to be here. You'll get to think of every single bad choice you made that brought you to this point, buried under rock all alone, and how you could have chosen something different every time. Starting with not believing you were some Indiana Jones character and winding back all the way to not killing my parents."

Seth stopped and neither man spoke for a while, Seth simply satisfied to savour the moment and Petrela sensing the completeness of the trap he'd fallen into.

"Let me out." He said eventually in a small, beaten voice. "You can have it all, everything I've got. It'll make you a rich man."

Seth snorted derisively. "Valon was right you've gone soft. I could never have got away with this on the *krye* who built the *organizatë*, or even the punk who killed my father. You're pathetic."

Again there was no response from Petrela.

"Do you believe in a god Petrela? If so you'd better start praying 'cause he and I are the only people who know you're not dead. And I'm not listening."

"What if I choose not to eat? I'll die quickly and you don't get your revenge."

"It's up to you. I don't really care. I'm not going to know anyway am I? Once I leave you I'm not coming back. Nobody is coming back, nobody will know when your worthless carcass finally gives out. You'll be like Schrodinger's cat. Dead and alive and neither and both all at the same time. The difference is with you no one'll give a shit."

"I've still got the gun, I could kill myself." Petrela whined.

"You certainly could, it's your choice." Seth breezed and then with a deadly calm that slammed Petrela back into a room twenty years ago, standing above a kneeling man and watching his son for signs of fear, "Life's all about choices kiddo."

Seth turned from the erratic, finally tearing himself away from the moment and walked away.

29

Day 437
19:34

Seth waded through the surf, pulled himself on board the fishing boat and pushed off aiming to get away from the island as quickly and as discreetly as possible.

He wasn't worried about anyone finding Petrela now but it always paid to be careful. To that end, despite the fact that this side of the island received only a very few visits from the occasional monk, he had spent twenty minutes filling the outer chamber with concrete Jacob had stashed on the island two months ago.

Taking inspiration from the Romans he'd filled the chamber with the powder and would let the sea water hydrate it. He knew full well modern concrete wouldn't stand up to this as well as the Roman variety but it would outlast the prisoner inside and that was all he needed. Finally he'd rolled the outer erratic back into place.

That would almost certainly be enough but to be completely comfortable he had already rigged the erratic inside, if it was moved from the entrance the roof of the inner chamber would be brought down by enough explosive to kill anyone within ten metres of the opening. He'd specifically chosen an explosive that would degrade to stable so as not to cause unnecessary damage (or draw unnecessary attention) but there was always a chance it would go off prematurely. Just another option for Atropos.

Throughout the process he had worked in silence, ignoring Petrela's increasingly muffled attempts to talk, cries for help and shouts of rage. Halfway through his work cold, silent tears had started streaming down his face. He hadn't noticed until his face was soaked.

Now that he was done he planned to reverse the route they'd used to get here, heading north before turning back to the south once out of sight and then return the boat to the rental shop with a story about how they'd decided against spending the night in Sannox after all. Then he'd walk the four miles into Brodick and stay overnight in the hotel there before heading back to the mainland in Valon's car.

Once he had got the boat travelling in the right direction he triggered a message from his phone to the scrapyard as Petrela, telling whoever was currently manning Valon's post to drive Sarah blindfolded to the centre of town and let her go. At the same time he rang her mobile a couple of times and left her increasingly frantic voicemail as Ben telling her Petrela was dead in a shootout with some rival gang and he was coming for her as quickly as possible. He texted her the same and left an answer machine message on their home number.

All of which left just one unpleasant thing to attend to, Siobhan. Curiously he felt strangely reluctant to do this. He knew it was necessary and ordinarily that would be enough for him but still, he wished he could come up with an alternative.

There were options, he knew, he'd toyed with some of them during the early planning stages but none of them included a route to get the rest of what he now wanted to achieve. He could do it if Ben disappeared but, as he'd started to realise this morning and had finally fallen into place in his head while talking to Petrela he had no wish for that to happen. He'd started to enjoy being Ben, it was like being able to show the best parts of himself to the world. Well, most of them. Normally his outward faces had been so restrained that he never felt like he was being himself. Ben was different.

I must be getting emotional, he thought with a smirk. *It still needs doing, omelettes and eggs and all that.*

He looked at his mobile phone. He could trigger it now and it'd be over. No. He'd ring her, he owed her that much.

Anyway, he thought, rationalising, *I need to know for sure that the other two are in the bungalow.*

If one of them were left out this would get very messy.

Aware this wasn't his best idea he decided to do it anyway. He'd make the call once he'd got the boat away from the island to the point where he needed to turn back to Lamlash. That way he could find somewhere to drop anchor for a few minutes and concentrate on this. He tapped an icon on his phone and, in the background as he piloted the boat, an application discreetly opened up the webcam on Siobhan's laptop so he could see if it started to spiral out of control.

*

Day 437
19:53

Siobhan saw it was Ben's number, hit answer and launched into speaking as soon as it connected.

"Ben, I've been thinking about the Latin in that riddle. I don't know Latin but there's something odd about the translation. It makes perfect sense."

"That's good isn't it?" He said, drawn into the conversation despite it being pointless.

"Not really. It's a machine translation. They're never very good. It makes me think it was translated into Latin the same way."

"It doesn't matter Siobhan, don't worry about it."

She stopped, disoriented by his lack of interest.

"Ben you don't understand. It can't be real, it can't have been written in the 1400's if somebody used an internet translation service to put it into the Latin. And once I started thinking about it I realised I don't buy the reference to the great summit either. Who in 1400-and-whatever would know that was the Gaelic name for the mountain on Holy Isle?"

"Yeah, maybe you're right. Siobhan, look I need to know are Petrela's men still with you?"

"Erm…Yes, Zef is sleeping. Pjeter is watching TV. Ben what's the matter?"

"Nothing," He answered.

Then why didn't he care? And then all at once the answer appeared, fully formed, in her mind. He didn't care because he already knew.

As ridiculous as it seemed the idea acted like a flashpoint. It was the missing bit of information her brain needed to make sense of the last few days.

A dam broke inside her mind and all of the recent events were re-evaluated in a cascade that flowed across her synapses, each newly understood memory triggering a change in the next. As though seeing the events play out on a stage in front of her she saw the same things but from a different viewpoint. A twisted viewpoint she had no desire to believe. And horrifyingly they made more sense.

The riddle pointing to the Holy Isle, well okay she'd worked most of that out herself but when she'd been stuck he'd basically given her the answer to Saint Molaise that got them to the right place.

The Cardan grille disc was made of gold so there was no effective way to tell when it was made, assuming he had access to enough money he could have made it at any point.

She'd decoded the missing manuscript pages but it was him who'd got them in the first place. She only had his word that they'd been in the National Archives. A reference in a computer database was all too easy to fake, as she knew better than most.

And even if they were in the Archives she had no proof they were genuine. She'd never seriously questioned it, she'd just assumed they were the original missing pages because they were in the same style as the rest of the Voynich manuscript and the letter had referred to them.

But the letter had been found with them so if the pages weren't genuine the letter wasn't really any proof at all. It could be a fake too. He could have easily written it and encrypted it in a Playfair cipher that was readily available on the internet, safe in the knowledge that a modern day computer would break the code, no need to nudge things along there.

Even the idea that the pages would be with Wreath's papers had come from him and Ardian. She had no idea how clever the young gangster had been before Ben had mysteriously managed to fight off his supposed attack and kill him but was it really likely he'd found a completely new source of documents that had eluded dogged investigators for decades?

Even the idea to look for the pages in the first place might have come from her but he'd jumped at it.

It was all Ben. He'd played her.

The only thing she couldn't see his hand in was the original letter and she'd never even really seen that. She had only Oliver's word for it existing at all. *Wait, Oliver.*

"What happened to Oliver?" She asked.

It was the first thing she'd said aloud but the delay and her tone meant he knew she'd worked it out. He didn't bother denying it.

"There never was an Oliver. But the actor who played him is dead."

"What do you mean actor? I spoke to him for months, how could that have been an actor?"

"No you didn't Siobhan you spoke to him once. He was dead a day later. Every other interaction you had with him was over email."

"But an actor? Why would someone do that?"

"He thought he was playing a part in an alternative reality game for rich men. Petrela saw the same guy just in case you compared notes. Not that that was likely but I had to allow for the possibility."

"The emails were from you I guess?"

"Yes."

"The whole thing was you. Was any of it real? Was there even a letter from Voynich?"

"No."

"That's quite a lot of work."

"Yes it was. But necessary. And anyway that's sort of how it works, human minds always look for explanations but they tend to settle on the one they're given and go for simplicity. Is it easier to believe that this is all real or that someone would go to these lengths to fool you?"

"So if you could do all that why use me at all?"

"Two reasons really. Verisimilitude and bandwidth. Ben isn't supposed to be able to do any of the stuff you can. Also there's a limit to the number of parts I can play at the same time. Added to which you're good at what you do."

"Not good enough to spot you earlier than this."

"Most people wouldn't have spotted it at all. You are good. Which only makes this all the more unpleasant."

Siobhan could see where it was going and was typing furiously as she spoke, desperately trying to record and stream it out over the internet.

"But why me?" She asked, delaying the inevitable.

"You asked a similar question when Oliver, well, let's call him Oliver, recruited you. You asked how he found you and why you were suitable. Do you remember what he said?"

She did. He'd gone off on a riff on combinatorics. About how he'd looked for someone with an exceptional degree in mathematics, specifically number theory to be sure they understood the basics, followed how many of them moved to Cheltenham (from the electoral register) because that pretty much meant they'd gone to work for GCHQ, then seen how many of them showed up as unemployed (available on employment websites) after more than three years, apparently an arbitrary amount he'd chosen that he believed would give them enough exposure within GCHQ to become competent. Each stage filtered out large numbers of candidates but he was left with enough possibilities to give him options. He'd delivered it quite well for someone who apparently had no idea what he was talking about. She'd completely fallen for it. She still couldn't quite grasp that he was just an actor.

"I remember." She said.

"Well, it's basically true but missed the last few steps which included not having people who'd miss you. Don't be offended. Lonely people are ten a penny, the key criterion was brilliant and you've demonstrated that."

*

On the top half of his screen he watched her through the webcam, brows furrowed in concentration and fingers moving rapidly across the keyboard.

The bottom half of the screen was divided in two.

On the right were five graphs representing sensors under Siobhan's bungalow. They were tracking the concentration of methane accumulating under her floorboards as he spoke to her. They currently averaged 4.12%. All five lines were heading towards red lines on their respective graphs set at 5.00%, the lower explosive limit of methane. Once any one of the graphs hit that red line he could trigger an explosion, if all four of them did then there would be nothing left of her home or the occupants. Out of completeness he'd also built in an automatic trigger before the concentration got too high to explode (known as the upper explosive limit and 14% for methane) but it was really just an intellectual exercise since if the concentration got that high she'd have smelt the additive in the gas and no doubt evacuated.

The bottom left of the screen showed the progress of her cyber attacks against the firewall he'd erected around them. It was quite impressive, though futile. She must be beginning to wonder why it wasn't being successful.

"I'm afraid whatever you're trying won't work," he said. "I routed your connection through me at the beginning of this conversation. It's no longer hitting the outside world. Everything you're doing now is happening in a sandbox."

The look of despair on her face was saddening. She raised her hands from the keyboard and tried a different tack.

"Zef can hear all of this. He'll tell his boss."

"Not very convincing Siobhan, I thought he was asleep? And in any case it wouldn't matter if he could hear. Petrela's phone doesn't have any signal anymore."

So he'd killed him too. She made a last stab.

"What about Sarah? I thought you loved her."

"Yes, that's interesting. I thought I didn't. Turns out I think you might be right."

"Then how could you put her through this?"

"She hasn't been harmed and when, or if, Ben needs to disappear she'll be taken care of."

"Taken care of like you're about to take care of me?"

"No." He paused, feeling an uncharacteristic need to explain himself. "Look, your death is a necessary part of the plan. Think of yourself as collateral damage. You've helped me take a dangerous man off the streets. The police would be thrilled."

"I somehow doubt they'd be thrilled when they realise a more dangerous one was left on it."

"I'm quite sure they won't ever realise that. I'm sorry Siobhan, I'll genuinely regret this. The world needs more intelligent people not fewer."

"You'll regret it but you'll do it anyway. What the hell are you Ben?"

"Focussed."

He tapped an icon on his screen. The average was 5.03%, one corner would not be quite as dramatic but it'd do the job.

*

In Siobhan's bungalow a spark jumped across wires that appeared to have been exposed by rats gnawing on them.

The bungalow was completely destroyed.

Epilogue

Day 466? / Day 29?
12:21

He looked through the window at Sarah waiting for him on the lawn of the big house. They were renting this place as part of their recuperation but shortly he was going to have a distant relative die and get them an inheritance.

She knew he had no family so he would be just as surprised as she was when a long lost uncle died and left him enough money to make a large downpayment on a nice house with a garden.

She had turned out to be surprisingly resilient, which he was pleased about, but she did like being outdoors a bit more these days and a place of their own where they could spend time in the garden together would help her get over everything.

"Bo-oss?" Jacob, over in Taunton House, called in a sing song voice from the other end of the video conference. There was no distortion of voices on this line, no silhouetting of their figures, the video conference was simply to prevent either of them having to travel (still encrypted to prevent eavesdroppers of course).

Jacob was running the remains of what had been Petrela's *organizatë*. Turning Seth's hastily conceived idea to take over the gang and use it as a method of establishing a physical power base into a reality.

The footsoldiers or *ushtarët* had resisted at first, Jacob very clearly not belonging to the small group of Albanian families Petrela and Valon had drawn on to populate the *organizatë*. That resistance had evaporated when Jacob's small, highly trained team had been introduced and begun a focussed campaign of education.

Once the *ushtarët* came on board Jacob was quick to show them the benefits of belonging to the new organisation, continued ability to engage in their chosen activities and remain breathing, chief amongst them.

"Yeah, sorry. I'm listening. Carry on."

"No you're not. 'Cause I just asked you a question." Jacob grinned. Seth racked his brain but Jacob was right he hadn't heard a word. "I asked what we should do about the Bridge Boys."

*

Sarah was spread out on the picnic blanket enjoying the sunshine. Summer was over, had been before all of that nonsense with the manuscript began really, but they were having an Indian summer and she was making the most of it.

Ben had persuaded her not to press charges.

He'd explained that Petrela and the other men in charge had all been killed by some rival gang who had chased them up the country on the hare brained pursuit of gold from the manuscript.

"Did you manage to decode it for them?" She'd asked him a couple of days after they were back together.

"Of course not." He'd replied. "It can't be decoded, I think it's made up. I just went along with it and kept talking nonsense until we got a lucky break and that other gang got him."

There was lots she didn't understand. How Ben had survived and got away. Why Petrela had got his men to release her as he died. But frankly she didn't care. She was just glad the whole thing was over and she didn't take a lot of persuading to keep the police out of it.

The only person she could have identified who wasn't dead was Enver and since he had tried in his own way to be good to her she had no desire to get him in trouble.

If they'd involved the police they couldn't have done anything and the whole affair would have been dragged out longer. Better that she and Ben sort it for themselves. That's why they'd got this place for a bit and put off returning to uni for a month.

And slowly things were returning to normal. This morning had been the first time since it was all over that he'd played his old battle with the alarm clock.

Ever since she'd known him he had refused to look at the clock in the morning in the childish belief that if he didn't look at it he didn't know the time. And if he didn't know the time he wasn't late. He'd tried on one occasion to convince her that it was a serious attempt to refuse to collapse the wave function of time. The idea being that he would be held in some superposition of states, both late and unlate at the same time. The universe, more specifically that part of it that had employed him, had yet to play along.

Mental, as she'd told him at the time. But she was really pleased that he'd done it again. It was a good sign.

They'd picnicked every day now. Her request. She liked to be able to feel the wind on her face. Even when it had rained they'd dashed out to a gazebo he had set up and eaten underneath it, the rain pelting off it and driving in from the sides.

*

"Kill them all." Seth said simply.

The remains of the Petrela family were now firmly on board with the new arrangement and a number of smaller neighbouring Albanian families were falling into line quickly as well.

But Seth's ideas did not stop at the current end of Petrela's family, nor even the wider *Mafia Shqiptare*. Without a monopolies and merger commission insisting on competition, expansion was limited purely by a combination of brain and muscle. Historically muscle power, or at least firepower, had had the upper hand. Seth intended to change that. Organised crime was a pure meritocracy and there was no reason to restrict that meritocracy to such a crass measure of merit. He intended to spread this view across the whole of London and eventually further.

Paul Bridges didn't share his view. Or perhaps he did but had his own view as to who should be sitting at the top.

Paul had begun capitalising on the gap Petrela had left even while Seth was dragging him around the country in search of his own money and he'd continued to take advantage in the first couple of weeks that Jacob was getting established.

To some extent Seth blamed himself for Paul's currently strong position. When he needed Valon irritated and Petrela distracted and looking weak it had suited Seth to give the Bridge Boys some headroom. But not anymore. Now they represented a problem.

"You want us to go to the mattresses?" Jacob asked and laughed. He was enjoying his role as gangster in chief but wasn't above having a bit of fun with it.

Seth laughed as well.

"Screw the mattresses, go to Google Maps. Find 'em, tag 'em, kill 'em. Kill them all." He said again. "The old ways are just so inefficient. None are them are logical, none of them follows anything through to a conclusion, all this dicking about with reputation. Put the word out, from now on you work for me or you die. And then make the Bridge Boys the example, I want every last one of them dead in one go. Get me a complete list of who we'd need to take out to make sure there's no one left who could possibly strike back and we'll work out the details together. We'll nudge Paul to make some gobby comment and then we'll wipe them out publicly."

He had no desire to be the next Al Capone or Sam Giuliano or anybody else you could name. No. He would arrange it so that he had all of their power and none of their fame.

And he would make it clear, there would be no war because he would crush anyone who stood up to him. His very own Pax Sethi.

It'd be unpleasant for a couple of weeks but then it'd all be over and he and Sarah would be safe.

He would keep them safe.

*

He was leaving the house now and coming toward her, a basket over his arm. She waved at him and he waved back, his hand clasping a bottle of something.

*

Can this really work? He thought as he let the door close behind him and waved to her, careful not to drop the bottle.

Perhaps he was having a midlife crisis? Certainly there was no useful reason to want either of the things that were occupying him at the moment. *Ambition?* He had always thought he was immune.

Did this now count as part of the plan? Should he extend it? What was the goal? None of it was clear.

How long can I keep this up? He'd done a thorough enough job creating Ben that he could live as him forever if he chose to. The question was: Did he want to?

He definitely wanted some of it.

No, all of it.

He definitely wanted all of it. He just wanted more as well. And there was a good chance they were mutually exclusive. How to reconcile the two?

He was still counting the days against the plan, perhaps he should stop?

What if she began to suspect?

This was not planned.

He smiled and sat down beside her.

"Hey you!"

- **THE END -**

Author's Note

Cleft Lip and Palate

My daughter, Beth, was born 10 years ago with a cleft of the soft palate. Like most people my wife and I knew next to nothing about clefts at that point and had no idea what to do. Within 4 hours of the doctors discovering her cleft a team of specialists from Birmingham Children's Hospital had swooped in and taken us under their wing.

Children with a cleft cannot suck properly so they need to have special bottles to help them get any milk. The team from the hospital explained how to use the bottles to feed Beth and gave us the bottles free thanks to the Cleft Lip and Palate Association (CLAPA). That team and the information and equipment provided by CLAPA helped prevent that first day of Beth's life being a blind panic. Over the next few days they visited us regularly, helping us understand the various procedures that might be necessary as Beth grew up and the support that was on hand both from themselves and from CLAPA.

Six months later Beth had repair surgery carried out and, with the exception of a minor operation to help her hearing, has been fine ever since.

Beth was lucky. She had a very minor cleft and we live near a world class centre who were able to treat her. Since her cleft was only of the soft palate she hasn't had to endure some of the repeated operations and stigma that many children with clefts have to face. Lots of children all over the world are not so lucky. And it is 'lots', about 1 in 700 children are born with a cleft in the UK and US, with rates similar the world over.

CLAPA and the Cleft Palate Foundation (CPF) in the USA exist to support parents and the children themselves right through to adulthood. They are funded largely, and sometimes solely, through charitable donations.

Fear not, this isn't a request for money, by buying this book you are already supporting the fantastic work that these two charities do (half of the proceeds go to CLAPA and CPF) but I would love it if reading this raised awareness of cleft lip and palate so that other parents are a little more prepared than my wife and I were. So please, when you put the book down take a look at one of the websites www.clapa.com or http://www.cleftline.org/ and read up a bit about the condition and the things that they do to help (and while you're there, if you want to donate, please do (okay, I said it isn't a request for money but they're charities, they won't turn it down!!)).

Obviously, it goes without saying that neither of the Cleft Lip and Palate organisations who are supported by the book in any way endorse its contents. It is a thriller and as such has plenty of scenes health care professionals should rightly distance themselves from. All of that is my fault alone!

This book

Clearly most of this novel is precisely that, a novel, a work of fiction, however, it weaves in several real world people and events so it feels appropriate to distinguish some of them.

There are a couple of real world things I've changed to make the book work (or just because I could):

1. The approach suggested by Siobhan of using the words under the zodiac signs as a crib to break the manuscript wouldn't work as they appear to have been added later in the manuscript's history and are written in a Romance language.

2. The manager of Voynich's London shop was in fact a gentleman named Herbert Garland, a man about whom I know far too little to use in a story and therefore replaced him with the fictional Henry Wreath. Should the real life Mr Garland have any living descendants (unlike, to my knowledge, all of the other historical characters in the book) then I trust they will not mind their ancestor forming the basis for a cameo performance.

3. Ben states that the last ferry leaves Holy Island at 1845. That isn't true. There is no ferry from Lamlash to Holy Isle after 1630 and it usually goes straight back so that'd be about 1700. However, the timing of the story meant that it was already past 1700.

I'm not aware of any other liberties I took consciously, and if I took them unconsciously then I absolve myself of any guilt and class them simply as mistakes! A neat segue to: if there are any mistakes I haven't spotted, please feel free to contact me (though I might not fix them).

More interestingly there are a number of things that seem unlikely but are true:

1. Both Wilfrid and Ethel Voynich were spies in their youth.

2. Ethel Voynich did write a novel, *The Gadfly*, that has been a bestseller in Russia since its publication.

3. The description of the Domesday 'book' is accurate, it really is two books in five bindings.

And from about 1600 it really was kept in a chest with three separate locks whose keys were held by three different officials. Just like nuclear launch keys.

4. The missing folios from the Voynich manuscript are real. Ben's description of the way they are missing is also true, most of them have clearly fallen out but the ones used in the book do appear to have been cut out. And one of them is almost certainly a horoscope of Capricorn and Aquarius.

5. The crypt under the Priory Church of St John is genuinely a 12th century crypt which has remained intact under London. Even knowing that, like Terry Pratchett's Ankh Morpork, London is built mostly on London, it still amazes me that a room can have been in use continuously for 900 years. And that it passes mostly unseen as we go about our daily lives.

That manuscript

The official Beinecke collection entry for what they lovingly refer to as MS408, and the rest of the world calls the Voynich Manuscript, can be found here: http://beinecke.library.yale.edu/collections/highlights/voynich-manuscript

However, Yale seem to (sensibly in my view) discourage the hype that surrounds their manuscript and therefore there is little of use to the would-be conspiracy theorist here.

By contrast I found the following two websites of immense use in exploring various elements of the manuscript itself, its history and the various theories that seek to explain it.

http://www.ciphermysteries.com/the-voynich-manuscript – Nick Pelling's blog on a number of different cipher mysteries. This link is to the section specifically on the Voynich Manuscript but the rest is equally worth losing days reading through! I used this site primarily to research the history of the manuscript and the attempts made to decipher it.

Nick has also written a gripping, non-fiction account of the history of the manuscript, *The Curse of the Voynich* which is available here: http://www.compellingpress.com/voynich/

http://www.voynich.nu – René Zandbergen's website pulls together much of the research carried out by a loose working group (including René himself) since the 1990's. It seeks to present an opinion free description of the manuscript and the current state of research. I used it for most of the physical description including the missing folios.

Anyone with an interest in the manuscript could do much worse than consulting these sites. Be warned though, it is dangerously addictive.

So, finally, do I believe the manuscript can be translated? Out on a limb moment: no. (Though I reserve the right to change my mind!) There is, however, much to be learnt in the attempt, and there are plenty of other fruitless ways to spend your time that don't require learning history, linguistics, statistics or cryptanalysis. So go for it and who knows, maybe you'll prove me wrong.

Acknowledgements

I am an arrogant man. I've always been quite comfortable with that (but then I suppose I would be, I am an arrogant man…!) It is therefore tempting to say, and is certainly true at one level, that I did this, "Little Red Hen"-like, myself. But, like all stories, one level barely begins to tell the truth. It seems appropriate then to take the chance to properly thank some people who deserve it.

Firstly, two women whose belief in me beggars my own. In order of appearance (!):

My mum whose unflagging, quiet support is at least partly responsible for the arrogant man I am, it's always the mother's fault! Thanking her for something specific seems somewhat redundant but since these are acknowledgements for a specific book, I will anyway: thankyou for proof reading this Mum.

Verity, my wife, has always demonstrated a faith which I find staggering. There was no better example of this than her simple, unhesitating "Yes" to my ludicrous request to take six weeks without getting paid to write a book for no purpose other than that I've always wanted to. Thankyou so much.

Secondly, my children, Connor, James and Beth who all contributed to this book and more importantly put up with me being at home for six weeks and having a single topic of conversation for six months. Cheers guys.

Michael Lancashire
December 2013

ABOUT THE AUTHOR

Michael Lancashire lives in the Midlands with his wife, three kids, five chickens, four guinea pigs and two reptiles.

The Voynich Deception is his first full length novel.